WILL OF THE WIST

Will of the Wist

BRITTANY CARR

Brittany Carr

Dedicated to my husband and my children - I love you with all of my heart. Thank you to my friends for being my editors. To my inner child - I told you we would be an author one day. Thank you to all who read my story, I hope you love my characters as much as I do.

With love, BLC

CONTENTS

~ One ~

FAR FROM STÓNGRAST

Crunch, crunch, crack.
Heavy boots pounded through the forest, crunching leaves and twigs under each fall of leather. Harsh breaths echoed through the trees, bouncing off the branches, filling the forest with palpable anxiety. A man, young, but old enough, ran hard into the thick growth of trees with seemingly no destination, or hesitation at the dark and mysterious woods. He felt his knees ache as his feet slammed into the earth, he felt his lungs burn, deep inside his chest with each gasp, panic trickling down his spine filling him with ice - he ran harder to get away from the feeling. He needed to get away, to get *out*. He needed to *run*, as fast as he could, to out distance the cold and desperate feeling that filled his chest. He felt trapped, as though no matter how far he ran he just couldn't get away, couldn't avoid his destiny. The panic filled him deeper and deeper as he ran, until he felt as though he couldn't get air into his lungs. His body started to slow with exhaustion and despair as he realized he couldn't escape his own mind, no matter how fast he went. He couldn't be free for even just a moment, forever trapped within his own

thoughts. The dread was heavy in his aching bones, full with the futility of it all.

He ran deeper into the woods, stumbling over roots and righting himself on bark. Scrapes formed under his long white sleeves through the holes the bark tore. He strayed off the path, eyes too full of tears in his growing panic to notice, his breath caught in his throat, hitching between sobs and gasps. He kept running, kept trying to get away, though he knew he couldn't get far. Their voices rang in his ears and no matter how much distance he put between himself and them, they grew ever louder inside his head. He mourned deep in his heart, and yet life and its expectations from every direction held fast to his every move, preventing his healing, keeping him constantly on edge with no hope. He ran despite his lungs burning and begging him to *please* stop, still trying to drown out his own thoughts screaming inside his mind. A heavy sob heaved from his throat, tears spilling onto his cheeks. He was so trapped, so tired of it all, so alone.

He ran, but a protruding root from a nearby tree grabbed his booted toe. He tripped and landed hard on his knees, his breath letting out in a harsh *whoosh* at the sudden fall. The hilt of his sword clanked against the ground and the forest was quiet again, his sobbing breaths all that could be heard. He laid on the moss, whole body sprawled out on the ground. He closed his eyes for a moment feeling the cold ground under his cheeks, the low hanging branches of the tree a cocoon over his head. His scraped palms, still outspread in the moss from his fall, slowly reached up onto the bark of the tree - a willow, he recognized blearily. He pulled himself against the tree trunk, resting his forehead there, and let the tears finally, uncontrollably and freely, roll down his cheeks for an impossibly long moment. The forest seemed to absorb time. He hugged the willow's trunk as he hunched over himself, unable to hold back his tears. The low hanging flowers tickled around his body as the wind tousled them closer. He felt as if the tree were reaching soothing hands to comfort him, embracing him, as the flowers hung low and brushed over him softly. The fragrance was calming as he kneeled there holding the trunk, his overheated and desperate body grateful for the shade.

He didn't know how much time had passed before he sniffed away the last of his tears. His knees felt numb and his forehead felt sore from the bark after leaning into it as he cried - he imagined he had been there a while, not quite caring how long it had been. The blood on his palms had dried and he looked at them with a frown before wiping his tears with what was left of his ripped sleeves.

"Are you alright?" He heard behind him suddenly, the voice soft and gentle. He grabbed his sword and spun around, startled. He ignored the groan of his legs at the sudden movement and stumbled, his feet tingling from lack of movement leaving him out of balance. He stared in surprise - a woman stared back.

"It would be unwise to unsheathe a weapon to anyone but an enemy, sir," she said softly with a quirked lip and a teasing smile. She raised an eyebrow at his hand still holding the sword, looking at it pointedly. He looked down at his hand for a moment before sliding the blade back into place, not even realizing he had grabbed for it at the suddenness of her approach. He supposed it hadn't been sudden, though, and blamed himself for his lack of attention that she had been able to sneak up on him. He looked back up at her, his hands now empty, still wearing the surprised expression on his face.

She sat down on a bed of moss that seemed to mold to the curve of her legs. Her dress was earth colored, beige, and slightly too short. He could see her calves and bare feet as she rested on the ground, her skin surprisingly clean for having been barefoot in the soft mud and grass.

"Well?" She prompted, gesturing to the moss under the willow tree. The branches tickled his shoulder as he sat, swaying over him softly. He noticed her hair was laced with tiny versions of the leaves and flowers blooming off the willow, a delicate pattern, almost flowing naturally from her long curls that pooled around her shoulders and lower back. He looked at her again, with deep confusion as he felt the damp moss underneath him. She looked back with impossible eyes glowing with interest, and a hint of a smile behind her lips.

He sighed then, his shoulders dropping. A woman in the forest, to find him when he is the most distraught and out of his own comfort zone - what was the point in keeping up an appearance? *Now? Here? There surely was no point at all,* he thought.

He leaned back against the tree, feeling heavy and defeated. A frond draped over his shoulder, and he allowed himself to feel comfort from its light graze.

"I wouldn't trouble a stranger with my worries," he said finally, the tremor in his voice made him unable to say anything else. He wasn't certain of what she wanted him to say, anyway. Years and years of etiquette training had not taught him what a maiden in the forest would find appropriate, and he was woefully uncertain on how a young woman would react to an unmarried man in her presence with no chaperone. *Though she could very well be married, of course,* he thought with a grimace. He looked up at the cracks in the trees, seeing the small bits of sky that peeked through.

"A stranger deep in the forest would have the best listening ears for one's worries, don't you think?" She smiled, leaning back on her palms, her feet stretching out in front of her. He noticed the smoothness of her soles and once again thought it odd how clean her feet were in the muck of the forest around them. "A truly unbiased opinion may do you some good, sir," she said kindly with a smile, "but of course, I am not one to pry." He could tell from the raise of her brows that she fully intended to pry, her curiosity plain across her face.

He sighed, again, and looked at her fully. He took in her soft face, speckled with freckles, and the moss green of her eyes, close enough now that he could make out the green and the brown in them, so much like the earth they sat on. He took in how well kept she looked despite a certain wildness, evident in her clothing and bare feet. He took in the loose fabric of her dress, falling over the full curves of her form. He felt almost rude by how deeply he was staring at her, but she stared back at him with equal fervor, her gaze unflinchingly matching his.

"I have been under a lot of pressure lately," he said in a low voice, coughing gently to clear his throat. "My family have all told me it is time to take a wife," he all but whispered as he tried to keep his emotions held tight, "but between defending the port, and being a part of the King's Guard, and taking care of my mother's home, I don't know how it's possible to fall in love." He rubbed his cheek, deep in thought, wondering what else he should say to explain just what he was running from.

"I told that to my family, and," he turned his eyes to her then, "and they just laughed, telling me that love would come later." He was grateful when she ignored the tears as they spilled, though he was mortified to have her witness his emotional breakdown. He continued to speak as he tried to let himself feel comforted by her quiet and reassuring presence.

"They scoffed at the idea of finding love first, or at least it had felt that way. Since then I have been introduced and reintroduced to just about every woman in town. Even the ones at least ten years younger than me, barely old enough to be a wife let alone a mother," his tongue felt heavy as he said it out loud, disturbed that one of the girls he'd met was only a child of fourteen. How her mother thought it was a suitable age for a bride, he wasn't sure, and his mother and sister quickly responded to the suggestion in an equal horror to his own. His mother had thankfully not been the one to bring the offer to him which he was grateful for, but was disturbed all the same as his baby sister was barely five years older than the girl. "They're perfectly tolerable women, *nice* women, even, but..." he trailed off for a moment and stared at his hands before he began again, unable to fight back the queasy feeling he had as he thought back on the meetings with that...*child,* his mind supplied. He let out a shudder at the thought. He was surprised he even said as much as he did, as he'd never told another person of his worries before this moment. He couldn't help but continue to tell her more, her silence was enough to convince him to keep talking.

"It became too much to deal with, and on the one day of the week I am not on patrol, I tended the garden to find a semblance of peace. My mother and sister started questioning me about the fact I hadn't chosen a woman to marry yet, and how several maidens would be making calls upon the house for brunch," he bit his lip, the sudden anger at the memory billowing up and out of his mouth. Though they had only asked him a few questions about his ideal wife of choice, he had felt a chokehold over himself as they spoke. The words he let out burned his tongue, tasting of loneliness and frustration, as he explained to the woman more and more about his stress for the situation.

It was not nearly enough detail to entirely explain *why* he felt so alone, but he didn't want to say too much. Life kept moving, no matter the amount of grief in someone's heart. He didn't want to think of the loss of a man he'd seen as a father figure in his life, of the way he'd found him outside of the walls of the Port after another attack. Despite everything continuing like normal around him, he couldn't find it in himself to also keep moving forward. His frustration that life was forever out of his control, his dreams just out of reach as he tended to others before himself, tainted everything around him. His pain was unseen, perhaps because he hid it so well, but he wanted *someone* to notice. No matter the kindness he was spoken to with, his mother and sister's gentle words always filled his ears with a venom he couldn't explain, as if the simple life he wanted was a mirage he couldn't grasp. It seemed as if the more he was told to *try* for the life he wanted, the more he felt his family wasn't listening to what exactly he was looking for. He felt like they only saw him as an object, pushing him toward a life they wanted for the sake of his happiness, but not quite understanding what he needed to be happy. All he wanted was a place to belong with someone he loved by his side.

"But how," he continued, voice pained, "am I supposed to marry someone I don't know? How do you live a life with someone that you only tolerate?" He focused on her, eyes unintentionally pleading for an answer though he knew she probably didn't have one. His voice quietly cracked on the last word, and he wiped his cheeks and rubbed his eyes, trying to clear the thoughts away.

"Well," she began with a deep breath, and leaned her elbows onto her knees in front of him. Her dress pooled between her thighs and showed a shocking amount of bare skin. He was momentarily distracted by her legs but lifted his gaze back to her as she continued, "sometimes tolerating a person is longer lasting than love," she said.

He looked down, and his eyes scrunched shut as he sniffed a deep breath, tears tracking down his cheeks. He wiped his cheeks again before he looked at her with a pained expression, sharp blue eyes bright with glistening tears.

"I didn't think it would be like this," he said softly. She touched his knee in comfort, and he finally noticed how she had inched her way closer and closer to him as he spoke. Her hand was cold, but it grounded him.

"Oh, sir, you still have youth on you," she replied, smiling gently, "and you are a man after all. Just tell them *you'll* tell them when you get married and not the other way around. If you are the man of the house, it is your right to do as you please, is it not?" she squeezed his leg. "You have time to find a love, soldier," she said as she settled back onto the moss, straightening her dress back down over her now stretched out legs.

"Too much is happening for me to have that choice," he said while wiping his face on the ripped sleeves of his shirt. He thought of the incidents along the port's border with those strange attacks on travelers, of the attack on a man he had cared for so deeply. He thought of the rise in illnesses as deliveries had been unable to be fulfilled, of all the people that had gone missing, or were found in pieces. Time was certainly not on his side, at least not now.

"Keep looking," she said simply. He was grateful for that comment, and felt a weight lift from his shoulders at the thought, though it felt futile. He needed to hear someone support him in his desire to find the right wife, to find the love of his life, without a bias. He still felt helpless and out of control, but hearing her words gave him a sense of sanity about him, something he hadn't felt in a while. "Keep looking, and then come back to tell me how it goes," she continued, reaching into her sleeve. She pulled out a small cloth and handed it to him, "but first, take this to clean your cheeks."

He took it gratefully, suddenly concerned at how dirty he must be after today, and scrubbed it across his face. She stood then, fluidly, without using her hands, and reached out to him. He took her hand in his, small and delicate, and let her help him up. He stood with a groan, body aching as he wasn't one to stay idle for long and hours must have passed since he'd entered the forest and sat on the moss. He felt his age in the aches of his joints, *I'm only twenty-five but I still feel impossibly old,* he thought as his body creaked. He noticed the forest was getting darker, and that the sun would set soon. There was light enough for him to get home safely, though, the sky still blue. His hand felt warm inside her grasp, though her hands were still chilled. She smiled at him, giving his hand a gentle squeeze before nudging him back onto his path. He walked steadily along the trail, feet slow but sure.

"Don't forget to come back and tell me how your search is going," she called after him, "and don't dawdle in this part of the woods!" Her voice was a whisper in the wind behind him, he shivered at the sound of trees rustling around him but kept walking.

Before he knew it, the man made his way through the wall bordering his town, surprised at how he even made it there in what seemed like a blink of an eye. He hoped his family was asleep and didn't ask him about his torn shirt and scrapes, and certainly prayed they wouldn't complain that he had bailed on their brunch ambush.

He thought of the woman in the forest and he could still feel the touch of her hand in his palm, soft and cold, fragile and firm. Her hand had filled him with a warmth he couldn't describe, but her words had left him feeling hopeful and light - something he hadn't felt in a very long time indeed.

He clutched the small handkerchief tight in his fist, absorbing as much courage from it as he could before finding his way home.

...

The days continued as they always had, full of training and patrols, and scattered meetings of more single women. It was as though he had never even stumbled into the forest at all, never had a break from the monotony, never had a conversation with a random stranger in the woods. He patrolled the port where the trouble had been occuring the last few moons, the unexplained disturbances perplexing and increasingly more violent in nature. He continued to joke and laugh with his fellow soldiers and friends while fielding his mother and sister and their suggestions for a wife. He acted normal, unbothered, completely at ease, and from the outside no one could see what he was hiding. He was gracious to the women his mother kept introducing him to, kept up friendly conversation with them, and while they were all *fine,* he felt nothing for them. And surely they were beautiful, and would make good wives for someone - he had just thought there'd be a moment where he would know, with unfaltering, unwavering certainty, that he had found the one he was destined for. *How would I even know?* He thought to himself, certain he missed his soulmate somewhere along the way and didn't even realize it.

In his pocket he kept the small square of fabric given to him by the woman in the forest. Now clean, its soft texture would ground him back into the present whenever his thoughts would get too desperate, though he was unconscious to the action at all. It became a constant comfort to him, a gentle reminder to be hopeful. Whenever he gripped the tissue in his hand, his thoughts would turn to the woman's words. Her need to hear about his search for a wife had made him smile as he reflected on it later, his mind going over how he'd update her on his seemingly impossible task. For a while, he was certain he was incapable of love or attraction at all, but he remembered the woman's bare legs in the forest and the blush it had brought to his cheeks. He was still a man, after all, he told himself, and those base desires were healthy and normal. He only wished it had come from a person he was encouraged to marry, and not a stranger in the woods, though at that point he wasn't sure his mother cared *who* he married, just that he *did*.

Despite everything that clouded his thoughts in an endless storm, he made it through each week by the hairs on his head. While he was struggling internally, he didn't let anything pass through his guise. He painstakingly crafted his social image to exude the airs of a well-off bachelor - whether or not he wanted to be seen as that at all didn't matter to him, and he was sure to keep it from upsetting his family. He wanted to make everyone happy, but it seemed to come at the cost of his own needs, his own desires, his whole future entirely. Throughout the days, he frequently thought of the different things he wanted to tell the odd woman in the forest, of all the people he had met. He wanted to keep the promise he made to her, to give her an update of his search, though she probably forgot about him already. He thought she would love to hear about a conversation he had with a strange fellow he'd known his whole life, a man ever shrouded in mystery with a demeanor as solid as stone.

Teg was always at the tavern, always ready with a gruff laugh and a philosophical notion while he gazed into the fireplace as though it was full of answers only he could see. The man never seemed to go home, yet his stories were of wild adventures he'd had in his youth. He thought she would surely enjoy hearing of the silliness in his day to day routine, and at the very least, telling her of the amount of villagers he needed to placate daily would make for a funny story. But who would want to hear about the troubles between the chicken and egg carts at market, or the drama between two families on neighboring farmland in the midst of a turf war over a strip of wheat fields?

As suddenly as he would have those thoughts he would be abruptly dragged back into the present, and would have to deal with whatever new woman his mother introduced or whatever new threat he had to fix on his patrol, rarely ever an actual problem that needed to be solved - only ever obstacles. He never let himself wonder at *why* he wanted to share his day with her, or why he felt the urge to run back to that tree to see her again despite only having shared a few moments with her. Luckily, he was always busy with other things and was able to brush the thoughts off easily.

Unfortunately, each night, conversation would turn, inevitably, to his marital prospects despite his best efforts to warp the conversation into any other direction. He gripped the handkerchief tight in his pocket, fists going white with the pressure he squeezed. It had been months, the seasons were changing, as were the leaves on the trees, but he held that handkerchief tight almost constantly. He gripped it as though it would will patience and calmness into his very being.

"Oh she is a fine woman, her family very well off, too, Arden, and she would make such beautiful children," his mother sighed as his sister nodded in agreement as they finished up dinner one night. It was colder, now, as autumn pulled through the Port. He had met the woman in the beginning of summer, not quite hot yet but warm enough, so much time yet so little as he sat there feeling as if he would never find a wife inside of this town. No matter their family ties or connections that would benefit himself and his family should he accept a proposal, he just couldn't put himself into a position where he married a stranger. He hung his head, biting his tongue, hiding the anger and sadness there, and let them continue to talk to him. He tried to drown it out but failed, their words filling his ears, poison that he could taste on his tongue. How many more times could they have this conversation without him pulling his hair out in frustration? How did they not see the pressure they piled on him? No matter what he said, they continued to ask him when he'd marry, who he'd marry, where, and everything in between no matter the relevance to Arden.

He knew in the back of his mind that he was exaggerating his mother and sister's words as they also talked about the issues in the Port, with only a few mentions of marriage during the course of the day. However, their sound was amplified in his ears, making him feel as if it were his only purpose in their lives, no matter how supportive they were of his decisions. It was hard to separate his feelings of inadequacy from what he felt they thought of him. His sister had told him long ago, when they were still children, that he took things to heart too much and needed to find his own sense of purpose, and leave others' words behind him. He'd do well to follow his baby sister's advice, but his desire to make everyone around him happy first took away his choices and left him feeling suffocated.

He didn't know what was wrong with him, to feel the way he did about everyone's words. It was as if things said to him were morphed into something more, feeling as though his short-comings were on display and everyone would find out he wasn't the man they thought he was. If his mother made a suggestion or told him of another woman looking for a husband, he'd take her words as if she thought he was a failure, that he couldn't even handle finding a wife on his own, let alone be in a success-ful marriage. He tortured himself with everything he heard and supplied his own fears in the spaces between them. He wanted to stop, but he didn't know how, and only felt trapped. Reality blurred within his head, the dark part of him beating himself down and amplifying his flaws.

The man gritted his teeth as he quietly listened to his mother and sister discuss the new fashion trends, at least for a moment before the topic turned again. He wanted, desperately, to walk out of the house, down to the market and hope - *beg* - for a distraction. He wanted to find a wife randomly at a shop and need not look any longer, to just casually bump into his future wife - but it would never happen as he was always too busy avoiding people to spare a moment for conversation that involved a woman at all, in case it gave them the wrong idea about his intentions. If he spoke to anyone for too long, smiled at a woman for too long, his mother and sister would start planning a wedding immediately - and he could not risk it. He daydreamed of running away forever just to keep himself sane, if for a little while longer.

~ Two ~

DEEP IN TONSILTA

In a forest full of flowerless trees, there stood one different from the others. Slightly shorter than the rest but by far the most beautiful, a single wisteria tree with sparse blooms of white blossoms grew from the earth surrounded by moss. Its roots grew elegantly along the ground, cradling a small cottage that emerged from under the tree almost blending it into the woods, with a well worn path leading around the house to a garden. Around the garden growing seemingly at random, sprouts peered through the dirt. Nothing was sectioned off and the fruits growing from bushes looked to have grown on their own with no outside assistance. They lead the way to a small river with an outlet pouring into a creek in between the fresh berries.

There was a small pool of water, fresh and filled with a gentle current circulating from its mother river. Smooth rocks lined the bottom, and in the center of the pool, a small woman stood with her dress tied around her waist. Her toes curled in the chill waters and her nose lifted to the sky. Tiny freckles lined her cheeks from the kiss of the sun, a soft glow around her. A large breeze swept through the forest then, rattling the leaves. Her hair fluttered around her and she breathed deeply, the garden scents filling her lungs. Another wave of wind, stronger than the one before, promised a rain storm this time, and the woman pulled herself from the pool and fixed her skirts.

"So the routine begins, Wilmayra Wisteria Willow," the woman murmured to herself, the only voice that could be heard through the forest for miles, the only language that could be understood by Man for many miles more. She walked slowly as the sound of wind promised rain for her gardens, a long awaited watering for the life in the forest. As she walked on, her wet toes drying on the moss, her true name came whispering back to her from the trees. Their leaves fluttered and waved in the wind, offering a gentle feeling of support and fondness as she walked towards her home as the breeze grew slowly stronger.

The trees groaned under the continuous wind, grateful for the coming rain but protesting the heavy gusts all the same. Wilmayra Wisteria Willow trotted through the garden with her bare feet and small basket she picked up from next to the water, trying to secure the ripened fruit and vegetables before the storm began. She laughed to herself when a fat droplet of rain fell on her nose and surprised her as the smell of petrichor drifted from the direction of the coming storm. The trees responded with a laugh of their own as the wind twirled around them, calling her the name bestowed upon her from her family tongue. Though her name had no true translation, the closest it could be explained was a cool spring day with a playful breeze, as the sun peeked through the leaves. The trees did their best to call to her and she smiled at them in turn, grateful to hear their usually stoic voices. The promise of rain made them louder than usual, and she was loath to go inside so soon.

She filled her lungs as she gracefully danced on the moss toward the fruit that was most ripe, ready to be picked. Her toes dipped deeper into the dirt before she pulled the last of the items from the vines and branches, finally heading around the small house underneath the lightly flowered tree. She let the low hanging branches graze across her shoulders without ducking to avoid them, the leaves a soft kiss on her cheeks. With each caress, the soft murmur of her true name floated around her, a welcome sound, reminding her of who she was despite no one around. It promised with a whisper a somber and loving support, always nearby, above and below growing deep in the earth and high into the sky. Though she was alone, she was never truly alone thanks to the trees around her that had been there since before she was born, watching her grow over the years.

She placed the basket by the front door before walking slowly around the house and securing the storm shutters on each of the windows, clasping them tightly at the center before locking them. In the slots at each side and at the center of the frames, a wooden post was slipped in. It blocked the windows and the shutters with a heavy layer of protection to the elements and with the vines growing over the wooden panels, the home looked uninhabited and empty. The sun would set in the next hour or so, and the sunset would be hidden from behind the heavy wood panels. Though the glass would be protected in addition to the Safety spell bound to the panes, she preferred the extra feeling of protection that the shutters gave her even if it wasn't quite necessary.

After the last window was secured, she walked back to the front door and collected her small harvest. The front door was a heavy wood with iron hinges, and the door closed with a groaning *clunk*. She pulled the matching heavy bar from along the edge of the door where it had rested and slotted it over the door frame much like she had the windows. With the outer windows secured, the home was very dark, completely devoid of the sunshine. The air in the home was cool yet when the windows were closed this way, she couldn't help but feel a sense of oppressing heaviness that the darkness left around her. Sighing to herself, she placed the basket on the counter in the kitchen and started towards the hearth.

Wilmayra Wisteria Willow, with practiced ease, deftly struck a match and tossed it into the wood. Her morning routine had her placing these items at the ready every day, so when she tucked herself into the dark cabin in the evening, they would be available without fumbling in the dim light. After the first several times of being alone without being able to find anything in the darkness, she quickly realized how important setting up the necessary items for the night was, like fire and dinner supplies, in order to keep her from fumbling blindly around the house. Eventually, she stopped eating dinner in the dark and would eat her meals when the sun was up to avoid the tediousness of bringing the fire to a low blaze, to eat quickly and clean up after supper just as fast before the fire began to burn out. A big fire would take too long to turn to ember and since she wanted to avoid a house fire, she had no choice but to limit the length of time the hearth would be lit. It ensured her to be an early riser, going to bed as the sun set, so that she could begin the day anew and maximize the use of the sun.

The storm coming, however, pushed back her schedule a bit as she had to scramble to shutter the house before the rain poured. Though she had to begin the nighttime routine early, she moved no quicker and accepted the day for what it was. There'd be more time tomorrow, of course, to do the same thing she had done today and the day before. She breathed heavily through her mouth in a puff as she poked the wood with the fire stick, and pursed her lips, thinking of all the things she would have to do come morning. She shook her head to herself to bring her back to the moment, and continued bringing the fire to life.

After a small flame was crackling in the fireplace, she moved back to the kitchen in the low light and pulled out containers for the fruit and vegetables. She would rinse them tomorrow, but for now they'd be safe from the storm blowing in. After settling the produce, she turned and grabbed the leaves and herbs she had collected and placed them on a cloth to dry out. She would be making several different healing ointments with the ingredients, and some tea blends, to bring to the trading market during the next full moon.

By the time everything was cleaned and put away, the fire was down to its last small flame. Wilmayra Wisteria Willow padded across the floor with silent footsteps and sat in the orange light, flickering and cracking around her. Sitting close to the window, she turned her ear toward the sound of wind and rain as the storm grew stronger outside. Sound usually wasn't able to get through the shutters, but the storm brought with it a fierce strength as it pounded the walls of her home. Small rumbles could be heard, and the woman was certain by the time she saw the last ember glow, the thunder would be right above her. She sighed before stretching out and slowly stood on her feet, toes curling against the cold ground beneath her. The only sounds she could hear were of the storm, and her own breathing.

She walked down the pitch black hallway by memory and opened the bathroom door, and unbuttoned the front of her dress. She left the dirty dress in a pile on the floor, knowing she'd clean it up in the morning as she usually did as part of her routine. She gently closed the door behind her before dragging her hand along the wall as she walked to her bedroom, feeling the grooves in the wood and the door frame as she felt her way down the hall. She felt the open doorway and walked inside, counting her footsteps to find the bed. Her feet felt the bed frame first, and she climbed into the blankets, cold on her bare skin, and pulled the comforter over her nude form. Finding clothes in the dark would be too tedious, and she was exhausted from the long day. A long, repetitive, tedious, day. She pulled the blankets tighter around her body and sighed again, her eyes open and looking towards the ceiling but seeing nothing. She blinked hard, colors bursting behind her eyelids, the only light she could see, as a frustrating feeling at the overwhelming weight of the air around her filled her belly.

Outside the storm continued, getting closer and closer, the rumble becoming a *crack*. Small flecks of light appeared behind the shutters where streaks of lightning snuck through, though not enough to light the room behind the heavy shutters. She breathed deep, trying to smell the rain beyond the walls but couldn't. Her eyes kept tracing the window frames for more of the lightning, the occasional flicker a welcome sight even though it was fleeting. She shuddered when a tickle burned in her eyes, she fought back the strong sensation of crying and ignored it with a bite to her lip that was peppered with cracked, raw skin. She forgot to put on the hydrating balm again and tasted the sting of blood on her tongue. She tried to keep herself from running her teeth over the same split but the habit was old and hard to fight back. She felt so, truly, undeniably alone even from the elements as she lay there in the dark. The storm swallowed all the noise around her and not even her breathing could be heard over the sound of the rain, now pounding hard against the roof.

She rolled over and suppressed a tear, fighting it back with a sniffle. She went over her checklist for the morning routine

- put on a clean dress, wash the dirty clothes, open shutters, wash produce, make the meals for the day, collect firewood, collect healing ingredients... The list went on and on and on. At this point, she was uncertain why she even bothered to run through her mental checklist when she had memorized it years ago. Another habit she had formed, through the practice of a daily regimen. She had tried to mix it around a few times but was left feeling groggy and confused come morning, and decided if she were to be stuck in the forest she'd at least make the most of the endless flow of days. Her "traveling apothecary" had helped many forest folk in the last several years, and she continued to study the art of healing, with a focus on fertility. She had become a true Master Healer in the Kagdah forest through her dedication to education, pushing herself through the years to keep spreading more of her knowledge to those in need. Those days began to dwindle as storms became more frequent, and travel began to slow around the forest as the tree dwelling people grew tired of finding spontaneous shelter in the dangerous winds. They even began limiting Trade at the Hanlan Outpost despite Wilmayra Wisteria Willow's desire to continue sharing her knowledge to fellow healers and patients. Every other full moon, now, was there a trading event at all, and the last time she'd gone to the outpost there was talk of cutting it down even more than that.

Sniffling slightly, she closed her eyes again and tried to drown out the sound of the storm and fall asleep. Knowing it was pointless, she tried to doze to the sounds of the raging storm, wind beating against the tree branches and rattling the stones and shingles atop her home. She thought of her chores, again, a now endless loop in her head, and calculated how many more tinctures she should bring to the next Trade Moon. Tomorrow she would do it all, starting from the top of the same list of things she had to do every day, like always, again. And again the day after, and the days after that.

The weight of the perpetual tasks of chores, and the ache of solitude rested heavy in her gut. She would do it all over in the morning and find herself here, tucked back into her bed naked and bare in the forest, with nothing but the leaves and flowers for company. She thought back to a time of laughter when her only friend would visit her quiet place in the woods, thinking of all the giggles and late nights they would share. All too soon they would go home, their parents picking them up on the way back from the Trading, or a visit from Lexman Yur where they went to school with Wilmayra Wisteria Willow. Sometimes they would leave her with supplies to make new tinctures or other recipes, supplies to store in her shelves and add to her collection. She ached to see them again, unable to travel further than the Hanlan Outpost. Her home was too small to keep a horse and carriage, and caring for them in the empty forest without a stable would be impossible. A brief flush of frustration washed over her body but she tucked it down, swallowing hard against the painful emotion. She refused to acknowledge the feeling that came with thinking of her friend and the effects solitude had on her. She could count on one hand the amount of times she had seen them at all in the last two years, and for only a handful of days at a time if she was lucky.

The coming day would start the loop over again. She sighed into the night preparing for a repeat of the exact same, and hoped that even for a moment, that something - *anything*- would change. A single tear rolled down her cheek as thunder rattled the windows in their frame - she knew tomorrow would be the same as every day before. The small flame of hope burning in her chest grew dim, flickering painfully, as another day ended the same as the ones before - alone, in the dark, with nothing but trees for company.

Wilmayra Wisteria Willow's last thought before succumbing to sleep was that if she never woke up in the morning, no one would know for a very long time that she was even gone.

...

The morning came quite the same as the others, though it was a bit more muddy from the storm than usual. The trees were still happily soaking in the water, though some grumbled over the loss of branches. Wilmayra Wisteria Willow dutifully opened the shutters, placing the long bars of wood back on the bracket under the window frames ready for the next storm. She continued harvesting the rest of the garden and by the time the sun was high in the sky, she had finished collecting the last of the produce that had survived the storm.

Wilmayra Wisteria Willow sat on the bed of the small pool by the river, now overflowing from the rain. Her dress was hiked up to her waist to avoid it getting wet, tied on her hip in a knot. She watched as debris floated down the river and wondered how the rest of the forest fared, or if it was just Tonsilta that had been affected. She washed her dress from the day before dutifully, wearing a new clean one she had found in her drawer. She slowly rinsed it before climbing out of the water, hanging it to dry on a bare branch from a nearby tree. She smiled at the tree gratefully as it grumbled at her teasingly, pretending to detest her behavior but enjoying her company all the same. After untying her dress and letting it fall over her knees, she sighed quietly before grabbing the basket and turning towards the front door.

Suddenly, the trees around her started murmuring to each other, their voices growing louder and louder. Wilmayra

Wisteria Willow quirked her ears toward their voices to hear what they were saying.

A man is in the woods, they said.

She gasped and dropped the basket before peering around the side of her house. She heard the sound of footsteps falling through the woods and echoing around her as the sound grew closer and closer to her home. She creeped further around the house and heard a gasp followed by the heavy sound of a body hitting the ground, making her wince. Just as suddenly as the forest erupted into noise, the trees became silent, listening intently. She could only hear the sound of crying. A strange feeling filled her, an overwhelming sense of *right* despite the pain in the voice of the person that found themselves at her home.

Wilmayra Wisteria Willow stepped further out to see who was now under her tree, how they could possibly be crying in such a pitiful and distraught way. She was curious at the sensation in her veins, almost pulling her to whoever was there. Her arms ached with the effort of reaching out to them. First she noticed that it was a man. Then she noticed he was very fair, with soft brown hair that curled around his shoulders. She stared at him a moment longer before her gaze traveled over his body, noticing how torn and dirty his clothes were as her eyes trailed over him. She let him cry, the painful sobs muffled under the branches of the wisteria. She and the trees were the only ones to hear the heartbreaking sound. They all continued to listen quietly, the sadness palpable. She was certain the man would be exhausted soon, and sore by the looks of his body covered in small scrapes.

She was startled to see his forehead leaning against the bark of the wisteria, his palms open and flat against the bark. Blood from his hands stained the wood exactly like in a Binding Prayer. Even though she hadn't seen it before, she recognized the pose from stories of her grandfather's joining of the Trees long ago. She could only see his left side from where she stood, but everything in her body told her to run for her healing kit, in the house, to fix his wounds, to help him, to comfort him - but she'd surely disturb him if she moved further, and who knew what a stranger would do if surprised? Tentatively, she stepped closer and closer along the moss, the sound of her approach muffled by the padded ground.

Finally after what felt like hours, though the trees hardly moved even for a breeze with the sun still bright in the sky, the man finally moved from his position. His voice sounded rough after crying for so long and Wilmayra Wisteria Willow had to fight back the urge to cry in sympathy at the sound, she could only imagine how much the man would be suffering to weep so openly and without holding back. He leaned back onto his feet, his legs trembling as he moved. He looked down at his hands, his brow furrowing at what he saw. Wilmayra could see the blood and dirt dried onto his hands from where he stood, and knew the man was surprised at the state he was in as he ran his eyes along the rest of his body.

Wilmayra took a deep breath and bravely stepped forward, her heart pounding in her chest. She felt nervous and uncontrollably curious at the same time, with an absolute need to approach him. With her feet steady and her hands trembling, she gently called out to the man.

"Are you alright?"

The man's eyes turned to her, wide from shock, and his body wobbled as he tried to stand quickly while pulling his sword from the hilt on his right hip. Wilmayra bit her lip, trying not to laugh - he was in a sorry state and she frankly couldn't help but find him silly. She was not the least bit intimidated by his stumbling stance.

"It would be unwise to unsheathe a weapon to anyone but an enemy, sir," she said, her words a warning but she knew the smile was fighting hard on her lips to break free. She wasn't sure when the last time she had spoken to anyone was, especially not a Man, and she felt unimaginably giddy. She glanced at his sword with a quirk of her brow and he followed her gaze, and gently tucked it away with a sheepish expression. Still he looked surprised, so she let out a breath before sitting down on the moss in front of him in a welcoming and calming way. She hoped she seemed calm enough for him to trust, at least, and by the way his shoulders drooped, Wilmayra knew he would stay. She wondered if he felt the same unsettling feeling of companionship when he saw her, too.

He dropped to the ground, settling his legs in front of him and leaned back against the trunk of her tree. She smiled softly to herself when he settled against the wisteria and tilted her head to get a better look at him. He was handsome, his light sky blue eyes and scruffy face were kind, but sad at the same time. He had an air of melancholy for someone so young, though she supposed she had no real idea how Men typically aged - he was the only one she'd ever encountered. His curls rested around his cheeks, the wind blowing them out of place. He brushed the strands behind his ears without any notice, the action unconscious. She could tell he was fighting for words, unable to explain what exactly he'd done to get here in such a state.

"I wouldn't trouble a stranger with my worries," he said finally, voice gruff and deep. Wilmayra felt a shiver up her spine at the sound before she replied.

"A stranger deep in the forest would have the best listening ears for one's worries, don't you think? A truly unbiased opinion may do you some good, sir," she murmured gently, trying to get him to open up to her. She bit her lip to fight back the desire to jump toward him and ask question after question about what happened to him. Quickly, she added, "but of course, I am not one to pry," and hoped she was convincing. He met her stare as she openly looked him up and down, he glanced her over and his gaze lingered on her legs. She wiggled her toes under his scrutiny but waited it out, seeing where this would go. She leaned back on her hands to get comfortable.

She couldn't help but feel a strong pull of wonder at a man in the forest, her home, seemingly running from some kind of terror as he found comfort under *her* wisteria. His eyes were glassy from the shed of tears, his face reddened from running and crying. She again had to grab the moss with the effort to not run for the healing kit to patch up his injured hands and arms, and fought the desire to wipe his face clean of dirt and blood and tears. He looked so scruffy, but also soft. She kept still, waiting patiently for the man to respond to her words, though quite a few minutes had passed. Eventually he shrugged and looked up at the sky again, seeking its warmth as it peered through the leaves of the tree.

"I have been under a lot of pressure lately," he said finally, in a low voice. "My family have all told me it is time to take a wife, but between defending the village, and being a part of the King's Guard, and taking care of my mother's home, I don't know how it's possible to fall in love." He rubbed his cheek, and Wilmayra watched as he smeared more blood and dirt along his cheeks.

"I told that to my family, and," he paused, "and they just laughed, telling me that love would come later." Wilmayra pretended not to see the tears that fell down his cheeks, nor the tracks they left. She patiently waited for him to tell her more, her heart sad for the kind man looking for love.

"They scoffed at the idea of finding love first, at least it had felt that way, and since then I have been introduced and reintroduced to just about every woman in town. Even the ones at least ten years younger than me, barely old enough to be a wife let alone a mother," he said in a low voice.

"They're perfectly tolerable women, *nice* women, even, but..." he trailed off, staring at his hands. Wilmayra stared at him, wanting to know more but heart breaking for him all the same. The curiosity burning despite her desire to comfort him, she waited it out for a moment longer, squeezing the moss as her heart ached in sympathy for the man.

"It became too much to deal with, and on the one day of the week I am not on patrol, I tended the garden to find a semblance of peace. My mother and sister started questioning me about the fact I hadn't chosen a woman to marry yet, and how several maidens would be making calls upon the house for brunch," his words grew heated as he continued speaking, and she ached to reach out to him, "but how am I supposed to marry someone I don't know? How do you live a life with someone that you only tolerate?" A single tear trailed down his face forming a track where the dirt had dried, and she really wanted to wipe his cheek clean - she bit her cheek to fight the thought, and frowned at his sad face. Each time he spoke and looked away from her, she scooted closer to him. Barely perceptible, she moved slowly toward him - she just couldn't fight the urge to make him feel better and allowed herself this small comfort, for both him and herself.

"Well," she began with a deep breath, and leaned forward, "sometimes tolerating a person is longer lasting than love," she said softly in a comforting tone. It was what she had been told, at least, and she wasn't married so had no way to know if it was actually good advice. But she knew many people who'd had the same mindset, her mother included, who found that stability was more important than love. She knew from his reaction to her words, though, that it wasn't what he had hoped to hear.

"I didn't think it would be like this," he said. Wilmayra touched his knee in comfort, unable to ignore his obvious distress.

"Oh, sir, you still have youth on you," she replied, smiling gently, "and you are a man after all. Just tell them *you'll* tell them when you get married and not the other way around. If you are the man of the house, it is your right to do as you please, is it not?" she squeezed his leg. "You have time to find a love, soldier," she said as she settled back onto the moss, straightening her dress back down over her now stretched out legs. She hoped that was the right thing to say this time and that she wasn't giving him the wrong advice. Afterall, how would she know how it worked in the Human Ports?

"Too much is happening for me to have that choice," he said while wiping his face on the ripped sleeves of his shirt. She sighed, the moss under her palm soft and cushiony, and thought for a moment on what to say next.

"Keep looking," she said simply. "Keep looking and then come back to tell me how it goes," she said as she reached into her sleeve. She knew he'd be compelled to come back to her whether he wanted to or not- the Old Ways now bound him to the forest. She said nothing, though, as she pulled out a small cloth and handed it to him, "but first, take this to clean your cheeks," she said, finally unable to hold back any longer.

After he took it and wiped his face, Wilmayra stood fluidly and reached out to him. She tugged on his hand and helped him to stand up. He stood with a groan and she fought back a giggle - she knew the feeling of sitting too long in an uncomfortable position, frequently forgetting time as it passed her by.

"Don't forget to come back and tell me how your search is going," she called after him, as he walked away back toward the port he'd come from, so far away. "And don't dawdle in this part of the woods!" she added just in case. The trees whispered a goodbye as he walked further and further, and Wilmayra asked them to keep him safe and guide his way home. She also asked for them to tell her when he finally stepped foot back inside the borders of where he belonged, and was grateful they agreed. Trees could be just as nosy as the forest folk and luckily it fell in her favor that they'd keep track of him for that long.

Noticing then the fall of the sun's rays, Wilmayra quickly started her nighttime routine before the sun went down any further. She brought everything into the kitchen before wandering back outside and listened for the trees to tell her when the man finally made his way home. Once they murmured his safety to her, she went inside and locked the door before dressing for bed. She pulled her blanket, cold and cozy, up to her chin and smiled to herself. She wondered at how the man had found her, all the way out in the middle of the woods. Though improbable, she was grateful he had found her. She blushed at the memory of his hands and forehead resting against her tree trunk, as he sat on his knees before it. A Binding Prayer. She imagined how his hands would feel if they hadn't been covered in scrapes and muck. Would they be soft despite his profession? She chased the thought away, unwilling to entertain thoughts of someone that was innocent of the ways of the forest folk. To the forest folk, a Binding Prayer was a marriage of sorts, even if she hadn't completed her part of the Binding in a traditional sense.

Wilmayra laid in her bed, a light feeling in her chest. For the first time in a very long time, she felt something blossom there, where it was usually a cold and empty feeling. She wondered at what that could be, what she was feeling, but couldn't quite name it. Her thoughts drifted over the interaction, thinking about each word said between them, and each expression that had run over the man's face as they talked. She wondered if he would come back and share with her his progress, or if the next time she saw him he'd be married. She wondered if he would ignore the call of the woods, the call back to her. She wouldn't blame him of course, he seemed as though he would do the honorable thing of finding the best maiden in his town. She pretended the thought didn't make her frown.

Finally, Wilmayra dozed with thoughts of the man running through her mind. The last thought she had before she succumbed into the most peaceful sleep she'd had in years, was the recognition of the feeling she couldn't name.

She drifted off, *hopeful,* for the first time in her life.

~ Three ~

UNDER THE TREES

Eventually the ache in his heart couldn't be ignored. After his family ate dinner and the topic came about again, he stood suddenly and rose from his chair. It was midway through autumn, the weather turning colder the way he had always liked it to be. He needed to be away from this place, and the forest seemed like a dream this time of year.

"I will be going hunting this weekend," he said loudly, voice filling the room from the sudden declaration. His volume surprised them all, including himself. His mother looked shocked and his sister looked excited, hoping it meant he had met the woman he would marry. Though he wasn't certain how his desire to spend a weekend alone meant he had found a wife, he just ignored them and hoped they didn't press him for any more information. He didn't acknowledge their looks and continued to his bedroom, not even pausing as he said goodnight.

His sister and mother were left staring after his form as he all but ran from the room, confused at the outburst but curious nonetheless. After all, there was no real need for him to hunt.

Arden knew they were thinking they could get meat from the butcher, and were most likely discussing his behavior over tea and dessert. He pretended that it didn't annoy him, and readied himself for bed. In the morning, he'd say his goodbyes and make his plans officially. It felt like a relief that he was taking a whole weekend to do... Well, to do anything he felt like without worry for anyone but himself. It was an invigorating feeling and he wondered why he hadn't done it sooner.

Because you hadn't met her *yet,* his mind supplied. He chased the thought away, shaking his head to clear it. After stripping off his clothes, he pulled the handkerchief she had given him out of his pocket. He squeezed it in his hands for a moment before placing it on his desk before he settled into his bed with the blankets tucked around him. He fell asleep with a small smile on his lips. He couldn't wait to go back into the forest and break free of the monotony of his days trapped in the port.

...

When he woke early the next morning, he told his squadron that he would be taking the weekend for himself, and planned on a new guard route for the soldiers in town for patrols. He said nothing to anyone about why he was leaving for a few days, but everyone was excited for him. Maybe not for the same reason he was excited, but the fact remained he was one of the wealthiest bachelors in town and anything he did was of great interest. The other villagers were excitable in general, and he tried to ignore their whispers. He only hoped being in the forest for a few days would clear his mind. He also thought, maybe at the very least, it would help him find a woman who was grateful for a soldier who could hunt as well as defend - though he admittedly didn't think of that until it was suggested to him by a particularly enthusiastic matron in the market.

Throughout the day, Arden kept thinking of what his father would think of his desire to find love. He was never home, after all, and resided in the King's Guard up in the mountains. He visited every few months, sometimes years, and they all cherished the moments he was around. A wise man, who loved to entertain, he was truly the life of any party. Arden wished he was around more, but he felt as if his father held out hope that Arden would join the Royal Guards one day. They both knew that Arden wasn't the kind of man to wish for that life, though, and was already a quarter century old - young, but past his prime. It was apparent the Port would be his home, forever. He'd never made it known his desire for *more*, especially not to his father that he hardly ever saw, and certainly not often enough to consider him a true parent. He was bitterly reminded of the loss of a man he'd looked up to his entire life, someone who'd taught him what it meant to be a leader.

If it had been up to him, he would have followed Bartrum in the Cahlin's family butchery, and live his life happily in Bartrum's footsteps. He'd been taken from them too soon, and all Arden could think was that would have been a life he'd have wanted for himself, too. An honest profession, something the town always needed - he knew he would've been an excellent man of the market. At the cost of himself, he chose to follow in his father's footsteps and he'd have to live with it forever. It was what everyone had expected of him, and he'd been unable to stop it. His thoughts ran over these memories and ponderings endlessly, and wondered if the woman in the forest would know what to do about it. His thoughts cycled over and over before he'd shake his head to clear it - a motion he was doing more and more frequently - and continue with his day, pretending to be deeply invested in the usual goings on of the Port. He held a hand in his pocket nearly all day, holding tight to the small strip of fabric hidden there. It felt like the only thing keeping him tethered to the ground.

In town during his patrol, he made sure to say a small farewell to his friends. Teg left him with a somber notion of remembering to look between the leaves of tomorrow before they become the muck of yesterday. He just laughed and thanked him, wondering what he could possibly mean by that. His friends, the ones he grew up with and who had joined the Guard with him, all told him he deserved a break and were glad to see him finally take time for himself. Arden was surprised at their kindness, but felt sad that he didn't immediately think his peers would wish him well. *I really do need this break,* he thought, *my thoughts are clouded and tainting my relationships.* He didn't want his frustrations to paint the rest of his life and he promised to himself, no matter what, he'd make sure to be kind to everyone, especially those he cared about most.

He said goodbye to his family with a kiss on each cheek after dinner, telling them he would see them at the week's end. His sister gave him a warm hug, and Arden was surprised by the action. He felt guilty for ever feeling as though his family didn't care about him in the ways he wanted them to as she squeezed him lovingly.

"I want to see you happy, Arden," she said as she kissed his cheek. "You deserve a family of your own and a life you make for yourself," she continued, hugging him tighter. "You do too much for me and our mother, and we only want to see you happy. You deserve to be happy, love," her voice was soft and Arden had to blink away tears from her earnest expression, overwhelmed by the love he saw in her gaze.

"I love you, Juna," he kissed her cheek, "I'll be back in a few days. I just need..."

"You need space from our matchmaking," she laughed, "I know. We've been haranguing you haven't we?" She pulled away from his hug with one final squeeze. "We were just trying to help, especially since you never take a minute for yourself–it's always work, or aiding the townsfolk with work. You'll wear yourself thin, and we only wanted to make it easier for you." She scrunched her nose, "though we may have been sort of aggressive in our search I'll admit," she added with mirth. Arden rolled his eyes dramatically at her, and she swatted his arm laughing.

"I'd say you've been *quite* aggressive in your search," he shook his head but couldn't help but laugh with his sister. Her words brought him a sense of peace and understanding, that he hadn't been wrong about their attempts at setting him up, but he hadn't been entirely right either. They'd only been trying to help. As he looked at her, he remembered a time when she was small, braided hair full of daisies and leaves. It was simpler for them both back then, but now she was a young woman who'd soon start her own family. The thought immediately took away his good mood.

"You know not to settle for anything less than you deserve, right Juna?" His voice was abrupt, and even his sister was surprised at his suddenness, but easily matched his energy with a solemn and proud expression on her face.

"I won't accept anything less than perfect, Arden. I promise," she said, voice full of honesty, eyes round and innocent. He knew she would tell him the truth and though she was a few years younger than him at nineteen years old, she knew to trust her brother indubitably. Atleast, Arden hoped she still trusted him that way. He kissed her cheek with one final farewell before heading to his bedroom. When he was alone in his room, he packed a small shoulder bag with spare clothes and a hunting knife before going to bed early to rise with the sun the following day.

He set out on foot at dawn, bag on his back along with his bow and quiver full of freshly sharpened arrows. He didn't know exactly where to head in the forest, but he marched for hours until the sun was high in the sky and he could see it between the leaves. He began to get frustrated when he couldn't seem to find the willow tree, or any familiar markings at all. He kept walking, and started to get scared at how far he was going into the Tonsilta Woods, a place no man dared to go alone. He realized he must have stumbled into the forest and accidentally taken the wrong turns when he had originally found the woman in the forest. He suddenly thought about what that might mean about the woman, if she were even human at all, when he suddenly tripped over an overgrown root - that *same* overgrown root as before - and landed in a heap at the bottom of the willow tree.

A peal of laughter broke through the forest and he turned his head to see the woman standing in the moss, her long dress blowing in the wind. Her face was split in a huge grin, her snicker still echoing around them. He smiled sheepishly, standing up as he wiped his knees off.

"Well," she asked pointedly, her laugh still under her voice.

"I didn't find anyone to marry," he said with a shrug, "so I'm going hunting."

"Ah," she replied, "a logical thing to do when one is looking for a wife." Her voice was teasing and he immediately felt comforted by the sound, his shoulders relaxed and he took a deep breath that felt like the first real one he had in months.

The forest was calming, and he wondered if that was why this odd woman would choose to live here. The flowers in her hair seemed fuller than last time he saw her, the soft vines flowing out from her wavy curls. He fought the urge to touch them, curious at how they twirled around her head. He wanted to ask why she wore it like that, but it seemed rude to ask a lady why she wears her hair a certain way, so he held his tongue. Her honest eyes caught his, so much like moss and earth and he had a hard time looking away from them.

She looked back at him curiously, as though she could feel him looking at her. His face was clean of dirt and blood this time, though he was sweating underneath the leather he wore. He wondered if she thought he had a handsome face, as he'd been told in the past by others. His cheeks were sharp and covered in a light beard, not quite long but not short either. His eyes a bright blue, the same as his father's and were hard to look away from, especially when in the role of Commander. Many of his friends had teased him for being so *pretty* but he never took it hard. After all, being good looking was hardly a problem. He'd always thought his eyes seemed sorrowful and full of emotion, though, difficult to not express everything he was thinking on his face. He noticed how much taller than her he was, she had to look almost straight up to meet his gaze. Her toes wiggled in the moss as they stood together, not talking, just staring. He wondered if she was cold in the changing weather, though she still wore no shoes. The silence around them was comfortable and effortless, and he quite enjoyed the sense of familiarity. He tried not to think about the relief he had from just being in her presence though, certain he didn't want to unpack what that could possibly mean.

"Would you like some tea?" she asked, finally breaking the silence.

"Sure," he nodded, and followed her under the willow, wondering how they'd have tea under a tree. The branches tickled his arm as he walked underneath them, his tall body bumping some of the thicker branches. He ducked, slightly bumping his head on a low branch, and rubbed his forehead. He heard the woman cough a laugh under her breath, no doubt she had seen him stumbling. It was a jovial sound and he smiled in response, feeling light, though the flush of embarrassment spread over his cheeks.

They continued under the willow, which wasn't a very large tree by any means, deceptively small - it was the flowing leaves and dangling branches that made it appear longer and wider than it really was. The low hanging branches guided a path into a small cottage, framing the front. The fronds dangled in front of the door, draping delicately onto the roof. It was almost encased in the thick of leaves and flowers and branches, hugging tight to the stone. It felt safe, and invisible. He hadn't even noticed the cottage was there, just behind him, this time and last he was here. The flow of branches dangling over his head camouflaged it well, as the moss gave way to a path of smooth stone. His boots clacked against it, a loud sound after being surrounded by such quiet.

"Leave your boots inside the door," she said as she walked inside, opening a heavy wooden door. Her bare feet stepped onto a small woven rug, he noticed her toes curl around it. He contemplated taking his boots off for a moment -- it was her home, after all, and he couldn't be rude and ignore her wish despite his trepidations. He pulled them off, and left them neatly by the door. He felt odd to be in socks in front of someone other than his mother and sister, but the stone floor was soothing on his toes, cold and firm, so he didn't mind.

He walked into the cottage and looked at the furnishings. The front door entered into the far right of the house. At the entranceway where he stood, there was a very small foyer with a plant and a window to the right, and a small seat built into the sill. The window looked out to the base of the willow tree, the branches arching over the frame. It was like peering into a fantasy world as they were encased in the leaves and flowers. It was hard to imagine they weren't a part of the woods themselves as he took it all in. Next to the door on the opposite side of the window alcove, was a recess in the wall that held several hooks for coats. He noticed a gardening apron hung on one, still coated with dirt. Just through the foyer was a long hallway and a few doors. A bedroom and bathroom, surely, but he wouldn't ask. He didn't want to be invasive, of course.

There was a small living room to the left of the house, with a couch and comfortable chairs leaning against the windows. The chairs looked soft and the couch looked plush, and the throw rugs all around the floors made it feel cozy. There were lots of blankets and books in the corner of the living room, almost tucked away in between the couch and chair on a small table with shelves underneath it. The whole room was covered in windows, from the door to the corner, and then around to the adjacent wall. He noticed a kitchen the further he walked in, full of jars of herbs and leaves. A window above the sink in between the cabinets of the kitchen overlooked deeper into the forest and he imagined winters would be beautiful here, and cozy. He'd like to come back and be snowed in here, though he wasn't sure that would be a proper thing to request.

There was a chimney between the living area and the kitchen, empty of a flame but he could see fresh ash from previous use. There was a small wooden table in the center of the living space with a rug underneath, much like the rest of the house. It was closer to the kitchen and the long counter top made it seem as though they flowed together. There were stools perched under the counter and beautiful wooden chairs tucked under the table.

The closer he looked, and the deeper he walked, he noticed more cabinets and storage hidden in plain sight. The house was an off center square and he didn't know what to make of it, it was seemingly small and yet so full and well lived in and functional - it was almost the exact opposite of the house he was raised in.

The woman was in the kitchen once he was done looking around, and he followed after her. She reached for a kettle hanging on a hook and quickly filled it with water and brought it to the fire place. She hung it on the iron chimney crane, and pushed it out of the way. She quickly lit a match, and tossed it into the center of the wood already nestled in the ashes. The wood was dry and a flame blossomed almost immediately. She turned the crane until it was holding the pot above the flames, and quickly went back into the kitchen. She opened a cabinet and drew out two mugs, tea bags, and some honey.

"I have many types of tea, but considering how things are going for you currently," she said, pressing her tongue to her top teeth thoughtfully, "I think I'll recommend lavender tea." Her smile was wide and he huffed out a laugh as she teased him and nodded, though he'd have accepted any of the tea she offered.

Soon the water was boiling and she expertly withdrew it from the flames. Her movements were fluid, almost as if she danced through tasks with practiced ease. She poured water into the mugs and placed it on the wool coaster as the tea leaves steeped.

"Honey?" she asked him quietly, pouring some into her own mug.

"I'll have some, sure," he said, not actually sure if he wanted honey.

"It works best to ease worries when you pair both honey and lavender," she said and offered him the mug. She walked to the small seat by the book corner next to the small table he noticed before, wedged between the couch and the seat. He noticed then that it was overflowing with different books, worn and well loved. She took a sip of the tea before she sat down and placed it on the surface of the end table, sliding one of the books out of the way. She sat with her feet tucked under her, the fabric of the dress falling around her knees and calves.

He stood there dumbstruck for a second, holding his mug, when he realized he was staring. He quickly sat on the adjacent couch, holding his tea delicately. It was softer than he expected, he sank into it with a plop. He couldn't remember the last time he felt so at home anywhere before. He gingerly sipped at the tea and all but melted into his seat, settling into it as if he'd always lived there.

Moments passed in the comfortable silence, and the woman finished her tea and abandoned the mug on the small table. She gazed out the window, watching the wind blow through the leaves. She smiled, and her gaze caught the man's eye. He turned to see a deer as it walked into view and ate some of the weeds growing around the trees. The large animal grazed only an arm's length away from the glass panes. They watched together until the animal walked away, its hoofs not heard through the glass. He realized then just how thick the panes were, almost certain they couldn't be broken by storm or man. Arden slowly turned back around, facing the woman again. She looked at him curiously, head cocking to the side. She made a face as though she were thinking. He put his cup next to hers on the table and sighed, running his hands through his curls.

"Are you going to make yourself comfortable, soldier, or are you going to wear your bag and weapons all evening?" she asked finally. Her eyes glinted with humor, but her tone was pointed. He looked down at himself and laughed.

"I forgot I was wearing them," he replied honestly. He stood then, pulling the strap off his shoulder, she stood with him and reached an open hand out to take his belongings. They walked to the front door, and she hung up his bag on the hook in the small alcove next to it. He gently placed the bow and quiver next to his bag.

She turned back to the couch and was about to sit back in her chair, but stopped and looked at Arden pointedly. He hadn't realized he had been staring at her in the center of the living space with an odd look, and she paused where she was before she mirrored the look back at him comically.

"Is there something you need, sir?" she asked, hands on her hips. His gaze traveled over her curves unintentionally and he shook his head to come back to awareness, the curls bouncing around his ears gently.

"Forgive me, it's just -" he pursed his lips, "who are you?" he asked, blue eyes sharp on her own green.

"My name is Wil-" Arden's brows raised in curiosity as the woman's eyes widened slightly and darted to the side. He wondered at her pause, having hardly noticed her voice trailing off as she spoke. "Yeah." She breathed with a nod. "You can call me Will." A surprised look formed on her face as though she had shared too much, but she lifted her chin in a proud way. He wondered what she was thinking to make a face like that after giving her name. "Goodness, sir, what a glare you have on you, " she laughed at the look on his face.

"I'm sorry, I didn't intend to be rude. I'm Arden," he said, extending his hand in the typical greeting of men. "My sister has told me my resting expression is rather angry looking," he offered shyly. She walked quietly over to him before placing her hand into his, firmly shaking it as she laughed at the admission.

"A pleasure to meet you, Arden," she looked up at him and smiled sweetly.

"And you as well, Will," he said back, a small smile lifting his still pink cheeks.

Will turned around and walked to the kitchen, and rummaged through the cabinets. Arden noticed she had most of the storage in use on the bottom shelves, and that the tops were mostly bare. He looked at her slight frame and his eyes rose at how small she really was. He wondered how he hadn't noticed at first, but she was easily the smallest woman he had ever met.

Like a wood nymph, he thought suddenly.

He remembered stories of times when nymphs and fae would go to the ports for trade, but they hadn't been to his town in decades easily. Stories his mother assured him were just town gossip and nothing that could be proved, but he and his sister would wait for even a whisper of one in the streets, and in the halls of school. Stóngrast Port was known to be a quiet and unassuming port as far as trade routes went, but it seemed to be a hub for magical beings if there were any truth to the stories.

Thinking of those stories, he began to wonder at how she was living alone all the way out here away from town. He supposed she most likely had inherited the cottage young - he wasn't sure how else she'd have gotten it, and she seemed very young to still wear flowers in her long hair. She had an old presence that he felt comforted by, though, an odd mix of traits. Each moment he felt more and more relieved by her, more and more at ease, as though they'd known each other a very long time.

He trailed behind her slowly as she walked to the kitchen, and watched as she filled a pot with water and rice. She placed it into the flames she had just used for the tea, and with a quick poke to the embers, she brought the fire roaring back to life. He stayed quiet as she continued to prepare a meal with various vegetables and spices.

When most of the food was sliced, she finally looked at him. He had made himself comfortable on one of the stools along the edge of the stone countertop. He was leaning his chin in his hands and slouching over the table, watching her patiently. She leaned back, placing her elbows against the sink and quirked her head.

"It's almost dinner time, now, and I don't know what your plans are," she said, as she ran a hand down her long curly hair. A flower fell as she played with the strands.

"I told my family I would be gone for the weekend," he said as he watched the flower fall. Her toes tapped the ground and he looked back up at her as a smile started forming on her face.

"Arden, there are no inns anywhere near here," she laughed. "I don't even think there are any within a day's travel. You found yourself pretty deep in the forest, sir, and look," she pointed out the window at the darkening sky, "there is no way you'll be able to make it back to town even at a sprint before the sun sets."

Arden thought about it and for a moment was slightly concerned, "I mean, I could very well run home..." he trailed off as her laugh burst through the room.

"I have a guest room and you're more than welcome to use it," she said, still tittering. "Grab your stuff and I'll show you," she pushed away from the counter and started walking to the hallway at the front of the house.

"That really won't be necessary, I'll figure something out," he started, "I really don't want to put you in a bad position." He followed her to his bags, and she turned to look at him with an eyebrow raised.

"Where do you plan on sleeping during your weekend long hunt? A tree?" She smiled softly before continuing, "A creature would eat you up as soon as you got comfortable."

"I think I could handle a night's camp in the woods," Arden said loftily, offended by her words. Though he agreed with her, and had no desire to spend the night alone in the woods, especially with the attacks that he'd seen around the Port.

She patted his shoulder, squishing her nose up with a smile, "oh I know you could, sir, but these woods were not meant for a solitary human after sunset." Her words were light, but he felt an edge underneath them and he was suddenly scared at what lurked out beyond the trees, the strange marks on the bodies of those found come morning. A small shudder went up his spine that he did his best to pretend didn't happen at all. Will saw but didn't react, but squeezed his arm as she passed him again. He grabbed his bag and weapons and followed her down the hall. They passed one door, and then another, and she opened up the last door on the right. She gestured inside, but didn't go in.

"This is my guest room, there are extra blankets in the trunk at the foot of the bed. You can close the curtains, as well, and I'll be closing the shutters before we go to bed, " Will said, "and also, there is a bathroom just here," she pointed to the second door they had passed, "if you need to use it." She turned back down the hall to the kitchen and let him settle in.

Arden was baffled by the kindness she had shown him so far and didn't understand how a woman living alone in the woods would allow a strange man into her home so openly and without fear. He had a terrifying image flash through his mind of her allowing the wrong type of man into her safe quarters - and grew sick at the thought. He quickly tossed his belongings onto the chair in the corner and walked back out to meet her.

Will handed him a bowl of rice, vegetables, and fish. It smelled delicious, and he sat across from her eagerly. She placed her bowl on the table, and then grabbed glasses and filled them with cold brewed tea, and handed him one.

They ate quietly together and the sun was close to setting by the time they finished eating. Arden felt warm in her presence, he had forgotten what it was like to have a peaceful dinner with no surprises or disappointing conversation. He wondered what it was like to live in the quiet, dealing with the empty solitude of the forest when the sun went down. There was always someone moving around the Port, and he couldn't even begin to imagine what it must be like to live in a place so devoid of the liveliness of the market.

With their bellies full, Will stood up and cleared the dishes and quickly washed them. She let them dry on a towel and brushed her hair away from her face, petals falling in almost slow motion around her. She sighed tiredly, and turned to see Arden staring at her with an equally tired look. Turning around, she opened a drawer and pulled out several candles. They were round and thick, and she lit them before placing them on small metal candle plates. One went on the kitchen table, and the other two she brought to the corner table next to the couches. She then walked past him to the front door and he wondered for a moment what she was doing, not certain why she needed candles before the sun went down.

"I'm closing the shutters, if you would like to join me. You'll see why we needed the candles when I'm finished," Will told him, "otherwise, make yourself comfortable," she smiled at him before walking out the door. He thought for a moment if he wanted to sit and do nothing, but he couldn't help but feel curious so he followed her outside to watch as she shut each shutter carefully. She was purposeful and sure in her movements, barely stopping to smile at him cheekily between windows. By the time they made it back around the front door, the sun cast an orange glow in the sky, beautiful and radiant.

They walked inside the cottage, now completely dark and devoid of outside light. The shutters prevented barely even a slight glint of the sun. He realized she was right about needing the candles, and thought her forethought was impressive. *She's been doing this a long while,* he thought, *of course she's prepared.* He followed her to the couch and watched as she plopped down onto it indelicately. He laughed under his breath and followed suit into the chair next to her.

"So what brought you back to the forest so soon, Arden?" Will asked with a yawn. "Not many are traveling lately, you know," she looked at him, eyebrows raised.

"It's been months," he laughed, rubbing his eyes. "It isn't 'so' soon," he glanced at her, with a wide smile.

"But a blink of an eye amongst the trees," she replied cryptically before throwing her head back in a laugh, unable to keep a straight face. She had sounded so much like Teg for a moment that he had been stunned, but quickly joined her. They laughed together for a moment before quieting down, gazing out the window and then back to each other.

"I have been feeling trapped in that town lately," he said finally, "it seems as though the walls I grew up in are getting smaller and smaller. And somehow, things just keep getting worse no matter what we do."

"What do you mean?" Will leaned forward, curious.

"I mean, things keep happening *near* town, or on the road out of town to the other Ports." he looked at her. "In the forest outside the boundaries of the Port, people are going missing and things...things just keep happening and there's no explanation for them." He sighed, not sure how to explain it. "We've had a hard time with deliveries, as well, and many of the shipments we need haven't been recovered."

"Wait a moment, you were going to wander the woods where people have been vanishing, and then camp in them?" she laughed but made a face, clearly alarmed.

"Not exactly," he pursed his lips and crossed his arms.

"What do you mean," she laughed, "that seems like *exactly* what you were going to do."

"I came looking for you, and knew I wouldn't be in danger," he shrugged.

"Oh," she said in surprise, "but how could you trust a complete stranger in the very woods people are going missing? What if it had been *me* behind it all?" He gave her a bland look. He knew he should be wary of her, especially by the implication that she may be dangerous, but couldn't find it in himself to be worried at all as he took in her expression.

"Because you're not," he said simply.

"I'm an herbalist, Arden," she leaned forward, elbows resting on her knees, "I could have poisoned you, like, eight different times tonight." Arden blinked at her, not understanding but then his eyes went wide and he looked at the tea mugs still on the table from earlier. Will threw her head back laughing, again, as though she couldn't even fight against the humor of Arden almost being poisoned. He looked back at her with a frown and rolled his eyes.

"That's not funny, Will," he huffed.

"Yes it is," she cackled.

Arden couldn't help it, the straight face couldn't hold against her laugh. It was sharp and silly sounding and he started laughing with her, tears forming in his eyes from laughing so hard. Arden couldn't remember the last time he had laughed so thoroughly before.

"Well, I guess it's almost time for bed. Unless you want some more tea?" Will asked before stretching out her legs. "Or you can tell me more about the mysteries of the Port," she offered.

"No thank you, but I appreciate the offer," he said with a smile as he stretched his legs, too. "Why do you close the storm doors before bed?" he asked as curiosity creeped strong in his mind. It was odd to close them just for the night, unless she knew there would be storms in the area.

"That's actually a good question," Will said as she stretched further over the couch. "There was a time when I didn't think it was necessary to close the curtains or shutters at night, so unless I knew it was going to storm they stayed open. But one night, I woke up feeling off and thought, maybe a glass of water would help me to fall back to sleep." She twirled her hair as she tapped her feet on the floor before glancing up at Arden.

"So I opened my bedroom door and felt *something* standing outside." Arden's eyes were wide and he leaned closer, completely enthralled with her story. "From my doorway, I can see into this window pretty clearly," she gestured to the one behind her, "and all I could see was this giant bear with eyes that I *swear* were glowing yellow." Will shuddered.

"*Yellow?*" Arden felt a chill in his spine at the image in his mind. "Gods," he mumbled as she continued.

"Oh yes, glowing yellow eyes. Its body easily took up the whole window pane. The only thought I had was 'well this is great, live alone in the woods, die alone in the woods.' I didn't think I'd be eaten by a bear, though. Always thought I'd just choke to death on a berry or something," she said with a laugh, though Arden immediately worried about the truth in her words. "But since then, I have never gone to bed without shutting the storm doors first - I want something more than glass and fabric between me and whatever beast is out there. And I always bring a glass of water to bed with me - just in case something *is* outside the window waiting for me."

"How long ago did you see it?" He wasn't sure he wanted to know, but asked anyway.

"Actually, it was a few weeks after we had first met," she said, making a face as she thought about it. "I remember it being right before the full moon, the day before the Trades meeting. I was exhausted from staying up all night," she told him. Arden shuddered, hoping that it didn't show its face here ever again.

"What kind of bear do you think it was?" Arden asked.

"I have no idea, and no one believed it even happened when I told my friends when I saw them on Trade's Day. They said it must've been a nightmare and not a memory." She looked at him with her eyebrows drawn tight, "but I'm telling you I didn't sleep at all that night. I just waited for it to push just hard enough on the glass to get through." Arden looked at her with an uneasy look, and glanced at all the windows to make sure they were properly covered, though he remembered her locking them tight not long before.

"I'll get us some water glasses to bring to bed," she said, eyes twinkling, before walking to the kitchen, and quietly filled up two cups of water. She came back and handed one to Arden after blowing out the candle on the table.

"Are you just telling me a campfire story to tease me?" Arden asked as he took it from her, wondering if maybe she wanted to scare him a little bit.

"Oh no," she laughed, "I am absolutely serious. That bear is out there and I am wildly concerned about him finding my cottage again," her laugh seemed to fill each word as she said them. Arden sensed that for Will, she had to either laugh or cry about her situation. He wondered if that was why she was so giggly, if laughter was her only relief to the solitude and fear that living alone in the woods brings. They were quite the same in that their lives seemed to have them bound to loneliness, though in slightly different ways. "But don't worry, we can close your curtains, too, on top of the shutters." Arden suddenly yawned and rubbed his eyes.

"Come on, soldier, let's go to bed," she reached her hand out to him and he grasped it, standing. He rubbed his eyes again, and she rubbed his arm, "you came a long way and you need some sleep." She reached over and grabbed the remaining two candles from the end table before walking down the hall.

She led him to his room, and helped him close the curtains and placed one of the candles on his bedside table. "You know, there are more windows in this room than mine. I thought guests would like to wake up and gaze out to the creek out back, or wake up to a blanket of snow." She smiled as she tugged the last curtain into place. He put the glass on the end table next to the bed and then sat on the mattress watching her.

"It's been nice having a friend over, again. It's been a long time," she said with a sad tone, "good night, Arden."

"Good night, Will," he answered. He didn't say it, but he felt the same. It really had been a long time since he felt this level of friendship with someone, and he was glad to have stumbled quite literally into it.

She turned out of the room and shut the door behind her, leaving him in the candlelight. He felt around the bed for the blanket corner and tugged it down. Before climbing into the cold sheets, he blew out the candle. In the pitch dark he realized he still was wearing his leather vest and his belt and shirt, so carefully slid them off, and tossed them over the side of the bed. He tucked himself deep into the firm mattress, taking a deep breath when he was comfortable. A moment passed before he fell asleep, quickly lulled by the enveloping silence and the exhaustion of the day, the plump pillow under his head a soft and welcome comfort.

...

When Arden woke up, he was disoriented and confused about where he was. He blinked and rubbed his eyes, and sat up before he remembered with an excited flutter in his stomach. Briefly he wondered if Will was still asleep and then heard a door open and small footsteps padding around the kitchen. He threw his legs out of bed and tugged on his shirt, the ties at the base of his throat loose and out of place. He didn't see a mirror and was still half asleep and was too tired to attempt lacing the shirt back up, so he didn't bother. He rubbed his eyes again and ran a hand through his hair hoping it tamed his curls down slightly. He didn't want to look like a fool stumbling barefoot through a lady's house at dawn, but wasn't sure it mattered anyway. He wasn't even certain he knew the time at all, it was still very dark with the shutters closed. He did see faint light peeking through the cracks, though, so he supposed it wasn't too early.

He walked out to the kitchen to see a small fire already rumbling to life, and Will filling the kettle with water at the sink. She wore a nightgown that was slightly rumpled with sleep and her hair was tousled out of place. He noticed the flowers were still there and surprisingly not wilted, and he was baffled at how well they had lasted through the night. He sat on a stool as she turned the water off and turned around.

"Morning," she murmured with a sleepy voice and a soft smile.

"Morning," Arden answered, his breath catching in his throat at the sight of her. He had seen she was beautiful when they first met but now he realized she was striking, truly taking his breath away as she stood in the fresh morning sun with messy hair. The shutters were open, and he supposed she must have opened them right after starting the fire. Her dress was slipping over her shoulder and he couldn't help but glance at her collar bones under her hair, but a yawn forced him to finally look away.

I need to be more mindful of how I stare, he thought to himself, *friends don't ogle friends.*

"You like coffee, Arden, or would you like tea?" she asked.

"Coffee would be great, thank you," he said.

When the water was ready she added it to the press and they waited while it brewed and steeped. She poured it into mugs and slid him one, offering him what looked like powder.

"What's that?" he asked.

"Oh, it's powdered cream. Living out here, I don't always have fresh dairy or meat, mostly what grows naturally around in the forest. So I stock up on this as often as I can, since it lasts a long time," she explained as she spooned it into her coffee before stirring and sipping it.

"That's interesting," he said, "I wouldn't have thought about that. I drink mine black, though, so it wouldn't be an issue for me," he laughed, voice still husky from sleep.

"You'd do well in the forest then," she laughed back.

"What made you move out here?" he asked, sipping from the mug.

"It wasn't exactly an active choice. I kind of just...ended up here," she yawned then, then took a big sip from the mug. "But anyway, what about you?"

"What do you mean? I don't live in the woods," he said in a teasing tone. She laughed and shook her head.

"No, I mean - you told your mother you were hunting, right?" He nodded in response before she continued, "Well, what are we hunting today? You can't go home without something if you've been gone overnight," she reasoned.

"Ah," he said, stretching his back, "yes, I should probably bring something home then."

"Yes, probably," she threw her head back with another laugh, "it would be a good idea to do what you said you were going to do," her laugh was contagious and Arden joined her, amazed at how whole heartedly she could laugh at even the smallest thing, every time, and not show any sense of getting tired of being silly.

After they had coffee and a small breakfast, they sat with their mugs on the couch and watched out the windows together in the quiet. It was a lovely morning, and sitting next to Will felt so *right*.

Around midday, they went outside and collected berries together. Arden felt naked in his slept-in clothes and bare feet, and couldn't remember the last time he'd been in the garden with no shoes on. He felt like a child, the innocence of spending time playing in the mud and digging up bugs flashing through his mind. He felt at peace as they ate berries straight from the bushes, and watched as Will produced a large melon from seemingly nowhere. The autumn chill was still in the air, the ground cold under his toes but it was refreshing in a way he didn't understand.

"What is that?" he asked, voice high with surprise.

"Have you never seen a watermelon before?" Will laughed, as she dropped it hard on a smooth rock by the river's edge. It burst open and she broke it into quarters, and gave him one of the chunks before taking a bite of the bright colored meat, juices falling over her hands. "The season's ending so I'm glad you're here before they go away. I wouldn't have been able to finish them all in time before the first frost," she told him as she wiped her hands on her skirts. He took a tentative bite of his own, pleasantly surprised by the gentle sweetness of the large fruit.

They ate more until they were full off of the things they found in the garden, before eventually Arden knew he had best head back to the port, and go home. They went inside and cleaned themselves up, though he wasn't ready to leave. Arden changed into his fresh clothes, storing his laundry in the bag and then grabbed his weapons before walking to the front of the house. Will put on slippers and a sweater before she turned to him.

"I'll come with you until we're closer to town," she said as she opened the door and led him out. They walked in silence until they heard a crunch in the distance, twigs breaking softly. Arden withdrew his bow and nocked an arrow into place, but kept it held at his side. He didn't hunt often, but he was a good shot and knew it would be easy to catch the creature.

"Arden," Will whispered comically loud as they approached a large deer, "if you kill that animal, how are you getting it home? It seems rather large," she started to snicker under her breath. Arden made a face and looked at her perplexed.

"You always have to do that, don't you?" he asked.

"Do what? You mean, voice logic?" she laughed quietly.

"More like, rain on a parade," he glanced at her with a frown, though there was nothing more than mirth in his voice.

"Okay, then, how *are* you going to get it to town?" she smirked at him.

"I'll toss it over my shoulders, Will," he said, voice haughty, though the laugh that threatened to leave his throat was hard to hold in.

"Maybe you should find one closer to your town before you travel that far with a huge weight on your back. You can't be walking in these woods at night, especially not with a dead animal," she said. Will put a hand on his arm and he sighed at her, knowing she was right. He noted how nice her hand felt on his arm and hoped she'd do it again.

They walked on, talking quietly with each other and enjoying one another's company. They teased each other back and forth in an easy way, and if Arden wasn't reading too much into it, he felt as though Will was flirting with him. Finally, though, Arden found a suitably close deer and Will whispered a small farewell, and they parted ways regretfully.

"You are always welcome in my home, Arden," she whispered, her expression a little sad, "until next time."

After Arden killed the deer, he picked it up and carried it on his shoulders all the way to town. The sun set was nearing fast but he made it home in time before darkness fell. Something about Will's words worried him about the forest, and he was grateful to have made it home safe without any issues.

When he reached town, he brought his hunt to the butcher's where they would save the fur and antlers and have it sent back to Arden's home for use. The meat would be used up and the leftovers Devon would buy from Arden, whatever they ended up not using. Having grown up with the butcher and his children, he was very well educated on the processes Bartrum had used. When they'd gone to school together as kids, he would come to play with Devon after classes let out. If he was lucky, Bartrum would teach Arden about the butchery profession on the days he visited, and it was his absolute delight each time the man kindly shared his knowledge. His heart ached painfully as he spoke to Devon as he left the deer with him, so much grief within them as they existed in a shop once run by arguably the kindest man in the Port.

Arden walked through his front doors and was greeted by his sister, who had been watching out the window and saw him walk up.

"Good afternoon, brother, how was your hunting trip?" she asked excitedly.

"It was good, I left a deer at the Cahlin's," He said as he took off his bags and shoes. They were covered in muck and Felisia the housekeeper took them from him to be washed by her daughter, Alise, the maid. Arden sighed, already frustrated by the presence of so many people despite being grateful for their help and kindness over the years.

"Mother was asking for you all morning, apparently she forgot you were going on a trip," Juna murmured low in Arden's ear, "I don't think she really forgot, she just wanted to be theatrical, running around and calling your name," she giggled, "she missed you."

"Of course," Arden laughed gruffly, not surprised at all by his sister's words. She often teased their mother on her behavior as she was prone to being dramatic. His sister wished their mother was more down to earth, and it caused many arguments over the years between the three of them. Arden was certain it was because Juna favored calm, quiet, and mellow activities like he did, whereas Alvenia preferred social excursions. She was a loving and kind mother, of course, but she did tend to like making a big to-do of all the small things, and laying about the chaise with a hand to her head to lament if her children were too busy for her and nowhere to be found - it was one of her most frequent activities.

Arden had the feeling she missed having children in the house, little ones to spend time with her, and it was half the reason she kept pushing him for a marriage. He couldn't blame her, of course, but it was too much pressure for him to even want to acknowledge it, especially when he didn't want to marry a woman and risk never being able to love her. He shook his head hoping his sister didn't see his thoughts on his face, running a hand through his hair before quickly giving her a peck on the cheek and murmuring that he'd be back downstairs soon.

He went up to his room to bathe and change out of his well worn clothes, now dirty and bloodstained from carrying the deer through the woods. He looked out the window, gazing out at the forest with an ache of longing in his belly. He already missed the quiet and comfort of the trees. Already missed Will with an aching sense of loss, though he was surprised at the depth of the feeling. He procrastinated in his room with the white handkerchief for a while, just staring at it fondly, before finally succumbing to the hunger in his belly, and made his way to the dining room.

Dinner was served and Arden dined with his mother and sister. It was much the same as usual and he had to bite his tongue to try and maintain a gentle expression on his face. He could see the effort they made to hold back their incessant questions, a small thing that made him feel grateful. No doubt Juna had mentioned to their mother to stop asking persistently on his marital status - he wished he felt grateful for it but he only felt guilt. Finally though, the two women couldn't hold back any longer, but at least they had made it through most of the meal.

"Oh, Arden, I was wondering where you went and I just completely forgot you were going on a hunt! It's just so silly I would forget where my own son was going!" His mother laughed. Alvenia truly loved her children and would do anything for them, and Arden knew without a doubt that she was fully aware of his location at all times, or tried to be. She just liked to pretend she wasn't worried for him when he was out of her sight, to pretend that he was a boy for a little longer and safe in her care nearby. He loved the two women at the table with him, though they were tiring in a lot of ways. He supposed that was family for you, though, before he smiled warmly at his mother.

"So where did you go, brother?" Juna asked, leaning forward onto the table.

"I went to a friend's," he answered plainly.

"A friend's? Where?" his mother countered.

"A friend in the forest."

"Well, who is the friend?" Alvenia was intrigued. Arden could read her feelings clean across her face, her thoughts had always been an open book. He could see her thinking, *well who has friends in the forest?*

"Will," Arden answered easily before scooping more food into his mouth, chewing slowly.

"You have a friend named Will who lives in the woods?" Juna asked, nose scrunching. Arden wondered if her cheeks were starting to hurt from hiding a laugh, "that's weird," she said finally with a cough, but their mother just shrugged.

"So your friend Will has a house in the forest?" Alvenia asked, her eyebrows raised, Arden could see her trying to elaborate more of even the smallest ounce of information about his weekend adventure.

"That's right."

"But why is the house in the forest?" Alvenia said with growing confusion. Arden knew it was because she had been born and raised in the Port and couldn't fathom the idea that someone were to live in the middle of nowhere without any distractions around. He saw her face pinch at the thought of being without any friends for company.

"Because, mother," Juna offered, "that's where Will *lives.*"

Arden tried hard not to laugh when his sister responded. He shoveled as much food into his mouth as he could, hoping he'd be full by the time they stopped talking. Or at least be finished eating before they could think of more questions to ask him. He was vague enough that they didn't seem to care about where he went, other than the fact the house being in the woods was weird. He just hoped they would leave him alone about his friend, and was dreading when they'd bring up marriage again. So far, though, he was pleasantly surprised at his reunion with his family.

When they headed upstairs to bed, Alvenia gave him a warm hug. He was no longer a small boy and towered over her, but she still kissed both of his cheeks before bidding him a good night with love.

Arden thought how grateful he was to have people to love him, and how it was so much different in this house full of so many compared to Will's empty home alone in the dark out in the middle of the woods. For a moment he was struck with homesickness, his whole heart aching confusingly, before he finally fell asleep to the sounds of a lived-in home.

~ Four ~

VISITING HANLAN

Wilmayra laid in her bed for a while, thinking over their night together. She didn't remember the last time she had been able to laugh with another soul the way she had today, save for the rare nights her and a friend would stay up late as they giggled by the candle light. She was also concerned for Arden's safety - if he had wandered any other dangerous path no others had followed and blindly walked into a stranger's house, she would be upset to say the least. Something terrible could happen to him and she would blame herself for it. How could a man be so trusting and kind? It really made no sense. Sure, maybe she had let a man into her home with no source of protection for herself, and it was basically the same thing as what Arden had done, but she brushed the thought away.

She had found him in the Binding Prayer position, a pose she had thought she'd never see in her lifetime, and certainly not to her own tree. He was truly innocent of the ways of her kind, especially since he'd sealed his fate to her unintentionally. She felt guilty, but she couldn't pretend that she didn't find him safe. She wanted him around her and craved his presence when he was gone, even though they hardly knew each other at all. Paired with the fact that she didn't think him capable of harming another being, it made it harder for her to remain objective. After all, he'd be married soon enough to a lovely human woman from his Port and move on, forgetting about the lonely woods altogether. Her brows bunched in thought, remembering his kind manners and easy way about himself. His reaction to her supplying the idea of him being poisoned by her was comical, too, and she was glad he hadn't found her crazy with how shrill her laugh was.

It took a very long time for her to fall asleep, just thinking about having a man in her home. Not a friend, not a parent, but a *man,* in her *house.* She honestly didn't think it was ever a possibility, especially since it was so rare for anyone to travel in Tonsilta at all anymore. To meet anyone at all was difficult, and this man found her and then came *back.* It was just too much to believe but she was grateful in a way that words couldn't even stress. She had never even thought it possible that she'd ever marry or have a family. She'd always thought she'd be destined for eternal solitude out in the empty woods. Her thoughts continued racing wildly around in circles before Wilmayra settled and found a dreamless slumber.

When the morning sun rose, Wilmayra awoke naturally from the ingrained routine. It took her a minute but she eventually remembered the guest in the room down the hall, and tiptoed to the kitchen and put water over a fire she quickly brought to life before she headed out the front door to open the shutters. She left the guest room shutters closed to let Arden sleep longer, and made her way back into the house to brew the coffee and waited for the man to wake up. She was surprised when he did finally stumble out of the room and down the hall, his shirt askew and falling open, revealing his broad chest and exposing dark hair.

She begged her cheeks not to heat and looked away as she greeted him and offered him something to drink. She hadn't spent much time around men in such a relaxed setting but knew staring at his body while biting her lip was definitely not proper etiquette, even for forest folk. She brushed the thoughts away and pulled a coffee press from the lower cabinet before adding coffee grounds to it when Arden's gruff voice affirmed he'd like some. Her cheeks did heat then, at the sound of his sleepy words, the rumbling deep timbre of his low voice. She hadn't expected she'd have any kind of reaction to the voice of a Man, but she considered she had just never been in this specific situation before and couldn't help but feel as though she should behave a certain way. She was unsure of how exactly she was supposed to act though, and was certain her mother never told her how to deal with an overnight guest from a far away town before.

After having their coffees, they spent the day together. First having breakfast and a simple grazed lunch, they teased each other back and forth as the trees watched and listened. Wilmayra showed him a watermelon that he had been surprised to see, and thought over a list of other produce she would be able to surprise him with. It was easy, the way they were able to talk and laugh. As though they'd been friends their whole lives. Wilmayra really didn't want him to leave, she knew the silence would be deafening as soon as he was gone.

After all too short a time, Wilmayra regretfully had to finally say goodbye and send Arden on his way. She almost asked him to just stay, but knew it was for the best. After all, it would be dangerous to be in the forest too late in case he was stuck out in the open when the sun went down. She wondered when he would be back again to visit, or if this was the last time she'd see him. She forbade the tears to fall out of her eyes though they burned with the effort as she turned around and went back to her cottage.

That night it was hard for her to fall asleep again, but for different reasons than the night before. She felt alone, a deep ache in her chest. It felt deeper than the usual loneliness she typically felt. After having been in someone else's company for so long, even only a day, the silence was painful and hard to adjust to. The cost of finding a friend made solitude sharper, a knife to her gut. Wilmayra almost felt as if it hadn't been worth meeting Arden at all if this was how it would feel every time he left her behind. She sniffled into the dark room and hoped that maybe going to the trading outpost later in the week would relieve some of the ache in her heart. She hoped to see her friends there, too.

...

Wilmayra spent the rest of the week packing up traveling bags full of dried mixes of herbs and oils, and several blends of teas. Each one was placed in small jars or linen bags that she had sewn from scrap fabric she had lying around. There wasn't as much as she would've usually liked to bring, but trade was slower than years before and she didn't have enough supplies to make more than the small tinctures with the changing seasons limiting growth of new ingredients, and she didn't want to delve into her reserves especially if there were fewer items worth trading at the outpost. Her stores in the basement were rather excessive, but she wouldn't bring a large supply of stock unless someone showed up with a delivery cart on the next Trade's Day. If the need is there, she'll have it scheduled for pick up next time. She knew she was only going to the Trading Post to break the monotony of being alone all day, which was the only reason she ever really decided to go to Hanlan, anyway, if she was being honest.

The morning finally came for her to go to Hanlan, and Wilmayra filled a large knapsack to the brim with small bottles, and a shoulder bag full of the loose leaf teas. She wondered who would be there, this time around, since fewer and fewer people had been making the trek. Not for the first time, Wilmayra wished she had a horse to make the distance quicker to travel. She put on her hiking boots and a thick traveling smock before donning the bags and headed out for the long walk as soon as the sun rose in the sky. She skipped a sweater to avoid sweating during the hike.

She had been caught in the night of the woods before, and the trees helped guide her the last distance home, thankfully, but she had not enjoyed the feeling of complete darkness save for the moon high in the sky. Though it had cast enough light on the ground, it was still hard to make out any landmarks she frequently traveled over the years and knew by heart, especially following the creek with its loud bubbling. She shivered remembering the strange bear that had looked in her window that one night, and knew she would never set foot in the woods past sunset willingly ever again, especially after knowing what lurked under the moon.

Hours passed as she walked as quickly as she could, whispering back and forth to the trees. Frequently she stopped and explored the local flora hoping to pocket a few pieces of plant life to propagate in her own garden, smiling as the trees thanked her for bringing new life deeper into the forest. Naturally, she had a green thumb and each new plant she harvested did well under her care. The small baby propagations all but sang in her pockets as she continued walking along. When she got to the outpost, she'd make sure she traded her supplies for small plant vases and dirt to nourish them while so far away from home, even a few hours would have them wilting and she didn't want them to be uncomfortable.

By mid morning, Wilmayra was finally at the outskirts of the Hanlan Trading outpost. The creek passed through the center of the small town-like market, a watering hole for anyone in need. There was a small inn used for emergencies, though not many had needed it as of late since no one had been traveling far enough to need overnight lodging. Usually she could hear people chattering by the time she reached this point, but so far it was eerily silent aside from the sound of the trees in the wind, and the creek bubbling along unbothered. Not knowing what to expect, she kept her footsteps from making noise and hoped the small jars didn't clank around while she tiptoed along.

She was grateful to see that a few of the regulars were milling around the main market stall, a breath of relief falling from her lips. She recognized an older man in the distance, standing gravely with his back to her, and she made her way over to him.

"Teggert," she said as she reached the man, calling him by name. The man turned and gave her a somber smile and Wilmayra was immediately alarmed at his expression. Gert was never one to mince words or offer advice that wasn't right or warranted and for him to have such a serious expression, she was concerned. Considering the lack of people at the market- she saw only three people from where she stood, not including herself- she knew it must be bad news. She almost felt the need to sprint back to her cottage and drop everything in her bags at Gert's feet, to flee whatever it was that was scaring everyone in the forest. None of her friends had come since the time she'd mentioned the bear to anyone, months ago. It seemed something far worse was lurking in the forest to keep everyone so far from home.

"Wisteria," Gert greeted her with his gravelly voice. He reminded Wilmayra of stone, strong and heavy, reliable- someone she trusted completely, and over the years he proved again and again just how reliable he was. Like a river rock, down to the roots the trees grew around, a presence that grounded all who sought his company. Wilmayra saw his solemn smile and reached out for a hug. "I had hoped you would stay home, if I'm being honest," he said as he hugged her back, a gentle squeeze so familiar. He wrapped an arm around her shoulder and pulled her to a small bench close to the inn. It was so quiet, the hairs on the back of Wilmayra's neck started to stand as goose bumps covered her arms and legs. She fought a shiver as it tried to overcome her body, and leaned in close to Gert's tall form. The small propagations in her pocket tittered with curiosity.

"Gert, what's going on?" Her voice was a whisper. She was scared that someone would overhear them but knew it was silly, since Hanlan was all but abandoned .

"Wisty, love, there have been an increased amount of strange things happening around the entire Vesphnion Kagdah forest. No one is traveling at all because of....." his gravelly voice tapered off, and he looked like he was trying to find the right words to explain to Wilmayra what was going on. She waited, though she couldn't say she waited patiently, for him to continue as her whole body started to feel like it may tremble and quake right off the bench. It seemed that Gert couldn't begin to say what he wanted, and after a few minutes Wilmayra nudged him and tried to bring him back to the moment. Finally, he continued.

"Wisty, there has been some peculiar goings-on in the Kagdah," he ran a hand through his grey hair, "people have been going missing." He furrowed his brows and Wilmayra leaned closer, shoulder pressing against his arm to hear his words clearly.

"What do you mean by 'missing'?" Wilmayra asked quietly.

"Well, to put it quite frankly," he looked in her eyes then turned away before murmuring, "they aren't exactly *missing*."

"Gert, please, what do you *mean*?" Wilmayra said, voice still a whisper but she was growing frustrated.

"'M sorry, love, it's hard for me to say it out loud," he said sadly, nodding to himself as though he were trying to gain the strength to finish what he was trying to say. Wilmayra sat on her hands to settle herself down, knowing that whatever he had to tell her would clearly be terrible news. When he finally continued, she was unsure she even wanted to know anymore.

"Fae folk have been disappearing in the forest," he said gravely. "At first, it seemed as though only humans were going missing. But after the autumn equinox last month, there was a steady increase in missing people of all kinds."

"What does that mean?" Wilmayra asked, pretending her voice didn't tremble with fear. For a man who had such a steadfast presence to be so concerned that he couldn't even voice it out loud - she was afraid. Her heart began to pound in her chest, threatening to break free of her rib cage in anticipation.

"Well, at first, it meant nothing. Coincidence," he murmured, leaning back into her where she leaned against him, "at first it was all coincidence. But from town, I heard from my brother some news that the humans going missing around town were found."

"Where did they go?"

"They hadn't gone anywhere, except for a walk after the sun went down. But they were eventually found...though not whole."

Wilmayra shook her head and a tremble made its way from the base of her spine to her neck, breath hitching in her throat.

"Pieces were recovered, strewn about the outer walls of the human Port. Grin let me know what was happening, and who the victims were. It was clearly something large consuming its prey," he continued, finally sounding as though he knew how to say it without second guessing himself, though it was gruesome. "It was also clear that after a few attempts of eating humans, they weren't the intended victims. The humans were never...finished, if you pardon the description," Gert said apologetically as Wilmayra's face went green at the thought. " It wasn't until the first Fae victim that the disappearances increased, and we realized whatever this thing is, it's searching for Fae."

"So something is...*hunting* Fae?" Wilmayra's voice was barely a whisper, barely a breath of air between them.

"I'm afraid that's not the worst of the news," Gert said levelly, looking into her eyes, "it's targeting Wood Nymphs."

Wilmayra blinked at him and shook her head, unable to process the information. She was suddenly terrified for her family, so far away and she was unable to check on them. She was scared for Gert's brother, Teggrin, and what that could possibly mean for them now if the forest they had no choice but to live and grow in was no longer safe.

"The Willow family is safe, it seems as though it won't cross stone barriers. Stóngrast Port has stone walls around it, and so does your family's grove. It doesn't seem to either be able to get through stone, or unwilling to try, which we should be extremely grateful for."

"What about your brother?" she asked, still worried.

"Trust me, our roots are protected by lots of stone. There will be no pruning of the Teg's without our compliance," he smiled kindly, sounding almost like his usual self.

Wilmayra felt tears prickle in her eyes, so unsure of what they should do or what she *could* do, living by herself out in the middle of nowhere with no support of family or even a stone that wasn't dug into the earth around her.

"There's more you should know, Wisteria," he said. Her stomach dropped at his words, she was certain she didn't want to hear anything else from him. "It will attempt to lure out the nymph by attacking its tree. Any sound, any attempt to defend the tree *will* be fatal. I won't tell you how I know this to be true, but *trust* me when I say the only way to avoid it hunting you and killing you, is to completely disappear."

Wilmayra immediately thought to herself the hidden basement in her home, completely undetectable to the outside world. That would be where she ran if she even thought she heard a branch snap in the woods around her. The entrance was hidden under a rug in the kitchen, underneath the table and chairs. It dropped down over a dozen feet underground, cool and dark. It was where she stored all of her jarred and preserved food, and medicinal supplies. She had been stocking it and keeping everything fresh for years just in case something happened - unfortunately, she hadn't expected that something that lurks in the night would be the reason she needed to hide in a dark hole under her house. She was grateful that she had the forethought to put a bedroom in the little cave, though her mother had told her it was slightly excessive with the Protected windows. She made a promise, then, to herself, that she would sleep in that dark hole every night just in case the creature found her. It would be worse than the bear incident, and a tear slipped from her eyes then at the thought.

"Gert, I don't want to be eaten," her voice was unrecognizable. She sounded like a little girl lost in the woods, alone with no one to rescue her.

"You'll be okay, Wisteria, but you need to be prepared," he told her with just as much fear as she had in her own voice, "just make sure you stay close to the tree if it's nearby. It's not safe to leave it behind to hide, in case it hurts the tree to lure you out and you are unable to repair the damage right away. It would also be fatal to leave the wounds to the bark - we have seen many succumb to infection that way. I've been in contact with a few of the fae families and we are getting a better idea of what we can do to keep everyone safe," he explained, "I have theories on what's going on and how best to handle this, but the research isn't complete. I need more time, but I know I'm close."

"How many have been hurt so far?" Wilmayra was afraid to know the answer.

"We aren't certain. There have been many in hiding since the rumors started, and many more still receding into solitude to remain undetected." He stared across the empty market, devoid of all the usual life. "I would imagine close to a couple dozens of Fae that have been taken away from us too soon. And many still we haven't been able to trace at all - they could be anywhere."

"I just don't understand why this is happening to us," she whispered.

"Something woke up a sleeping beast, long lost to time. We don't know how it happened, either, but it hunts during the night when the moon is high in the sky," he trailed off, eyes unfocused. Wilmayra waited for him to continue, staring at the grass and cobblestone. "Before it only ate every few weeks, the attacks were sporadic at best. But now, it's nearly every week that we hear from a relative that they were not able to escape."

"It's getting hungrier each time it eats?" A shiver trailed up her spine.

"Yes, it seems to be so." His brows were drawn tight, a river of emotion flowing quickly over his face.

"What will I do, if it comes for me?" She hesitated before asking.

"As long as you remain unheard, hidden in your home, you will be okay. Do not let it know you are close," he rumbled solemnly.

"But how exactly does it know what tree will lead it to a nymph?" A breeze pulled a strand of hair into her eyes and she brushed it behind her ear. "I don't understand how it can find one of us, our trees are almost indistinguishable from the others."

"We don't know how it knows, but we think it can smell the life force of the tree," he supplied, running a hand over his chin.

"Does it follow a path that can be tracked?" She asked, wondering if it could be hunted itself.

"It manages to evade tracking, and all but disappears when the sun rises," he stated, looking at her then. "Luckily, it hasn't made it through Hanlan yet. Myself and another have been staying in the inn for the last few months, and haven't heard whispers or even the trees to warn us that it's close."

"Hmm," Wilmayra murmured softly, thinking.

"The ones that are lucky enough to have evaded the beast, say the trees go silent when it's near. It seems like they know they may lead it straight to the nymph by making any noises."

"So it can speak our language?" That was worrisome, though not as upsetting as the fact that it's eating whole nymphs.

"It's fae, and an old one at that, so yes it seems to be so."

"I really don't like this, Gert," she tried to swallow the sudden lump in her throat at the overwhelming emotions brought on by the news. "I want to be with my family," she continued but trailed off, the words wouldn't even roll off her tongue. To voice the loneliness, to give a real description of the empty feeling of being in that house day after day, alone, *everyday,* was hard enough let alone to have to experience it all anew with a fresh reason to be isolated even further from everyone she ever cared about. The conversation made her feel even more alone, even more tethered to her tree and bound by the roots that grew there, so far away from what should have been her home. Not for the first time, she cursed that her mother had decided to travel from the grove while pregnant at all, and that the waters of the womb that she grew in had to land on the ground and sprout so many miles away from where her siblings would spend their days together without her. She could weep at the thought and always forbade herself from thinking about the reason she had grown up alone. And now she was even more bound and trapped, no freedom offered by the quiet cottage and gentle garden of trees surrounding the humble grounds she spent every moment.

"Your home isn't far from here, if you want to stay at the inn with us. There's still room for you yet, of course. You'd be able to make it to your tree in case the need arose," Teggert offered kindly, "though it seems you've found something to keep you where you are," Gert said as he raised his brows and looked at the flowers growing around her head. They'd gone into a full bloom recently, having flourished almost immediately after meeting Arden. She wondered how Gert could tell.

For a moment, though, she considered staying with Gert. To be here with someone she knew, with protection and company, almost saying yes. But then fear struck her heart at the thought of Arden coming to find her in the woods, and being left out in the darkness with the beast on his own with no one to help him. Dread filled her belly, thinking of Arden meeting the beast. She knew he'd attempt to fight it, to protect himself and Wilmayra even if he couldn't find her, and even if he was a strong fighter - she doubted that he'd be able to take down a fae demon that was consuming grown fae. He would succumb to it, and she wouldn't know until long after he was gone. None of her training would be able to revive that which was lost, and the ache of him finding harm was too much to bear. She'd rather be lonely with his occasional visit, than for anything to happen to him.

"I need to be at the cottage, Gert, but I thank you," she said as she wrapped her arm around his, clinging to his elbow. He squeezed her hand that laid over his arm with his other hand, with a reassuring pressure and a smile.

"I knew you'd say that," he chuckled, "I'd like to meet them, someday soon maybe," he winked at her.

"How did you know?" She asked with a laugh.

"Your blooms are different, someone has Bound to your tree," he said simply. She was surprised he was able to tell just by her flowers. "I've also always been sensitive to the scent of Bindings, the life force that holds a pair together is very distinct," he explained. "If you change your mind about staying in your cottage, we will be here. Don't forget," He assured her with his stone-like voice, grounding her where they sat.

"I'll remember," she smiled gratefully before frowning. "He is soon to be married, though, to another human. He won't be around for much longer, I'm sure," she told him sadly.

"I wouldn't count him out, just yet," he said with a kind smile, "a Binding Prayer is hard to deny whether he's aware of it or not." She looked at the ground, still not convinced. His words helped reassure her, though her hope was small. After another minute she turned back toward Gert, remembering the supplies she brought with her.

"Here, take these," she said, pulling the bags off of her from where they hung on her shoulders. "They're labeled for use, it'll be best to have them in case you need them," she said, "better to be safe than sorry."

"Thank you, Wisty," he rumbled, voice full of gratitude as he slipped them over his back, before he stood up and tugged

Wilmayra's hand and led her to the inn. "I have a bag for you, as well," he said with a small chuckle. "I had a feeling you'd be here today and wanted you to have this," he guided her to the bar inside, completely empty and barely lit by a single candle. He pulled a leather wrapped satchel off the counter and handed it to her. She noted how weighted it felt but wasn't sure what it was. He then pulled another bag, round and full with whatever was inside of it, from behind the counter and draped it over her shoulder. "And this is dried meat and other food you may not have had in a while," he smiled as he watched her tug the strap over her arm to get a better grip on the satchel he gave her, heavy with food. She moved it to open the small leather bound item he had handed her first.

"It's a blade," she gasped as she unwound it from the leather, "what will I do with this? It looks very old," she whispered in awe. It was almost rusted, the hilt held four dull gemstones though she imagined they used to be brighter. The large stones were settled into the metal of the hilt that melted directly into the blade, a single long and tapered instrument. Each gemstone was a different size, the largest red, then yellow, then grey, and at the base of the hilt was a dark yellow stone, smoother and clearer than the rest. It hummed with energy, and it almost felt like a heartbeat. She noticed then that there were vines wrapped around the hilt as though they held the gems from within the blade. Like it was forged over the limbs of a tree. She brought it closer to her face, trying to make out more detail in the full light of the inn's tavern. She could see the blade clearer then, and saw that it was almost branch-like in its shape, where she thought it had tapered off in a style of welding, it was really the rolls and knots of a tree branch. It felt *alive,* and as though she had known it for her whole life. It had a warm presence to it, and looked at the blade in wonder as Teggert watched on.

"You can feel it," he said, nodding at her recognition.

"Yes, it's almost thrumming with energy," she rolled the blade back into the leather and hugged it to her breast.

"It was forged from the Old - a branch of the first Nymph, stones from the first witch who Bound them with protection sigils carved into them, and metal from the first Man. It is older than we even know it to be, still full of the life it was given and full of the life it protected." Teggert explained, voice growing louder with a storytelling flare. Wilmayra always knew Teggert and Teggrin, brothers, had a knack for telling wild tales and had always enjoyed tricking the Fae of the forest with their identical faces. Though it had always boggled them when Wilmayra seemed to know which one was which, she enjoyed teasing them about it immensely. His storytelling voice brought her back to those simpler memories, and she wished for the simpler times to be here once again. She'd never tell them how she knew long before she saw them who was actually at the Hanlan outpost, that the trees whispered to her who traveled past her humble home quietly in secret trying to remain unseen by Wilmayra. The trees seemed to giggle at the shock from the men as they realized she never got it wrong who would be at the outpost - and she'd let that secret die with her because it was one of the only simple joys she had - a teasing of her friends. It gave her an air of mystery about her, but really it was only ever the trees of her home giving her the secrets of those around her. She was suddenly brought back to the moment, the happy memories fading away back to reality when Gert continued.

"It was used to destroy the Beast before, when it last was awake. We know now that it only slumbered all these years. It needs to be destroyed for real this time." His voice was grave and serious.

"And this blade is the only way to do it," Wilmayra gathered.

"Exactly, love," he smiled. Wilmayra handed it back to him but Teggert put up his hands. "You'll need to take it with you," he told her. She blinked at him, unable to fathom what he was saying.

"What am I going to do with it?" She asked him plainly, brows furrowed.

"You're the only nymph that's alone with a home that is not surrounded by stone," he said, "and you'll be the only one able to stave it off because of this."

"I can't be the only one who needs protection," she hedged, trying to hand it back to him anyway. He shook his head, pushing it back.

"Okay, you're the fae my brother and I want to protect most, especially since you were entrusted into our care all those years ago. Let this be our way of keeping you from harm," he said softly.

"But," she whispered, not sure what to say, "there's no way I'll be able to fight it off with this tiny knife, Teggert," her voice grew panicked. She couldn't even hunt and knew no combat moves to fight off an intruder let alone a *Beast!*

"Oh, but you won't be alone, now will you?" His eyes twinkled in the candlelight mischievously. Her thoughts flashed to Arden, making her cheeks heat. Gert only smiled at her with his all-knowing eyes making her laugh despite the tension in her shoulders.

"No, I suppose I won't be alone," she smiled, the hope blossoming in her chest once again. They turned to leave the inn and walked back into the light of the sun.

"You should head home now, Wisteria, before the sun starts to set," Gert said as they stepped toward the empty market. Wilmayra smiled at him as the bags on his back clinked when he shifted to give her a brief hug. She hugged him back with a tight squeeze and pulled away before he continued. "Make sure you leave no traces of life when the sun is down. If it is dark, you do *not* exist." His cryptic words were grave, but she understood. Make no fires or smoke, tread light and leave no trace of having been in the garden. "Listen for the trees, as well, for if they were to go quiet - you'll know the Beast is near and you must remain undetected. Until the time is right for the blade to be used." He hugged her again, before turning her toward the dirt road she arrived on. Everything he told her felt heavy in her gut, fear making her fingers and toes feel cold in the bright sun.

"I'll see you soon, Gert," she said softly. He watched her as she walked away, and when the outpost was out of sight Wilmayra *ran* home. She ran as fast as she could, lungs burning. Her boots pulled heavy on her feet as they hit the ground, though her footsteps still made almost no sound as she ran on into the forest. The sound of the river covered what noise she did make and occasionally she'd peer behind her to see if her steps had accidentally made any tracks leading straight to her home.

By the time she made it to the outskirts of the cottage, her garden ahead of her in the distance, she sank to her knees and wheezed. She didn't know how long she had been running, but she gasped in breaths, hands outstretched in the dirt in front of her as she bowed her head trying to regain air in her lungs. She coughed and sputtered when dirt blew back into her face, and leaned back onto her knees to wipe the dust from her nose. She was grateful to be home, and stood up to make the last trek of the trip. She started to shutter the windows back up before stepping foot into the house, though the sun was still high in the sky. She didn't want to risk having to come back out and close them close to sundown. She murmured to the vines growing over the shutters to wind over and make the house as invisible as they could. The vines and trees around agreed, all sending out gentle reassurances. They had been listening to her talk to Teggert, and knew something roamed to be wary of. They solemnly vowed to grow wildly, to cover the garden with overgrowth and cover any signs of life beyond the forest creatures, making sure nothing but plants and wildlife would appear to live here.

Wilmayra sighed then, closing the last shutter at the front of the house before walking under the wisteria willow tree. It held the life blood of her heart, the roots growing strong and deep inside the earth. A well grounded and lively tree, always twirling fronds around those who spend time in her shade. She was a representation of the soul inside Wilmayra, vibrant and playful, and Wilmayra was grateful to have such a steady presence around her in this lonely world. She placed her hands on the bark, carefully avoiding the marks Arden had left behind all those months ago, stained deep into the wood from his life blood and forming the Binding Prayer. Though accidental, it was still bound in all ways. She didn't want to complete it without his understanding of what that would mean, though, and wrapped her arms around the trunk of her tree in a warm embrace. It had been a long time since she sought out the grounding feeling of holding what was essentially her own self, but she needed it today of all days.

She murmured into the trunk the warnings Gert had given her, the trees around her listening intently at her words. After she told them everything, Wilmayra told herself she would do her best to make sure nothing happened to her wisteria tree. The tree was her life, without one the other would cease to exist, too. She'd protect her home as best she could, and held the bag that carried the blade tight for a moment as she rested against the cool bark of her tree. Finally, she let go and made her way around the back one last time and deposited her collection of propagations at random around the woods.

"I'm sorry to leave you out in a new place with the cold moving in. I won't have enough sunshine inside to keep you with me, so grow strong, little ones," she murmured as they whispered excitedly in their new home. The trees offered their support on the new lives joining them and she felt relieved that they'd at least be well taken care of with the help of her friends, since they wouldn't survive inside in the dark.

As she walked into her now very dark house, she relied on memory to find candles. After lighting one, she realized she was starving after the long day. After not having rested or eaten since the sun rose in the sky, she put a hand to her growling belly. At that moment, she remembered what she had been sent off with - the satchel. She pulled the heavy bag off her shoulder, having forgotten it was even there despite its weight in her fear and sprint through the woods, and pulled the food out that Teggert had given her. There were more dried meats than she had had in months, not being a good hunter she tended to eat a mostly vegetable and fruit diet. Though she was better at fishing if she needed to eat some kind of protein, she still didn't like to prepare the raw meat. She stuck to baking and would make her own dough for breads and noodles, and had a large stock of rice in a container in a low cabinet.

She ate some of the jerky before wandering back outside with a basket and collecting as much ripe produce that she could find. She washed it in the river and ate directly from the bushes and trees, filling her belly before bringing the extra food into the house. She idly missed the days she'd cook outside, making a fire and sitting under the sun while roasting fresh food she found in the garden - the simple days when she wasn't scared of the woods, back before she'd seen that bear with strange eyes. She brought the food to the kitchen and then went back to the door to lock it, pulling the wood slab tight over the heavy oak door.

She made her way back to the kitchen and pulled the table closer to the lounge chair in the living room. She opened up the space covered by a rug, revealing a small handle. She pulled the handle up, and then laced a long ribbon through the now open hatch to the storm room and tied a pine cone to it on the underside of the secret door. She pulled the ribbon until the pine cone was tight to the bottom, and then tied the other end to the inside of the throw rug that had a button hidden underneath for attaching the piece of fabric. With the length connected to the emergency room door, she'd be able to pull the door straight down along with the rug to keep her underground room safe from discovery should the front door be broken through. Because the button was quarterway under the rug, it would completely cover the door when she pulled the pine cone on the end of the string once the door was closed.

Leaving the hatch open, Wilmayra climbed down the narrow steps leading to the room that was deep underground. After a dozen steps, she reached the bottom and saw the emergency candle stash that was hidden right at the base of the stairs. She lit one and walked down the hall. Along the walls were shelves stuffed to the brim with other important supplies, like canned foods and jarred goods and other apothecary items for injuries and health related necessities. It was meticulously organized and stocked abundantly. Over the years, Wilmayra had wanted to keep it up to date with what she would need should an emergency arise, or a large-scale disaster. And this certainly felt like an emergency, but she would run through the safe room to make sure it was still good for living in.

Wilmayra made her way down the hallway running her hands over the shelves full of things before she found an open doorway leading to a small room with a bed, and more shelves. The shelves lined the whole room, with blankets and clothes and more candles, and even some other things like books and shoes. She laid the candle on the shelf closest to the door and then made her way to the bed. She pulled back a burlap rag that had been laid on top to avoid the blankets from getting musty and dusty underneath and rolled it to carry upstairs. She fluffed the pillows before turning to the other door on the right side of the little bedroom and opened a tiny bathroom with a sink and toilet, and a small washing basin. It was directly under the bathroom of the house for the plumbing. Because of this little bathroom, it made the storm room a convenient place to "disappear" for weeks at a time if Wilmayra found it necessary to do so. There would really be no need to go up the stairs for as long as the supplies lasted - and she supposed it could be a few months with modest supply use, should she need it to last that long.

She walked back to the small room and looked at the two small storm windows that lined the ceiling. They were about a foot long and a few inches wide, and stared out in the direction of the wisteria, and one straight to the river out back. The windows were tinted on the outer sides and nothing could see into them. Along with gentle Protection spells that prevented anyone from noticing them, they were also lined with small stones and flowers. Anyone looking outside would only be able to see flowers, but looking up at the windows from in this room, you could see clearly from underneath the stems. It gave the room access to a small amount of natural light that made it more livable and not the equivalent to a dark cave, like the rest of the house.

Wilmayra made sure the wooden posts were there to make sure the windows could be locked, in case something *did* find them even with the extra protection. Much like the front door, the slabs of wood were slotted over the glass panes and when they were locked, all light was blocked out. The slabs were tight to the walls in the locked position, pulled flush against the windows where they were held by the thick metal brackets. For now, she decided to cover the small window facing the back of the house into the garden and left the one facing the base of the wisteria open, just in case. The slabs were lying on the top shelf where she left them, but she had to climb on the lower shelves to reach it. She realized then that if something were to look in the windows, they wouldn't be able to see over the length of the highest shelf - it would look like the windows stared straight to the ground from the outside. If she had to, all she would need to do is hide in the corner between the two windows, or in the hallway to be extra safe. She would also have to make sure there was absolutely no chance of a fire being seen casting any light from within, and told herself she'd have to blow out candles as soon as the sun even remotely started to set.

She sighed to herself, grateful at least that the sun didn't set as early this season, though it would change very quickly from here on out. She wished it were summer, so she could enjoy the outside for longer without fear of cutting it too close to dark and leading the Beast straight to her. A shiver climbed up her spine. She left the candle in the room and made her way back upstairs to collect more food for dinner. The sun was midway to setting and she had a few hours of light left, and wanted to collect one more round of fruit and vegetables from the garden and a fresh jug of water from the river before she locked herself away.

When she stepped outside, she breathed as deep as she could to preserve the feeling of freedom and hope for as long as she could, and quickly hustled around the garden plucking every-thing she saw before grabbing the water tin and making her way back into the house. The candles were lit on the counter, and she placed the food on the counter next to them before going to the door and locking it tight. Then she brought everything down into the basement storm room, and lined the candles in the hallway. She climbed up the storm stairs and pulled down the hatch and locked that too. Next, she tugged on the pinecone holding the string to the carpet and listened for the *zip* noise to know that it was in the right position.

Satisfied that her hiding place was completely hidden, she went into the hallway and pulled a small stool that was tucked into a shelf and sat on it, eating her simple dinner. She had brought down the bag of food from Gert, as well, and dug into that. When she was full, she blew out the candles and went into the small bedroom. The sun was beginning to set in the distance and by the glow coming from the small window above the shelves, she knew it was time to lay down and blow out the final candle. She laid down inside the cold covers of the soft bed, surprisingly squishy for being in disuse for so long. Small things to be grateful for, she supposed. She laid in the bed until the sun set, growing more and more anxious. Nothing happened, though, and eventually she fell asleep.

...

She woke up to the birds chirping and the sun beaming gently through the window. She was surprised and disoriented for a moment before remembering the day before, and quickly climbed out of bed and made her way upstairs. She continued basically the same as before, only listening closer to the trees and the forest to make sure nothing was lurking in the distance.

Days passed like this, collecting her garden contents quietly, bathing in the river, locking herself in the storm room. After the third day, she thought it was silly to keep locking herself in the basement and closed the storm door with a scoff. But when the sun set, and the floor creaked under her toes, she sprinted in the dark - tripping a few times with the dim candle - before closing herself into the basement.

She lost track of the days after that, and tried again to sleep in her actual bedroom without trembling in fear. The compromise she gave herself was to leave the storm door open and sleep in her room. Unless she was scared, only then would she make her way down the stairs. She seemed to do better though by the second night she tried that, and continued with her new routine well into winter.

When the frosts came followed by the first fall of snow, the house was almost entirely hidden in the white blankets of ice, the wisteria cocooned softly in the snow's embrace. Will was able to harvest much of the garden before the cold came, and jarred or dried everything so it would stay for the season.

It was boring, and tedious, the sheer amount of time that she spent in the dark. She found solace in the hidden room, seeking out the sunshine through the small windows. She held tight to the rays, clinging to the light with a painful desperation. But with the layers of snow, days would pass before she caught a glimpse of the sun again. She was lonely, and painfully bored, and began making different syrups and tonics with ingredients she hadn't tried yet just to break the monotony. She didn't dare hope that Arden would come back, especially not in this weather, but each day that passed brought with it more hopelessness. Each snowflake felt heavy in her heart as she watched them fall, soft and slow, delicate little fluff drifting through the air. Each flake felt like a reminder of how alone she was in the world.

Finally, though, the snow melted around her and left the ground soft but safe to walk on again. She had just come inside after a long day of walking in the sunlight for the first time in ages, and was reaching for her candle to take to her room and go to sleep, but the breath in her chest left her as a sound suddenly echoed through the house. Her blood ran cold as she spun toward the sound, a chill tingling up her spine.

There was a knock at the door.

~ Five ~

WHAT LURKS THERE

A few days passed and Arden once again felt ready to run straight into the forest. Between the constant buzz of people in his house, asking him question after question, and seemingly the whole town asking him about which woman he was going to marry, he had had enough. Right after patrols, he would hurry to his room and hide away until it was time for dinner once again. He continued the cycle to keep himself sane, doing everything he could do to avoid unnecessary interactions with those around him in order to prevent himself from hyperbolizing everything anyone ever told him.

After he had talked to Juna before his last trip to the woods, he was able to begin to separate his own anxieties from what people actually said to him. The overlap had been quite drastic in that he had been hypercritical of *everything* said to him for the last several months, if not years. He felt guilty for having been so wrapped up in his own insecurities that he projected them onto everyone he spoke to, sure that they saw what he did, too. It wasn't true, of course, and he had support from his family and friends in everything he did. But it was a hard habit to break, though he was making progress on it. He couldn't shake the pressure he had put onto himself, and needed to escape once again. At the end of the week, he left patrol early and packed a bag to go back to the woods.

"Mother will miss you if you spend another weekend away," Juna said as she saw Arden pack up, "especially so soon."

"Tell her I'll find a wife on my own time," he said, then kissed her forehead and walked through the front door, "don't worry about me," he said softly. A shriek tore through the house as the housekeeper yelled for help, and Arden heard his name called by everyone nearly simultaneously. He closed his eyes and sighed, putting his bag down and turning around. He would help those in need, even at great cost to himself, even if it weren't an actual emergency and he was only needed to help pull a splinter from someone's finger. He sighed, before making his way back to his bedroom. The sun was setting, and there was no time to go to Will's, now. He would try again next weekend, and hoped the timing was right. He pretended to ignore Juna's sad expression as he walked away from them after having solved the fiasco they had made in the kitchen involving a rolling pin and a now broken plate. He didn't want to think about why she looked sad for him, and he knew he'd only spiral again should he think more on it.

Each week brought with it another emergency or training accident that prevented him from seeing Will yet again, and as the colder season blew in, people in the Port grew ill, too. Many of the soldiers and their families were incapacitated with fevers and other illnesses, leaving patrols spread thin without the proper coverage. The Fairwoods were spared, but their house-keeper and her family unfortunately were not. The D'Misios all fell ill and he and his sister, along with their mother, had to nurse them back to health. They'd long been very much a part of their family, though on paper the Fairwoods were very well off compared to them. Felisia had been friends with Alvenia for a long time, and none of them could imagine a life in which they weren't all here together. It was a trying time for them all, though, and with the snow and ice the winter brought with it, Arden wasn't sure he was able to breath the entirety of its length. Even Alvenia, who was always able to command an audience, was feeling the strain of the Port's struggles. Arden heard her speaking to her cousin, a physician, about the lack of medicine for the bouts of illnesses around them. He felt trapped, not sure what to do, and prayed to the gods that they'd make it through winter.

When the final frost melted and flowers popped through the earth, Arden *needed* to escape from the Port. He wouldn't make it one more minute away from Will, and needed to see her immediately. He didn't care if she weren't there when he got there, or if her life had continued without him when he was stuck in place. All he knew was that if he didn't see her soon, he was sure he'd lose his mind. The only reason he hadn't seen her in the winter was his fear to travel during the snow season, in case his footprints were tracked. He hadn't wanted to accidentally doom them both to a horrific fate if his path in the snow had been followed. He only hoped she'd understand, though he wouldn't blame her if she didn't. He wondered if she'd be happy to see him after what felt like an eternity had passed with no contact. His heart squeezed in his chest as anxiety bubbled up from his belly. He huffed a breath to clear the intrusive thoughts away and made his rounds in the barracks.

He left patrol early that weekend after adjusting the new patrols after more people grew ill. He had stayed late a few times the following week to even out the gaps in the schedule, and hoped it was enough. Luckily because of the adjustment, he had been able to leave when there were still a few hours of daylight left and knew exactly what he'd do with this opportunity. He gave a very quick farewell to his sister and mother, hoping his abruptness would spare him from being held up again on his attempt to find Will, much like the last several times he tried to visit her. He walked quickly, trying to beat the still early setting sun. At first he wasn't worried about the time, but as he neared the woods and the sun crept lower and lower, he grew more and more concerned. He started jogging and aimed to be at the cottage in an hour, using the colors in the sky as a clock of sorts, gauging the sunset by the hues of orange and blue.The sun seemed to set even quicker than normal as he traveled on, and was just about to start sprinting when he caught sight of the tree and cottage a short distance from where he was, portions of it still covered in snow.

Breathing a sigh of relief, just as the rays soaked the sky and the trees in a golden hue, he ducked under the branches of the willow tree and knocked on Will's door. He heard a flutter of footsteps and a creak of the old hinge. Will's surprised face met his gaze.

"It's so dark!" She exclaimed, grabbing Arden's arm and pulling him inside abruptly. Arden looked at her confused as she peeked out the door, scanning the trees, before she shut the door and bolted it shut. "You shouldn't be out here, Arden," Will said as she pulled a long beam of wood and slotted it over the door.

"I wanted to see you," he said in a low tone. He was startled by her abrupt manner and was curious to know the reason behind it, feeling unease creep up his spine. It seemed he was right to be afraid on his way here, though he hardly regretted coming. Will sighed and ran a hand through her messy hair, before pulling it out of her face and tying it up with a ribbon she had in her pocket.

"I am glad to see you, Arden, these days have dragged on very slowly for me," she murmured, pulling him into a hug. Her small frame fit into his arms perfectly as she squeezed around his waist. Her cheek tucked into his chest as she sighed against him. He wrapped his arms around her just as tight, surprised by her affection but grateful for it all the same. She pulled away after a few minutes and smiled up at him before leading him to the couch bathed in the light of a few candles.

"What have you been up to?" She asked curiously. He rubbed a hand over his face as he grumbled.

"Not much, but it seems like *everything* all the same," he sighed. "I wanted to visit before the snow, but I was pulled in every direction and wasn't able to," he said sadly.

"That's okay, you have an important job so I understand," she told him easily, eyes honest and open. He knew she was telling the truth, but felt bad all the same.

"What have you been doing?" He asked her as he took in a basement hatch he hadn't seen before. He understood why she'd moved the table away from that area the last time he was there, it looked a lot like a storm cellar. Will sighed before running her hands over her face, her skin pale. She looked very fair and almost sickly and he wondered what happened.

"I think it would make you sad if I told you," she said, but continued anyway. He would have asked her to tell him even if she didn't want to, as she seemed unwell and he was worried. "I've had to stay inside all season because of the snow, I couldn't risk my feet leading something to my front door. I've just been here," she said sadly. His heart dropped, remorse filling his belly as she spoke.

"I should have brought you to the Port with me," he told her, holding his hand to his forehead.

"Oh no, it's okay. Arden, really," she said before standing and moving to sit next to him, sliding up to lean on his shoulder and gently rested her head against him. "You couldn't have known and you have your own family to worry about. I'm alive," she murmured. "But you did miss some of the stories I heard at the trading outpost about the strange events we've been seeing," she continued.

"What kind of things have been happening?" Arden asked as he sat next to her, his arm moving around her back to sit more comfortably as she leaned into him.

"Well, I kind of know what the beast is, now." Arden turned to gape at her, making her laugh at his expression. "I'm sorry, I don't mean to laugh," she took a deep breath and continued. "Someone told me that something in the forest is...*waking up*," she shuddered, "nothing has happened here at all, at least I haven't actually been able to check. But I know people have been going missing or worse, and Teggert seems to know why," she explained. He bit down a wave of jealousy at the mention of her friend's name, swallowing the feeling with a minute shake of his head. "It's been months since I've seen anyone, though, so I'm afraid I don't know much more than that."

Arden pursed his lips, wondering what her friend knew that they didn't, before he thought back to his patrols. "Actually, the attacks have been less frequent lately now that I'm thinking about it. But we assumed it was the lack of travel in the winter," he shrugged.

"I'm not surprised, it seems the creature has gone past here and went deeper into the forest. And the snow would also mean less travelers to attack, so both theories hold weight." Will agreed quietly, face somber in the low light.

"Have you seen it?" Arden asked, wondering if she'd know what it looked like.

"No, I'm certain I'd be dead if it found me," she looked up at him hauntingly, not an ounce of dishonesty on her face. He shuddered, trying to put the thought from his mind as she kept talking. "Most of the people we normally see weren't there. There were only a few people there at all, it was completely empty. And my friend didn't say what exactly it was, just that it was very old and very hungry. It must be very dangerous, though, if the trading post was so empty. Nothing stops us from going there, not even bad weather. Just this."

"What about that bear you told me about?" Arden thought out loud, the thought coming to his head suddenly. Will's eyes widened as she looked up at him, considering his words.

"I hadn't even considered that thing," she said through a tremble. "It's eyes... It was certainly *something*." She peered at him with a grimace, shuddering as her eyebrows furrowed, "I'm sure I'm just spooked by the story I was told, but living alone will make you crazy if you let it. It's been a really long winter for me," she looked down at her hands, cheek still resting on his shoulder.

"Well, living *with* people will make you crazy, too," Arden laughed gently, trying to ease her sadness. "I can imagine how unsettled you feel, though, and I'm sorry. But at least now you aren't alone in the dark. I'm sorry it took me so long to come back this time," he added, "you must have been very lonely."

"Thank you for coming back," she smiled, "we can both be scared in the woods together," Will said with a quiet laugh, and smiled at Arden with humor in her eyes. "I was lonely," she added quietly as she looked away from him. He tightened his arm around her and rested his cheek against her head. A creeping feeling crawled up his spine when he thought of what could have happened to them both if he were only a few minutes later showing up at her house. "Teggert has never been one to make up a ghost story though, which is the most worrisome of it all."

"You think he's right?" Arden asked. His stomach then growled suddenly, and he put a hand over his belly. "I forgot to eat at home, I was in a rush to get here." Will laughed and stood up, walking to the kitchen. She filled a bowl with the fruits and vegetables she had sitting on the counter. He followed her to the kitchen, taking a seat at the counter on a stool as she handed him a bowl.

"You remember what room you used last time?" Will asked. Arden nodded in response around a mouth full of strawberries. "I'm going to go to my bedroom now, I want to straighten it up before I go to sleep," she brushed a hand across his shoulders as he finished his meal and quietly started toward her room, blowing out candles as she went. She left one lit for him on the kitchen counter next to him, and left him to dine in the flickering dim light, "stay up as long as you want," she whispered as she rounded the corner with a smile.

Arden ate quietly, enjoying the fresh fruit and vegetables though it hardly felt like a dinner to him. He finished it in only a few minutes and walked the empty bowl to the sink to wash it out gently before laying it to dry. He went to glance out the window overlooking the sink and saw that it was all boarded up, and realized she must have been living in the dark this whole time. He felt his stomach drop at the realization, understanding why she looked so pale and unwell. She had been cooped up all this time, with no one and nowhere to turn to. He felt awful, as if it were his own fault, as he remembered her story of the strange bear. The beast staring into her window and terrifying her while she stood alone in the dark. He shuddered at the idea of experiencing it himself and was glad the windows were bolted tight. He looked across the kitchen to the living room windows and saw the curtains in the room had been drawn over the glass, hiding the shutters behind them. The curtains were still drawn back in the kitchen, so Arden pulled them closed and tried to listen to the outside world. Nothing but the gentle flicker of the candle could be heard over the thick slabs of wood encasing the house. A relief, though, as it meant no one outside could hear within the walls either.

He picked up the candle and walked toward the guest room to get ready to sleep. He noticed Will's door was wide open, and paused a moment before glancing inside. He saw her sitting up on her bed, knees drawn to her chest with her head resting on them. She turned to him when he peered in the doorway. Her face surprised him, he hadn't expected her to appear so afraid.

"Arden," she asked him, her voice sounding tentative.

"Yes, Will?" he asked, stepping into the room slightly, leaning against the door frame.

"Arden, will you sleep in here with me tonight?" For a moment, he thought she meant that she wanted him to sleep on the chair in the corner, or even the floor. But then she pulled the blanket down and gestured to one side of the bed and looked at him with eyes wide, completely devoid of any ulterior motive. Instead, she just looked frightened and in need of some form of comfort and safety. And surely, she didn't seem to even know most of the usual customs he grew up with, living alone in the woods. He was almost certain she didn't know the implications of what she was asking. All Arden knew was that he should say no as an unmarried man and her an unmarried woman. Their friendship was inappropriate enough as it was, and he certainly didn't want to cause a scandal.

"Okay," he said, surprised by his own words. But his body was already moving, settling his candle down on the bedside next to the other one, he pulled his over-shirt off and tossed it onto the chair as he stepped out of his boots. After he blew out the candle, he slid under the blanket she had opened up for him and settled in next to her, the blanket warm already.

"Thank you," she said, gratefully.

"Of course," he murmured, before she rolled over and tucked the blanket tight around her. He mirrored her, and closed his eyes. How lonely must she have been to invite him to lay beside her as she slept, though he was grateful she did. The idea of sleeping by himself with whatever lurked in the darkness was terrifying, and he was sure he'd have laid awake all night if he'd gone into the other room.

He fell asleep to the sound of her gentle breathing, her feet tucked against the back of his legs. He'd never felt so at peace in his life.

~ Six ~

WITHIN THESE WOODS

Dark room, she stands up. Something is calling her. Her feet are cold as she walks, slowly, slowly, slowly. It's not a voice that calls to her, but she walks. Her whole body says to stop but she ignores it. A faint gurgling noise echoes around her, she can hear nothing else. She sees nothing but her feet as she walks, the white linen of her dress tickles her ankles with each step. She's in the hallway now and pauses, still looking down to her feet without glancing at anything else. She walks around the hall, around the table and counter. She walks to the window. There is too much light coming from the windows for the middle of the night, but she ignores the thought, ignores the fear, and keeps moving. Against her own will, she walks to the windows. Her eyes never leave her feet. She wants to stop moving, she wants to get back into bed, but something pulls her on. She won't lift her head. She walks to the couch, toes padding over the carpet, and finally lifts her eyes to peer out the window. Her eyes are met with a beast, large, so large, it blocks out anything behind it. She doesn't understand how so much light fills the room with its massive frame filling the window frames entirely. All there is in the window is the beast. Black fur, a mountain of what looks like a bear, but not. Slitted pupils stare at her, into her, peering and hungry as it looks through the window at her directly, unblinking, unfeeling. Her body trembles at the unwavering gaze, she sees saliva pool out of its mouth as it stares at her. She can feel its hunger in the gaze as it presses its massive nose against the glass. The window fogs up as it breathes deeply, in and out, trying to smell her. Her body freezes with panic as the glass fractures under the pressure, slow spider web patterns cracking along the glass. The beast presses forward, nose cracking more of the window before it breaks through the pane. Its nose sniffs into the room, smelling for its dinner. Its teeth pull back into a snarl, and it presses a human looking hand against the window frame before pushing its head through the window, shattering it completely. Its mouth opens, a long reverberating growl pouring from its throat. The beast snarls louder, revealing massive fangs to the woman standing there bare but for the plain linen over her body. She opens her mouth and lets out a shriek, pure terror filling her with lead and ice. The beast opens its mouth wider, reaching for her with its disturbingly human hands. She screams and steps back as the sound bellows from its massive throat as its hands reach for her, slowly, but quickly, as if time is frozen on this one moment. There is nowhere to run, she steps back blindly. Her eyes never leave its strange pupils, slitted, rectangular, completely empty of emotion. Its hand grazes her throat before it lets out a roar, her screams barely heard over the depth of the sound.

Wilmayra jolted awake, gasping for air. She clutched her throat where she swore she could still feel a massive hand around her, squeezing her skin. She heaved in a breath as she blinked in the darkness, terrified, looking for signs that someone or something was breaking in through the shutters she swore she had put up months before. Suddenly she felt the other side of the bed move, and hands reached out and touched her shoulder. She almost screamed, but the feel of the hands was warm and gentle, so different from the nightmare, but still she trembled against them.

"What happened?" Arden's voice was thick with sleep and confusion as he sat up and squeezed her shoulder. He tilted her chin to him with his other hand, blinking at her face with alarm though it was hard to see in the dark. She had forgotten he was here but was overwhelmed with relief that someone at least would be able to comfort her, for the first time after dozens of bad dreams over the years, and dozens during this month alone, and leaned into his grip with a sniffle. She trembled again, a chill rolling up her spine at the memory of the dream.

"I saw it," she whispered, barely able to voice what exactly she had seen. "It was like I was there again, and it was *calling* me. I think it knows I'm here," she shuddered. Arden pulled her close, tucking her head against his neck. She breathed in his scent, relaxing into his embrace and pulled her hands around him, nestling deeper into his arms. He was strong, she could feel the strength of his grip, his muscles pulling against the sleeves of his tunic.

"What do you mean?" Arden asked, voice still confused and a little tired. He settled them back into the bed, still holding onto her. Wilmayra wiggled against him, getting comfortable and tucked her arm under her chin, letting her right hand lay over Arden's chest, feeling his heart beat within. Arden yawned and rubbed his eyes with his left hand, curling his other arm around Wilmayra.

"The beast," she whispered after a moment, blinking tears out of her eyes. She didn't want to say anything else, she didn't want to voice it into reality. But Arden's hands were comforting in the dark room, and she knew she needed to tell him why she had woken him up in so much distress. She could feel him still tense next to her as he yawned again, and Wilmayra yawned involuntarily at the sound. She took a deep breath to try to gain the courage she needed to share her deepest fears out loud.

"The beast," Arden murmured, prompting her gently to continue.

"When exactly did the animal attacks stop happening around your home?" Wilmayra started, mapping out her thoughts before she explained further.

"They stopped in the summer," he said, thinking. "About the time that I first met you, they had, by then, slowly lost frequency until one day, they had just stopped altogether." Arden paused, thinking, "I hadn't realized just how much time had passed since that day."

"It's always like that, here. Time is just different in Tonsilta," Wilmayra murmured. She stopped thinking of the passing of time in the same way others did, long ago. Nothing changes in the woods besides the weather - it's hard to notice time passing at all with no one to talk to. Though this time, she had felt the passing of each day with agonizing clarity. Arden squeezed her a little tighter after she said that, and Wilmayra realized how lonely she must have sounded with her words. She took a deep breath and pulled a hand through her hair, flower petals sprinkling around the sheets with a faint nectar scent floating around them. Arden picked up a loose flower and held it to his face, looking at it perplexed. She almost laughed at his expression, full of confusion, but continued to share her thoughts. Despite wanting to swallow it down and ignore it, she knew it needed to be said.

"I think I know why the attacks were happening in this area for so long," she said quietly against his side, trailing a hand over his chest. "It was right after I met you, the strange bear had looked through my window, maybe two or three weeks later. I've lived here my whole life and never used the shutters unless I knew a storm was coming. But since then, I've bolted my windows shut," she shuddered at the memory again, "that creature was horrifying. In all my years I'd never experienced that before - I've even slept out in the meadow for whole seasons, on the moss."

"So, the bear..." Arden said almost to himself as if he were working it out the same way Wilmayra did.

"You were right last night, the bear has to be the beast in the forest," Wilmayra agreed, looking up at Arden with a dark expression. "It was looking for me, and when it couldn't find me that night," she trailed off.

"And when it couldn't find you that night, it searched deeper," Arden finished. "That would explain the sudden attacks, and the way it just - stopped one day." He murmured almost to himself. He rubbed his chin, a deep breath leaving his body. Wilmayra rose and fell with it as she laid almost on his chest, her hand resting her chin over his ribs. He looked down at her as she peered up at him, her expression bleak. "But why would it be looking for you?" Arden asked as he looked at her.

His eyebrows were pinched in thought, wondering at her reasoning. Wilmayra wasn't sure if she should tell him and sighed, considering. They had slept in the same bed together, deep in the forest all alone. Arden had Prayer Bound himself to the wisteria willow, inadvertently promising himself to Wilmayra without knowing what he'd done by offering his blood, sweat, and tears to the tree. She'd have to tell him eventually, she knew, but still she was afraid that the idea of an accidental fae marriage would overwhelm him, and send him away from her forever. She sighed and rolled back onto the bed, disentangling herself from Arden and stretched, procrastinating on voicing the truth. Arden rolled to his side and looked at her, hands tucked under his cheek.

"Well," she said, haltingly, not sure how to begin. He just raised an eyebrow, lip twitching as he held back a smile.

Wilmayra calmed at the sight - he was a kind man and knew he'd at least be nice about the truth of her being a part of the forest. "Have you heard of nymphs?" She asked finally, throwing an arm over her eyes to avoid his reaction.

"I've heard of them, yes..." he said quietly.

She said nothing but her hands clenched and unclenched with anxiety, waiting to see if he'd piece it together. Suddenly she heard a sharp intake of breath and the bed dipped. She lifted her arm to see what he was doing, to see if he would run home now that he knew what she was. Arden leaned over to the bedside table and lit the candle still sitting there, bathing them in a warm light. When he turned back to her, he made a face she couldn't recognize, not quite scared and not quite happy. His hand reached out suddenly and she startled at the movement, but his hand went to her hair.

"So that's why you have flowers in your hair - they *grow* like that," he said. He was curious then, she thought, as he poked at the petals and tiny leaves entwined in her hair. She laughed then, relieved by his reaction, and not a little bit surprised.

"They only grew in recently," she said with a smile, before plucking a tiny white flower and holding it in her hand for him to see more clearly. "I was a late bloomer," she smirked at the pun.

"When do they usually start growing?" He asked as he inspected the petals.

"Usually when the tree blooms, it doesn't take long. A few years old is typical, but mine came well into my teen years." She explained.

"Why's that?" He looked up at her then and she could see his mind filing this information away, he was very intrigued by it.

"I think it's because I was born very early. And I was essentially raised alone out here," she made a face and quirked her lips, "I also think being alone for too long stunted my growth. Usually we're surrounded by our family trees but I only have me, here, in Tonsilta." She watched as his brows furrowed, she noticed the flash of anger over his face before he blinked it away.

"Well why did they leave you out here by yourself?" His voice was like ice and she laughed again, sitting up.

"That's a long story, but essentially my mother went into early labor with me, and unfortunately my roots grew here before they could make it home in time." She pulled her hair out of her face and tried to straighten out the mess of curls. "For a long time I was angry about it, but I realized there's nothing to be done about it now. I'm alive, and healthy, and I'm here. I'm just glad my siblings are safe in the forest at home where they belong," she sighed and looked down and twirled a strand of hair in her fingers, frowning. She *was* glad they were safe. But she wished she'd been there, safe, too, especially now with the beast in the forest. She feared for them, and knew it could easily take months for her to learn if something happened to them whether good or bad. She had never let herself think about that immense loneliness, that pit in her belly, and always maintained a schedule to avoid dwelling on it.

Arden reached a hand out, twining his fingers through Wilmayra's. She lifted her eyes from where she twirled a strand of hair in her fingers to meet his gaze, her expression sad. She didn't try to hide the look, she knew she couldn't even if she wanted to. Bound to the forest alone forever - she couldn't pretend to be okay. It was too overwhelming, the realization that the beast had been looking for her and could very well come back when it couldn't find more Fae. *When it couldn't find more unprotected Fae,* she thought grimly.

"It'll be okay, Will," Arden said gently as she frowned again. She couldn't look into his eyes any longer, the kindness he held in them was too hard to accept. But she squeezed his hand back where it still clutched her own and sighed deeply before stretching and yawning.

"Let's have breakfast," she said finally with a gentle laugh. Arden agreed as he quietly stretched, and so their day began. Wilmayra tried to swallow the overwhelming sensation of comfort and *right* that she felt starting her morning with this man, who had literally stumbled into her life not long ago, at her side. She was afraid to allow the feelings to bubble out and give a voice to them. There was no way this would be a forever occurrence, and she knew it well, so she would try to enjoy these moments as best she could until the season ended. She ignored the part of her whispering *he came back after months, he will stay.* So she tried to enjoy the moments as they happened around her, the small ways Arden's presence filled the tiny house with life and joy. She let herself bask in it, at least for now.

"I'm sorry I don't have much more for you than this," she told him. "Soon enough the forest will bloom again and I'll show you more of what grows around here."

"I'll be looking forward to it," he told her with a smile.

They spent the morning doing small things around the house in the candle light. Will was too afraid to be outside yet after having spent so much time inside, but Arden didn't push her and graciously accepted her boundaries. All too soon, he had to make his way home.

"I won't be this long, again," he told her at the door after he put his boots back on. She smiled though she was doubtful. She knew he meant it, but she also knew that sometimes life was out of their control and all she could do was be patient.

...

Arden visited twice more before spring finally came. He would spend the night each time he came and her heart was heavy each time she watched him walk away. With the break in the weather, she was grateful to at least be able to see the sun again. Her color was finally brightening back into a healthy pallor after being unable to go outside for months on end.

As the berries started growing, Will showed Arden where she usually collected fruits and vegetables from the forest, and showed him how to find the ripest berries. She found herself laughing at the pure wonder on his face, his enthusiasm endearing.

"What kind of garden is this?" Arden asked after filling two baskets with blueberries and squash, and other things he didn't remember the names of. Wilmayra led him to the riverside and sat on the edge of the small pool of water, river rocks clear to the eye above the depths of flowing water. She pulled her dress almost to her hips before she noticed Arden's reddened cheeks and hastily shifted the hem to tie around her thighs instead. She tucked the length underneath where she sat so it wouldn't fall in, before answering him.

"It's not really a garden, if I think about it," she said as she slowly dunked a basket into the river pool. Dirt and debris from the fruit rolled around the water before finding the current and trailing away. "I find offerings from the forest, and remember where they are, and eventually patches of what I harvest make their way to me." She pulled the basket out of the water after the dirt cleared, and pulled the next basket in. Vegetables tended to take longer to clean thoroughly having lived in the dirt, but she didn't mind. Usually she'd wash them in the sink inside but she was loath to go back into the house before the sun went down. She also knew it would be too dark in there to do anything anyway, so she took her time rinsing the squash, zucchini and the radishes that had popped up one day not long ago.

"They just show up?" he asked as he hiked up his pants and rolled up his sleeves and settled next to her to help wash the vegetables. They both scrubbed and brushed the dirt off, enjoying the company and the breeze as it ruffled the leaves of the trees around them.

"Well for a long time, we got most of our produce from the Hanlan Trading Outpost, but after I was left here to live by myself full time, I had to learn how to forage close by my house. I was scared of traveling alone so I made do with the things I could find and on Trade Days - which were more frequent back then - my friends would sometimes visit me and it wouldn't be so bad." They scooped the basket from the river and sat it to the side, kicking their feet into the still chilled water.

"So the trees just started planting things for you?" Arden asked, turning to her. She laughed, and leaned into his shoulder.

"No, but yes," she giggled, "the forest kind of shares stories with itself, like whispers on the wind, and eventually they learned there was a small Fae in the forest who needed a garden." She waved behind her, pointing to the ivy overgrown on the back of the cottage, a heavier coat than its been in years. "Those vines are thicker now because I asked them to hide me away," she continued to point in each direction where they had found the different fruits, growing at random. "The zucchini was a surprise, but I had asked the trees over there for something new to try. Over there the radishes - I actually don't know where they came from but they have been fun to eat," she laughed.

"I didn't realize how much the forest had to say," Arden whispered as the leaves fluttered around them. He looked up as some of the trees felt like they were bowing to the wind despite the breeze having faded.

"They're laughing at you," Wilmayra laughed, throwing her head back. Tears came to her eyes as she heard the trees snicker about how the human *obviously* couldn't have known about their complex communication system. Arden started to laugh with her, the sound of Will's laughter was contagious. She had been told many times by her friends in Lexman Yur during her school years. She tried not to think about why her laugh was the loudest - *it's always the saddest souls who laugh the hardest.* She let herself feel warm and comforted by his presence, enjoying the depth of his laugh and the brush of his shoulder against her as they basked in the sun together. After a moment, Arden quieted his gentle laughter and his brows furrowed in thought before he turned to her.

"They *laugh?*" he whispered in a voice between shocked and disturbed as he finally realized what Will had said. The leaves rumbled again around them, fluttering in what a passerby would assume was a strong breeze high in the sky. Wilmayra felt her belly start to hurt from the laughter spilling from her lips, for once unperturbed by anything at all. His reaction was honest and adorable, but she couldn't help but find it funny all the same.

"Oh, yes, Arden," Wilmayra finally was able to wheeze out, "there's many things they do that man doesn't remember." She couldn't help the bubbling laugh that escaped her lips when Arden shuddered at her words. The leaves fluttered again, and she nodded at them before continuing, "Trees never forget, either," she side eyed him with a grin.

"Oh, no," he said, "the amount of times I've-- " he stopped abruptly, eyes wide. Wilmayra threw herself back onto the dirt, feet kicking in the water, as tears formed in her eyes from laughter.

"You peed on some, didn't you?" She gasped between breaths, holding her belly with each giggle.

"I'd rather not say," he murmured back at her, a smile threatening to appear on his pink cheeks. His eyes glanced down at her bare legs before catching Wilmayra's eyes again, his blush spreading down his chest. She propped herself back onto her elbows, looking at him curiously. She wondered for a moment at his blush and sat up, brushing her thighs off from where dirt had fallen from the vegetables, but quickly shook her head to herself and brushed the thought away.

The days he spent with her were filled with moments that Wilmayra wanted to freeze in time, to hold onto the laughter forever. She found that the more she smiled and laughed with Arden by her side, the deeper the melancholy settled into her belly. She wanted to ignore it, to push it down and exist purely in the moment - but all she could imagine was how eventually, Arden would leave and only the faint memory of laughter within the woods would be left behind.

~ Seven ~

A CALL TO HELP

Arden was glad he'd been able to visit Will a few more times before spring came, but he felt like it wasn't enough. Each time he left he knew he needed to go home, and that he had stayed as long as he possibly could before leaving at the very last minute. But the feeling of utter loss at the idea of being home again, alone under his covers, listening to the sounds of people around him as he struggled to fall asleep, actually caused an *ache* in his heart that he couldn't ignore.

As he trudged home each time, sadly but surely, he practiced his best friendly smiles to put everyone around him at ease. Collecting fruit with Will had been easily the most fun he'd had in years, if he were honest with himself. He knew that when he was married, he wouldn't be able to visit her in the forest anymore, and was loath to stop seeing his closest friend. He couldn't imagine getting married at the cost of losing her, and had all but stopped even considering the idea at all. He was sure no one would approve of his excursions to the forest to spend time with a woman outside of marriage, but he wasn't ready to stop seeing her. He didn't want his family to know that he was struggling coming to terms with the mere idea of marrying a stranger, let alone actually having to start a new life with people he didn't know. He also didn't want them to know that she was an unmarried woman he'd been seeing, for obvious reasons. His mother would faint if she knew, and his sister would be positively titillated.

His thoughts would circle and he'd consider his parents and their paths in life, wondering about their choices in marriage. They were both passionate people with strong beliefs in what they wanted for their lives, though Arden hardly understood them by any means. Alvenia wanted to be a mother, and raised what Arden would agree to be the best children in their Port, who also became well-rounded, smart, and kind adults. Arden's father wanted to be the best Knight in the King's personal guard, and that's what he did, too. His parents gave their dreams priority over their marriage especially as they were married quite young and for the same reasons Alvenia expected Arden to marry, or at least that's how it seemed. They would see each other a few times a year, but Arden's father was always bored of the local Port and wouldn't stay longer than a week at a time. He had hardly ever been home often enough to be considered a parent as he'd climbed the ranks and made it into the Guard. He left them with little to no contact, though Arden and Juna received letters throughout the years from him.

Arden had always felt sorry for his mother, always guarding the home and protecting the family's status as well as her children and running the household efficiently all alone. She really was always a reliable source of comfort in the town, and many deferred to her when they needed help managing their own estate and affairs. While Arden knew Alvenia would play into dramatics quite frequently, he knew it had no actual bearing on her strengths and skills as a homemaker. He admired that of her, and hoped Juna would be spared from marrying for anything other than love, with a partner that cherished her and raised a family by her side.

With those thoughts in his heart, he made it through town and back home before supper. He was perplexed, though, as he swore time was different when he went through that forest - some days it would be a really long hike, but days like today he made it home with hours of sun to spare. He shrugged it off though, and figured it was just the changing of seasons making the sun stay out longer. At home, he bathed and changed and had a light dinner before retiring early for the night, too emotional to want to do anything besides sleep. He fell asleep quickly, the long walk catching up to him all at once.

...

Another month passed that way, with nearly weekly visits to Will in the woods, whenever there was a space in patrols that he could squeeze in for himself. As he thought about the last visit he'd had with her, a smile came to his lips as he fought back a laugh. There'd been a moment so ridiculous, and yet so funny, that they hadn't stopped laughing even as they parted ways.

Willow had started gathering fallen sticks and brought them to the side of the riverbed. She lifted stones into a circle and placed each stick purposefully in the pile before pulling a pack of matches out of her apron pocket. She struck one and threw the lit match into the loosely made fire pit, and his eyes widened. He stood there, unsure what to do as she burned the branches of the trees around her.

"What's the matter?" She asked him as she turned around and reached for another stick.

"What's the matter? What are you doing right now?" He asked, exasperated.

"I'm making a fire to have tea with you?" She said, but her voice rose into a questioning tone as he stared at her. "Like we've done before, though it *has* been a while," she added with a laugh.

"You're burning yourself," he said slowly. She looked down at her hands and patted her dress, giving it an inspection.

"I'm not burned," she smiled and showed him her hands.

"No, the *wood*," he said, pointing to the fire. She blinked at him before glancing at the fire and looking back.

"Arden, what are you talking about?" She asked after a minute, confusion on her face.

"You're burning trees, Will!" He said louder than he meant to. She only blinked at him, before her brows slowly rose and a faint smile rose to her lips.

"Are you upset that I'm burning trees?" She asked, biting her lip. She looked like she was about to burst into laughter and he narrowed his eyes.

"Aren't you made of wood?" He asked finally, not sure how else to ask. "Aren't the other trees your *family?*" Will's laugh cut through the forest, sharp and abrupt. She dropped to her knees as she howled with laughter, holding her belly in near tears. Arden stood there making a bland face, waiting for her to stop laughing. He bit his inner lip to keep himself from joining her, and begged his cheeks not to burn.

"Arden I'm burning dead tree branches," she gasped after a few minutes, "and no, I'm not made of wood, but my wisteria is," she wiped the tears that pooled in the corner of her eyes and stood up, coughing from laughing so hard. She shook her head and wiped her hair from her face, before looking at Arden. She nearly fell into another laughing fit, but managed to stay calm as she continued explaining to Arden what she was doing.

"I'm collecting fallen branches that have been shed by the trees around us," she told him calmly. He stared at her with pursed lips, not convinced that she wasn't cannibalizing her fellow trees. "Would it make you feel better if I told you that the trees said it was okay for me to use those pieces?" She asked him. He thought about it before nodding.

"Yeah, that does actually make me feel better," he admitted as he ran a hand through his hair. She started giggling again, and the forest around them also seemed to titter and giggle. He put his hand to his hair as he shook his head.

"The lot of you are menaces, I was *worried*," he grumbled at the sound of Will and the trees laughing at him, "standing here thinking you were massacring your fallen brethren." Will grabbed his arm and nearly fell to the ground once again, knees weak as she giggled. Before long, he started laughing, too.

"I should have told you before," she wheezed, "learning about tree nymphs is a lot but the little things certainly seem weird," she told him.

"I should say so," he agreed, his words making her snicker.

"Oh please, go grab some more sticks," she told him before swatting him away with her apron.

"I don't burn my hair if it falls out," he mumbled to himself as he picked up a carrot. The trees trembled in delight around him, certainly enjoying his existential awareness of life in the woods. He rolled his eyes, pretending to be cross with their snickering, Will's the loudest of them all.

He found himself sitting in the home library, staring out the window into town after he'd freshened up after a long day of training new recruits as he remembered that day. If he could bottle up that day and keep it forever, he'd be a happy man. He stood before walking to the windows, peering out at the deep hues of the sunset. From this floor, he could see the whole Port market overlooking the south shore. As he stood at the window, hands linked behind his back in relaxed soldier form, he felt a presence behind him and turned his head to see Juna looking at him with a smile from the doorway.

"I thought I heard you stomping around in here," she snickered and bumped her shoulder to his as she sauntered up next to him. She was quite tall this year, not as tall as him but she had grown several inches in the last few months and could easily look into his eyes now to tease him more directly. He loved their ability to still be silly together, even though he was past his childhood now. Some things never changed, and for that he was grateful.

"I got home earlier than I expected so I'll actually be ready for dinner with you and the heckler tonight," he said, hiding a smile.

"Oh, don't call her that out loud! She has ears everywhere, you know," she giggled, but mirrored his stoic military pose. Arden thought she would make an excellent Commander like himself one day, with her direct and purposeful approach in life. "I'm actually certain she's buying dresses today because her friend's boutique finally got their shipment. We could potentially have dinner alone tonight," she continued as they both stared out the window in the direction of the boutique, waiting to catch a glimpse of their mother holding ribbons and accessories.

After a few minutes with the coast clear of any sight of Alvenia, they made their way to the dining room, still laughing quietly down the stairs. The table was already set by their housekeeper, and sounds of her moving around the kitchen could be heard as they seated themselves in their usual chairs. She finally walked through the doorway carrying two plates and laid them on the table gently, patting them each on the head before she turned back to the kitchen humming softly. They ate in silence for a few minutes before Juna started chattering about her weekend while Arden was away.

"So when are you bringing Will to the market?" Juna smiled mischievously as Arden almost inhaled his last bite of food.

"I don't think sh - Will would come this far from home just for a day," his voice trailed off and he felt his cheeks heat as his words slipped.

"Oh I am sure that sh-Will would love to join us for just *one* market day," she giggled. Arden almost groaned out loud but the sound of the door swinging open abruptly startled them.

"Not a word," he murmured to Juna, begging her with his eyes to keep it to herself. Juna stuck her tongue out at him and snickered, but said nothing. The sounds of Alvenia bumbling through the house and talking at the top of her lungs sent Juna into a fit of more giggles before she finally burst through the doorway to join them for dinner. Arden was barely holding himself together, he felt as though if he let one single word out of his mouth, he would lose it entirely.

He was grateful that Juna redirected every question their mother threw his way. He kept sipping the tea Felisia had placed out on the table for everyone before she swept their plates back into the kitchen quietly with a smile. Arden smiled back and watched his mother and sister gushing over the ribbons she brought back from the boutique, and small fabric samples of the dresses she was waiting on getting resized perfectly. Arden glanced at the clock in the corner of the room, a grandfather clock quite literally as it had been commissioned by his maternal great grandfather, and breathed a sigh of relief at the time. He took the last sip of tea he had left in the cup and opened his mouth to speak when he was interrupted by Alvenia and Juna.

"Did you hear what I said, Arden?" Alvenia asked him with a gentle smile.

"Oh, I'm sorry, I was just thinking about something," he said. Not quite a lie, but Arden knew he wasn't exactly telling the truth. He cursed himself for not escaping earlier and pretended not to see the smirk on Juna's face as he was dragged into what he was *certain* was a trap of some kind. He clutched Will's handkerchief in his pocket absentmindedly, running his fingers over the soft fabric as if attempting to absorb strength from it.

"Well Mother was just telling us about the fare of the apothecary right now," Juna started as Alvenia nodded.

"We've been getting fewer and fewer shipments of almost every kind of medication. The apothecary stores are dangerously low for a Port of our size. We've stretched it to last as long as they could. But there was a spread of a fever through the school districts again, the third time since winter, and it hit the families hard," Alvenia's voice was stern and smooth, Arden was always amazed at how she almost seemed to become another person when discussing important details with him and everyone around them.

"Naturally, the reserves are now critically low, borderline nonexistent. Travel through the roads is near impossible as of now, and soon so the ships shall be. The Captains have told us of the troubles at sea, along with the high demand of the products we need," she continued in a low voice.

"Most of the poultices and serums we use in this area are made with plant products," added Juna with a nod and a pointed look at Arden. He was afraid to know where they were going with this but he nodded his understanding before Alvenia continued.

"We have officially put out an alert to neighboring areas for assistance in the medicinal products we need. As of now, if another fever sweeps through the port, there would be no medicine to save the lives of the very young and the very old. But our hope isn't going to sustain us and I'm certain no aid will come, as we are not the only ones that have had shipment issues." Alvenia glanced at Juna, and frowned in thought for a moment. Arden could see the motherly fears rolling through her mind with that look. A fever could take down even the healthiest adult, and he knew she feared for their safety.

"Mother is asking anyone for help, even novice gatherers with a knowledge of the local flora," Juna said with another pointed look at Arden. He tried not to flare his nostrils at the mere *hint* of what he knew they were going to say.

"Arden, your friend Will that lives in the forest," Alvenia finally said as she looked into his eyes. For a moment, Arden was stunned to see the watery eyes of his mother. He knew whatever she asked, he would do everything in his power to make sure it happened. The look of pure motherly fear emanating from her was enough for him to want to promise her whatever she needed for the rest of his natural life.

"Yes," he murmured, waiting for her to continue.

"Your friend Will must know about any of the plant life in the forest that could help us, even a little bit," Juna said. Arden took a deep breath and nodded solemnly. It wasn't a question and he knew Will could help. She knew plants better than any-one and he flashed back to one of the first times they had spoken, and she had told him she was an herbalist. He knew she would help even if there was danger in the woods, especially if she knew how dire the circumstances were if she *didn't* help. He couldn't imagine her turning away innocent children in need of medical care.

"Will is an herbalist, with a very good understanding of me-dicinal products," he told them. He could visibly see the relief in his mother's eyes as she processed what he said.

"Oh thank the stars, will they help us?" Alvenia leaned forward and reached her hand out to her son. He caught it and gripped it tight, silently reassuring her in the only way he could.

"I'll have the squads reconfigured and go tomorrow to get Will's stores. Hopefully Will has what we need and we can fix this before it gets any worse," he rubbed her hand in his. He tried to ignore the thrill in his belly at the thought of seeing her again. He was immediately excited and could barely swallow it down. He smiled at his mother before standing, and gave both her and Juna a kiss on their cheeks.

"I'll be back later, I'll need to sort things out before I go," he called over his shoulder as he headed to the door.

He hurriedly made his way to the barracks, an old converted school, and informed his soldiers on the change in routine. He had expected many to be frustrated by the very sudden and last minute change, but only saw relief in their eyes when he said what he was aiming to do. He suddenly remembered the families and small children most of his peers had at his age, and knew they must have experienced the panic of the fever the last few weeks. They gratefully accepted the change and thanked him genuinely. Quite a few had dewy eyes full of unshed tears at the hopeful news. He made his way home quickly and told Felisia to have him woken up before first light, so he could have everything they needed to collect whatever Will was willing to spare. He fell into a fitful slumber, anxious at the thought of bringing Will home.

...

Immediately upon waking, he was on his feet and grabbing bags and jars and anything else they would most likely need to transport a large amount of medical supplies. Finally, though dizzy with exhaustion, Arden made his way to the stables. He knew they needed a quick form of transportation to ensure

Will's safety and the safety of the items they needed. He hoped she would be ready and willing to help - though he argued, she *would* be the type to want to help whoever she can. He twirled the small square in his pocket as he thought before letting it go with a sigh, ready to make his way back to Will.

As soon as the sun started to peak over the horizon, Arden mounted the horse and started at a brisk gallop. When he made his way through the stone wall borders of the port, he began talking, seemingly to himself if anyone had been watching. He told the trees to warn Will he was coming and that the people of his home needed her apothecary knowledge desperately, and he was coming to get her. He begged them to help and knew they heard him when he saw them shuddering around him, ahead of him, beyond even where he could see in the distance. Atleast, he hoped it was them listening and not actually a high wind catching their branches.

He pressed on, pushing the horse as hard as she could go but listening to her breathing for if she sounded winded. He didn't want her to get hurt in his mad dash to save the day, but he needed to be as efficient with his time as he possibly could. He couldn't remember the last time he had ridden this hard, let alone ever in his life, and reflected on the urgency of the moment. He wondered if he had been too caught up in his own thoughts and doubts to realize what was happening in the port all this time, the lack of medications amongst other things. He felt guilty for having spiraled at the thought of getting married. If he hadn't been so obsessed with his own problems, he would have seen what everyone needed before it had gotten to this point. He should have taken her to Stóngrast well before the harvest, to keep her from living in a dark cottage for the entirety of winter. It would have saved people from another illness had she been there sooner to prevent it. He felt guilty even more because of that, not only had he not kept Will safe but he'd neglected his home, too. Will would have thrived in the port, and so would the townspeople had she been there. He tried to brush away that feeling, and hoped at least now there would be peace for everyone he cared about.

The horse began to slow as they headed into the thicker part of the woods, right on the border of what the myths used to call the human realm. Though it had gone by Tonsilta for the last several decades, he had only just remembered its name in one of the last few months he had been coming this way. He had been reminded by Will when she had said it out loud during one of his visits. He could now recognize the sudden change from the human realm to the fae forest quite easily, but he supposed it was because he was more intimately acquainted with its secrets than he had been before he knew about Will's fae heritage.

A home in this forest with Will would be lovely, he thought with a smile before quickly correcting himself - *not* with Will, *like* Will. He shook his head to clear the thought away, wondering where exactly that had come from. He told himself not to think about it again and brought the horse back up to a faster speed. He noticed then that the trees had started swaying back towards him, as though returning a response to him. He wished he knew what they were saying, or if they were just moving to the breeze, but he kept the horse on course and hoped all the same.

As they ran he thought more about what he wanted from Will. Primarily, he wanted her to be on board with his urgent but optimistic plan. That she would be what they needed to keep his home safe, and everyone he ever knew or cared about safe. He thought of ways he could try to repay her for whatever she was able to help them with, in the instance she needed the monetary compensation to make more, or to buy more supplies. He knew that all of the families in need would give her whatever she wanted as well, so long as she was bringing medicine, or ailment relief, or even just a strong tea to aid an upset stomach. He didn't know what he would find once he made it to her home, but he was full of anticipation at the thought and rolled through every possibility in his mind.

Finally, after what seemed like ages, the wisteria tree blooming tiny white flowers finally came into view. He sped up until he heard the horse's hooves meet the moss, and then slowed to a walk almost to her front door. He paused for a moment to listen, when he heard frantic whispering from behind the house, closer to the river. The trees were still shuddering and trembling so Arden supposed it was the wind after all - until he finally made out what Will was muttering.

"I heard you already, I'm going as fast as I can gathering an arsenal of herbs and everything I can find that *makes* anything important!" She comically whispered, as she looked up at the trees before wiping her hair out of her face. Her hair was quite literally a mess, full of leaves and small sticks and he was almost certain he could see a family of ladybugs lounging on the flowers atop her head. She must have heard him then, because she jumped nearly a foot in the air with a shrill cry before she blinked at him in recognition. He didn't have time to do anything but smile before she shouted again.

"Oh thank *goodness* you're finally here! See this leaf?" she tossed a small leaf into his hand, it looked almost like a green flower petal, "they're on that side of the river - please fill this basket with them so I can find more of *this* leaf!" She raised another one in his face before spinning away.

He blinked at her form as she ran away surprisingly fast, deeper into the forest. He dismounted off the horse and led her to some grass before running to the other side of the water bed, grumbling for a moment that he was definitely going to be soaking wet, when he saw the large rocks at the bottom of the river. Perfectly laid out, he walked right over the river with barely a wet shoe and was grateful that Will seemed to think of everything around here. He filled the basket easily and crossed back over to the horse when he noticed a shape at the backside of Will's home.

A travel cart! He immediately ran to it and brought it over to the horse. He would definitely trade for a better one when they went to town as the wheels were not quite in the best shape. It may add time to the journey but the sun was still very low in the sky, so he knew there was at least a few hours of wiggle room before they needed to come back to Will's home. After hitching the cart to the horse, grateful he had the foresight to pack the necessities for that job, he jogged over to where Will was collecting what looked like berries.

"What's next?" he said to her as she then pulled each leaf off the fruit into a separate satchel altogether. She looked up at him and his eyes widened for a moment at the sight of her, on her knees, skirt tied around her waist, barely covering her legs let alone anything else. He begged his cheeks not to heat though he knew they definitely were already burning. She blinked up at him and pulled her messy hair back into a knot with the ribbon she liked to use, and wiped her forehead. She smeared dirt on her face as she did so but he knew that he would tell her before they left so she wasn't embarrassed at the market.

"As soon as I heard you were on your way, I pulled out as much as I could from my personal stores as possible. I loaded everything into the doorway, it was everything I had been saving up until now. I of course left some for emergencies for myself, but it's only enough supplies for a few months. I can make more, but given the times we're in now, I wanted to make sure I was being smart about it before giving you the entire store," she laughed before picking more leaves off the berries. "There's a lot, all labeled, and all concise written instructions are on each poultice, tincture, salve, and anything else I've made."

"Thank you, Will," Arden said with a sudden burst of emotion. His chest felt so full he wasn't sure he was breathing right, let alone talking right, but hearing her say those things gave him a heavy feeling of relief and gratefulness. Immeasurable was her aid, and he knew it. Even without knowing what's going on, she was just willing to help him, no questions asked. She smiled up at him again with a tilt to her head. He couldn't believe his luck, to have met her at all.

"You have no need to thank me, of course I will help you and your home," she said with a gentle squeeze to his boot. She tapped his leg and waved her hand at him to go and get the bins of whatever she had in the house.

He gasped when he saw just how much she had and was willing to share. He couldn't fathom how she could have made all of the goods but his chest swelled again, paired with a funny tickly feeling in his belly, and went to work filling the cart with the containers. He wondered what she would charge for everything after she brought it to market and noticed the different labels on each bag or bin. Some were labeled delivery, some were labeled childbearers, some were labeled with burns, belly aches, infection - she had a whole hospital worth of medical supplies. He was stunned, but continued filling the cart until the home was empty of them all again. He dusted off his hands before heading back to find Will and to offer her another hand in gathering anything.

He found her still covered in dirt, completely disheveled. He felt his belly roll at the sight of her again, and averted his gaze. She turned to Arden with a full burlap sack, struggling to lift it to him but trying all the same, and he couldn't help but smile at her in a way he never smiled at anyone else before in his life. She was stunning, absolutely glowing, as she stood there under the morning rays.

~ Eight ~

FILLING A CART

Wilmayra woke early as usual, and for a moment forgot that Arden hadn't stayed the night. Immediately upon remembering, she felt her stomach drop in utter disappointment. It took her several minutes to breathe deeply enough to calm herself down, the feeling of loneliness absolutely unbearable and stifling all the way down to her toes. Finally, though, she was able to make her way through the dark house and start her day. She went to the bathroom, she washed her face, she changed her dress. She did everything she could to feel alive, or at least tried to do her best at feeling okay with being alone again. She really didn't know how much more she could take of this feeling, the inevitability that Arden would stop visiting one day, and most likely she wouldn't know when the last time she'd ever see him again was. *How could it be worth it to feel this way constantly*, she thought to herself with a sniffle.

She sighed heavily, upset with herself for the overwhelming sense of abandonment. It hadn't been longer than a week since she'd last seen him and there she was, near tears from loneliness. She wasn't sure she'd survive Arden's marriage when it finally came. She made it to the kitchen after dragging her feet through the house at a slow pace, her feet heavier than usual, and grabbed the coffee press with the coffee and cream powder before heading to the front door to have an outdoor breakfast. The walls were suffocating and she wanted to get out and be free after so long inside. As soon as she opened the door, she was struck by the sounds of the trees whispering very loudly to her. The sun had only just risen, but the trees were insistent she listen to them immediately and be *ready*.

"Ready for what?" she asked, in a bout of panic. She almost dropped the coffee straight onto the stones leading to her doorway in fear. The trees urged her again, but this time gentler.

He is coming for you, you must be ready.

He needs help.

Your medicinal library is in immediate need.

Gather everything you have and enough to make more.

He is coming!

Wilmayra immediately sprang into action and brought the coffee back inside. Part of her was filled with excitement that Arden was coming for her, but the other part of her was worried about why he needed her help in this way. She ran back out after putting the press down, and opened up the shutters in the living room, just enough to cast a light into the room she needed to access. Running back inside, she threw open the hidden stairs and climbed down to grab each container of everything she had prepared, bottled, and labeled for the last year or more, and collected them into the doorway of her home. She had been making them for the Trade Days, however since there hadn't been any, she had accumulated quite a lot of medical necessities. In her opinion, she had become quite the nut if the hoard she had acquired was anything to go by.

"I guess it was actually good I had kept making these even though I couldn't share them at Hanlan," she muttered to herself, already sweating and out of breath. She managed to pull everything out of the basement shelter, after what felt like ages, and moved onto gathering as many leaves, berries, bark, and herbs as she could find. She wondered how exactly she'd bring everything to his home in one day and back in time for sunset - but suddenly remembered there was an old trade cart folded away behind her house, barely visible under vines and branches. She hurriedly ran to pull it out, struggling under its size, but managed to pull it out from under the foliage and unfold it. The wheels went back on surprisingly easy, too, and she murmured a gentle incantation to promote strength into its old bones.

"Let's go, old boy," she smiled at the perfectly intact cart that was easily over five years old at this point. She couldn't actually remember how long it had been but knew the poor old thing was severely neglected, and she would have to tell Arden to take it easy on the walk home. They would definitely both have sore arms when they made it to town, pulling this big thing all the way down.

After the cart was settled, Wilmayra ran back to her task of collecting as much as she could to make as many tonics, poultices, creams, and anything she could possibly think of that would benefit the sick or injured. Her mind went wild with scenarios, trying to piece together why exactly Arden would need these products, especially in this level of urgency or volume, but she knew the trees wouldn't exaggerate - well, they wouldn't exaggerate that excessively on something this serious. She stood on a fallen tree trunk to scope out the area, and listened to the gentle urging of the trees telling her which places to look for helpful plant life and roots.

She hopped down after making a list in her head and took a moment to hike her dress up as high out of her way as she could. It was a very taxing and messy job on a good day, to collect all that she needed, especially the roots and pieces of tree bark hidden under ivy and flora. She needed mobility, but since she knew Arden would be showing soon she couldn't exactly drop her skirts as she would usually do. Finally knotting the fabric as best she could into a makeshift satchel, she ran toward the first task she set for herself and began to dig. Periodically, the trees would let her know of Arden's pace and she would quickly rejuvenate her own, trying desperately to have enough supplies to replenish everything one time over. Logically, she knew it was unlikely to find that amount of leaves and whatnot, but she knew she had to try her very best to do so. At the very least, she would be able to show their medics how to make some of the potions she made.

The sound of a rhythmic clomping sound interrupted her thoughts suddenly, after maybe an hour of foraging and collecting. The trees suddenly started yelling at her, urging her to keep going because he's almost here, leaves fluttering around her. Finally she couldn't listen to their murmurs any longer after having been rushed and urged all morning.

"I heard you already, I'm going as fast as I can gathering an arsenal of herbs and everything I can find that *makes* anything important!" she said, voice rough with frustration. Suddenly overwhelmed, she blinked back tears that threatened to spill down her cheeks. She could hear Arden in the distance, closer and closer with each heavy sound that could only be a horse, and looked up into the trees to keep the tears from falling. One managed to escape despite her best efforts, and she wiped it away before brushing her hair away from her face. Aside from the trees still whispering urges to her, rattling their branches and holding on to whatever Arden had told them in the first place - she would need to ask him as she had never quite heard the trees this frantic - she realized then that it was quiet in the forest.

She tilted her head listening for his approach and was startled to see a large figure behind her, looming. She let out a shriek before she realized it was Arden and *not* a beast in the woods. She felt embarrassed for a moment, but then remembered why he was here and smiled at him before holding up a leaf in her hand, hoping he didn't see the redness of her eyes in her sudden fit of emotion.

"Oh, thank *goodness* you're finally here! See this leaf?" She handed him a tiny and soft leaf, almost a frond, and continued, "They're on that side of the river - please fill this basket with them so I can find more of *this* leaf!" She held up a completely different leaf, bigger than her face, and ran in the other direction.

After only a few minutes, she had collected enough poultice leaves and made her way to the very last fruit and leaf she needed. Everything else was accounted for and it would be the very last thing they needed before they could go to Arden's home. She heard him approach not long after she had started picking leaves off the berries, and looked up at him as he got closer.

"What's next?" he asked, his cheeks red.

"As soon as I heard you were on your way, I pulled out as much as I could from my personal stores as possible. I loaded everything into the doorway, it was everything I had been saving up until now. I of course left some for emergencies for myself, but it's only enough supplies for a few months. I can make more, but given the times we're in now, I wanted to make sure I was being smart about it before giving you the entire store. There's a lot, all labeled, and all concise written instructions are on each poultice, tincture, salve, and anything else I've made." She said, hoping she hadn't babbled too much with her words.

"Thank you, Will," Arden told her with the warmest voice she had ever heard. She almost trembled at the feeling spreading through her body but tried to ignore it.

"You have no need to thank me, of course I will help you and your home," she reached out and squeezed the closest part of him, which happened to be his muddy boot. She hardly cared, though, she was certain she looked like a wild animal in her current state. She waved him away before scrambling to finish the last mundane task that threatened to permanently cripple her fingers - fighting the leaves off each tiny berry was *painstaking.*

Finally though, each ingredient for as many medical products she could possibly think of were secured and prepared, along with all of the completed items in jars or small pouches. She pulled her basket and satchels to the front of her house to see Arden loading up the last carton into the rickety old cart. The wood barely groaned at the weight so she supposed that was good news, though she did murmur another strength incantation just in case as she ran her hand over the wheels. She smiled briefly at Arden when he glanced at her but looked away in case she looked like a fool with the dirt covering her entire body by now, embarrassed that he had seen her in this state, though not really sure why.

"I'm going to clean myself up and grab the recipe book I made for all of these," she gestured at the ridiculously large pile of everything in the cart. Arden nodded, smiling back at her as he started to throw leather straps around the cart. She didn't know how he knew what he needed to bring, or that she would even have what they needed at all but somehow, even the trees listened to Arden. For a second too long, she stared at him and really *looked* at him. Kind but sad eyes and a steady gaze met her suddenly solemn face. She felt an odd flutter in her belly as she looked into his blue eyes.

She realized then just how close they were standing, her hand almost grazing his as they both had a grip on the side railing of the cart. She quickly pulled herself away remembering the rush they were in.

"I promise I won't be too long!" she called to him as she dashed through the front door. Since the fear of the beast in the woods was at an alltime high, Willow had skipped heating water from the tap when it was time for a bath. Typically, it took too long to heat up and cool down and since she was not willing to have a smoke signal give away her position, she had been bathing in the cool water of the stream directly, or using the tap connected to the river for a cool shower. She dived straight into the shower and furiously scrubbed her entire body. She hated to wash her hair but knew it was beyond the ability of a brush to fix the tangled and muddy mess. She scrubbed until the water ran clean. Her thoughts turned to what a human market would be like, if it were anything like Hanlan. She had no idea what their customs were or what they expected of her behavior-wise. She was suddenly scared of what could happen or what they would ask her, but turned off the water and dried herself off before running in her towel to her room to figure out what she should wear.

I never expected that I'd be nervous to go to the human realm, she thought to herself, as she pulled a cotton slip from her linen drawer and pulled it over her head before gently brushing her wet hair. She checked her face over in the mirror, candlelight flickering around her. Even with the candle, it was still almost pitch black in the room because of the shutters. She had only opened the two in the front of the house to be able to see the cartons and pouches, but the rest of the house was still as dark as night. After she was done brushing her hair, she tried to look through her closet for a dress that would be suitable for a human market. She tried to remember what her mother had taught her almost ten years ago at this point, but found the memories were almost completely lost to her.

She pulled out a chemise folded neatly in the bottom drawer, and garters she had been saving since her twentieth birthday. She pulled a corset from the top drawer, wondering how she would even attempt putting it on if she had no one to help her. She bit her bottom lip wondering if Arden would mind helping, after all he would know what exactly a human woman would wear. She kept pulling out different dresses and blouses and bodices and ribbons, belts, accessories of every kind. She could barely make out the color of the clothes she was pulling out of the drawer because of how dark it was in the room. She frantically started pulling everything out of the closet that she could fit into her arms and stumbled her way to the living room. She threw everything onto the couch in the living room, startling Arden as he had been gazing out the window innocently watching his horse graze. She felt bad for a moment until the intense overwhelming anxiety rushed back to her, still frustrated by the lack of light in the room and the lack of knowledge she had on the fashion industry in another world.

"Arden, please help," she said frantically, hair still dripping wet down her back, making the slip cling to her skin. Arden blinked at her, eyes wide and cheeks red, as she shoved more and more items over the couch. She looked at him with pleading eyes, waiting for him to say something. She glanced at the clothes and then to him and grabbed a bodice from the pile, before holding it out to him in question.

"What are your customs in your home?" She asked, clarifying what she needed help with. Arden only spluttered and averted his eyes as she stood there in her slip, barefeet chilly on the stone floor. "Arden, please, I know nothing of your culture. I don't wear these here, and I don't know how they go on or in what order," she said, increasingly anxious about it as the minutes slipped by, "well I do know how to wear them but it's been ages since I've had to, and I can't remember." Arden closed his eyes and pinched the bridge of his nose before taking a deep breath and nodding to himself.

"Okay," he murmured, still not quite looking at her. He reached into her pile of clothes and grabbed for the wider corset and handed it to her without turning his head. "Put this on first," he said. As she reached out to grab it, their hands met. He turned to her then, his gaze dragging slowly over her body before he met her eyes. Willow's mouth opened slightly at the feel of his deep blue gaze, so intense she could have sworn she felt his hands on her.

An immediate flame kindled in her belly, the anxiety and fear from before disappearing from her mind altogether as she looked into his eyes. They both took involuntary steps toward each other, heat almost palpable between them. Willow glanced to Arden's lips as his tongue darted out, moistening them. Willow bit her lip at the sight when suddenly, a belt slipped from the couch and onto the floor, startling them both.

Will took a timid step back to put the corset on, unsure of what exactly just passed between them. She noticed, then, with pure delight, that Arden *definitely* felt the energy between them just now. For a second she would have assumed it was all in her mind, but a very noticeable part of Arden was very much at attention, and the fire in her belly threatened to burn her at the thought.

She raised her brows and wondered what to make of everything, while also desperately trying *not* to look at what he was hiding from her. He had hurriedly turned around after they were plucked from the moment by the sudden noise breaking the silence, and hid his arousal from her. She looked down at herself to start adjusting the corset, and realized what exactly Arden was privy to when she had stormed into the room, claiming his attention. The soft cotton of the slip was wet from her hair dripping down her shoulders and back, and left very little hidden. She started giggling to herself, knowing he had definitely liked what he saw.

She pulled the corset over her head, the ribbon already threaded and ready to be tightened. The corset was the same fabric as the slip, and the same shade, and Willow couldn't help but feel lovely in the ivory color. She tugged the ribbon a little tighter and tried to remember exactly what her mother told her about the secret to a well fitted corset, and was able to cinch it without pinching herself or making it hard to breathe.

"I did it!" She cheered with another giggle and a glance at Arden, who instinctively turned to her when she spoke. She saw his eyes widen, taking in the sight of her in her corset, the strap of the slip dangling over one of her shoulders. As he turned away, Willow's lips curled into a mischievous smile. She knew that this would *not* be a good game to play, but she was completely unable to deny how fun it would end up being if she did.

"What would be next?" she said, voice quiet but only to hide the laugh that felt lodged in her throat. Arden cleared his own before responding, turning delicately to the couch and rifled through some of the dresses and skirts Will had, until he stopped and handed her a light green dress. It was a heavier gown that she hadn't worn yet, soft purple threading along each seam in a beautiful floral pattern. There were petal fitted sleeves and a gentle, modest neckline, that had been a gift for her coming of age party. She took it from Arden before sliding it on over her head easily, fabric sliding so smooth it was like flowers on the breeze. It took a moment to slide it over her curves, having filled out more in the few years the dress had been waiting. But when she looked down at the dress, she knew it had never fit her better than it did that day. She thanked the gods for that, and gave the full gown a twirl before laughing again. Arden turned around to meet her with his own, and she tried to pretend she didn't know exactly what he had been hiding.

Arden nodded in approval at the dress, but dug through the pile of clothes again until he found stockings and tentatively picked up a garter that matched. Willow couldn't hold in the laugh that escaped, and tried slapping a hand over her mouth to hold it in. Arden gave her a bland look and puckered his lips, but Willow knew he was fighting against his own smile that threatened to escape as his cheeks twitched, a small dimple forming on one side.

She barely caught them as Arden tossed them at her, his laugh finally let out. She caught them with a squawk and a snicker and slid them onto her feet, hiking the skirts up as high as she could. For a moment she furrowed her brows in thought, staring at the garters and gauged her brain to remember exactly how they worked, but finally figured it out. They simply wrapped around the thigh, holding the stocking in place through tension - she knew the other garter in her drawer was connected to a pair of panties, and figured these would definitely be faster than trying to find the other pair at this point.

"I'm ready to go, now!" She cheered as she laced her nicest pair of boots, slender and light in the softest leather she had ever felt.

"You need to put your hair up," Arden laughed and shook his head.

"Oh my *gods*, what else could there be?" She ran to the bathroom and pulled a small compact mirror from the counter blindly in the dark and took several ribbons from the trinket box as well before running into the living room to Arden. "We are going to run out of time, so I'll do my hair on the way," she said, pulling a satchel off the hooks by the front door, and placing only the matching ribbons into it, along with a comb that had been in the kitchen along with the mirror, as well. She was grateful that spring was in full bloom with weather suitable for a carriage ride without a coat, knowing she would have made them late trying to find one.

Arden nodded in agreement and so they made their way to the door. Willow almost stepped out of the house after him but remembered that she would absolutely need to lock the door behind her, as she had never been this far from home before. *You've gone to Hanlan every month by yourself for the last twelve years,* her mind supplied. But she knew it wasn't quite the same, as she had never been around humans before this - Arden barely counted at this point, as far as she was concerned. She found the key still hanging behind the stone archway of the entry, covered in dust, and before she closed the door and locked it behind her, she pulled the curtains down in the living room, and made sure each one was locked from the inside with no way of opening them. After locking the door, she also pulled the shutters closed tightly, and that they were locked well, before walking up to Arden as he stood next to the horse pulling the cart easily. Arden reached his hand out to her, and helped her up onto the horse. She exclaimed in surprise at the movement, having thought she would just be sitting in the cart.

"It's way too full for you to sit back there, you may fall off if there's a bump in the road," he explained without her having to ask. She nodded at his words in understanding, before quickly grabbing the comb and pulling it through her now almost dry hair.

As Arden hopped up behind her, she felt her belly dip at the heat of him pressing along her back. She tried to ignore the feeling as she pulled her hair into a braid as best she could, but his arms wrapped around her belly as he pulled at the reins. She was certain this trip to Arden's home would be pure torture, as she could feel *everything* he did. The way he breathed, turned his head to look through the woods, his one hand still on her belly to keep her from falling off, the way his other hand held tight to the reins as though it were nothing, his strong thighs cradling her between them as she lay side-saddled on his lap - or atleast, *almost* completely on his lap.

She shook the rest of the thoughts from her head as she struggled with the mirror while tying the braid and then pulled it into a bun. She paused for a moment at the flowers in her hair and hoped they weren't too odd for the humans to see. She wasn't sure of their customs on that, and hoped she at least looked young enough for it to still be acceptable.

"Are you done with your hair?" Arden asked as he looked down at her, face impossibly close. She could see each freckle on his nose and the different shades of blue in his eyes. She couldn't help but glance at his lips as he spoke, drawn to them like a moth to a flame. She blinked at him for a second before answering.

"Yes, I'm all done, thank you," she murmured, averting her eyes.

"Hold on tight," he said as she put everything back in the satchel. She screamed then, as he suddenly snapped the reins and urged the horse onward. She clutched her arms around him as best she could, but felt one of his arms tighten around her belly again as it looped its way around her back, tucking her to his chest easily. She almost shuddered at the shiver in her spine at the feeling, and hoped Arden wouldn't be too uncomfortable riding a horse in a state like the one before when she was wearing her slip. She laughed against his chest as they hurtled through the forest, cart creaking behind them. She knew aside from someone taking an ax to it, it would stay secured with the incantation she had put on it. She thought of how long it had been sitting behind the home she had lived in her whole life, and was glad her and the cart were able to share a trip to a far away land she'd never been before.

It was an odd feeling for her, to leave in this way, her house just left behind and only a small key between them now. Her heart ached for a moment but knew she would be home soon enough, only a few hours really. Homesickness was not a thing she had ever felt before, having never really been far from home. She thought it must feel like this, an aching and empty feeling, unsure and alone, the world swept out from under your feet and nothing quite feels real anymore. Just a dream, never far from home but soaring above the clouds all the same. The only thing they could hear for a while was the rushing wind and the sound of hooves on the earth under them.

~ Nine ~

WELCOME TO MARKET

Arden held his breath as Will sat almost entirely in his lap. He prayed to every god he knew to *please* make this journey short and *please* do not let what happened earlier happen again in this close proximity - he would surely die of embarrassment. He could not believe he had become aroused seeing his closest friend in a state of undress in that way. *I'm only a man,* he told himself in a gentle voice, but he quickly brushed it off. He hoped Will hadn't noticed but was certain that even if she had, she was too naive to understand what exactly had been enticing in the first place. She lived alone after all and didn't seem to be acquainted with anyone besides himself as of late. Though, he didn't know what she did when he wasn't there. It wasn't fair of him to narrate her life as he really didn't know much beyond what they spoke of when alone with each other, he really didn't know of any of her other friends or her family. He was struck with guilt for a second but brushed it off, knowing they enjoyed each other's company and nothing else really mattered outside of their happy little bubble.

As they galloped along at the fastest pace the horse could run in the dense woods, he thought of how much Will was offering his home to aid in their trying times. There was no way he would or could have predicted the amount of stock she had stowed away, or that she would be willing to not only part with it all but also *make* more while there. She had even brought a recipe book! He was completely amazed by her, truly, and he knew Juna would latch onto her as well. His sister had always been able to detect someone's intentions, good or bad, and knew as soon as she even glanced at Will that she would love her, too.

Will looked around him as they ran, taking in the areas she had never been with her lips parted in wonder. Arden tried not to stare at her but in this position it was just not an option, there was nowhere to go and nowhere to turn that either of them weren't already there. He could smell the flowers in her hair, the shampoo equally as floral as her own natural smell. He was so used to the scent of her, he hadn't even realized that her home smells the same exact way that she did. He was always so comforted by the smell of flowers that everytime he stayed the night, he was always asleep in moments of laying his head down.

The horse suddenly ran over a large branch, and the cart jolted them up and almost out of the saddle when they landed. Arden used his thighs to keep Will from falling over the side, and used his hands to settle the reins and realign the horse from the fright. He led the horse into a jog and looked to Will to make sure she was alright. She was clutching him as tightly as her small frame could hold, eyes squeezed shut as she tucked herself under his chin.

"We're close enough to the border of Stongrast, we can slow down now and still make it with plenty of time," he assured her. She blinked up at him and he couldn't help but laugh at her expression - utter surprise and dismay at nearly toppling out of his grip. As he laughed, she narrowed her eyes at him before cracking a smile and laughing, head thrown back, and Arden couldn't help but think she was the most beautiful being he had ever seen. He traced the freckles over her nose with his eyes and delighted in the laughter they shared over a ridiculous moment, clinging to each other as if their lives depended on it as they traveled closer and closer to his home. After a few moments, Arden remembered what he had wanted to ask her earlier.

"Will, I have to ask about the supplies you're providing," he started, not quite sure if she would find it rude or not to ask.

"Yes?" she asked, looking at him with a curious expression.

"How much will you be asking for them?" He felt his cheeks heat at the direct question but knew he needed to ask it anyway. She turned her head to look at him directly and raised her brows in confusion.

"How much will I be asking?" She wondered, "for what?"

"I mean, how much will each item cost or are you offering it all in one large sum?" He said, trying to clarify what he meant.

"Arden," she said as she blinked at him, "I'm not 'asking' for anything," her voice was gentle.

"What do you mean?" He was confused, he figured she must also be confused, but before he could ask her again she continued.

"Everything in the cart is a gift, if your family and friends need help it is free for them to take," she smiled, "though if there's anything someone is willing to trade me for, I'll accept that, too." For a moment Arden couldn't speak as he processed what she was saying. He blinked at her with his mouth slightly ajar as he thought of a response.

"This is too much to just *give* away, Will," he managed to say, flicking his hand towards the cart packed to the brim. There was no way she meant what she was saying. If she gave away everything she had, for nothing - why would she want to? He blinked in dismay and shook his head, she'd have no money or goods to trade with if they took all of her stock. He wondered at her before realizing she was staring at him with a small smile on her face, her arms still clutching his waist.

"I can make more, Arden," she said with a laugh, "trust me when I say, making more will be easy and I'm certain by the end of the week I'll have made enough to replenish what was lost."

"A *week?*" he exclaimed, louder than he expected his voice to be. Will just laughed at him, throwing her head back.

"Arden, there's really not much I do aside from making my herbal recipes." Arden raised a brow at her suddenly solemn tone before she continued, "I have been too afraid to light a fire in case the beast were to realize I was hiding there and break into my home, so I haven't been able to jar anything that I used to fill my pantry with, I've only been eating what I find during a forage, especially after the long winter indoors drained those stores. But that leaves a *lot* of time to myself, so I have been making more than I need of everything in my recipe book." Her voice trailed off as she looked into the distance. "It's a book I have had since my mother taught me everything I needed to know when I was very little. She passed on her own mother's knowledge, and her grandmother's before that, too. It fills my days, and without having been to a Trades Day with other forest folk, everything I made in the last several months has just been sitting there and waiting."

Arden really didn't know what to say to that, so just tightened an arm around Will in a small hug. She laughed as she melted into the embrace and Arden felt his belly dip and roll, and prayed to the gods for maybe the tenth time that morning to *please* not let this arouse him, this innocent show of affection.

Luckily for Arden, the border was becoming visible in the distance. The trees had begun to thin out around them as pathways emerged. Once they were settled onto the first pathway that would lead to a road directly into town, Arden readjusted the both of them before sending the horse into another gallop, as fast as she could go. Though it was hardly mid-morning, he wanted to make sure there was no way they would be late to return Will home. He was scared of her even being alone in the woods at all at this point but knew he couldn't keep her here with him forever.

Juna and his mother would certainly try to keep her no matter what Will thought about it, he thought wryly.

In what seemed like minutes, they came to the first road that led to town and he pulled the horse into a trot, still maintaining speed but not as aggressively as before. With the slower pace, it was easier to hear everything around him. He took a moment to gather his thoughts before he asked Will a question.

"When we get there, I'll introduce you to everyone we meet," he started and glanced at her before looking away, back at the road. "What is your full name?" Will looked at him in surprise, eyes wide, and gasped. He was stunned at the response but waited for her to answer.

"I -" she started to say but looked away, cheeks red. He was curious as to why this would be the question that stumped her, but continued waiting patiently as he counted each marker along the pathway to measure the amount of time it would take to be in the market. Finally she continued as they met the last stretch of the road, but her eyes were shifty. Arden thought she seemed scared for some reason.

"Arden, I can't tell you my *full* name but you may introduce me as Willow," her voice was so small he almost didn't hear her. He smiled at her and didn't ask her to elaborate, he knew she must have a good reason to want to keep the rest of her name a secret. He assumed it had to do with fae culture, and didn't want to sound rude for prying so he didn't say anything else. He would make do with only knowing what Will was short for, and was happy to have the name Willow to go by for now.

He felt Willow tense as they finally came into full view of the Port. The land surrounding this side of the entryway of Stóngrast was cleared of most foliage, with only beautifully manicured trees wrapping around the stone wall enclosing the town inside. Willow turned and stretched her neck out as far as it could go to see as much of the town as possible from where they sat atop the horse. Arden pulled the horse to a stop before moving Willow upward and out of his way as he hopped off the saddle. He turned to Will and helped her down by lifting her up by her waist and gently placed her on the ground in front of him. She looked around uneasily for a moment, the morning sun still a ways away from the apex of its journey as the trees ruffled gently in her direction. Arden knew they must be offering comfort to Willow because she almost immediately relaxed and nodded before smiling at Arden.

"I'm just going to grab my recipe book so I can look through and see which recipes I have enough ingredients to make while we're here," she chittered nervously, pulling the book out and holding it tight to her chest.

Arden nodded and offered his elbow to her, as he held the reins in his left hand. She took his arm while still holding the small leatherbound book tightly. Her nervousness was palpable, and he hoped she wasn't uncomfortable being here but continued walking towards the main entry of the gate at a moderate pace. Willow kept looking around and over her shoulder as they passed through the wall and entered the Port of Stóngrast at last.

People were bustling through the main square of town, busy as they always were. If Arden didn't know any better, he would have seen a lively crowd. But under all the noise and people, you could see just how much his home was struggling under the onslaught of sickness and the sudden financial insecurity from shipments lost at sea and bandits in the neighboring Ports. Everyone had a heavy presence, and surely several had family and friends succumb to the recent bout of fevers as it tore through the town.

"Oh my, Arden," Willow murmured sadly as she used her opposite hand to hold his arm tighter around her elbow, "what happened to everyone?" He sighed, wondering how she could even tell when everything looked almost normal on a surface level. He should've known she would be able to pick it up easily, though.

"There has been illness spreading through here that we weren't prepared to handle, along with a rise in theft. Whatever is awake in the woods seems to have also awoken a lot of other troublesome beings," he told her quietly. He saw a man approach them and realized it was Teg, and blinked in surprise at seeing him in town square when he was usually always gazing into the fire at the tavern. He went to greet him when suddenly Willow slammed her book into Arden's chest and took off running.

"Teg! I can't believe you're here!" she cried as she ran into his outstretched arms.

"I was certainly not expecting to see you today," he laughed as they hugged. Arden could hardly believe his eyes, and wondered at the implications of Teg and Will's acquaintance - was Teg like Willow? His brows furrowed in thought as he watched them interact.

"So I'm sure you have met my friend, Arden, then," Will said as she stepped back and reached out to Arden. He gripped her hand with his own almost unconsciously and pulled her arm back through his, linking them together again. Teg smiled at Arden at his movement and he couldn't help but feel a warm fluttery feeling in his belly. He felt as though he was staking a claim over the woman between them, but knew that was a silly thought to have. He told himself this is only how friends behave, and it meant nothing more than that. He wondered at the mischievous glint in Teg's eyes, though, and looked away as he felt his cheeks heat. He refused to let himself think very deeply on it, and was grateful when Teg continued talking with Will.

"What brings you to town, Will," he said with a glance to the loaded cart.

"Arden's home needs some of the medical supplies I've had stored for awhile, and I wanted it to go somewhere useful before it went bad," she smiled and looked up at Arden, who's cheeks still felt like fire.

"You are very kind to help Stóngrast, Willow," he murmured as they started walking again. Teg stood next to Willow as they walked and he saw a brief questioning glance to Will before she turned her head with a giggle. He noticed her cheeks turning pink and felt happy at least that they both had matching blushes on, now, despite not knowing what it was that Teg said that had caused it.

Finally, they made their way into the market. The Market was along the actual port of the town, with storefronts and kiosks lining the stone walkways. Town square kept all of the important businesses and banquet halls, as it was easier for the cargo to be divided out to the shops directly from the port instead of creating cart traffic throughout town to drag it all the way back to the front of the border. They had changed the locations only a few generations ago, as they learned how easily bandits would make off with goods if they were directly next to the walls. To avoid anything else from being stolen or destroyed, they moved everything into more logical locations to make best use of each part of the town.

Will was practically vibrating from nerves at the amount of people she was seeing, Arden could feel her tensing under his hand and gave her elbow a gentle squeeze before pulling the cart up to a long empty kiosk. He didn't need to say anything at all before Teg and Will both started unloading the cart. They filled the kiosk to the brim with as many products that they could fit into it, quietly and efficiently. Lots of the potions had to stay in the cart, but Teg unhooked the old cart and looked to Arden.

"I'll take her to the stables and spread word of what you have brought for everyone," he said, clasping Arden's shoulder tightly before offering Willow a gentle smile. "She's a good one, Arden, I've known her family a great long time," he squeezed him again before turning with the horse, and making his rounds through town to help them.

Arden turned to see Willow aggressively flipping through her recipe book before landing on a page and reading through it. Her head tilted for a moment and he swore he could see her thoughts run across her face as she dug through some of the bins and bags for some of the loose ingredients. She also pulled one of the cartons out that was labeled "supplies" and began adding leaves and berries, and what looked like small vials of oils, before grinding it down with a mortar and pestle. As she stood there and made another paste, he noticed a young woman approaching from the side and turned to see Juna with a grin as she ran toward Arden.

"Arden!" she yelled from across the market, laughing as she ran faster. Arden braced himself as he walked toward her, knowing she would try her best to knock him over in front of everyone, giggling wildly as she did.

"Juna," Arden laughed gently before his little sister leaped at him in a hug.

"I heard you were here and I came to see what was going on!" she said as they straightened themselves. Juna looked over his shoulder and he could see in her eyes the exact moment she registered Willow, and put it together that she was his friend from the forest. She gasped in delight and jumped where she stood, hands clasped under her chin. "I knew it! Mother is going to *faint* when she meets her!"

Before Arden could stop her, Juna ran out to see Will with a devious giggle. He sighed for a moment and told himself this is what he knew would happen, he knew they'd be excited, so he tampered down his sudden frustration and walked over to introduce them.

"Juna, this is my friend Willow," Arden said with a smile, "Willow, this is my little sister, Juna," he continued. For a second, Willow's face flashed with fear at the introduction before she smiled and curtsied - he assumed she was afraid of not using the correct custom in front of Arden's family. He knew they hadn't discussed that aspect, and felt bad for not properly preparing her. But as quickly as the thought crossed his mind, Juna was ready to plow through the conversation. He watched as Willow tentatively placed the paste into a jar and wiped her hands together to clear them off as Juna spoke.

"You must be Will from the forest! Arden has told me *so* much about you," Juna gushed. Arden wanted the world to swallow him where he stood, and begged the gods to please make his sister be quiet as Will laughed.

"It's a pleasure to meet you, Juna," she smiled shyly, and Arden's belly dipped at the sight.

"What's all this stuff?" Juna asked with curiosity. With what seemed like a switch, Willow's whole demeanor changed. Both

Arden and Juna stood there, with what Arden was certain were the same expression on both of their faces. They listened in awe as Willow went through each item and explained their purpose and how exactly to use them.

"I was trained by the best healers I know, herbalists through generations. My mother and her mother gave me everything I needed in order to be the best healer I could be, a vessel of our combined knowledge. I went through extensive training and applied sessions in healing in order to grow into a true apothecary one day. I know how to make every kind of medicinal herbal remedy you may need, and some even you may not have known you needed at all. My specialty has always been in fertility, " Willow explained before pulling more of the items out of the cart, "though I'm well versed in everything else, too."

"These elixirs, tonics, poultices and more, are what we would need for a parent delivering a baby," she pulled one of the small vials out and handed it to Juna. "This is what I have had many childbearers deem as "The Miracle" as it takes a lot of the pain away and helps the body rest before delivering." Juna handed it back to her and Willow offered her another item, "This is a cream for the stretching and growing skin on a baby belly, and it prevents scarring or tearing during delivery as well, should you also use it as a lubricant for the baby," the jar was full of what looked like a solid white cream, "we found this out when a good friend of mine melted it by accident and it went *everywhere*," she laughed.

"This one is what we would use to induce a pregnancy that has gone past term to ensure the safety of the baby and the one carrying it. The rest of this carton is full of other remedies to relieve cramping, excessive bleeding, and anemia caused by what many of us have to deal with every few weeks, along with contraceptives and everything in between." Arden was stunned at what she was saying, blinking in surprise at the directness of her explanations on such delicate matters. Even Juna stared in awe and delight as Will continued, not even a blush on her cheeks as she spoke of menstruation and giving birth. It would seem Willow wasn't as naive as he had thought.

"This carton is full of everything you need for a stomach bug, whether its for hydration," she pulled a jar out that was full of an opaque pink liquid, "for nausea," she pulled a smaller vial out, "for food poisoning - though this really only helps settle the belly, there's no cure for food poisoning. It would work for any kind of nausea or diarrhea, so long as you don't take too much of it," she put everything back into the box and placed it into the cart. She continued to go over each item in the other boxes before turning to the kiosk she had filled when they got here.

"These are the most important ones, the ones I had a feeling you needed the most," she murmured as she held up a tiny vial of a dark liquid. "This will lower a fever within thirty minutes - it goes by weight and you have to make sure you're taking the right amount or it could weaken your system more than you can bear. I made sure to label each vial to assure everyone that there is no room for doubt when giving to a child or an elder," she placed the vials gently back onto the counter of the kiosk, tucking them under the lowest shelf.

"These are for infections - external infections take a poultice that's spread over the area and tied tight to the flesh using *this* leaf before being bound with a strip of fabric," Willow continued.

"Why does it need a leaf in between?" Juna asked, and Arden knew she could never fight against her natural curiosity. He was surprised, though, that it was the first question she asked after everything else had been explained.

"That's a really good question, Juna," Willow turned to her with a kind smile, face glowing with pride. "This leaf specifically takes actual weeks to start to wilt and decay, it stays waxy and solid for a very long time. It also doesn't absorb oils and liquids, so won't change the product in any way. If you were to apply this paste to a wound and bind it with a strip of cotton, the bandage would be wet almost immediately. Naturally, for avoiding infection, this is *not* ideal. The wound needs to absorb as much of the medicine as possible while the bandage stays dry. The leaf also acts as a natural barrier of protection for the wound itself. It keeps it from sticking and scabbing onto the bandage and makes it easier to change the bandage altogether while also ensuring it's fully absorbed by the body for the best possible results." Juna nodded as she explained, completely entranced by Willow.

"Now this vial is for internal infections, the ones that we can't see but know are there by fever, rash, or malaise in general," she lifted a vial of a red liquid, and shook it for a second until it turned dark purple, "it needs to be shaken before use to make sure it's properly effective," Willow demonstrated and offered it to Juna to see the small flecks floating around in it. Arden was impressed, he hadn't thought about what she was bringing specifically, and couldn't believe the amount of things she was able to actually make by hand in the first place.

"You *made* all of this?" Arden couldn't help but ask.

"Yes," Willow laughed as she tossed the recipe book to him before gesturing to Juna to look at the tea satchels on the top shelf. Arden vaguely heard the girls talking about different types of tea, from belly aches, healing, cramping, to enhancing your immunity, and for energy boosts as he turned through the pages of the small book in his hands.

The leather was very old, and very worn down. He could tell that Willow had been using this book almost her whole life with how aged it looked. He noticed different styles of handwriting on each page, some in script and some in childlike bubbly letters. He knew it must have been a mixture of Willow's handwriting through the years and couldn't help the warm feeling filling his chest as he watched Will interact with his sister in the full market streets of his home.

~ Ten ~

A FRIEND

Willow explained each tea to Juna who was listening with a wide eyed wonder for everything she said, making Will feel important for a moment. Willow kept going, kept explaining and clarifying as she enjoyed the company of another young woman for once in a very long time. It reminded her of years at Lexman Yur, a fae school in Coven Land that dedicated education toward the natural affinities a fae may develop, and for any with a curiosity for a new talent. Willow had been trained by her mother in her early years with all the knowledge bestowed on her mother from her mother's mother, but the lessons she learned in her years at Lexman were truly pivotal in her skill development especially after her family moved back to their orchard.

Her voice trailed off as she noticed Arden staring at her intently, a small smile on his face. Her cheeks felt warm and Juna glanced at her brother before smirking in a way Willow knew would be trouble, but couldn't help but laugh at her youthful glee from teasing her brother.

"Oh, Mother is going to be *so* excited to meet you, Will," she took Willow's arm in her own with a giggle. Willow blushed harder and ducked her chin, and tried not to burst into giggles at the grumbling sound Arden made at Juna.

"Give her some space, Juna," Arden grouched.

"Why, are you jealous?" she snickered. Willow quickly covered her mouth with her hand and tried to hide the laugh as it slipped out. Juna cackled next to her, before winking at Will. Will knew Juna and herself would have quite the fun together should they ever meet again, though that thought brought with it some melancholy. She wasn't sure if she would see them again after this. She knew Arden would choose a family life soon and she really couldn't blame him, this town was *beautiful*. The ocean glittered over the docks, boats and noise and people bustling around them. Though the town was full of sad and tired folks, she knew it was only temporary as they would be able to use the medicinal supplies she brought, and she would also make sure to leave the recipes for them, too.

"Arden," Willow said as she still held onto Juna's arm, "do you have an herbalist here, or an apothecary?"

"We do, it's more central to the town," he said pointing towards the homes along the street.

"Can you take me there, please?" she asked, hoping it wasn't too much to ask of him and already feeling silly for it. Juna laughed then, and pulled her forward, into the direction Arden had pointed.

"Of course we can go," Juna and Arden both said at the same time, sending the girls into a fit of laughter.

"What do you need at the apothecary, Will," Arden asked. Willow could hear the curiosity in his voice and smiled as they walked on.

"I'm going to check their stores and their recipes, and see if I'm able to offer suggestions on anything, and make sure there isn't an item you need that isn't stocked well enough yet. I can make more once I'm home, and you are more than welcome to take it," she trailed off as both Arden and Juna looked at her with their wide blue eyes, but she wasn't sure what they were looking at. Her cheeks flamed again, and she was afraid her face would become permanently red from what seemed like endless amounts of embarrassment even though she knew there was no reason to feel that way.

"That's very kind of you, Willow," Juna murmured with a squeeze to the arm she had linked in her own. Willow felt warm, pleasantly warm, and dreaded the moment she would be back home alone trapped in the dark.

Finally they led Willow down the streets of town until they met a shop center, a cul de sac of stores, and saw the apothecary sign at the end of the circle. Juna let go of Will as they walked a little faster to get there quicker, and Willow followed Juna through the doors as Arden held them open. The shop was small but tidy, dark aside from a few candles as the curtains were pulled tight. She looked around and delicately stepped around the cold room before she turned as Arden spoke.

"Hello, I've brought someone who wants to help you," Arden said to the apothecary owner, or so they seemed to Will. "This is my friend who was trained extensively in the art and she wishes to aid our town in recouping from the stress of the last few months." Willow tentatively walked up to the man standing there in a white cloak and curtsied.

"It's a pleasure to meet you, sir, I hope I'm not overstepping," she said shyly, unable to look him in the eye as he wore a stoic expression.

"You've come to help me?" the man asked, confusion lacing through his voice.

"We've brought everything she had in her storage pantry, it's in the market now," Arden supplied.

"Yes, and I've brought my recipe book for you to see my recipes and find anything you may not have but need," she said finally looking into his face. Dark brown eyes looked back at her kindly and she smiled, "I also wanted to know if I could take a look at what you have so I can try and bring more of what you need or see if there is anything that needs an update for maximum efficiency of the product." The man looked at her without an expression to give a hint of what he was thinking, before he broke into a full laugh.

"Oh, my dear, you have come at such a perfect time. I was well and truly hanging on by only prayer, trying to put together even one more tonic for one person, let alone the whole town." He pulled Willow into a hug as he spoke, and she could feel the relief in his squeeze. He pulled back from her to look in her face with a happy smile, and led her to the back rooms. She felt Arden and Juna behind her, following with intrigue as they crossed a narrow hallway into a large room, meticulously organized. There was a large window on the ceiling that gave everything a luminescent glow as the room was lit by the natural light of the sun.

"Wow," the trio murmured as they looked around the almost barren room. Willow went up to Arden and pulled her small book from his hands where it had been staying for the last few minutes, before opening up to the second page of the book and showing it to the physician.

"Here's a list for all my products," she offered him the page to read through, "do you have a pen and paper I can use?" She asked, trying to force herself not to feel guilty that she hadn't brought one along with her here and had to bother the doctor for one. He obligingly pulled a pen and notepad from his pocket and handed them to her while she strolled through the room and took notes on what were the staples in this area, and what they typically didn't stock at all. She walked around and wrote down each medicine's name and cross checked the ones she made from memory, and saw there were quite a few that they still needed, and some that were made with an outdated recipe.

"What have you been using for birthing babies, I'm not seeing many fertility medications or recovery items either," she asked out loud, more by accident than anything.

"We haven't actually had effective labor options for pain management in the last year or so, lots of the ingredients have become impossible for vendors to find," the doctor answered, offering his own recipes to Willow. She glanced through the book to get an understanding of where they were at in development - it seemed this human town was several decades behind on medicinal studies.

"I'm afraid to know what exactly is your birth survival rate, for both the delivered and the deliverer..." she muttered, flipping another page. "Okay," she huffed and closed the book, "are you willing to be retrained in *all* of these recipes?"

They all turned to Willow in surprise at her words and glanced at each other, but Willow didn't move or blink away at their heavy looks. She wanted to run under their penetrating gazes, but knew the cost of improper education on medications, especially if they were this behind on the herbal studies aspect. Lives were at stake, and not just for fevers and illness.

"What do you mean, my dear?" The doctor asked, curiously.

"I mean, all of these are extremely out of date and pose a threat to your entire town. Low birth rates are really bad for populations, and you've all been under extreme circumstances with sickness sweeping through the young and old," she spoke with a kind but stern voice as she wanted to be polite but also felt she had to state this plainly even if they didn't want to hear it. "Do you know what you get with low birthrates *and* low survival rates to illness?" They shook their heads at her question, eyes wide. "You get dying towns that cannot grow and replenish during times of stress," she finished. They blinked at her as her words sank into them, she could see each of them processing the idea of a barren town. The doctor seemed to break from the thoughts first, and stepped closer to Willow.

"My dear, it would seem you have been brought here for good reason and your dire words are certainly cause enough to take preemptive action. I'll take a look at your book and try to learn what I can," he spoke in the same tone she had, stern but kind, and smiled at her. In her experience, not many elders would agree to what she was urging, and would outright refuse to abdicate in that way to allow that room for error. She felt relief at his response, and looked to Arden who stood there with his brows raised, with an expression she didn't recognize on his face. He smiled at her when he noticed she was looking at him and couldn't help but beam.

"Okay!" She laughed before taking her book from the doctor and giving him back his own. "I actually carry another book for situations like this, with all of the copies of each recipe, and I can go over that with you in the market now," she said as Arden offered his elbow to her. She felt a warm feeling in her belly at the idea of being pressed up against him again, and immediately latched onto him while Juna held his other arm.

"I'll follow you after I lock up," he nodded at Arden who nodded back, and they started back for the kiosk where they had left her supplies.

The walk was much shorter on the way back and Willow wasn't certain if it was just her imagination, or if they were only moving faster this time. She hurriedly dug through some of the bags as Arden lifted anything heavy before she found the book, still crisp and neat, tucked neatly away with the empty jars and sachets. She had made this many years ago but had edited it when necessary, and made sure to write explicitly detailed directions on the process of making it, the precise amounts of each ingredient, along with the best methods for use and where to find the flora to make it.

She turned around and realized that Teg had come back and placed a long table by their cart and kiosk, making an almost full stall in the marketplace. Willow wordlessly thanked him with a squeeze to his shoulder before he walked off into town again. Juna was straightening the teas while Arden placed each carton on the table, and the extra underneath it. By the time it was organized and ready, the doctor had come back and placed his own notebook next to Willow's before looking at her earnestly.

"I know I'm no spring chicken, but I have always been fond of learning. I will be your pupil now, Miss -?" he asked, a charming smile on his cheeks.

"You may call me Willow, Doctor," she said with a curtsy.

"Oh hush, you may call me Fasomalo," he said as he stuck his hand out to her. She took his hand in hers before they shook them, and laughed as he continued, "How good it is to meet you, Willow!" She laughed with him, sharing a moment of relief, and ushered him to where Teg had laid out the table and had him look at the book she had made especially for an emergency like this. She was glad she had had the forethought to prepare a few of them, just in case one day hers was lost, or she was invited to Lexman Yur one day as a teacher in the art. Whatever her motivations had been on making them, she thanked her past self for doing so. It would save them time and translation issues in the future if the good Doctor Fasomalo had forgotten a small detail.

Willow felt eyes on her and turned to see Arden speaking to a woman who looked just like Juna, and realized with a sudden twist of nervousness in her belly that it must be their mother.

She took a small deep breath as she saw Arden gesture for her to come closer, and gave him a small nod before she turned to the doctor and told him she would be back, but the book and the entirety of what it makes would be on the kiosk or the table should he want to look a little closer. She braced herself before walking up to the two of them, shyly smiling and offering a delicate curtsy. She was worried of embarrassing herself but the look on the woman's face was one of very evident yet pleasant surprise.

"You must be Arden's friend, Will from the forest! How wonderful it is to meet you, dear!" The woman spoke in the same way that Juna did and she could tell by Arden's face that he was currently praying to the gods, his eyes were turned up to the sky as he muttered to himself. She found a laugh escaping her mouth before she could stop it, but the woman only laughed with her before pulling her into a hug that Will easily returned. "You may call me Alvenia," she murmured gently to Willow and she couldn't help but feel the kindness rolling off the woman's presence as it filled her with ease.

"It's good to meet you, Alvenia," Willow responded back quietly, as Alvenia pulled away from her.

"It seems you have come to our rescue, haven't you?" Alvenia asked.

"Willow is unfailingly kind," said Juna, popping up from behind the stall and linking arms with her mother. "She also knows more than the doctor, can you believe that?" Juna giggled to her mother, pointing at the doctor at the table. Alvenia made an impressed face and laughed, clearly delighted by the news.

"It would seem so!" Alvenia giggled in response to Juna. "Let us go and let the townspeople know that medical attention is available now, before it's too late in the day to get the message out," she said tugging on Juna's elbow linked in hers. Before she turned away, she embraced Will again, this time with Juna on her other side. They both kissed her cheeks as Alvenia continued, "Thank you for everything, darling, truly this is the most important role anyone could have in our home right now. My cousin, the doctor, is in good hands," she added with a smile.

Willow stood there blushing, holding her cheeks as the women walked away swiftly. She turned to Arden and suddenly her belly growled, she startled in surprise when Arden laughed.

"If you're hungry, there's a restaurant by the tavern just over there," he offered his arm to her.

"I'm *very* hungry," she agreed. They walked to the doctor to let him know where they were going should he have questions, or if anyone else showed up looking for something specific. So far no one had approached the stall though Willow knew once the sun fell past its highest point, people would be here shortly thereafter. It would be after meal times or during a lunch break that someone would finally come, after the people had been notified of the presence of the medications. It would take time but she was hopeful she would be home long before sundown at this rate.

"Doctor," Arden grabbed his attention, "we will be having lunch and will be back soon, will you be alright to man the table while we're gone?" he asked.

"Of course, I can stay if you want to familiarize yourself more before taking that responsibility," Will offered.

"Oh no, my dear Willow, go enjoy the town. I can handle this - you have done an extensive amount of organizing and labeling, I have no doubt I'll be able to handle this with your help making those guides for us!" Fasomalo laughed and waved his hands at them before diving back into the book, scribbling notes to himself into his own.

Gratefully, Arden and Will hurried to the restaurant. They walked down the street passing other vendors arm in arm, enjoying the noise around them while also enjoying the silence between them. She wasn't sure about Arden, but she was *exhausted* - and also starving. She supposed she had forgotten to eat anything while scrambling around her house. She was surprised that Arden had been able to hear her belly rumble at all though, with all the sounds around them.

She noticed something behind Arden when she looked up at him, and paused for a second to see it clearer before they walked past it. She tilted her head and squinted her eyes before the emblem on the doorway to the tavern finally became visible to her. She gasped and pointed at it, knowing the sign as she had seen it everyday for an entire decade, and let go of Arden before running to the door where it hung. She ran her hands over the small stone emblem, a decoration to anyone else, but she knew what it meant. She pulled the door open and walked in, not waiting for Arden in her mad dash to get inside. She felt bad for only a moment but could hear him behind her, and continued further inside.

She looked around the tavern, looking at each face, before her eyes fell on a particular person across the room. As if they could feel Willow standing there, they turned around, holding a now empty tray. Willow gasped again before jumping and running toward the person they hadn't seen in a *long* time.

"Sian!" Willow yelled as she barreled into the arms of one of the most mysterious people she had ever known, who met her in the center of the tavern. She could hear whispers and murmurs around them but she only laughed as she hugged her friend tight. "What are you doing here?" She laughed again, completely boggled at the presence of her favorite mentor from Lexman.

"I could ask you the same, Twig!" Sian laughed and pulled Willow back to see her face, calling Will by her childhood nickname. Willow felt Sian's eyes rove over the flowers in her hair, white and blooming. Sian raised perfectly combed brows in a pointed manner and glanced around the tavern before eyeing Arden. Willow knew Sian could sense soul bonds from the Binding Prayer and felt a flash of fear at the thought of Arden finding out like this, but she knew Sian would just tease her mercilessly before ever sharing a secret that big. She also knew how much Sian liked to make people squirm with the knowledge they had, so prepared herself to buckle down and brace for it should Sian find out how easy it was to make Arden blush.

"This is my friend Arden," Willow said pointedly, before holding onto his elbow once again. "Sorry for running like that," she offered Arden gently, "I just recognized that stone on the door and knew Sian would be here."

"Hello, Arden, it's been a while," Sian grinned, pointed teeth glinting off the fire in the dark lit tavern. Arden's eyes widened slightly, and Willow felt his grip tighten on her arm. She couldn't help but laugh before realizing people were still staring at them. She blushed for a moment and then shrugged it off, not caring if people saw her spending time with her friends, though they were quite different from one another. Sian's hair was shaved down low on each side but the mass of hair in the middle was long and braided intricately. Dark makeup covered dark grey blue eyes, and Sian's wardrobe was equally as dark and intricate to match. Arden stood there in his crisp and light washed clothes, shoulder length hair naturally curled with a light beard, blue eyes like the sky. Sian and Arden seemed to be opposing forces as she stood in between them.

She couldn't help but be delighted to see them both in the same place, no matter how odd it apparently seemed to others that she had such wildly different friends, if the people in the tavern gawking at them were anything to go by. She laughed, unable to contain herself at the wonder of being able to see *two* friends from miles and miles away from home along with many new friends that she had made today. She couldn't believe her luck, after having spent so much time isolated and lonely, that she would be able to experience a day like today. Bringing herself back into the present, outside of her own thoughts, she tugged Arden closer with the arm linked through his and then reached for Sian's hand.

"We're starving, Sian, do you serve food here?" She asked softly, "I would love to catch up with you while we eat, too."

"Oh, Twig, you know I can't resist a good gossip," Sian snickered, eyes sneakily glancing at Arden and back to Will with a single brow raised. Willow felt her cheeks heat but knew it was too dark to be able for Arden to see - though she *knew* Sian the sneakiest of fae could, as Sian cackled and led them to a table in the corner. Willow just smiled at Sian, knowing that they'd never actually embarrass her in public like that, and allowed Sian to keep being silly in the best of ways that she had truly missed after all those years alone.

"I'll bring out the specials, and don't worry Commander, I already know what you like," Sian winked and looked at Willow and cackled some more, before sweeping into the back of the tavern and disappeared through the doors behind the bar.

"What a trouble maker *still,*" giggled Willow as she settled into the seat Arden had pulled out for her, quietly thanking him as she finally felt the eyes of all the bar folk lose interest in their reunion. She was certain Arden would ask about Sian, as it was quite out of the ordinary for Will to know *anyone* besides Arden himself. Arden cleared his throat and looked around the room to spot Sian, before pulling himself closer to Willow.

"I have a question," he murmured, entirely perplexed. Willow let out a peal of laughter that was easily swallowed up by the sounds of the people around them, none of them turning to see her now that the scene they had made came to an end.

"You may ask me," Willow grinned.

"How do you know Sian?" He asked.

"We have known each other since we were very young, and trained together in school. Sian went off to travel the world a few years ago, and I haven't seen them in a while. But I know their sigil better than my own family's, and knew I'd find Sian here with that symbol on the entrance." Arden smiled thoughtfully as she spoke, and they sat together quietly in the dimly lit tavern comfortably in front of the fire.

Willow had a feeling though that the entire town would be gossiping about them within the hour, but she couldn't help but grin at the thought. Her and Sian were opposite in many ways, and had been fast friends when they first met at only seven years old. Sian had always had a muscular form, slender and tall, and aside from their eye color they generally had similar features. However, the energy that Sian exuded was very stoic and straight edged, a firm and sturdy presence that everyone could lean their trust on. Willow was certainly more whimsical in manner and appearance, compared to the dark leather and heavy boots and trinkets that adorned Sian from head to toe. She supposed her and Arden matched in that way, he was always wearing simple clothes and a natural look. *He'd thrive in the woods,* she thought with a sad smile as she looked at him across the table. He smiled back at her with what she swore was the same expression across his face, a sad smile on his lips mirroring her own.

They talked for a while, Willow mostly listening to what Arden explained about his home. He pointed out people in the tavern discreetly and told her what they did for a living, what they were like, and how they usually came to his mother for help regarding things around town that needed both fixing, or regulating. Her heart felt warm knowing how loved Arden and his family were, and knew it was well deserved. Even though she hardly knew them and they had only just met, she knew they were all unbelievably kind and intelligent people. They were deserving of every happiness, and that thought hurt her heart painfully as she knew Arden would find someone as kind as himself soon enough and the small world she found herself in would all too quickly disappear.

"What are you thinking about?" Arden murmured, having moved their chairs closer together to hear each other better in the lively bar. Willow sighed, not sure how to answer. She had never been anything but honest - well, about everything *but* the Binding Prayer, but that was only an omission as opposed to an outright lie. She still felt guilty, though, before she glanced up at him.

"I don't know, actually, I'm feeling rather...sad but I'm not sure why," she offered in a small voice.

"Oh, you must be very homesick," his voice was gentle and kind, and her heart squeezed painfully in her chest again, the sensation ever familiar now. She laughed before looking down at her hands that played with a utensil that had been left on the table to use, fiddling it around and admiring the unique design on it.

"I've left home before but I do suppose it's been a long time since the last time," she said.

"When was the last time you left home?" He asked, curiosity in his voice.

"Hmm," she thought for a moment before realizing something quite sad about herself, "I don't think I've left home aside from a day trip to the trading post occasionally." She paused to count in her head to make sure she wasn't wrong, "it must have been at least four years since I traveled anywhere longer than a few hours, but I genuinely can't even remember." She frowned, sighing heavily, only to see Arden staring at her with the most solemn expression she had ever seen, even more sad than Teg's face when he had given her the dagger.

"I should've brought you here a long time ago," he told her, his hand sliding forward across the table towards hers.

Abruptly, Sian placed a large tray of food in front of them both and chattered excitedly before pulling a seat over and joining them. Willow watched Arden's hand reach out to squeeze her own before handing her a heavily loaded plate of food. Willow saw Sian smiling pointedly at her, sharp teeth glinting against the fire behind them, and Willow smiled back while narrowing her eyes. She knew what Sian was saying with just an expression, just as Sian knew she was telling them to mind their business. Sian laughed before diving into the food just as Arden began to eat, too.

They ate quietly, but Willow knew it was because they were all hungry and nothing more. She had never had such a quiet and peaceful meal surrounded by so many people in her life, and before long their plates were empty.

"What are y'all up to today?" Sian asked them, curious.

"Arden brought me here today to share my herbal remedies," Willow smiled, trying to not sound arrogant or overly excited about being able to share it all here with people who actually needed it. Sian stared at her and made a face, interjecting quite loudly.

"Willow, you're professionally trained by several apothecaries, not only through a generational lineage of your family but also by *mine*. You have *been* over qualified to be an herbalist, at this point you are nothing short of an actual physician, if not moreso," Sian boomed but they placed a hand over Will's gently. "Start taking pride in your gift, give credit where it is due and for the *love of Ivokorresh* swing your dick around, would you?" Willow saw Arden blinking at Sian in surprise before he turned to her with a look of pride. She couldn't help but blush and look away from their intense gazes, unable to deny their kindness - *though Sian's was quite an aggressive form of love,* she giggled to herself.

"I can't help that I'm *modest,* Sian," Willow pretended to fluff her hair dramatically. Sian just laughed and rolled their eyes, before standing up and gathering everything back onto the tray.

"Go and get back to work, then, Twig, because we needed you here like a year ago," they lifted the tray with all the empty plates and utensils, "it took you long enough," they laughed before leaning down and kissing Willow's cheek, and all but stomped to the back room with the tray in tow. Arden smiled at Willow before standing and offering his arm to her, and they walked back to the market as fast as their full bellies could take them.

~ Eleven ~

A NIGHT AWAY

Arden was stunned at the way their lunch had gone, he had not expected Willow to know anyone from town let alone two of the most cryptic and bewildering members of society that seemed to have *always* been here. He couldn't remember a time where he hadn't seen either Teg or Sian at some point during a busy day, they were staples to the community. He couldn't wrap his head around the fact that they also have lives outside of the Port's walls, let alone that they were all *friends*. He truly had so many questions, though he wasn't surprised to learn that they'd known each other as children. They had an easy connection that everyone in the tavern could see as Sian and Will greeted one another, and Arden knew Will had plenty of stories about their upbringing if Sian's way with words was anything to go by. He couldn't wait to hear about them, if he was being honest.

They walked back to the market leisurely, taking their time, and he couldn't help but feel warm and happy as their arms were linked together, noise and life surrounding them. When they finally made it back to the stall, people had begun to gather around the old doctor, excitedly buzzing around. They were all looking at all of the potions on the shelves and the table, whispering to each other as they looked at the different labels. He could tell that Willow also noticed them, and started to pick up her pace before diving straight into the mass of people. Arden stood there, not quite sure what to do when he saw Willow wave him over.

"Arden, you can help me if you'd like," she told him over the sudden roar of the crowd.

"Tell me what you need," he said easily.

"If you can organize the people into lines based on their needs, that would be *amazing*," she said earnestly. Arden already knew he would do anything she asked him to, and immediately jumped into action. He used every ounce of his Commander's voice as he urged and guided everyone into lines based on needs - illness, discomfort, injury, and another line for miscellaneous options. He blushed a few times during those instances, as many of the items in question were for feminine needs, but he put on a brave face and channeled the ease in which Willow had explained everything to Juna and himself this morning.

He noticed then that the sun had dipped a little lower in the sky, not quite evening but mid afternoon, and he thought about the amount of time they would need to walk back to her cottage. He supposed he could take her on the horse again, and run back home before the sun went down, but he knew there wouldn't be enough time for a round trip. The horse would easily signal to the beast in the woods that they were nearby, and he couldn't take that risk. He would have to spend the night with her again, after taking her home, and he didn't find that he was upset by that idea in the least. He was excited about it, truly, but also felt guilty for wanting to spend more time with her.

He felt it wasn't kind of him to drag her along and tell her of the expectations he was under, and forcing her to listen to his woes on marriage. He would need to get serious about finding one, as he was nearing his thirtieth year, but only felt dejected at the idea of a permanent attachment to someone he didn't love. He supposed he would have to tell her soon of his plans, but didn't want to think about it beyond it being a general plan. For now, it would have to suffice, as he led people to Willow and Fasomalo, his mother's older cousin, and they continued to give items to anyone who needed it.

"How much will this cost us, I have four boys and two girls so we need quite a lot," a woman said as she spoke to Willow, clearly anxious. Arden waited to see what Willow said, curious as to how the woman would respond.

"Oh no, ma'am, this is a gift. I won't accept anything other than the health of your family as payment," she smiled kindly. The woman blinked at her in surprise before frowning in confusion.

"You can't be serious," she cried out, before saying again, "how much is everything altogether? I need a *lot* of everything as my children almost constantly have an illness!" Willow reached out to the frantic mother, who's baby was in a papoose on her back, and took her hand.

"I will give you enough of everything you need at *no* cost to you. The only thing I want is for you and your family to be safe and healthy," she smiled gently, before tugging the woman and pulling her behind the table. He watched as Willow used an empty bag to hold multiples of everything she had made, and offered the woman the full and heavy to bursting bag. The woman stared at it, still in disbelief, and Willow continued to hold it out to her. She waited, and waited, before finally the woman, with trembling hands, took the bag from Will.

"I don't know what to say," the woman's voice was watery with unshed tears.

"You don't have to say anything at all, just keep your family safe and healthy for me, okay?" She said softly, still standing close to the woman.

"I will," she said before tears started trailing down her cheeks. Her shoulders shook with the pressure of trying to keep the emotions detained. Suddenly, the woman reached out and pulled Will into a tight hug, the bag of medicine clinking against her back. Willow only laughed and squeezed her back, not in the least phased by her emotional outburst. The baby smiled at Will as she was pressed against the young mother, making Will smile back. "You don't understand how much this means to me, my babies were *so sick* I thought - I thought -" she sobbed, unable to say what she was feeling over the deep cries. Arden's heart ached at the sound and imagined his mother weeping in this way over her children, too.

"Nothing is as scary as the thought of losing your baby, I couldn't imagine how hard that must've been for you and your family. But they are safe now, and I have so many recipes to share with you that will help for a *long* time, so I hope that helps you feel safer." Willow said, words so wise and kind that Arden was certain he would weep, too, if he didn't start moving around again. He found he couldn't look away, though, and watched as Willow stepped back from the woman and held her hand and brought her to the furthest side of the kiosk, and rifled through the jars until she pulled out a large one filled with tiny cubes.

"These are an immune system boost, have you and your family take one or two a day - I typically prefer one in the morning and one at night but you don't have to take it more than once a day if you like," she put it in the bag before continuing, "I will make more and come back with it so you won't have to worry. I've also shared these recipes with your apothecary, so they should be readily available quite soon. Enjoy your children, don't fret too much, and be safe," Willow said before hugging the woman again and waved to the giggling baby.

"Thank you," the woman's voice was so full of gratitude Arden felt his own eyes well up. He took that as his cue to make his way back to the line, and began directing more and more people to Will and Fasomalo until the crowd died down and empty cartons filled the cart and table. They filled the cart back up and covered it with the table cloth they'd used. Fasomalo and a few other men began to pull the cart back to the apothecary for safekeeping, with the promise to study the rest of the recipes. When they finally walked off with the supplies safely tucked into the cart, Arden turned to Willow to let her know he could take her home now.

"Are you ready, Will?" He asked her with his hand out.

The wind suddenly picked up then, and both Arden and Willow looked out over the harbor as heavy, billowing clouds rolled across the horizon. Willow gasped and stepped forward before the trees rolled against the wind, surely offering a warning to Willow as her head tilted to listen.

"Oh, no," she murmured before turning around and tried to scan the sky towards the direction her home would be. She whispered to herself but Arden didn't hear what she said as the trees rumbled again, even the smallest trees that grew on the corners of the streets, and the trees around the wall. It was a foreboding tremble, and Arden knew if the trees were saying anything at all, it would be to tell them they would be silly to try and get through the woods under clouds as big as those.

Thunder rumbled low in the distance, the wind picking up as a flash of lightning lit up the sky. Willow turned to him, eyes wide, hands wringing in front of her chest.

"Arden, if I run, I can -" she started to say but was cut off by the start of heavy drops of rain landing on her nose. She sputtered in surprise, looking up at the sky as it opened up on them entirely.

"You won't be able to get home in this, even if you run," Arden said loudly, but not unkindly, over the sound of the raindrops on the stone. The wind howled around them, sweeping the rain right into their faces and drenching them through their clothes. Willow's hair started to fall out of her braid as flower petals fell to the ground around her. Arden tried to ignore the way his belly flipped at the sight of her standing there, dripping wet, staring into the clouds. She looked back at him sadly, and he noticed her lower lip trembling as she continued to turn around and watch the sky. In an increasingly frantic motion, Willow started pacing back and forth before running toward the path that led to the outer gates of the Port. Arden was surprised for a moment, but easily caught up to her as he noticed his mother and Juna running from the direction of the boutique.

Arden caught Willow's hand as she ran, and gently tugged her until she faced him. Her face was dripping with rain drops, and her eyes were full of tears. He ran a hand over her cheek, wondering which droplets were from her eyes and which were from the sky.

"Arden I have to go home, I can't be away from my tree this long," she heaved, out of breath, trying to hold back a sob though Arden could still hear it.

"Honey, no one is going to be able to travel through the forest like this," he said gently, close enough for her to hear without having to yell. "First thing in the morning we can go home but right *now* there is no way for us to do that safely," he continued.

"You don't understand, Arden, I haven't been away in years, I *need* to go back *now!*" Her lip trembled and she tugged on him, trying to pull her hand out of his. He tightened his grip on her when Juna and Alvenia finally caught up to them, both placing a hand on Willow's shoulder. She flinched for a second before she turned around to see them, lip still quivering as the rain continued to soak her through.

"It's okay, Willow, we have a warm bed for you and we'll make sure you have supper," said Juna, squeezing her shoulder.

"Come on, love, before the rain gives you a chill," Alvenia added, squeezing her other shoulder. Willow straightened and looked up at Arden before putting her face in her hands, a sob leaving her as her shoulders shook. Instinctively, Arden pulled her to his chest and rubbed a hand across her back, and his mother and sister leaned against her gently, hands rubbing against her arms.

After a few moments, Willow lifted her head and shook herself and blinked. She wiped her face before sputtering as rain went up her nose. She finally laughed and turned around shyly, glancing at the women in front of her. Wordlessly, they reached their hands out, offering their kindness to her in the purest, most innocent form, like children in the school yard. Arden watched as the three women in his life walked home in the rain, holding hands, as he followed behind. He could feel his cheeks start to hurt from the smile he wore, but he couldn't wipe it from his face even if he wanted to.

Suddenly, though, it caught up to him. He thought back to how upset Willow was at not being able to go home because of the storm, and immediately the smile dropped from his face. The idea that she didn't want to be here *that* badly upset him, and also reminded him that she was only here because Arden had requested her help in the first place. It was his fault that she cried, as he should have taken her home as soon as the stall was set up instead of playing merchant with her, and handing out medicine. The apothecary could have easily done that tomorrow, and now, because of his selfishness, Willow was trapped in this human town. He felt a pit of despair in his belly at the thought of hurting Will, even by accident, so he promised himself he would apologize to her properly.

They made it to Fairwood Manor, not far off from the center of the market. They ushered Willow inside the warm home as they shivered from the rain. On the port, the winds from the ocean were chillier with a storm, but the housekeeper had the fire roaring in the main living room so no one would be cold. Arden watched as Juna tugged on Will's hand and led her upstairs. Will flashed a look to Arden, afraid, and he knew she was unsure of what to say or do. He followed them up the stairs, Alvenia already running into her own room that was in the far back of the home on the ground level.

"Brother, I am going to show Will around and find her some clothes after a bath," Juna called over her shoulder with a giggle. Willow smiled finally, and nodded to Arden, wordlessly telling him with her expression that it would be okay, and they turned down the hall. Arden walked to his own room, through the doors that led to the attached bathroom so he could immediately take a bath of his own. Though they hadn't been in the rain very long, he was soaked down to his bones. He stripped, and stepped into the tub that was filling slowly with hot water, and sank down as low as he could. He was glad they had finally gotten a larger bath for this bathroom, as he could not fit in the old one after he had his last growth spurt as a child. The tub was old now, of course, as it had been a long while since they had gotten it, but it was still perfect.

Arden almost dozed off after cleaning himself up, and barely managed to put his house clothes on before there was a raucous knock at his door, with giggling beyond it. He rolled his eyes comically to himself before opening the door.

"Can I help you?" He asked, biting his cheek to keep from laughing.

"Look at Willow's hair!" Juna said, jumping and clapping.

"Look at my hair, Arden!" Willow laughed before twirling around to see Will's intricately braided hair. Each strand looked meticulously combed and tied, the flowers flawless and white on the crown of her head, though a few had started to line the lower parts of her hair, and filled the braid in a delicate way.

"You look lovely," Arden told her honestly. Juna pretended to gag at his words, but laughed and pushed him away from the door, ducking into his room and flopping onto his bed. Willow started to belly laugh when Juna had pretended to be sick, and followed after her onto the bed.

"Thank you," she said softly, cheeks dimpling. "Oh, and Juna showed me to the guest room that I'll be using, and also gave me this gown to wear to bed. *And* she gave me a robe!" Her voice grew in excitement as she ran her hand over the dark yellow dress and matching robe happily, and looked to Arden with a soft gaze.

"I'm letting her keep them because it suits her better than it suits me, I'm not sure why I ever even bought it," Juna laughed. " I suppose life works mysteriously that way, it must have always been for you," she nudged Will's shoulder. The girls laughed and Arden felt his heart twinge at the sight. "Oh, Arden, she's going to stay in the room that's on the other side of your bathroom. The maid told us she was getting it ready, the other guest room is being redecorated." She made a sneaky face at Arden and winked at him, and he almost choked on air at her insinuation. Willow must have known Juna did something silly, and started laughing quietly. A knock sounded at the door then, and they all turned to see the housekeeper standing there.

"Dinner will be ready soon, Madam is taking her dinner in her bedroom tonight as she is tired from the rain. Would you like to eat here or in the dining room?" She asked.

"We'll follow you to the dining room, I couldn't trust those two with food in here," Arden said airily as he stuck up his nose teasingly. Juna threw a pillow at him before running after the snickering housekeeper, who was long used to their shenanigans. Felisia was a kind woman, and had always been a part of their lives. She was pivotal to their household just as much as Alvenia was, and they had all expressed this to her whenever they could.

The Fairwood family believed in respecting everyone's profession, especially when their livelihood benefited the ones they worked for, too. It was one of the things everyone in town admired Alvenia for as she set the standard of the ones born into a higher income bracket, and encouraged fair wages and treatment to *every* employee. He was proud of his family for being as kind as they were, and Arden hoped that Willow could see them at their best before going back home, though he was sure one night would most likely not give her a chance to see anything of merit. Still, though, he knew his mother and sister had played a large part in bringing Will here without her exploding with emotion, so that had to count for something.

The trio made their way to the dining room as Arden thought about everything, when they were greeted with a large bowl of soup at each seat. Willow gasped at how big the bowl was, and the large soup spoon to go with it. He watched her excitedly sit down across from Juna, as he sat at the head of the table. She placed her hands on her lap and looked to Arden and waited to see what he would do. A maid brought out another bowl full of fresh sliced bread, and a butter dish. They all thanked her simultaneously, and Arden told her they could get home before the storm could get any worse. He knew they only lived in the lot next to them, their property a part of Fairwood Manor, and it wouldn't be long enough for them to become drenched from the rain. Best to leave now, before the wind picked up any more than this. Not for the first time, he was grateful his forefathers thought to build their home this way.

Long ago the family had been given the option to start the Fairwoods on farm land in order to build a large Manor as the name of their home suggested. But the founding Fairwood of Stóngrast said no, we will live with our families and share our lives and experiences, and be humble and gentle hearted to all. Arden admired that, and was proud of his ancestors for preferring a more humble lifestyle than some of the nobles further inland. As he started to eat his dinner, a thick bisque that he loved ever since he was a child, Juna interrupted the sounds of spoons on bowls as they followed his lead and began to eat.

"Mother was talking to our cousin in the market today while you both were having lunch," she started before dipping her bread into the bisque.

"What were they saying?" He asked between bites.

"Cousin Fasomalo was telling Mother that she must have prayed *really* hard to be sent such a gift from the heavens," she used her bread slice to punctuate her sentence, "he had been telling her the inevitable fate of our home had no one brought a miracle soon."

They both looked to Willow as she put a spoon into her mouth, and she looked at them sheepishly before placing the spoon back into the bowl.

"What else did they talk about?" Arden asked while still looking at Will before holding a bread slice toward her. She smiled, taking it, before biting into the bread shyly and digging back into the bowl.

"They had been talking about the epidemic in the area brought on by the lack of medications, and the loss of the professionals who were dedicated to learning and relearning the apothecary trade." Arden was struck by how similar Juna was to their mother, and listened with rapt attention that her storytelling voice commanded. "He had apparently begged her to help him, since she has an almost unnatural ability to manifest solutions to any problem no matter how big or small. He had asked her to figure out a way to save the town from tragedy." Juna took another bite before continuing, "he swears Mother has a gift of manifestation, but she only shushed him - though I do think she does have an unnatural ability to get things done her way," Juna laughed. "But anyway, Mother said she had never been one to care for the herbalist career, and had reminded him she had not been good at it when they were kids. She said she felt awful for that, and that she had assumed this was a punishment for not trying harder to keep everyone safe - she should've listened to our Auntie when they were young so that she could help Fasomalo personally. That's why she told us the other day, in tears, that she wasn't sure what we would be able to do to fix this problem."

"I hadn't realized she was that upset about everything," Arden murmured sadly.

"She must have been worried for a long time before bringing it to you," Willow commented, a frown on her lips. Juna nodded, chewing bread thoughtfully.

"She told me when we were walking to the boutique that she *had* been worried for months about this but had been trying to find a solution without worrying us needlessly. But I think by telling us about it, she *had* found the solution we needed all along." Juna smiled at Willow, who smiled back.

They ate the rest of their meal quietly, while Arden thought about how their lives had all inevitably been twined together from the moment Arden had run into the forest, all those months ago. *Well, it had been nearly a year at this point,* Arden told himself as he reflected on just how long ago he had found himself on his knees in front of the beautiful and mysterious woman in the woods. He'd met her during the early summer, only a few more months until one entire year passed them by - he was baffled that time moved so fast and yet so slow at the same time. It had truly been a miracle to find Willow, indeed, and he couldn't imagine his life without her in it now. His heart hurt at the thought, as he accidentally thought about the inevitable fact that they would both be bound to another person for life, no matter where their lives led them in the not so distant future. He shook his head to clear the thoughts of even the mere idea that Willow would marry another man. He refused to acknowledge it. He also refused to even wonder about *why* he felt that way.

When their bowls were empty, Juna offered to take the dishes to the kitchen for them. Arden was grateful as he was ready for bed, and couldn't handle the thoughts rolling through his head, he hoped he would be able to fall asleep quickly after such a long day.

"Will you lead me to my room?" Willow asked as they stood from the table and made their way to the stairs at the front of the house.

"Of course," Arden smiled and he guided her to the room Juna had told them the maid had prepared for them. "Good night, Willow," he said softly. Willow turned around with a hand on the door and looked up at him, blinking slowly. They were close enough that Arden could count the freckles over her cheeks and the bridge of her nose. Her moss green eyes blinked at him innocently, before she tilted her head with a small smile.

"Good night, Arden," she whispered before she swept into the room and closed the door behind her.

Arden walked into his bedroom and sighed after closing the door behind him, and went to the bathroom before climbing into his bed. He tugged his shirt off and threw it on the floor, and stared at the ceiling in the dark for a few minutes thinking over the day. He should have apologized to Willow for having been the reason she was trapped here. He knew he couldn't have known that it would storm and keep them from Tonsilta, but he felt guilty all the same. He also felt bad that he *liked* having her here, liked watching her interact with the important people in his life. He heard the thunder rumble then, louder than before and a flash of lightning crossed across his windows. The storm was in full swing, it would seem, and he hoped that the sound of rain put him to sleep quickly.

As he laid there, he thought he heard someone in the bathroom and realized he hadn't closed the door to give Willow privacy, and sat up to close it for her. She closed the door from the inside before he could move any further, so he laid back down and rolled to his side. He laid there with his eyes closed before hearing the door jiggle again, quietly squeaking as it opened. He blinked his eyes open and turned to see Willow standing there in her nightgown, hand on the door frame.

"Arden?" Willow whispered into the dark room. Arden wordlessly pulled the blanket down for her, and she immediately tiptoed into the bed with a giggle. "Thank you," she told him earnestly, "I have never slept anywhere other than my home and I was scared in that big room," she continued with some hesitation in her voice.

"I'm so sorry you were stuck here, I should've taken you home earlier," he scooted closer to her, sliding his hand across the bed to reach her.

"Oh no, I had a lot of fun today, I'm sorry I cried at first, though," he could hear her smile in the dark, and she scooted closer to him and grabbed his outstretched hand in her own.

"I felt awful, like I'd let you down," he told her honestly. Her fingers grazed his cheeks, softly stroking.

"I know, and I'm sorry I upset you, for a moment I was..." she trailed off for a second before continuing, "I was overwhelmed with the fear of being anywhere but my small little house. I really *never* leave so - it was a scary feeling that swallowed me up for a minute."

"I'm glad you came," he said as he wrapped his other hand around the one she rested on his cheek. "But you have a lot of questions to answer, Miss Willow," he said teasingly.

"I knew this was coming," she laughed, "go ahead and ask me," she scooted closer before tucking both of her hands under her cheek.

"Well first of all, how do you know Teg?" he asked as he mirrored her position.

"The Tegs have known my family forever, I think they were a trade merchant between the fae and humans once upon a time, but they've been in my life since the very beginning," she told him.

"How big is the Teg family?" he asked, curious about her wording.

"I think it's just the two of them left," she said, "at least in the area." He supposed that was enough, and continued with his questions.

"How in the world do you know *Sian?* I know you went to school together, but there has to be more to it," he asked curiously.

"I've known Sian since we were around seven, when I joined their classes. We learned together for a few years before Sian mastered their craft, and then Sian continued on as my teacher for quite a bit longer, even though we're the same age," she explained.

"What did they teach you?" Arden wondered. "And is Sian actually as intimidating as they look? Because I've been scared to death of upsetting them accidentally, I avoid them a lot because of that," he said honestly. "Sian looks like they would easily be able to break me in half through spite alone," he shivered. Willow started giggling, unable to hold in her laughter.

"Honestly, Sian has told me the *exact* same thing about what they want people to think any time they walk into a room," she gasped through her laughter. Arden laughed with her for a moment before they quieted back down. "But to answer your question, Sian taught me a lot of different things. Sian's family has healers, and other magics. Since Sian's healing isn't as prominent as their destruction, they taught me how to *apply* the knowledge along with a lot more that would be confusing without a demonstration. And no, Sian is as soft hearted as they come. But you didn't hear that from me," Willow laughed. Arden smiled softly as he listened to Will, a warmth filling him as she told him about her life before he knew her.

"It's been nice having you here," Arden whispered.

"You have a lovely home, and your family is *so* kind," she told him.

"Yeah..." he trailed off, feeling guilty for being frustrated by them over the last few years. "Ever since - nevermind," he said hastily before rubbing his eyes.

"Ever since what?" Willow asked curiously. Arden sighed, and braced himself. He knew she would want to know and at this point, she was probably entitled to some of the details of his life that he had been keeping close to his chest.

"I haven't talked about it," he warned her, "I haven't even let myself think about it."

"*Please* tell me," she urged, getting even closer to him and putting her hands on his.

"Do you remember how you found me in the forest?" He asked her, knowing the answer already.

"Of course," she smiled, he could hear it in her voice.

"And you remember *why* I told you I was in the forest?" He continued.

"*Yes,*" Willow said emphatically.

"Well, there was a bit more to that than just the concept of marriage," his voice was so soft there was barely a sound.

"You have to tell me before I yell," she laughed, rattling his hands in her own.

"Well, it's not a very happy story," he pursed his lips.

"I wouldn't assume so, you were very upset that day. My heart broke for you," she murmured. Arden sighed and allowed himself to share his struggle with Willow, who undoubtedly would support his feelings as she had always done since the day they first met.

"I had been on patrol, right around the time people had started going missing. By then, we were finding them after they had already passed. It was gruesome, and we had to start assigning random soldiers to help clean up the scenes, and help bring the bodies back to their families." He paused to take a breath but Willow only stroked his hands until he continued.

"One day, we found another body. I hadn't been on patrol, but it was my rotation for cleaning up the scene, so me and the rest of the small crew prepared for what we knew would be there to greet us. But when we got there, soldiers were weeping." He sniffed, fighting against the emotions the memories brought back with them.

"It was Bartrum, the butcher, a man I -" his voice caught, and he paused to give himself a moment to recover. He took a deep breath and tried again. "Bartrum was closer to me than my own father, he had taught me everything I know about being a good, honest man." Willow slid across the bed and tucked herself under his chin and stroked his back, wordlessly supporting him.

"His children had been sick, and his grandchildren caught the illness too, and so he had to go into the woods early that morning to stock the shop. He had gone alone, not unusual for him, he had done it so often before. He had passed the job to his eldest son who was a better shot than him, and they had worked together for years that way seamlessly." He felt Willow move with his breathing and was surprised at himself for being able to even voice these words out loud at all.

"His son had told his dad the night before how scared he was that his children had such a high fever. I was friends with Devon as a child, he's the same age as me but married young and now has three children. They *all* had a fever that night and he and his wife were terrified. Bartrum had told him to rest when he could, and he'd handle the hunt this week, and that was the last time anyone had seen him." Arden whispered, eyes welling up with tears.

"I had to clean him up, and bring him home, and tell his family what happened to him. Naturally, they blamed me as the commanding officer for not having more patrols to keep us safe. And I agreed with them," a heavy sadness filled his words.

"After a few days, the town had seemingly gone on as if nothing happened. Devon took over the Cahlin family's butcher shop, begrudgingly as it wasn't what he wanted to do as a career. But everyone lived life the same as we have always done," he finished finally.

"I'm so sorry, Arden," Willow murmured into his chest.

"It's really not the worst part for me, either," he said, frustration lacing his voice. "What was worse, was that everyone told me to basically get over it and move on, he wasn't family, and I needed to start my own life myself."

"How can anyone just 'move on' after such an experience?" She said angrily.

"I was told to get married and forget about it," he sniffed, the unshed tears giving him a runny nose. "Well, it seemed that way at least."

"What do you mean?" Willow asked curiously.

"Do you ever unintentionally take someone's words and hear them incorrectly?"

"Oh, yes, I do that, too, and worry my perceptions are wrong," Will agreed as she laid with him, still nestled against him. He felt relieved that she understood what he was trying to say, that she knew the feeling of being told one thing, and hearing another.

"Thinking about it now, it seems as if they were encouraging me to move forward instead of holding on to a ghost. At the time, it was devastating to hear. I felt as though the man who taught me how to run a butcher shop, how to prepare different animals for harvest and use every part of them without being wasteful, the man that taught me how to be a lead, how to be kind, and he..." he trailed off, "he taught me how a father is supposed to be," he whispered as the tears finally fell from his eyes, "I felt as though a man I admired wasn't as important to everyone else if they wanted me to merrily skip past his death and into a stranger's arms." Willow pulled him tighter to her, and his arms wrapped around her small frame easily. She gently stroked his back, offering what little comfort she could give. As the tears began to fall freely, Arden could only feel grateful for her presence. He hadn't dealt with the complex emotions of his grief, a raw and aching wound that refused to heal, even with time. It only would get easier to ignore, if his experiences were anything to go by.

"I'm glad you can see now that they only wanted to offer their support, but I understand how upsetting it must have been at the time. I'm proud of you for moving on in your own terms," Will kissed his cheek, soft and sweet, and rubbed her hand on his back in a comforting way.

Arden dozed with Willow tucked under his chin as she continued to run her hand along him, a soothing gesture that made him feel like a small child again. His release of those pent up emotions had exhausted him entirely, and he felt himself falling into a deep sleep slowly. Her body curled up sweetly against his own. Warm, safe, and peaceful. He tried to remember the last time sleep found him so easily, but the thought eluded him. He was nearly dreaming by the time he remembered; the last time he slept so easily, he was with Willow then too. Sleep finally found him with a small smile on his face.

~ Twelve ~

COMING HOME

Willow woke to sunshine warming her face as the birds chirped next to the window. She was warm, snuggled up on her side as a weight behind her wrapped around her body, a hand on her tummy. She remembered then where she was and smiled, placing her hand over Arden's as it curled over her soft skin. She opened her eyes, blinking as she registered Arden's hand under her nightgown, it having bunched under her waist in the night leaving her skin out in the open. She tried not to giggle and wake him up in this position, and took a deep breath to calm herself. Arden stirred behind her and unconsciously pulled her closer. She felt something pressing into her back and almost gasped, realizing what exactly it was. *We meet again,* she thought hysterically, a hand over her mouth to keep the laughter in. If she woke him by laughing, she feared he'd think the worst. That she was making fun of him, and not enjoying this pleasant surprise after a good night's sleep.

She rested there for a while, dozing with Arden's nose pressed into her neck. He breathed a little deeper and she couldn't help but flinch at the ticklish sensation it caused, and giggled before nudging his cheek with her fingers. He grumbled and ducked his face further into her neck, nuzzling into her hair, and she laughed louder.

"Arden, you're tickling me," she whispered.

"Hmm," he grumbled again before rolling onto his back and yawning. Willow stretched, arching her back and relieving the muscles that were tired from having been stuck in that position for too long. She laid there, stretched out for a minute as Arden rubbed his face and kept grumbling. She turned to look at him and smiled, his shoulder length hair sticking up from where he had been laying on it, and she couldn't help but pat the hair back down. He turned to look at her then, finally awake, and smiled back at her.

"Breakfast and then back home?" His voice was gruff with sleep. She nodded in assent and stretched again, a loud yawn escaping. Arden stood up and walked to the bathroom, pants hanging low on his waist. His skin was fair and smooth, his broad shoulders on display as he had taken his shirt off the night before. She shivered at the memory of his strong arms holding her tight, and shook her head to clear it away. She stood regretfully, the warmth of the bed enticing but she knew it was past time to go home.

Arden spent a few minutes in the bathroom before coming back out, hair neat and tidy before he gestured to Willow that she could use it next. She went quickly, and stepped back into the room she was supposed to have slept in and looked for her clothes. She noticed an outfit had been placed in the room with a note on top that the outfit was a gift to her. She smiled before changing back into the delicates that had been dried out from the rain and changed into her new dress. She quickly pulled her shoes on and turned around to go to the bathroom and check herself in the mirror. The doors to the bathroom were both still open, and Arden had a blush on his cheeks and she knew he must have gotten an eyeful of her changing. For a moment, his eyes shifted away from her as she pulled her hair back into a bun, but he eventually shrugged and stood in the doorway and watched her do her hair.

She wanted to feel embarrassed for having forgotten to close the door behind her, but she found herself not actually caring in the slightest. She wondered at what that meant, knowing she definitely knew the answer but refused to let herself reflect on it. She smiled at Arden's reflection and he smiled back sweetly. Finally, her hair was done and they left the rooms through Arden's doorway, only to be met by Juna in the hallway. Her eyes flicked back and forth between them and the door, and suddenly a cheeky smile lit up her face. She giggled and raised her eyebrows at them pointedly.

"Did you *sleep* well, then?" She grinned. Arden looked gobsmacked and the girls both started laughing, unable to hold it in as he sputtered at Juna's insinuation.

"Juna, go away, would you," he grumbled as his cheeks turned red. Willow smiled and took his elbow and the three walked downstairs in search of breakfast. Willow found she really liked Juna, she was very silly and easy to talk to. She would miss her when she went home. She would miss a lot about this place. It had been so long since she last felt so at peace, so long since she had been around people in a familial sense like this. Market and trade interactions weren't quite as gratifying as being around people, physically close to them, engaging on a deeper level. She knew the loneliness would creep in soon if she let it and tried to enjoy her last few minutes in Arden's home to the fullest she could.

They ate pastries quietly, though there were still interspersed giggles throughout the meal. The sibling bickering made Willow

miss her family, though she really hadn't had much of a connection to them as she had been left to fend for herself from
a very young age. Missing them was laced with bitterness, and
she hated the feeling and discreetly tried to shake it off. It felt
strange to her, to long for siblings she'd never met. But it was an
ache she couldn't explain, a hollow feeling in her chest. Finally
though, Arden and Willow made their way to the door and said
their goodbyes. Alvenia embraced Willow in a deep hug, having
been sitting in the family room when they had passed her by.

"I can't thank you enough," she murmured into Will's ear,
and kissed her cheek.

"There's no need to thank me, Madam, it's been a pleasure to
help," Willow smiled. Juna dove in for a hug after Alvenia let her
go, and also kissed her cheek with a little more force.

"I know we'll be great friends, Willow, and I can't wait to see
you again soon," she still had the mischievous glint in her eyes,
and Willow's heart throbbed at the thought of Juna's words
turning out to not be true. She just smiled and nodded, and
didn't mention the unlikelihood of that happening.

"It's been lovely spending time with you," Willow said honestly. And with that, they walked outside and started toward
Willow's home arm in arm, much in the same way they had
entered the town just yesterday morning.

They walked quietly, Willow lost in thought. She wondered
what Arden was thinking about as they continued on through
the paths just beyond the outer walls of Stongrast, and in no
time at all they were deep into the woods. The shift happened so
quickly they both seemed surprised, the trees gently whispering to her in greeting. They asked her if she was okay, and she
whispered back to them about the time she spent with Arden.
They were always curious, but she had known them all for so
long that she treated them like friends and easily shared with

them everything she experienced. In turn, they offered their insights and company, and she knew without them, she'd have easily gone mad in solitude long ago.

She glanced at Arden as they neared her home, she could smell the creek and the wisteria from here. She noticed his brows were furrowed in thought and his steps looked heavy, though she supposed he was still exhausted from traveling back and forth so many times in the last few days. They trudged along, her own feet suddenly feeling heavy, too, until the cottage finally came into view. She had almost been afraid that it would be gone with the storm, though she knew the thought was irrational, and almost skipped to the door at full speed.

As she turned the key, she realized that she had forgotten her recipe book at Arden's house. She would need to have him bring it back to her eventually, though she knew she had two more still in the basement safe and sound, waiting to be used with perfectly scripted letters and sketches. She pushed through the door and breathed deep, smelling her home and feeling relieved to be back even though she had enjoyed her time with Arden in his own home, too. She tucked the key back into its nook and turned around, pulling the door shut. She grinned at Arden as he had caught up to her, and he smiled back.

His smile was laced with a little sadness, and she really wanted to ask about it but also wanted to open the shutters for a moment today, even just for a little while. She pulled them open, and then remembered the mess in her room, and ran to the other side of the house to open that shutter, too. She needed the light to clean up the disaster she had left behind. Finally, she walked back around and noticed Arden inspecting the shutter, running his hand along it and checking his hand for paint.

"What are you doing?" She laughed.

"Oh I was checking their stability, I think there may be a better option for you to try," he said sheepishly.

"Thank you, I'd love to hear about that. I've been wanting to change them but...you know how things have been going," she said.

"Yeah..." Arden murmured, looking at his feet. Willow pulled his hand and led him inside, before leading him to the kitchen for a drink of water after their long walk.

"What's the matter?" She asked him after filling the cups and handing him one. He drank his quickly, but she sipped on her own waiting for him to talk. He sighed heavily, before pacing and standing by the window for a moment.

"I'm going to tell my mother that I'm ready to get married," he said quietly. Willow's stomach dropped, even though she knew it had been coming.

"Oh, you're ready now?" She asked, trying not to let her voice waver as loneliness crept in.

"No, not even a little bit," he laughed humorlessly. She made a face in question at that.

"Well, then *why* are you going to do that?" She was confused.

"I just have to, it's what you do," he shrugged, still gazing out the window.

"Arden, that's the silliest thing I've ever heard," she scoffed, not liking his tone. He sounded so forlorn and broken, and she didn't like it.

"I don't know what to tell you, Will, I just have to do this and get it over with." He started pacing again, frustration emanating from his tall frame. Willow didn't know what to say, not even the slightest. All she could think of was to argue about his logic, but he continued talking as he took steps around every square inch of her living room, "I just wish I'd meet someone, and have an instant connection with them like *we* did," he snapped then. Willow frowned at that, wondering what he could mean.

"I still don't get it, Arden," she said quietly as she walked up to him, "if you hate the idea of marriage you shouldn't get married at all. It's not fair to you or your wife," she told him.

"It's just that I don't want to marry someone I don't know well," he tried to explain.

"Well, Arden, *everyone* is a stranger at first, like we were when we first met in the forest forever ago," she laughed, trying to understand just *why* he wanted to get married at all.

"That's not the same," he sighed.

"How is it not the same? I can't see the point of marrying at all if you hate the idea of marriage this much, what good would it do if you hate it?" Willow walked back to the kitchen and sipped on some more water, shaking her head to herself thinking about how asinine this conversation was.

"I don't hate the idea of marriage, I hate the idea of marrying a stranger that I don't even know and not getting a choice on it at all!" Arden raised his voice, shouting in anger, finally explaining why he acted the way he did over the last year whenever marriage was brought up, and the expectations he was under, albeit of his own making. Her heart dropped, and knew in that moment, she had only *one* choice. And that was to finally tell him the truth. She took another sip of water nervously and started wringing her hands before pacing like Arden had.

"Oh - Arden I should tell you..." She trailed off, trying to find the right words, "No, Arden I *have* to tell you..." She trailed off again.

"Will, *tell me,*" he said in exasperation.

"It's going to be a rather long story - erm, well, an explanation, really," she stalled. Arden sighed heavily again, and made his way to the couch and plopped onto it dramatically.

"We've got some time now, don't we?" He gestured with her hand to continue before he looked at her pointedly. She sighed too, and closed her eyes before nodding to herself and pacing again as she started to speak.

"Okay Arden, just don't interrupt me even though it'll be quite long winded," she warned, but he just waved her on. "Okay, so, there are different ways of joining oneself to another soul. Your culture calls them marriages and weddings, my culture calls them the binding or intertwining of the souls." She spoke in the way of the story tellers in her family and all throughout the fae forest, voice enchanting and commanding but gentle.

"Long ago there were methods of this that humankind considered....kidnapping, for lack of a better word. Unsuspecting human folk would wander into the forest and suddenly, their family would find them bound to a fae, and they would not return home. Unfortunately, it was misunderstood, and for good reason, as it is quite unorthodox to "marry" someone who was, in every way, a stranger." She glanced at Arden and he nodded, still listening.

"However, the Binding Prayer was quite more intricate than these "tricks" that humans swore we committed, and no matter how much my people tried to explain it - including the ones who were deemed kidnapped in the first place - the practice became a death sentence to many fae." Arden made a sound at that but she put her finger up and shushed him wordlessly.

"Would you not protect your child from that fate? Having been stolen away, as far as you knew, with no hope of coming home without feeling attached to a being they knew not?" She hedged and he frowned, and she nodded as if she knew what he was thinking - no, he'd protect his child from an unfair fate at all costs and they both knew it.

"And so the tradition died out slowly, over generations, as many humans shared untrue versions of these weddings and warped the fates of their loved ones until our marriages were taboo altogether. The Vesphnion Kagdah forest became the Fae Forest, Tonsilta the bridge between them, and no man had traveled within these woods for a good, long time." She looked out the window, the sun still high in the sky as she paused for a breath.

"But the thing with a Binding Prayer, is that it isn't a fae tricking another soul to be bound for eternity. It is *multiple* souls calling out to one another looking for and finding each other, and binding together on another, deeper, spiritual layer altogether. It's not one choice, it's many choices, from deep within, that brings them together. Both souls have to be calling out in order for the Binding to work, but that's only the first part," she continued.

"In order to be bound to another soul, one must offer life blood of your own onto the bark of a fae tree from your palms, while placing your forehead against the tree in between your outstretched hands. In this Position of Prayer, you bind yourself to the Fae. It cannot be undone, even if the Nymph does not complete the Prayer as their life blood is in the tree, the sap that runs through and over the bark, over the offering of blood, and claims it as soon as it's there. However, the ceremony is complete only when all partners have placed their palms and foreheads against the bark and sap. But of course, that specific aspect is not necessary to complete the ceremony, it would still be a marriage accepted in the Fae community. All Fae can sense another's marital status if they marry in this way. It is like a soul print, or a change in aura that they can sense on another level." Willow kept pacing until she reached the counter, still on the side of the living room that Arden was in. He stood up then, brows furrowed in question, and took a step toward her. She knew he would try to interrupt soon if she didn't hurry up, but her words were getting jumbled in her head as she felt overwhelmed and *scared* about how he'd react.

"So Arden, what I'm saying is that..." she said breathlessly, "we have been Prayer Bound since our very first meeting. In fact, it was you that initiated the Binding, your soul called out to mine and the woods led you to me. The trees around me that day were chittering and telling me you were coming, but they wouldn't elaborate. And then I heard you, felt you, holding me. But you were so sad - and now, I've lied to you all this time, afraid of what you might think or say or do when I told you. I knew eventually you would leave me behind one day to start a family of your own, and I kept waiting for the day, knowing an old fashioned promise meant nothing in your culture." Her throat felt tight but she continued anyway, "I didn't want to hold you back when you found a good wife to make you happy."

"I knew it was wrong to hide it from you this long, but knowing everything you've shared with me last night and meeting your family - I just couldn't hold it in any longer, and when you marry for love, I don't want you to regret being my friend for all this time. After I hid such a big secret from you, and hurt you by making you unintentionally marry a stranger - the thing you hated the most about marriage in the first place - Arden, I'm *so* sorry," Willow finished finally, tears filling her eyes as she tried to meet his own. She could barely hold his gaze from fear he'd yell at her, but stood there and waited for him to react after he processed what she was saying.

"Will," Arden started. She turned to him wordlessly as the tears finally spilled over her cheeks. Her lip trembled, waiting for his ire. He stepped closer to her and reached out a hand, but she ducked her chin in fear. Arden only stepped closer and put his hand on her cheek, his thumb stopping a tear in its track.

"Will, I thought you were going to tell me that *you* were the beast in the woods eating people all this time," he laughed quietly. She sniffed out a surprised laugh and finally met his gaze.

"No, that was definitely not the secret I've been keeping from you," she smiled watery.

"Willow, I can't tell you how I feel, I don't even know how to explain it," he whispered.

"I'm really sorry, I would've stopped you from touching the tree if I knew where you were," she said as more tears trailed down her face.

"I'm not sorry," he said earnestly, taking her face in both of his hands. She blinked at him in confusion before he grinned at her. *"We're married,"* he laughed, shaking his head, "Wilmayra I am *so* relieved that it's *you.*" She was stunned, not a word in her mind able to voice what she felt, but she didn't have to. Arden stepped closer to her and trailed one of his hands down her neck until it cradled the back of her head, and slid the other one down to her waist. He pulled her tight against him and pressed his lips to hers.

Willow gasped and wrapped her arms around him, clutching him frantically as he kissed her lips. His tongue grazed her mouth and she welcomed it inside her own, pulling his hair to bring him even closer. He dropped his hands and grabbed her by her backside and lifted her onto the counter so she was level with him standing there. He slotted her legs around his waist before diving in to kiss her again, forcefully, eagerly, and she continued to hold onto him like her life depended on it.

"So, you're not mad at me then?" She breathed into him, a small giggle under her breath.

"I'm so far from angry that I can hardly stand it," he laughed, kissing along her neck.

"Well, then, take me to bed," she whispered as his tongue teased her throat. Arden hoisted her up and tossed her over his shoulder. She squealed in surprise and laughed as he carried her to her bed and tossed her onto the mattress. She bounced and laughed, landing on her back and Arden crawled over her. She smiled up at him as he looked down at her, his face so sweet that it made her belly flip. He kissed her softly before standing and taking his overshirt off, and unbuttoned his pants. Willow bit her lip, and almost drew blood as she gawked at him. She sat up and pulled her sweater off, and raised the outer skirts of her dress over her head. Arden stared at her, a dark look over his eyes before he dropped to his knees at the edge of the bed and pulled her close to him, hands around her waist, until they were pressed flush together.

He kissed her again, tongue delving into her mouth. He tasted so good, she could hardly breathe. He pulled away from her then and gently rolled her slip up and over her legs, until it bunched around her thighs. She scooted up and he pushed them all the way around her hips before he tugged her panties down, over her legs, and tossed them into the pile of clothes littering the floor. Willow went to take his shirt off, and slide it over his shoulders, but he pushed her away and laid her down, before pulling her knees over the edge of the bed and draping them over his shoulders. Willow's belly twisted realizing what he was about to do, as he kissed up her thighs slowly. He looked at her as she laid with her elbows propping her up, and she nodded giving her consent to whatever he wanted to do to her.

His lips met her core, already wet and dripping, as he gently ran his tongue along her. She sighed, trying not to make noise when he pulled away and looked at her sternly.

"No, you'll let me hear you," he told her before he pulled her to his face and plunged his tongue deep inside her. Her head dropped back onto the bed as she moaned at the sudden onslaught of his tongue. Her fingers desperately grabbed at the blankets, before finally finding purchase on Arden's hair. She gripped his curls with one hand as the other clutched the sheets, and writhed under his ministrations.

"Arden," she gasped as he slid a finger into her, *"please,"* she cried. He started rhythmically moving his tongue and fingers until he found a pace that she praised the most, listening to her pleading as a way to know what she needed. She all but screamed when he added another finger and curled it *just* so.

"Oh my gods, Arden, *there, please,"* she begged, arching against him. She felt like she would explode if she didn't finish soon, her breath wheezing. He sucked on her clit and curled his fingers repetitively, until she came with a scream.

"Oh *fuck,* Will," Arden said against her, fingers still curling. Her body trembled as wave after wave of pleasure hit her, warmth rolling through her body. She caught her breath before sitting up and kissing Arden hard, tasting herself on his tongue. She tasted of wisteria, of sweet flowers, and the combination of his scent and her own was intoxicating.

She wanted him inside her, and tugged his shirt all the way off before desperately pulling at his pants. He laughed and started tugging on her corset, and they finally both stripped themselves on their own, and stood there and took each other in. Willow's mouth watered at the sight of him, his cock standing proudly between them. She wanted to taste him, too, but wanted him too badly to try that now. They'd have time, later, she knew, and sat back onto the bed before laying in the middle, and reached her hand out to him.

He stepped onto the bed with his knees and crawled closer until he was between her thighs, her legs pleasantly warmed against his skin. Arden laid his body over hers, elbows holding his weight, and she wiggled her body until she felt his length press against her where she wanted it most.

"Are you sure?" Arden breathed.

"Arden, so help me *gods,* please fuck me," she begged.

"Oh my - *Will* -" he grunted, she felt his cock throbbing at her words. He gently pressed himself against her, slowly, before he entered her. He went so slow that she thought she would die, and wrapped her legs around him to pull him inside completely, fast and hard. Arden groaned into her neck, clutching her waist with his hands before sliding one of his hands over her ass. He shifted her leg on that side and Willow moaned as he went even deeper and hit that perfect spot.

"Please," she begged, and he finally started to move. He rolled his hips against hers and she met him in perfect sync. She held onto her leg that Arden wasn't gripping and used the leverage to grind against him when their bodies met, meeting him in the middle. She cried out as he lifted her hips and held her to him as he thrusted in quick succession. She reached down and rubbed herself as he pounded into her, gasping at each movement. Arden watched her touch herself, and leaned down to kiss her furiously, tongue sweeping through her mouth before he bit her bottom lip.

"Willow, you better come soon because I can't hold back," he whispered against her now bruised lips. He changed his pace to a little slower than before, and angled his thrusts in the same way he used his fingers on her moments ago.

"I wanted you so much it hurt," Willow whispered into his ear, eyes closed in pleasure, "and now I want you to come with me," she told him between moans, "I just need a little more *just like that,"* she gasped as he pressed into her with a sudden deep thrust and knew if he just did that, just a little more, she would finish again. He noticed her reaction, and hit that same spot over and over and over until Willow felt her body go taut, white hot, *burning,* as her orgasm rolled through her body, harder than before with Arden's cock still throbbing inside her.

"I want you to come, Arden," she begged, and his thrusts became erratic before he gasped into her ear.

"I'm coming, my love," he moaned before he grinded against her core, aftershocks quaking through him.

They laid there like that until Willow gasped out a laugh and Arden rolled over, an arm over his eyes. Willow tucked herself against him and pulled a small flower from his hair that had gotten on him while they had been making love. Arden just snorted and swatted the flower away before holding Willow against him and stroked her arm.

"That was not how I expected today to go," Willow snickered.

"Yeah, me neither," Arden laughed and kissed her forehead, "but I'm so glad it did," he told her softly.

"Me too," Willow agreed and kissed his shoulder as she laid on it. They laced their hands together and basked in the afterglow, happy and sated, with no intentions of leaving the bed any time soon.

~ Thirteen ~

TOGETHER

Arden laid there for a moment, looking out the window with a smile on his face. He couldn't even believe where he was and what just happened, and looked down at Willow still snuggled against his side, dozing with a soft smile mirroring his own. His stomach flipped as he reflected on Willow's brazen words, completely surprising him. Of course, as a man, he naturally wondered how she would act in this scenario, as a beautiful and unmarried woman, but he was a gentleman too and refused to let his dirty mind taint a kind woman. However, he did not expect her to have been unapologetically direct and outright *filthy* minded, but he found he really wasn't all that surprised. He already had ideas of how they'd spend their days together now, and he laughed then as he felt like the weight he had been carrying for so long, for *so* long, was gone. He felt lighter, he felt happy, and most importantly, he felt relieved.

His laugh made Willow open her eyes and peer up at him before she let out a yawn and stretched. He took her in, watching as her skin stretched taut over her ribs, her breasts full and enticing. He didn't spend as much time lavishing them that he'd have preferred, but smiled that he would definitely be better acquainted with them quite soon. As Will stretched, Arden ran his hand along her belly causing her to jump in surprise before she laughed and laid there, arms tossed above her, and let Arden stare all he liked.

"You like what you see?" she teased, skin twitching as he trailed his fingers over her so lightly it tickled.

"Oh, I do," he murmured, grinning at her, before kissing up her belly, the valley of her breasts, and kissed her deeply on her lips. Her tongue greeted his and he knew without a doubt, this was heaven.

When he pulled away, Willow rolled out of bed and started dressing, and threw his clothes at him as she rifled through the mess on the floor. He'd barely recognized the mess at all before, distracted by something much more important. Will threw a shirt at his face and giggled when he sputtered at the impact, but when Willow turned around and he saw the globes of her ass, he stood and smacked her on that perfect mound and laughed when she squealed.

"Naughty," he scolded, trying not to laugh. Willow only blinked up at him with faux innocence, and Arden realized he was done for if she gave him that look again. *She's going to wear me out,* he thought before she smiled and laughed before pulling her panties on, and tossed the only dress left in the closet over her head.

"I think you'll come to find that you *like* naughty, Arden," she said daintily and sauntered out of the bedroom. He rolled his eyes and pretended to be exasperated, but his laugh gave him away and she cackled as they went back into the kitchen. Willow filled his water glass back up and drank the rest of hers greedily, worn out from their activities.

"I'm hungry, do you want some lunch?" Willow asked him with a smile. He nodded and she started filling a basket with noodles and a jar of seasoning before reaching her hand out and taking his own. They walked out the front door and around to the creek, right next to the rock bed.

Willow pulled stones from the creek bed that lined the bottom of the alcove she used to wash vegetables, and made a circle right against the creek. She walked over the back of her home where she lifted a door off the ground, revealing a dug out hole hidden there uncovering a large pile of dried logs and sticks, and brought them to the circle she'd made with rocks. She must have collected more during the time between his last visit, after the incident with the trees and fires. He hid a smile at the memory and kept watching her with rapt attention. She pulled a tied bundle of sticks from the basket that had been in there already and used some dry and crunchy leaves from the ground to ignite the fire with a match. After a few minutes, the flames began to strengthen.

"I'm going to get something from the kitchen, you can wait here or follow me if you want," she told him. He smiled at her before sitting on the grass and started to stoke the flames. She grinned and ran to the house and brought back a pot of water and a grate, laying it over the flames with each leg of the grate standing on the stones. She placed the pot of water on top, and poured in dried noodles before reaching a hand out to Arden.

"Let's find some vegetables, now," she said as he linked his fingers through her own. They walked through the woods a short distance before Willow found the carrots, still safely buried in the soil. She took three, and pulled Arden along further before she found tomato plants. Her pockets bulged with the vegetables and Arden snickered at her, but she only laughed and continued guiding him over the moss and grass.

"How do you remember where each one is?" Arden asked as they circled back around toward the creek.

"I do it all day, every day. It's just ingrained into my memory, now," she said easily. Arden squeezed her hand and looked at her sadly. He felt heartbroken for her, that she lived this way for so long. He held tight to her hand hoping that his gentle pressure over her fingers conveyed his support, that she would feel him telling her he's here now, too, with no words needed. His heart swelled with a feeling he couldn't name as she smiled in a way that made him feel whole, seen, and for once in a very long time, *happy* down to his bones. If he was able to keep Willow in his heart, make a home with her, start a family - he would be this happy forever, of that he had no doubt.

He couldn't believe that she had been holding that to her heart this whole time, just waiting and hiding it thinking of how upset he'd feel. He understood why she hadn't said anything, since it had been something fae had been punished for in the near past. But with her explanation, and his own feelings on their immediate connection, there was no doubt in his mind that she was telling the truth about it being a mutual *soulmate* connection. It was just undeniable and he couldn't believe they had made it nearly a year without addressing their absolute need for each other. Arden knew he had done everything in his power to keep himself from thinking about Willow, and what she meant to him. He supposed this was why, though he hadn't consciously known.

After finding a medley of vegetables, she led the way back to the now boiling pot of noodles and began to clean the vegetables with Arden's help. He washed them under the water as she sliced everything and added it to the small pan that she pulled from her apron pocket. Will had pulled the knife and spices from her pocket, and she easily prepared their meal relaxed and happily. They kept sharing knowing smirks with one another and eventually, everything was mixed and cooked, vegetables fried and noodles seasoned, and they ate in comfortable silence. Will cleared everything back up the way it was before they had come outside, stones back into the river bed, pots cleaned, and they walked hand in hand back into the house.

The sun was only at its peak, so they knew they had more of the day to spend together before needing to lock the shutters and hide away. Arden knew he wouldn't be leaving after everything she had told him, and everything they had shared, but felt a little guilty that he hadn't warned his family first. But then he remembered what Juna had said to them this morning and rolled his eyes. She absolutely *knew* he wouldn't be coming home today and most likely the whole town already knew, too. He chuckled to himself, wondering how Juna always seemed to know things before they happened. He found that he didn't care as much as he thought he would, now that he knew the insinuation hadn't bothered Willow in the least. They walked through the front room and Will guided him to the couch before filling up some glasses of water.

"I'm sorry I only have water right now, I haven't been willing to attempt an indoor fire because of how long it takes for the chimney to stop smoking," she apologized, "but I can go back outside to brew it if you want," she offered. Arden waved his hand, dismissing her thoughts.

"Don't worry, water is perfect, thank you," he told her honestly. He didn't care much for tea, he liked it but didn't necessarily feel like he was missing out on anything tonight. He waved her to the couch and gestured for her to sit next to him. She laughed and put her cup on the coffee table, sliding next to Arden on the couch.

"If you're not staying tonight, you should leave soon so you're not in the woods in the dark," she said softly as he linked their fingers together.

"I'll only leave if you kick me out," he told her blandly. She threw back her head and laughed, bringing a smile to Arden's face.

"Good, I don't want you to leave," she told him with a sweet smile. He reached over to her and pulled her up and over his lap until she was straddling him. She raised her eyebrows, with a knowing smile before she leaned forward to kiss him. He met her lips softly, and they savored the moment lazily as they deepened the kiss, tongues meeting. Arden's hands trailed over her waist until they were at her shoulders, and pulled her forward against him. Using one hand, he lifted her dress over her hips until she was bare against his length save for her panties and his pants. Willow must have read his mind because she started unbuttoning his pants and released his cock from his underwear. She leaned forward on her knees and slid her panties to the side and sank down on him easily, already wet for him.

Arden gasped, not believing she was so eager to ride him, but the evidence was undeniable. She readjusted her knees again, until he was completely seated inside her, their bellies flush as they breathed into one another. Will cried out when Arden lifted her hips and thrusted up into her before putting her hands on the couch behind his shoulders for leverage as she met his hips roughly.

"You feel so good," she breathed into his ear, clutching his neck while the other hand still pressed against the couch, pushing herself onto him relentlessly.

"So glad I found you," he kissed her deep, and bit her lip as she rolled her hips. Arden was struck with the need to see her breasts, and pulled her dress over her head. He slowed his hips as his mouth watered at the sight of her bare in front of him, as he was deep inside of her. Her cheeks were pink, and he smiled at her before drawing her breast to his mouth, and gently bit the hardened peak, taking turns with each one.

"Mmm," Willow hummed before pushing him away and dragging him into a kiss, her hips slowly rolling before she picked up the pace. Arden had to fight against the sudden overwhelming feeling of an impending orgasm at her brutal pace, but Willow only laughed in pleasure, not caring in the least. "You can come," she whispered into his mouth. He groaned and grabbed her hips again and rolled his up and into her, the curve of his cock reaching the bundle of nerves inside her. As she screamed and her thighs quaked, he knew she was close and kissed her as his thumb circled her clit.

"Oh gods, Arden I'm coming --" she cried before letting out a scream, head thrown back as her pussy squeezed around his cock. He wrapped his arms around her before plunging into her, so close to his own end. Will kissed him before meeting his thrusts, bringing him closer and closer, her own body still spasming around him. Finally, he gasped and spilled into her, moaning. His orgasm was so intense, he could only feel her gentle body still holding him inside, her soft kisses raining over his face. His entire body felt warm and he leaned his head back panting. His vision finally cleared and he blinked his eyes open to see her smiling at him, cheeks still pink from exertion.

"I don't think I'll ever get tired of that," Willow giggled before separating from him and stumbled to the bathroom. Arden could only laugh, too dazed to think of any way to respond. He at least pulled himself back into his pants before she came back into the room and laid on the couch next to him, her head resting on his thigh. She hummed as he ran a hand through her hair, and Arden was once again blown away at the ease they've always had with one another, their connection so pure, their friendship immediate.

"I don't think I could ever get tired of this, either," he said. Wordlessly, Will wrapped her arm around Arden's belly, holding him tight as he played with her hair. They easily rested for half an hour before Willow yawned and stretched, and moved to put her dress back on. Arden also stretched before going to the bathroom, and when he came out Willow was gazing out the window with a soft smile on her face.

His belly flipped at the sight, her gentle beauty gave him butterflies and he couldn't remember the last time that had happened to him. In fact, he was certain only Willow had ever made his stomach roll, the only one to ever fill a part of his heart that he'd been hiding away in the fear of finding himself in a marriage quite like his mother and father. A marriage on paper of course, but the reality was that they were *at best* estranged. The idea of spending his life that way had depressed him, and then being expected to move on as if nothing had happened to the man who was an actual father figure to him, broke his heart and froze him in time. Marry someone who doesn't love you and never will, while grieving for a father that he wasn't supposed to care about, knowing he wasn't even an uncle or related by blood - he had only ever been kind and caring to him and showed him what it had meant to be passionate for a career you love, and finding pride in the family you created.

He showed him how men should be - open, inviting, understanding, yet also stern, patient, and loving. He would never have known his role in life as a man of a household had he not been taught by Bartrum what it meant to delegate tasks and provide leadership in the most direct way, and still make sure everyone is being treated with well deserved respect. His mother of course had instilled the same values, but she had been that leader for everyone in town and it was easy for Arden to forget that she loved him too, even though it felt to him that she was always distracted and attempting to solve everyone's issues on her own. Over the years, she had settled into herself and was able to show Arden how difficult true leadership is, that being able to find solutions through honesty and hard work was tedious, but rewarding. Her lessons had paired perfectly with the lessons Bartrum had shown him - that it was possible to lead without being overwhelmed, that it was possible to find love in the little moments, after years and years of practice.

Everyone around him told him to pick up the pieces of his heart that had been broken from grief, and fill it with a wife and children with no other thought. The entire foundation he had stood on had crumbled that day and the way no one saw it or understood his feelings, had made him feel trapped and abandoned at the same time. Of course *now* he was aware there was more to people's words about moving on. He'd created his own version of reality through his grief, hearing too many voices telling him to move on. They hadn't understood because Arden hadn't explained it, and that was on his own conscience. He had pushed it down and down until it became cataclysmic and he had found himself sprinting into the dark woods and landing at the bottom of a wisteria tree.

He was still devastated that Bartrum had met a terrible fate, but he knew it wasn't for nothing. His family was still here, and if fate had let Bartrum choose, he knew he would have gone hunting that morning without hesitation. His son, Devon, would be spared that fate, and he was able to continue raising his children because of the sacrifice his own father had made -- going hunting that morning instead of Devon had saved Devon's life. His heart still ached over the loss, and seeing the Cahlin family at the funeral would always sit heavy in his memories as he watched their grief unfold before him. He was sure watching Bartrum's grandchildren and children weeping for him would never be easier to bear, but he hoped with time, it would at least be easier to push the memory away to hide the pain. His own father had gone years without a visit, and Arden wasn't sure he'd even shed a tear if he were lost in battle - he barely recognized the man when he *did* show up. And that thought was a tragedy in and of itself, too.

He couldn't believe his path in life had led him here, as Willow turned to smile at him under the glow of the sun. Arden remembered then, the most important thing Bartrum had taught him: a family has many different minds and many different gifts, and that each difference was a blessing for them all to share. He supported his sons, daughters, and wife, and his in-laws, in each branch of the new family they were lucky enough to welcome into their lives. He showed Arden how happy and fulfilling life could be, how wonderful it is to grow your heart through the eyes of your loved ones, and Arden knew he only ever wanted to live like Bartrum Cahlin. The man had it all because of his heart, and Arden knew that that's the life he wanted and deserved for himself, and wouldn't have settled for less than that no matter the pressure he was under to live a normal life and fill it with children. He knew Bartrum would have been so proud of him for finding a place where he belonged, a place that he was happy to share with a family of his own. A place he didn't think he'd find until mere hours ago. A place that gave him peace and fulfillment, a feeling of belonging - and there she was. Sitting on the couch smiling with a hand holding her chin as she watched birds outside picking at the ground, bringing him more peace than he'd ever known before.

What amazing luck, was all he could think to himself.

"Hey Arden, remember when you told me you were going to get married even though you didn't want to," Willow called to him, still smiling, though her eyes glinted with mischief and he almost choked on a laugh.

"Hey Willow, remember when you told me you married me in secret, by accident and then didn't tell me," he rolled his eyes, biting his cheek. Willow shrieked in laughter and stood to meet him in the living room. She clutched onto him as she laughed so hard, her eyes couldn't open. When her feet started to stomp as her shoulders shook, no sound coming out of her mouth, tears in the corner of his eyes, he couldn't help but join her in hysterics.

"I was so jealous at the thought of you getting married, though I knew I shouldn't be," she finally said, still quaking with laughter. "I'm glad you found me," she looked up at him, cheeks pink.

"I was jealous too, thinking about how you knew Teg," he said honestly. Willow burst into laughter again, knees weak as she fisted the fabric of his shirt. Arden led her back to the couch as she wheezed before calming down enough to answer.

"The Teg brothers have long been a friend of the Willows, they helped our roots grow. They were actually the ones who diagnosed my parents with their ailments," she told him, rubbing his arms.

"Your parents? Are they okay?" He asked with a frown, not wanting to bring up anything awful.

"Oh, they're fine, it's just that when they had me, I was born too early and they couldn't make it back to their home in time - my roots grew here, a very long distance from where I was supposed to be born, but I told you that already I think," she pursed her lips in thought. "Well, anyway, my parents decided to build a home here for us and raise me until I was old enough to handle a trip that long. With the fae school nearby, Stóngrast, and Hanlan's Outpost, they didn't see the need to be anywhere else. So a home was built, and years went by until I was eight years old and they came down with an illness." She explained gently, a story she must have thought about every day. Arden's heart ached at her words, the sadness palpable though her words were steady.

"They got ill enough to go looking for medicine - my mother was a master healing expert but when nothing she did worked, we feared the worst. After traveling to different physicians and apothecaries with no results, we found ourselves at Hanlan on the way home from a short trip nearby, when Teggert approached us along with his brother, Teggrin. They said they had sensed something and were able to track us down." She sighed before continuing, Arden stroking her back, "They told us then that their trees were dying," her voice was a whisper. "By the time we found out the problem, and what the solution was, I was only nine years old. They had separated from their tree, their roots, their *soul*, for so long that their tree had started to die. The only way to heal the tree is to reunite with them, breathe into them, feel their bark under your hands as you feel it holding you back. The only way to save yourself is to go back home. So my mother and father had to beg the Teg brothers to take me to my new home in Lexman Yur, where I studied daily for a year until my cottage was fully built and functional, and then I would travel during the weekend to come here by myself, and live all alone, before returning for more schooling." Arden pulled her into a hug, squeezing her gently. She sighed in comfort, nuzzling his neck.

"My family could have saved their trees and prevented their illness by moving to and from their orchard and me. My mother had cried to me, she felt so guilty, and told me that she had only wanted me to grow big and strong, to protect my little sprout from harm, apologizing so many times," she murmured.

"I told her it wasn't her fault of course, she only wanted to be my mama and no one could have known that this would happen, but it was still devastating knowing they would never be able to return to me without risking death itself. But my siblings get to grow up happy and healthy, and for that I am grateful," she kissed his cheek, her voice trembling as her lips grazed his skin.

"I'm sorry, Willow," he said, though he had more questions. She peered up at him with a smile, eyes narrowed.

"You look like you want to ask me something," she scrunched her nose at him, "you go like this when you have something on your mind," she told him.

"You weren't even looking at my face," he laughed.

"I could hear it," she said, rolling her eyes, as if it were an obvious conclusion to come to. Arden laughed again before holding her back to his chest.

"Is your name Willow or is that your family name?" He asked, running his fingers through her hair. She sighed deeply, cheek resting against his chest.

"Well since we're married, I'm sure it's okay if I tell you one more secret," she said. Arden's brows furrowed and he looked down at her wondering what other secret she could be hiding.

"In fae culture, a name is powerful. To know someone's full name is to possess not just a word, but the person entirely. You can do a lot of harm with a name, through spells or other magic. I was told not to share my real name with anyone for my own safety as I lived alone out here," she explained. She shifted back onto the couch, making room between them, a small smile on her lips.

"My name is Wilmayra Wisteria Willow, first born daughter of the Willow family," she grinned, "it's very nice to meet you!"

"It's nice to meet you, Wilmayra Wisteria Willow. I'm Arden George Fairwood," he extended his hand. She held her own out to him and they held hands, barely a handshake at all, but Willow grinned all the same.

"Come on, Arden George, let's get dinner situated before it's too dark," she said before pulling him along. Arden smiled and followed along, not caring in the slightest where they were going.

"Do you want me to hunt for anything?" He asked, wondering if she wanted any meat for their next meal.

"As long as you know how to cook it," she laughed.

Arden and Wilmayra collected everything they needed for dinner. Arden was able to find a bird and Willow found vegetables to roast, and the two of them ate until they were full. By the time the sun was peering beyond the trees, they made sure to collect everything and bring it into the kitchen. Wilmayra went back outside, and Arden noticed she was locking the shutters once more before the sunset. He lit the candles in the kitchen so it wouldn't be dark when she came back inside. Wilmayra had also brewed them tea before they had taken the small fire down. Arden sipped on his as he waited for her to come inside, stretching out on the couch leisurely.

Finally, Willow came inside and locked the door behind her, the soft glow of the candles flickering around them in a soft orange. He felt warm and comforted here, he had since the first time he'd met Will, and as she placed her mug next to his own he couldn't believe how blessed he had been to get to this point in his life. She draped herself against him, her cheek resting on his chest with her hand on his belly, his own arm around her shoulders.

"I should have noticed there was something more between us, well before today," he whispered in the dark.

"I know, me too, I hadn't really known that the Binding would make us so connected," she whispered back, "so much time had passed that most of what I knew was always known to me as myth or legend. Despite it being the way my own father had married my mother, it had always seemed so distant from me, so unreal," she trailed off, holding Arden's shirt in her fists. He leaned down to kiss her on her forehead making her giggle, and they laid there comfortably until they both started to yawn.

~ Fourteen ~

INTRODUCTIONS

"I'll put the mugs in the sink and blow out the candles," Arden said with a quick kiss to her cheek. Will blushed at how sweet his gentle and loving touch felt and smiled shyly. After using the bathroom, she brought the candle to her bedroom and remembered there was still a mess on the floor and started cleaning it. She bent down to hang everything back up, knowing that she did not want to wake up to the same mess. She would want to ignore it for days more if she didn't do it now. She went back and brought the rest of the clothes from the living room floor where she had pushed them off the couch and put them away, as well. She reached down for the last pair of pants on the floor, and suddenly felt a presence behind her. In the dark and candle lit room, she turned to see Arden looking at her in a way that made her belly flip.

"Why are you looking at me like that?" She laughed, taking a step toward the closet and quickly folding the pants. Arden swept up behind her and held her to his chest, her backside pressing against him. He trailed his hands up her belly and over her breasts, making her giggle as he tickled her with that gentle touch.

"Why do you *think* I'm looking at you like that, wife?" She laughed at his response and he kissed her neck with a chuckle. He put his hands on her waist and guided her to the bed, laying her on her belly. When she tried to roll over, Arden laid his hand on her back. She hummed and laid her head on her hands and looked over her shoulder to watch him undress. She laughed when he threw his shirt at her and tried to throw it back at him, but he crawled behind her and nestled himself between her thighs, draping over her back. He slid his right arm around her belly and brought her onto her knees, and leaned in to whisper in her ear while his other hand held him up.

"Just like this," he kissed her cheek again, delicately. She smiled and nodded, knowing there was nothing else she wanted to say. He pulled her dress higher over her legs, over her waist, her breasts, until finally he threw it to the ground. She squirmed under his gaze and wanted to see him from where she faced the bed, but he only gently laid her forward with her ass in the air. He pulled her panties off until they were trapped around her knees and she instinctively squirmed to get them off. Arden only laughed before swatting her bottom, taking her panties off her legs before leaning over her again. He trailed his fingers over her belly, down toward her center.

"I don't need you to do that, I'm already ready," she breathed, squirming.

"Already ready?" He snickered, teasing her while testing how wet she was. She laughed breathlessly as he laid his weight against her from behind, and she prayed Arden didn't make her wait much longer. "So impatient," he kissed her shoulder. Willow grumbled before she leaned her weight forward and stretched her hand underneath them, grabbing Arden's cock and guiding it to her pussy.

"Very impatient," she agreed as he groaned. He leaned back and shifted his legs closer to her ass, and she obligingly spread her legs wider to take him in. She moaned when he seated himself inside of her, not quite as deeply as she craved him, and braced herself against the mattress before pushing herself back against his length.

"Fuck," Arden bit her shoulder before pulling her hips into his hands and rolling his own, grinding against her. Willow cried out, desperately trying to push back against him to get friction. She wanted him to pump into her hard and deep like he'd done earlier but he only tortured her with *just* enough movement, merely stoking the fire in her belly.

"I swear to the gods, Arden, move your body now or I'll scream," she heaved in frustration, trying to reach her hand to her clit and make her own pleasure.

"Oh none of that," he said easily, still grinding slowly before taking both of her wrists and holding them to the mattress.

"You're gonna kill me," she groaned, a thrill filling her as he teased her and held her down. He laughed, seeing her expression as she pressed a cheek against the sheets.

"You love it," he said with a deep thrust, finally moving himself fully into her before pulling back and hitting the same spot that made her eyes roll. Willow's hands clutched against the fabric as she wailed, Arden rolling his hips against hers. He wrapped his hand around her waist and his other under her arm and over her shoulder. He pulled her up, until she was flush against his front while he pounded into her at a deeper angle. His left arm cradled her right shoulder, wrapped entirely around her while his right arm held onto her left hip. Her legs were spread over his lap and he fucked into her from behind and below, and used her weight to bounce her against him even harder.

Willow wasn't even certain what noises she was making while experiencing that blinding pleasure filling her from her belly to her toes. She gasped at a deep thrust and Arden pulled her mouth to his, desperately tasting her, hand sliding from her shoulder to her throat. He held it there, warm and heavy, without putting pressure on it.

"I'm so close, Arden, I'm so close," she begged him. "Please can I use my hand now?" She moaned again as he pulled her down onto his cock.

"Yes, you may touch yourself now," he said with another grind before he picked up the pace. Willow's hand all but flew to her clit and she rubbed desperately, the heat in her belly so close to consuming her. Arden used his knees to spread her further over his lap and the slight change in pressure and depth made her come unexpectedly, her body tensing and exploding around his cock.

"I love you," she cried, sobbing in pleasure, her body still trembling with aftershocks while Arden was still buried inside her. He cursed before dropping her onto her belly before furiously pumping into her until he came inside of her, blinding and earth shattering.

"I love you, too," he kissed her cheek, her neck, over her shoulders before rolling over her and onto the bed. She hummed but found she couldn't move, and they lay there naked and spent until the candle wicks burnt out. They lazily rolled toward each other for another kiss before Willow went to the bathroom bleary eyed, feeling the walls to find her way along to clean herself up. When she slid back into bed, they linked their hands between them and curled toward one another, falling into a deep slumber in only a moment.

...

Wilmayra woke to warm pressure surrounding her whole body, engulfed in the softest heat she'd ever felt, much like the day before. She sighed, comforted by the warmth around her and smiled sleepily, before wiggling deeper under the covers. She couldn't believe the day they'd had yesterday, of everything they shared together between the secrets she had been hiding finally coming to light, to Arden's truth of why he felt the way he did about marriage. She felt lucky to have been found by the man holding her close, that he had gone searching for her that day when she felt lonelier than she'd ever had before, his figure holding her tree had felt like ice water on a hot day. She had *needed* him all along, and he, her. She hummed when Arden kissed her neck, slowly waking as he held her close. She found she had no interest in moving from where they lay, skin to skin, pressed together lazily with not a care in the world.

"Y'think 's mornin yet," Arden slurred in the dark room, shutters blocking out the light. She snickered, still sleepy at his grumble.

"I think so, my tree feels warm," she said, feeling the leaves basking in the chilly morning sun as Arden pressed his nose against the skin between her shoulder blades.

"Mmm, but it's dark in here it doesn't count," he said, voice still sleepy but more awake as the moments passed.

"Go back to sleep, my love, I'll make us some coffee," she pulled his hand that wrapped around her belly and kissed it, before sliding out of the bed to use the bathroom. Arden just sprawled out on his belly and fell back to sleep by the time she made it to the door. She paused to look around at him, in awe of the gift of being able to fall asleep in literal seconds. While she brewed the coffee, a smile lingered on her face as she sat by the edge of the river, waiting for the water to boil to add it to the coffee press. When the coffee was finally ready, she heard footsteps behind her and turned to see Arden walking her way. His shirt was half buttoned and hung loose over his hips and Wilmayra bit her lip at the sight, eyebrows raised in delight.

"Good morning," she said, pouring him a mug of coffee. He sat next to her on the cool moss where she had laid a blanket down and took the offered mug with a grateful smile.

"Morning," he returned with a yawn. They sipped their coffee peacefully, watching the birds fly from tree to tree as the gentle breeze played with their hair. Wilmayra felt the sun raise higher into the sky, but made no move to start the day. For the first time in months, she had no expectations of the day and how she'd spend each minute, counting down the seconds until sunset and fighting away the endless, restless, permeating and pitiful anxiety she had come to know and expect upon waking. With Arden she found herself to be at peace even if she was just sitting next to him. They hadn't spoken at all since he'd joined her, only to point at a unique bird or a nudge for more coffee, and Wilmayra couldn't imagine having spent her morning in any other way than by his side. She wondered at how time changed everyone, how they had gone from strangers to *this.* She giggled to herself as Arden looked at her curiously, a smile quirking his lips as he watched her.

"I was thinking," Arden finally murmured, smiles still lingering on their faces, "we should go back to Stóngrast so I can introduce you to my family."

"I met them already," she laughed, bumping her shoulder into his. He rolled his eyes and scoffed, before pouring himself some more coffee.

"I *mean* to introduce you properly this time," he sipped on his mug and raised his eyebrows at her, waiting for her answer. She frowned in thought, wondering what he could possibly mean when she looked at him and took in his hopeful face, with pink staining his cheeks.

"You want to introduce me as your wife?" She asked, grinning.

"*Yes,*" Arden laughed in exasperation, "of course that's what I meant."

"You were certainly not clear enough for me to understand," she lilted before tossing her hair over her shoulder in a mocking air. Wilmayra tried not to spit her coffee out as she took a sip when Arden's belly laugh took her by surprise, her mug almost tossing itself from her grip entirely as she giggled along with him. Arden finally stood up and reached his hand down to her, and they began cleaning up the fire and the coffee supplies, before heading back inside to get dressed.

It was still dark in the house, but Wilmayra had no desire to open and close the shutters needlessly, so she only lit two candles for them. She made her way into her room and dressed in a dark green dress, and a long hooded cloak to match. She hadn't brought a coat the days before and with the rain storm, she wanted to make sure that she was fully prepared this time. She had gotten quite good at packing things very compactly, and was able to also pack extra outfits in case she needed them. She hoped she wouldn't need anything else though, but she supposed Juna would share with her again should the need arise - though she certainly wouldn't expect it, of course.

She pulled the bag over her back and headed to where she stored her key and once again pulled it from its home for the last two decades, and placed it in her pocket. She had tied a long piece of twine to it as a child and braided it with stone beads that were still just as beautiful as the day she had made it with Sian in Lexman Yur all those summers ago. It was light, but it had a reassuring weight to it that she was grateful for as it made her feel its presence in her pocket. She had always been worried about losing her only key, but Sian had made sure her stone beads were carved with runes that would ensure it would never be lost, nor stolen. She blew out the candles on the kitchen counter and once again said goodbye to her home, excited yet nervous to meet everyone in a slightly different light this time.

After she locked the door, Arden reached his hand out to her. She smiled before linking their fingers together happily. They started walking back to town while Wilmayra wondered about the welcome she'd receive this time. The other day she had been helping them prepare medical supplies and so she knew they wouldn't turn her away as she had the things they most needed. But this time, she was afraid they would be disappointed in Arden's choice for a wife, or that they'd somehow come to the conclusion that she had tricked him into Binding himself to her much like the old myths humankind had believed only a few generations ago. Of course they had been kind to her, but that wouldn't exactly guarantee Arden's wife, that coveted position his mother had been encouraging him to fill, the same kindness. Almost as if she were projecting her thoughts into Arden's mind directly, he tugged on her hand.

"They're going to be very happy that it's you," he told her gently, pausing their walk as he pulled her into a hug. Will was surprised for a moment but gratefully wrapped her arms around him with a sigh.

"I'm just afraid they'll be let down that I'm not a woman from the port," she said quietly into his shoulder.

"After what you've done for them, I don't think anyone would have one negative thing to say about us being married," he squeezed her tighter, "and I especially know if I had returned without you, Juna herself would have marched her way out here to find you and drag you back so that I could wed you immediately," he laughed. Wilmayra couldn't help but feel a weight lift off her shoulders at his reassurances but still felt somewhat nervous. At the very least, she could trust that Arden was right about the people he loved the most and knew they'd be supportive of his choices.

"What made you think your family didn't care about who you married, just that you found a wife and started a family?" She was genuinely curious and wondered at how much of this involved the butcher Cahlin, and how much of it was Arden's perceptions of those around him. "I know we talked about it before, but I'm still curious."

"It was more so a frustration I was feeling about being unable to stop time, and being unable to feel everything I wanted to feel, with all of the limitations of pretending that I wasn't in mourning and maintaining that facade," he said, voice breathy as he rambled, "I'm not sure if that makes much sense, but when you see something awful and try to process it, try to put each emotion in the right place - that's hard enough. But when you have to process your grief, every stage of it, while still maintaining the persona of the leading Commander in the Port, and also be expected to casually interview all of the maidens in town to attempt a love match *and* have children while danger lurks in the not so distant woods..." He trailed off, his voice fading out gently. She squeezed his hand in quiet support, waiting for him to continue. "It could have been *my* family that was hurt, and that was terrifying to consider. If any of our lives had been slightly different, we wouldn't be here now."

"The idea of pretending I'm not scared of the state of the world, and that I'm not grieving the most painful loss I had ever experienced to date, was too much to bear. And it seemed as though my family couldn't see it even though I felt like I was suffocating, which *was* my fault as I had never actually told them how I was feeling and just expected them to be able to tell. Juna may have, but my mom only wanted me to live a life she couldn't, and I can't blame her for wanting me to chase after happiness when things were at the darkest. But because of that, it felt like I was being shepherded into being a husband and father without anyone asking me what I needed in order to be happy. It turns out, I only ever needed some space and some time to work it out on my own," he smiled at Wilmayra then, and she smiled back with a blush blooming over her cheeks as she took in his words. He was right, he did need to make the journey for himself instead of following a timeline that was decided for him. She did feel a little guilty for keeping it from him for so long, though.

"I'm glad you looked for me first," she told him honestly, her belly flipping at the thought of him marrying anybody else.

"Me too," he laughed easily, his eyes full of warmth as he looked down at her again. She couldn't remember seeing him look so carefree and realized just how relieved Arden must have been when he found out about their Binding.

"I should have told you sooner," she murmured as they continued walking, the guilt heavier in her belly than before.

"No, I think it was supposed to happen like this," he told her easily. His voice was gentle, and she couldn't hear even a hint of regret in this voice. She glanced up at him and he smiled at her, soft and sweet, and squeezed her hand. "We got to know each other properly, and without any expectations, and I'm grateful for that, Will," he turned to her and kissed her cheek, before drawing her into another embrace. They stood there in the middle of the woods, on the edge of Tonsilta, and swayed together for a moment. Wilmayra started giggling when Arden nuzzled her neck and he finally stepped away from her, his eyebrows raised.

"Why are you looking at me like that?" She laughed at him, eyeing him suspiciously as his eyes raked over her.

"Well we *are* alone out here, maybe we can," he grinned, and Will laughed again.

"You mean alone in the Fae woods with all of these *trees?*" She said pointedly, looking around. Arden grumbled and took her hand, before continuing walking.

"Well, you had to go there, didn't you?" He rolled his eyes comically, Wilmayra's laughter still bubbling from her lips.

"Oh, I don't mind at all, I just thought you'd might wonder what they're whispering about when we're *busy,*" she snickered. Arden's cheeks turned pink and he looked around at the trees surrounding them, his eyes narrowed. Wilmayra couldn't contain her giggles for the rest of the way to Stóngrast, the time melting away around them as they continued talking.

Stóngrast fell into view finally, after seemingly no time at all. Will unconsciously tightened her grip on Arden's arm, clutching his elbow to her with both hands as her nerves caught up to her.

"It'll be okay, I promise," he told her gently as they stepped onto the main road. Wilmayra could already hear all of the townspeople, somehow louder than she remembered from only a day ago, and looked around to see what was going on. She could see Arden's eyes harden as he scanned the town for anything wrong, but they both only saw smiling, jubilant, and friendly faces all around.

"I wonder what happened," Wilmayra murmured quietly, and Arden hummed in agreement. They walked further into town and passed by the market stalls when someone ran up to them.

"Commander! You brought back Miss Willow, thank goodness. We all wanted to thank her properly for providing us with all of this medicine," a woman with kind eyes and plain clothes reached her hand out toward Willow with a grateful smile on her face.

Will looked at Arden in surprise, not sure how she should react. He smiled back at her easily, though his brows were quirked in surprise. He nudged her forward but she kept their fingers laced together, she was unsure if she could even separate them at this point. Her palms were sweating between the heat of their hands and her growing anxiety as they were led further toward the stall they had set up days prior. She heard Arden laughing next to her and she turned to look at him again.

"You can breathe," he whispered with a smirk, she could see that he was trying to hold in a laugh. He tightened his grip on her hand as they met Fasomolo at the stand, a smile on his lips as he saw them approach.

"Willow!" He said, delighted, "It is so good that you've come back. We all wanted to thank you with something you'd find useful." He led them to the kiosk and gestured at what was sitting on the small shelves. Willow peered over to see fabric, jars, and a leather bag laid out. A small smile crept onto her cheeks, excited yet cautious at what she was seeing. Another woman came up to them and explained what the gifts were for, and Willow tried very hard to keep her eyes from welling up with tears.

"We know you said you didn't need anything except for us to be healthy, but we at least wanted to give you more supplies to use if you wanted to make anything more for yourself," as she spoke she gently packed the leather bag with everything slowly, and showed Willow as she went along. "Fabric for whatever you may need it for, cotton and burlap for bandages or satchels, tincture jars, and more jars in different sizes, and this bag," the woman smiled gently, and tentatively handed it to Willow. Willow held the bag to her chest, sniffing deeply at the familiar smell. Her breath caught in her throat as she fought against the burning in her eyes.

"Thank you," she breathed, looking at everyone around her. There were mostly mothers surrounding them, holding their little ones tight, as they waited to see her reaction to the small gift. "I love it," she laughed and draped the bag over her shoulder, admiring the weight of it and grinned. Arden's hand still held hers tight, and she turned to him while she squeezed his fingers. Arden's eyes flicked to the crowd and she noticed the murmur around them as everyone's eyes collectively fixated on the way their hands were linked. She went to pull them from Arden's grasp but he held tight and continued to smile at her. Heat filled her core at his gaze, a blush scorching her face.

Fasomalo caught her attention as she turned, looking as though he was ready to burst as they all watched their interlocked fingers. *This must be something scandalous in their culture,* she thought hysterically, moving to pull away from Arden for modesty sake. But Arden only held her hand tighter and shook his head slightly, barely moving a muscle. Her nerves calmed, and she found herself in a sea of people all offering their gratitude and small tokens of their thanks. Some pastries, some crochet supplies. Everything useful but small enough that she didn't feel guilty for accepting them as gifts, but vowed to bring more supplies in order to feel deserving of their kindness.

"I think this has Juna and Alvenia written all over it," Arden said as the crowd finally cleared.

"This bag is stuffed with so many things, I don't think I should take all of this," Wilmayra confessed, the excitement fading and bringing back a level of unease. "I feel as though I'm stealing," she said guiltily.

"Please, they all are beyond grateful for what you did for them. Of course you should accept their gifts," he told her gently. "You are giving everyone hope and health. A few trinkets are the least they can do to show you what that means to them." She smiled as she held the bag tighter, feeling like a little girl again, with a bag of goodies after a birthday celebration. A laugh bubbled from her lips in childlike joy and Arden pulled her along until they finally made it to his home. Wilmayra gently draped the bag over her shoulder before steeling herself a deep breath, and waited to greet her new family officially.

~ Fifteen ~

IT WILL GO

Arden tried to contain his nervousness but found that all he could do was grip Will's hand and smile, mouth dry, as he opened the door of his life-long home. There was a chatter he was used to as he tugged Will inside, a hum of noise guiding visitors into the lived-in home. Between his mother, his sister, the housekeeper and the maids, it was quite noisy compared to the cottage in the woods. He glanced down at Wilmayra and saw her cheeks blossoming red, a lovely color on her, and let out an almost hysterical laugh. Will looked up at him, still nervous, but she laughed along with him in the same pitch, and watched relief pour over her face as she realized how nervous he was, too.

Their laughter alerted his sister, he could hear her shriek his name from the far side of the house, and each stomp of her feet as she barreled down the halls after them. She met them in the lounge, just off the foyer, and saw their interlocked hands. Arden braced himself for what would surely be the most excruciating night of his life, as Juna and Alvenia realized exactly who Wilmayra was, and what they were to each other.

"Stop, Arden, I will *scream* right now -" Juna gasped breath-lessly, eyes near bulging as she locked her gaze onto him and Willow. Alvenia stepped into the doorway, nearly knocking into Juna, letting out a squawk in surprise, not expecting her daugh-ter to be blocking the way. She stopped in her tracks, eyes as wide as Juna's, and stared intently at their linked fingers. Willow almost let out a squeak but Arden could feel her start to tremble at the audience before them, and slid his hand out of her grip to wrap it around her waist. He looked down at her with a small smile and watched her cheeks dimple as she looked back at him, before they both took deep breaths and faced his mother and sister, finally.

"I want to formally introduce you to my wife," Arden said, voice clear in a tone he used for issuing orders. He felt that he needed the extra support of his Commander's voice, and knew it was the right call as the housekeeper and her daughters tiptoed into the room behind Alvenia and Juna. All of them clutched one another, eyes unblinking and mouths agape. They looked between Arden and Willow and back again, before at *last*, Juna broke into a grin. The girls held onto each other before squeal-ing and jumping around, while Alvenia and Felisia clasped their hands together, cheeks pressed together, before Alvenia burst into tears. Arden blinked in surprise and Willow made a con-cerned noise before the five of them began to laugh collectively. Arden huffed a low curse at the dramatics as Will gently elbowed him with a shush, a shrill giggle escaping.

Felisia led the still crying Alvenia to the chaise and sat with her on it, offering her a handkerchief and laughing as Juna, Annie, and Alise plowed into Arden and Willow in an aggres-sively excited hug. Willow laughed and accepted their embrace and kissed their cheeks in return.

"I *knew* it!" Juna giggled as she kissed Arden's cheek. The girls all nodded, and Will laughed, as Arden realized they had been gossiping about them as soon as they had met Willow in the first place.

"I recognize you from the market before the storm," Willow said after a moment, and Arden realized they had been in the crowd during the first sweep of the storm, only having asked for a few things before quickly returning home. "Did it help?"

"Very quickly, it helped," the girls murmured, still smiling. Alvenia finally settled down, and they turned to her as she started to stand up.

"Arden, I can't believe it," her voice wobbled and he was sure he'd start crying too if he saw his mother weeping for another moment. He was still unsure if these were even happy tears at all, but he bit his cheek and waited for her to continue. Felisia had more sense about her and gave Arden a hardy hug, and squeezed Willow just as tight with a kiss to each of her cheeks. She put her palms where she kissed her face, and smiled at her with watery eyes.

"My daughters were able to get my husband pain relief for his arthritis and it has been a blessing, seeing him moving around like he used to again," she whispered, trying to keep her voice steady. "Arden is lucky indeed to have found you, I'm proud of you both for finding your way." Arden saw tears forming in Willow's eyes before she blinked quickly to clear them as Alvenia made her way in front of them at last. Felisia snickered at Alvenia's expression, and Arden couldn't blame her as he took in her red eyes and gently smeared makeup. With her thumb, Willow gently wiped away a smudge of pink lipstick off his mother's cheek that had spread while she was sobbing, which only caused Alvenia to fall into another bout of hysterics. She gripped Willow tight, her nose pressing into Will's shoulder.

Arden made a move to separate them instinctively, thinking for a brief moment that his mom was being too rough, but Juna held his elbow suddenly and shook her head.

"Wait," she mouthed to him, and they all watched as Willow smiled into his mother's hair and hugged her back just as fiercely, her hands gently running along her back.

"I'm so glad it's you, Willow," Alvenia whispered, "my son is so deserving of a wife like you, I can hardly believe it." Her voice broke and Arden's eyes immediately watered, and he looked at the ceiling to prevent any from falling. "He has always been so strong, I was afraid he would lose his way after all the years of holding my hand," she continued.

"Mother -" Arden started but she waved a hand at him, making Willow giggle more.

"You have been my son's friend for a long time, he's told us about you, and I just knew from the first moment that this would be something special," she said, pulling away to look at Will's face, tears gently sliding down both of the women's cheeks.

"I knew it, too," said Juna loudly, making Annie snicker.

"She did actually say that months ago," Alise said as she held onto her mother's arm.

"Well, apparently Willow knew too," murmured Arden, making a face. Willow snorted, covering her mouth as a laugh slipped out before she agreed.

"He's right, I really did know before he did," she huffed. Juna was delighted and laughed, pulling Willow into her arms again.

"Okay, so," Alvenia clapped her hands together, "a ceremony. What are we thinking?" She asked Arden and Willow.

"I haven't thought about anything at all," Arden said honestly.

"I wouldn't know where to start," agreed Will.

"Well, the first question is - what *don't* you like?" Juna asked.

"I don't like the idea of decision making," Arden muttered, eyes wide as he thought about the amount of planning they'd need to do now. Willow rolled her eyes at that and nudged him, still smiling.

"I don't like the idea of anyone spending too much time or money on me, but that's the only thing I can think of that I'd be opposed to," she offered, which was more helpful for his mother, he could tell.

"Willow, can I ask you something?" Juna said gently.

"Of course," she replied.

"Do you know what it would cost to have one carton of your medicine made and delivered into our port, in the conditions it was delivered in?" Juna looked at her pointedly.

"Hmm, no. I guess I don't," Will frowned.

"To put it plainly, we could have spent enough money to buy and furnish an entire home *and* a new wardrobe, and still it wouldn't quite equal the value of *one* case of your medicinal offerings," she stated, Arden's brows rising in surprise. "Trust me, I went over it with mother's cousin Fasomalo. He gave me a list of what other ports are charging for the same supplies, with much less potency, and the prices were hefty to say the least. When I say - there is *nothing* you would be able to do to convince Stóngrast to give you a cheap wedding, it is not an exaggeration." Willow blinked in surprise at Juna's words, and Arden noted pride he saw on Willow's face as she watched his little sister use such a tone - a grown woman in her own right, though to him she would always be the baby. He felt pride on his own face, too, as he watched his sister speak. He couldn't believe his fate, that he was surrounded by a family that he loves with every fiber of his being, and that his wife was welcomed with the most loving of arms in every part of his home.

"In that case, I will be grateful for whatever we are gifted," Willow said.

"So long as it's not too extravagant!" Arden stated before his mother went into a tizzy.

"Party pooper," Juna sang, but giggled. "What are your favorite colors?" She asked Willow.

"Greens and yellows, and I do like purple too," she said. "Wait a second, actually there is something I would prefer," she said softly.

"Anything," Alvenia said as she wiped her eyes.

"My friend Sian actually knows some of these ideas, if you needed more help, but I would ask that any flowers or decorations we use come from fallen flora, so as not to damage any nearby plant life," she said, voice soft but direct. "I only say this because I'd like to make sure the area has enough flora to use for the medicinal stores, and I would also suggest everyone in the port to practice the same until we have enough stocked with a whole season's worth of supplies."

They all blinked at her before Alvenia broke down in tears again, hugging Willow in a crushing grip. Will only laughed and squeezed her back, and Arden wrapped his arms around them both easily.

"So lucky, Arden, congratulations," she weeped.

As overwhelmed as Arden felt at the thought of a wedding, let alone an *extravagant* wedding, he was relieved that his family had accepted the news with such joy. While he knew that they'd be happy, he had been anxious about them wondering about the match being a good one. Having met Willow only days ago had given Arden a reason to believe they'd take her in with no fuss. He had been right and his nerves had been for nothing, and he felt like he could breathe again.

They all made their way into the dining room as the house-keeper went to make some food for them to have brunch together. They all sat around the table as they listened to Felisia and her son cooking together, laughing from just beyond the doorway. She must have told Arick about the soon to be wedding because he popped into the room with two plates of tea cakes, one on each side of the table, and clapped a hand to Arden's shoulder as he made his way back to the kitchen.

"Congratulations, Commander," he said with a smile. They thanked him and started picking at the treats, and in no time at all their lunch was brought out, too. Felisia's husband came in after their sons, Arick holding their youngest. As they sat around the table talking and eating, the little boy wriggled free of his big brother and made his way over to Willow and Arden who sat pressed together at the furthest end of the table. There were chairs from the kitchen and the study lining the dining table to seat the extra people, and the little boy found his way to Will's side. Arden turned to watch them curiously, wondering what the boy would do. Willow looked down at him with a fond smile and the boy smiled back, reaching his arms out to her. She easily lifted him by his under arms and he sat on her lap as though he'd known her for years. Willow laughed as he nestled against her chest as he picked at the untouched cookie on her plate. The boy also held out another cake for Willow to eat, and she graciously accepted it.

"Thank you, little one," she told him. Arden chuckled and kept eating, and listened to them quietly talking together. "My name is Willow, what's yours?"

"I'm Amos and I'm this many," he showed her three fingers.

"Nice to meet you, Amos, I can't believe you're three! That's so big," she said as she patted his belly. He laughed, stuffing another treat into his mouth. Arden watched as everyone looked at

Willow interacting with the little boy, and knew his mother and sister especially were wondering about them becoming parents one day.

"She's good with children," Felisia whispered to his mother, who wiped a tear from the corner of her eye. He tried to feel scandalized at the thought but found he only felt excited at the prospect of having a family of his own one day, and smiled as they finished their meals.

After they ate, Willow carried the now sleeping boy to the quiet office, laying him on the couch with a blanket over his small form. His mother thanked her with a kiss to her cheek, and Arden led them to the living room where Alvenia and Juna brought out some tea. They laid about a while, chattering excitedly about ideas for the wedding, and talked about a guest list for the reception. His mother and sister offered to send word to Willow's family to come along, but she declined.

"The forest hasn't been safe for long distance travel in a good while, and I'm afraid even sending a letter to them may not be safe," she explained, "but worry not, as soon as I have word that it's safe once again I will call for them and we can have another celebration." They looked at her sadly, and Arden knew they'd have to explain more to them in the future but let it be for now since there wasn't much they could do to ensure their safety on such short notice. He knew they wanted to have the wedding within the next month or two, since they were already married there wasn't much need to hold a long engagement. The subject passed just as quickly back to more fun topics regarding the celebration.

"You don't mind having a big reception, right Will?" He asked her softly as they sat together, Juna and Alvenia discussing fabrics for table settings and gowns.

"I don't really have anything in particular I'd like, and I don't know much about what is traditional in your culture," she told him, "so long as the dress I wear is comfortable and not too extravagant, I can't say that I really care. We can let them have fun planning this," she added. He laughed at that, watching the faces of his mother and sister as they sketched out plans on a notepad.

"They do look like they're having fun, don't they," he snickered, "I agree with you, though, I don't have any ideas in mind and it's actually nice that they want to do all of this at all." Willow laced her fingers through his and leaned into his shoulder, not quite smiling but a peaceful expression on her face.

"The Binding Ceremony is pretty dry as far as my traditions go, it almost never has an audience at all aside from *maybe* the parents or siblings of the couple, and it's followed by a meal with whomever wanted to join them. Usually a gift of some kind of homeware, or garden supplies, in honor of beginning a household of their own is also given, but that's about it," Willow told him as they listened to more and more of Stóngrast's marriage traditions.

"I've lived here my whole life and don't know much about weddings, I've never been to one since I'm usually on patrol during a ceremony. I typically volunteered those shifts so that the others could attend with their closest friends and family, while I took their place," Arden explained. It had worked well for them over the years, and he never felt as though he was missing out on anything. He'd always figured he'd have his own one day, that the time would come for his team to take their place for him to attend his own ceremony. He knew without a doubt they'd volunteer to help him, even though he'd been off duty for the better part of the week. He was glad he'd had the forethought to let them know he'd be unavailable for the next few days when he'd originally sent out for Willow and her medical expertise; he would have missed several of his patrols had he not notified his subordinates in advance. It wouldn't do for a Commander to be missing in action with no notice, especially as the leader of quite a few soldiers.

...

The day passed them by quickly. They spent most of it lounging and eating, before they all went their separate ways. Alvenia told them she was running to the seamstress and the boutique for new clothes for Willow, and Juna went with her. The housekeeper and her family all went back to work, the little boy running out to play in the large back yard as his father continued to harvest more of the vegetables they grew there. Arden and Willow made their ways upstairs, a bath being drawn for them by Alise. She left them towels and soaps before heading into the kitchen to help her brother with the dishes.

After they took turns in the tub, they dressed in comfortable clothes and sat in the room. Willow found her recipe book and went to start making a new one out of a blank book she had been given in the market this morning.

"I'm going to the barracks to check in with my men," Arden told her as he laced his boots back on.

"I'll be here, I'm getting tired," she replied, leaning up for a kiss. He kissed her gently and smiled at her, a loving warmth filling his belly with butterflies.

He quickly hurried to finish the task of checking in with the other soldiers making sure the coming patrol shifts included himself. He wasn't certain yet what Wilmayra and himself would do for a living, but supposed they'd be able to add a stable to the cottage for a horse, so that he'd be able to ride back to the port each morning he was scheduled. He didn't think Willow would mind at all, and he also knew that Juna would insist on being a guest there as often as she could. She wouldn't have to be alone anymore, of that he would make sure of.

The soldiers greeted him in excitement, having either seen them in the market or the gossip had spread like wildfire and found their eager ears easily. Arden only laughed when they congratulated him, happy that they had made it to this point. Many of the men also thanked him for bringing Willow to the market in the first place, grateful for what she was able to help them with. More families had been touched by the lack of medicine available than he had originally thought, and many more were affected by the lack of travel, shipments, and being unable to safely navigate the woods during the recent months because of the attacks on civilians. Arden was humbled to know of their full support in his marriage with Willow, and he told them all how grateful he was that they'd show their kindness this way.

On his way home, he ran into Teg who was leisurely walking along the cobblestone path on his way to the tavern. They were going in the same direction, and walked quietly together before Teg spoke.

"She finally told you," he said with a smile.

"Yeah, she finally told me," Arden chuckled, "how did you find out?" He asked.

"Well, the flowers in her hair finally bloomed white, which is a telltale sign of a Binding. She had been a late bloomer and only ever had tiny leaves growing until recently, but we assumed it was from her premature delivery," Teg said sagely, but as Arden looked at him he only saw a fatherly love in Teg's eyes. "The flowers are smaller at first, from green to yellow, until the ceremony is completed, and then they bloom larger and whiter than they did ever before. It's also obvious to those like us when there's a soul bond on someone. You could say we can smell it in the air," he explained.

"Why didn't you bring her to Stóngrast before?" Arden couldn't help but ask.

"Her parents gave her a healthy dose of fear regarding the human markets, and especially about leaving her roots after what happened to them," he explained. "She wouldn't have come with anyone else but you." Arden was at a loss for words at the thought, but felt grateful Willow had decided to take a chance on him.

"She is a very kind woman, always thinking about others," Arden smiled. "She only came because I asked her to help our home with something that she has a gift for."

"I'm glad you did, she wouldn't have been able to make it on her own for much longer. She was very lonely and with the Hanlan Trading being completely empty, I feared for the worst," Teg murmured as they passed by another street, nearing his destination.

"We were both lonely," Arden said sadly, remembering the overwhelming emotions that sent him to the forest in the first place.

"A Binding Ceremony isn't considered romantic in this part of the realm anymore, but a long time ago it was seen as the purest form of love. They say it is the equivalent of a soul mate to humankind, and they're not far off," Teg said as he stopped on the corner by the tavern, "remember this: the sun will always rise, and so shall you." He turned to walk away with a nod, and nearly silently entered the tavern, leaving Arden to stand there with a curious expression on his face.

When he made it home, he stepped into his bedroom quietly so as not to wake Wilmayra if she were already asleep. He closed the door behind him, holding a candle he had taken from the foyer. He sat it on the nightstand and noticed Willow laying on the bed, hair flowing around the pillow she rested her head on.

He stepped closer to her, taking her in. Her dress was hiked up and the blanket was pulled down, and the sleeve of her night-gown was dangerously low on her shoulder, exposing her breast almost entirely. He immediately stripped off his clothes and slid into the bed with her, easily sinking under the blankets and slotting himself between her thighs. She squirmed in her sleep as he touched her lips gently with his own as he ground himself against her. She gasped awake when he trailed his tongue down her neck. She pulled him against her sleepily yet eager all the same.

"Missed you," she said between kisses, "need you." He only hummed in agreement as he slid her panties off and to the floor, and felt her wetness with his fingers. She moaned, covering her mouth to keep quiet as he plunged his fingers into her slowly. She was writhing in only a moment, desperate to feel him closer. He knew she would be begging him soon but didn't want her to be heard through the walls.

He decided to give her what she wanted, without teasing her for any longer. He pulled his fingers from her core and pressed his cock against her, making her hiss out a breath in need.

"Why must you torture me," she said in a frustrated whisper, "just put it in or I'll *ahmph!*" She cried out, surprised by his sudden thrust. Arden covered her mouth and rolled his hips to hers in a hurried pace, wanting to finish quickly to avoid anyone overhearing them. Willow seemed to be thinking the same thing, and shifted herself lower on the bed and pulled her knees up, using her feet to press against the bed with each of Arden's thrusts. By the desperate gasping she was hiding behind his hand over her mouth, he knew she found the perfect angle to reach her end. He made sure to keep the pace and the pressure, wanting to see her come apart on his cock.

"Come for me, my love," he whispered as he quickly aimed his cock *right there,* where she liked it most. Her entire body coiled around him before she threw her head back and panted against his palm. Her pussy clenched around his cock over and over as she came hard. He slipped his hand from her mouth to under her hips, and pulled her up against him.

"You feel so good," he told her, making her gasp as the pleasure still rolled through her belly, another wave of after-shocks stealing her breath away. He fucked into her hard and fast, knowing he would come in only a few more strokes.

"Oh my gods Arden, I'm gonna - again - I'm so close, Arden *please,*" she whispered desperately as she used her fingers to rub her clit in tandem with his cock deep inside her. Arden couldn't hold himself off any longer and came hard, rolling his hips through his climax. Wilmayra wiggled against him and her fingers before pulling him into a rough kiss, squeezing around his cock as she came again. He covered her mouth with his own as she let out a moan, swallowing the sound as she trembled from the overstimulation of her clit.

"*Arden,*" she breathed against his lips, their bodies grinding together one last time before they both gasped for air. He kissed her neck as he caught his breath before rolling off of her so he didn't crush her. They laid together for a few moments before Willow made her way to the bathroom to clean herself up. When she came back, she slid under the covers and gave him a kiss before flopping back onto her pillow and closing her eyes with a heavy sigh, and yawned loudly before rolling over and settling under the covers.

"I love you," Arden whispered, thinking she had fallen asleep after a moment had passed, having been in a daze after he orgasmed and couldn't form the words right away.

"I love you, too," she whispered back. She leaned over to give him another kiss before laying back onto her pillow and promptly fell back asleep. Arden snorted at how quickly she fell asleep before laying back against his pillow, his hand reaching out for a strand of hair that had landed between them. He twirled it in his fingers as he settled into his pillow and thought about their day, and of the upcoming reception after a formal wedding ceremony.

He still was in disbelief at how everything was unfolding in front of him, that he'd found a woman he wanted to spend his life with, and that she was already his best friend in the first place. And not only did she want to spend her life with him, but his entire family welcomed her with open arms without a question or a rejection on anyone's lips. They were all happy for them, and excited for what was to come. Things like that don't fall into anyone's hands everyday, and he swore to himself to always remember to cherish what he had every day because nothing was promised and the future was ever changing. He fell asleep to the sound of his wife gently breathing next to him as he held a lock of hair around his finger, a smile lingering on his face.

...

The next several weeks passed by in a blur. Arden didn't have much time to do anything other than patrol and wedding plan. He was happy and by the way Willow glowed after her long days helping Fasomalo, he knew she was, too.

"Do you mind being away from your tree until after the wedding?" He had asked her the day after they'd gotten there.

"It's close enough, and it's not a very long walk to get there," she had assured him.

They would stay in Stóngrast until after the wedding, and then most likely transition to here and there for a while. He was still worried about the beast, but since the sightings had all but ceased, he didn't know what else to do besides leave it at the back of his mind. He was far too happy and in love to think about it much, though, and continued on as Commander and came home to Wilmayra every evening after the sun had already gone down.

It was a hard adjustment on Willow, being outside after sunset. She almost refused to go out to the markets with him after he had gotten home one day, and told him it wasn't safe out there. But he reminded her they were in Stóngrast with a wall around the border of the town, with a patrol out at every hour of the day. She had been so used to isolating herself and hiding away that it broke his heart she had ever felt this scared in the first place. He hoped to be able to break her out of that mindset one day, though. By always being by her side when the night came, he hoped to alleviate her worries. He knew that it wouldn't be a problem eventually, as more time passed.

They spent nearly every evening in bed together, and would sometimes wake in the night with the need to feel one another once again. He was sure he was addicted to the taste of her at this point, and could hardly keep his hands off her for even a day. He did notice she was more tired after helping restock the medicinal stores, but attributed it to the longer days they'd had since coming to the port. It was a big adjustment, going from solitude to constant socializing. He knew it had been hard on himself to dive back into it, and felt bad for Willow on the days she was exhausted to the bone after he came home late.

On the day before the wedding, nearly two months after they had introduced Will to his family, Arden had breakfast with Wilmayra before his shift and noticed with surprise that her flowers had taken on a very faint purple hue, darker than he'd ever seen them.

"Your flowers are changing color," he said to her as he sipped his coffee. "I thought they were looking almost pink lately, too, but they are definitely purple now."

"There was a pink tinge to them for sure, but it was hard to tell. The purple surprised me this morning," she laughed, "I had thought it was supposed to happen right after we originally, er," she fumbled with her words, "as they say, 'sealed the deal.'" He couldn't help but laugh when she said that, and kissed her forehead as they sat together.

"Tomorrow's the day," he said softly, feeling nervous suddenly. Willow huffed a breath and leaned back, pushing her plate away.

"It's not too late to run straight for the cottage," she teased.

"No, I'm excited. It's just..." he sighed.

"Me too, I'm feeling very tired lately and my nerves are all catching up to me at once," she leaned her head on his shoulder. "I think it's making me feel queasy, I haven't felt right all week. I'm overthinking the details too much," she grumbled.

"That makes me feel better then, because I am also overthinking the details," he kissed her head again. "I won't see you tonight because of the tradition of not seeing the bride before the ceremony. Seeing you the day of is bad luck," he reminded her gently.

"What if I just close my eyes and you can still sleep in my bed?" She looked up at him hopefully.

"If I can find a way to sneak in, I will, but I think Juna has her guard dog aura on right now and I'm scared to test it," he whispered as he looked around, checking for his sister nearby. Willow laughed, her head tossing back as she smacked the table.

"She did tell me she was watching you and that she knows *everything*," she gasped between giggles, "I wouldn't put it past her to get you for the sake of tradition." Arden only groaned in response and finished his coffee before standing up and offering Wilmayra his arm.

"Walk me to the door?" He asked.

"Of course, husband," she said with a smile. He walked with her to the door both sadly and excitedly, the emotions whirling around inside of him. It was confusing for him, but he knew it was just anxiety making him feel like his mind was swirling around out of control with pent up feelings.

"I'll miss you, but I'll see you tomorrow, my love," he told her sincerely, pulling her to his chest. He kissed her cheeks and her nose before giving her a gentle, loving kiss on her lips. Willow's cheeks glowed pink and for a moment his breath caught in his throat, her beauty astounding him yet again. The flowers had filled out more, with each one holding a gentle gradient of lavender at the base.

With one final hug, he left toward the barracks where he'd get his horse from the stables and return to the wall's borders and take over as lead patrolman. He hoped the day would go quickly for them because he was certain he would be jittery for the rest of the patrol, especially because he wouldn't be able to see Willow tonight. His shift was a later one this time, and she'd most likely be asleep by the time he was done, anyway. He couldn't help but feel lonely at the thought and hoped he'd be able to find a way to sneak into her room at least for a good night's kiss.

He headed to resume as lead Commander for his patrol shift with a full heart and very heavy boots that seemed to want to lead him right back to the woman in the woods, with her beautiful smile and gentle hands.

~ Sixteen ~

A HOME GROWS HERE

Willow watched as Arden walked away, cutting across the town to the furthest end. She hadn't been to that side, yet, as she was either with Fasomalo near the markets or in Arden's home. The weeks had been the fastest time had ever moved for her, even the summers spent with Sian in Lexman Yur had dragged on endlessly. The pain of being separated so abruptly from her family was all consuming and hard to forget about, and so time moved slowly despite having childlike fun with her friends. But since the day they had announced their marriage, it had been a never ending list of things to do, and Wilmayra found herself having the most fun she ever had in her life.

When Arden finally slipped out of her view, she walked back upstairs to get ready for the day. She had to make a few more things for the stores, and then Sian, Teg, and Juna had plans later on in the day. While Willow knew that Juna only wanted to make sure Arden kept out of their room for the night, she knew his sister was excited to spend time with her. She wasn't certain what their night would entail, but most likely there would be tea, warm blankets, and an early bedtime.

As Willow dressed into her work clothes, a gift from Alvenia and Fasomalo, she looked in the mirror at her now purple flowers. She had only just gotten used to having a fuller bloom than before, and wasn't sure how she felt about the change. She was also surprised that it had taken so long to change to a light lavender. From what she remembered of the Binding Prayer, upon consummation it was supposed to change to a full bloom, deep and bright. She couldn't remember what the color was supposed to be, or how the flowers were supposed to look as she hadn't met many tree nymphs like herself in the last several years. She supposed it had to do with her premature birth, though, as it had taken until she met Arden for the bloom to fully erupt. She'd always had leaves and vine-like green in her hair, but since the Binding it changed from tiny, sparse flowers and buds to a full crown of them. And now, with the blooming purple, she felt as though she looked like she was glowing.

"I guess it's a good change," she murmured to herself, running a finger over her pink cheeks, following the freckles that lined them. It was still surprising to see, nonetheless, but it was good timing with the wedding ceremony coming tomorrow morning. She finished pulling her hair out of her face with a braid and tied it into a bun. After donning her apron, she set off down the stairs. She grabbed her bag off the coat rack and reached for the door when she heard footsteps behind her.

"Do you mind if I come with you today?" Juna asked slightly out of breath, having run from her room.

"Of course, I'm going to Fasomalo's first and then to see Sian for lunch," she smiled, glad for the company.

"Oh, good, I wanted to help with the medicine if I could," she linked arms with Willow and they walked down to the street. The sky was overcast and grey, but it was warm and Will knew she was going to be sweating faster than she was used to because of the extra layers of clothing she had to wear in the human port.

"I have a question," Juna said after a minute of walking, "but you can tell me no if you don't want to say."

"You may ask me," Wilmayra replied, curious.

"You're a fae, aren't you?" She turned her head to peer at Willow, though she was younger she was a few inches taller and had to look down. Willow looked up in surprise, immediately pausing her footsteps and stumbling. Juna held tight to her hand to keep her on her feet, to which Willow smiled.

"Thank you," she murmured before walking forward again. "What makes you ask?"

"I don't know, I just know," she shrugged.

"So it's not a question, then," Will giggled.

"No, I guess it's not," she laughed, "I think Arden knows, too," she continued. Wilmayra thought for a moment on how to answer, but found she didn't see a reason why not to tell Arden's sister. After all, they were getting married tomorrow and his family had given their blessing many times already. She assumed that had Juna not approved, she would have said something sooner.

"Well, Juna, you would be right on both accounts," she smiled, looking at her sister-in-law. Juna just blinked, before laughing again.

"I am *always* right about things," she told Will.

"What kind of things are you always right about?" She asked curiously, mind going to Sian unconsciously. Sian had said the exact same phrase to her the first summer they'd met, when Willow had asked about their Gift. They had been a witch blessed with many gifts, but their magical specialties had always been

Shifting and Destruction. They'd also had an unnatural talent for Erilaz, or protection runes, and Illusion. Willow wasn't sure how strong their gift of healing was, as they had never really felt a connection to it the same way Will had.

"Anything, really, I think I can see things coming. As if I'm solving a riddle in my head and can predict a likely outcome," she said, voice sounding as though she didn't know how to explain it, and had never wondered it out loud before.

"As if you have seen it before, almost," Willow asked.

"Actually, yes. It's like I can see multiple scenarios of the same event leading to different outcomes, and my mind will say pick *this* one and I'm just always right," she said in a hushed voice, looking at Willow as if she expected her to run away screaming, certain that she would label her as crazy.

"I think you should talk to Sian about that, when we have lunch later. Tell Sian exactly what you said to me, and they'll understand." Willow squeezed Juna's arm in her's.

"Tell Sian that I'm always right about everything?" Juna furrowed her brows in confusion, making Will laugh.

"Yes, trust me," she said through giggles.

"If you say so," Juna snickered. They walked quietly, lost in thought all the way to the apothecary. Willow knew that if Juna told Sian that exact phrase, they'd agree that there's no doubt that the girl most certainly had witch blood in her. Stóngrast was the closest human-kind trading posts local to Tonsilta, and it wouldn't be the first time a witch from Lexman had made ties with the port, though not in Willow's family. Her father's bloodline stemmed from Lexman, and had met her mother trading nearby their grove. Willow's paternal cousins had all traveled through the Ports at some point in their lives and knew of many witches who ended up growing roots in the human towns, finding families of their own. She wondered what the lineage of the Fairwood family was, and if their ties went back as far as her own. She paused her steps suddenly, an unthinkable thought on her mind.

"What was your mother's name before she was married?" Arden had told her that in human culture, the husband's name typically becomes the family name. In the fae culture, it's typically the childbearing parent that decides the last name. Her family is the Willow family, as her mother and foremothers were all Willow tree nymphs. Her father had been in the Ts'Kadvrok family, a family of weather manipulating witches.

"I think her name was Faelwyn before she married," Juna answered after a moment's thought. Willow let out a breath of relief, grateful at least that Arden wasn't a long lost cousin of some kind.

"Oh good, I do know that family, actually," Willow said. "They had always been regulars when trade was doing better, I would always see them. They were also a part of my education in the early days of my schooling, as they had been the eldest family of the healing Gift and knew more than anyone else," she told Juna who looked at her in surprise as they came to the door of their destination.

"I didn't realize they were so long lived," she answered as Fasomalo came into the room to greet them.

"Hello girls! It's so great to see you, but Willow, didn't I tell you to take a break today?" He teased.

"Oh I just couldn't stay away, and Arden had to help with patrols today since we would be taking what I'm told is called a honeymoon, though I've never heard of it before," she laughed, before she handed Juna a jar and a sheet of labels.

"We are going to fill as many of these as we can with the elderberry and lemon mixture. It's quite tart, but it does help prevent the majority of illnesses and it's also *very* potent and only needs a fingertip dosage," she told Juna as she and the doctor went into the back room where they prepare their medical supplies.

"Let's wash our hands first," Fasomalo said cheerfully before they all made their way to the sink. When they were clean, Juna began to copy labels and instructions on each label before adhering them to the jars, and waited until Willow had filled them and sealed them before adding them. In perfect synchrony, they were able to complete the task in only half of an hour.

"Here, we can all stand to take a bit now," she told them as the bowl emptied into the last jar, leaving behind only what was left still stuck to the sides. Willow dragged her finger through the pureed fruit and showed them how much she grabbed before placing it on her tongue. Juna laughed and swiped some for herself, along with the doctor, and washed their hands again before starting on the next task.

They were able to finish several more tinctures and poultices at the request of some of the town members for some of the ailments they had been dealing with, and even an order for a relative out of town to be delivered.

"I'm not certain if it will make it to its destination, but perhaps the tides are changing and we are entering a new era of peace," Fasomalo murmured hopefully, almost to himself, as he wrapped the parcel delicately.

"It's small enough to look like regular mail, I can't imagine it wouldn't be brought to its home," Juna told him with a hand on his shoulder, "I know it'll be okay," she told him with a glance to Willow. She smiled, and continued sealing the last jar before cleaning up the work space.

In the distance, the church bells rang out in song, a signal that it was midday and time for Willow to meet Sian. She quickly gathered up her bag with a few of each of the medicines, and met Juna at the door to be on their way. Fasomalo stopped them with a hug, before waving them off.

"Have a lovely lunch, and I will see you tomorrow!" He beamed. The girls giggled all the way to the tavern, talking about different wedding details they had been obsessing over for days.

"I can't express how much I love the details in the dress, the seamstress must have an embroidery Gift," Willow told Juna as they pushed open the tavern door and made their way to the seat Willow had been using each time she had lunch with her friend. She knew that Juna didn't come here much, that it wasn't typically her taste with the boisterous drinkers at the bar and the dimly lit room. But she didn't seem to mind as they sat down by the fire, warm yet cool despite the flames, and tried to read the menu in the dark.

"Please tell me you can't see anything in here, either," Juna whispered. Willow threw her head back and laughed, the words Juna said tickling her.

"Oh I can't see a thing, I don't know how Sian does it," she laughed. As if summoned, Sian appeared behind Juna who let out a squeak in surprise before moving over for Sian to sit between them.

"You get used to it, eventually," Sian said stoically, making Juna snort.

"Well, living inside this dark hovel of a place for a decade would definitely make you very well adapted for it," Juna said sagely, a mocking lilt to her voice. Sian slapped a hand onto the table, the other hand grabbing Willow's shoulder as they let out a cackle.

"Oh, I like you," Sian wiped a tear from their eye, before finally glancing at Willow. Sian let out a gasp and almost fell out of the chair, and Willow reached to them in surprise.

"Oh my gods, Sian, are you okay?" She asked, grabbing onto Sian's hand.

"Your flowers!" Sian wheezed, standing up and straightening the chair. When Willow looked up, she saw the Teg brothers standing behind Sian and Juna. She smiled at them in delight but was worried about Sian, and made no move to hug them in greeting. They pulled chairs to their table and sat next to Will and Juna, as Sian clutched Will's hand. Juna sat there with her eyes wide, unsure of what to make of what was going on. Willow felt the same, though she didn't want to cause anyone distress.

"The flowers change to a deeper color when you've consummated the Binding Prayer," she said to Sian, though everyone at the table heard.

"Ew," Juna said with a snicker, making Willow laugh. She shrugged with a grin, but Sian looked at her then, eyebrows scrunched.

"That's not what that means," Sian said.

"Yes it is, isn't it?" Willow murmured, now feeling alarmed. "What else would it mean if not that?" Teggert reached his hand forward, and put it on Willow's wrist. He was the closest brother to her, though Teggrin looked as if he wanted to also hold her hand.

"The flowers bloom white and full after a Prayer Binding," Teggert said in his deep, stone-like voice.

"Yes, but when you've completed the Binding..." Willow trailed off.

"The flowers change color after the Binding is consummated, yes, but that's not why they change color," Teggrin said softly.

"They change color when you are with child, Will," Sian said, looking at her finally, now that they had calmed down. Willow blinked at Sian and Juna, before furrowing her brows and counting back to the last time she had bled. It had been ten weeks since she'd come to the market, and had bled only a week before being with Arden for the first time. Since then, she hadn't had another cycle.

"Oh my gods," Willow said finally, "I'm pregnant," she ran a hand through her hair forgetting it was in a bun and sent flower petals flying. After a pause, Juna spoke.

"Well, at least you and Arden are married," she said with a shrug. Sian looked at Juna oddly, before laughing wildly and reaching for Will. Sian pulled her into a hug, and they stood there for a moment before Juna jumped toward them. She wrapped her arms around them both and laughed.

"How did I not even consider this?" Willow murmured into someone's hair. "I'm a fertility healer," she cried.

"We've been very busy," Juna offered.

"And you never think about yourself before doing anything for others," Sian scolded. Sian pulled back and waved Juna and Willow back into their seats, before running into the kitchens to get some food for them all. When Sian came back, they piled Will's plate up tall and slid it to her.

"Eat it all or I'll flip out," Sian said. Willow laughed obligingly, suddenly starving, and easily dug into the food. After a few moments, the Teg brothers spoke up.

"We have news from the Vesphnion Kagdah that is both worrisome and promising," Teggert said.

"The good news is that we have found a way to cure the injured and poisoned that have been attacked by the Riuvilish - the beast in the forest," Grin said, a chill going up Willow's spine as he said the name.

"We also were able to find a way of protecting the nearby trees of nymphs using an ancient tradition in our father's homeland," Gert explained. "It's an old way of making fabric out of stone that our troll ancestors designed. We were able to recreate it and use it on a poor fae's tree when it had attacked them. Luckily it had been near dawn and no one was hurt beyond a flesh wound."

"You're both of troll descent?" Juna asked curiously, though Willow could see goosebumps on her arms that showed the girl was more afraid of the turn in the conversation than she wanted to let on. Grin nodded at her with a wink before Will spoke again.

"What's the bad news?" Willow didn't want to know, but she *needed* to know. Juna looked at her sadly as if she knew what the answer was.

"The bad news is that the beast is turning away from the Kagdah," Gert said.

"We imagine it can only travel at night, and so it's moving slower than a typical beast, but it is still *very* fast," Grin added. "My brother has been in Hanlan, listening for fae that have been injured or worse, so that we may better protect those of our kind," he looked pointedly at Willow, and she knew that they had been doing everything they could to protect her from this evil thing that would be knocking on her door in a matter of weeks, or days even.

"After the wedding, we will go to your tree and bind it for you, we will wrap it with the stone cloth, or Textile Sarsen, we have made so far," they looked down at their hands and Willow noticed the blisters and the freshly healed slices on their fingers. She immediately dug through her bag and handed them pain relief and healing ointments, and they wordlessly applied them to their worn out fingers.

"It's a taxing task, despite being of Troll blood," Gert winked at Juna like his brother had, making Juna laugh quietly in response.

"We need a few more days to get enough Sarsen to wrap around your tree, we only have enough to cover a bough but that won't be very helpful to us. I wish I had been able to cover your tree before coming here, I didn't have enough time to loop back around and also make it to my brother in time with the information we needed -" Willow reached over the table and put her hand on Grin's.

"You've been helping the injured while also finding a way to keep me safe without jeopardizing others' safety. You have found ways to protect a fae from an evil beast who's name I can't even speak out loud or my bones feel like ice," Willow told the brothers in a sincere voice, "and now we will wait and acquire what we need in order to keep protecting everyone we care about." She unconsciously put a hand to her belly, scared for the baby she only just realized she was carrying. She would protect this small life with everything she had in her being, no matter what. "Sarsen sounds tedious to make, and I'm sure is a skill only possible by the hands of a troll," she said, almost a question.

"You would be right about that," the brothers said together.

"Then we will take as much time as you need to, to make what you need to make. Just give me a recipe to make for the poison antidote, or whatever you need *me* to make," She said firmly. Teggert reached into his pocket and pulled out a sheet of paper, and handed it to her. Willow squinted at the recipes and made a face when she realized what the ingredients meant.

"A sleep potion?" She asked, as she continued to read on to the antidote recipe.

"You'll have to take my word for this, but the poison acts as an *incredibly* painful toxin. To entice the prey out of hiding," Gert explained, "the poison will make the victim scream out until the Riuvilish is able to uncover where the fae is hiding to finish them off. The fae I helped had been sliced around their hip and was in so much pain, I could hardly bear it," he finished sadly.

"So you have to knock them out if they're attacked," Juna said.

"Completely incapacitate them as soon as the beast begins to attack the tree. It doesn't want to kill them, it wants to lure fae out so it is able to *eat* them. Which means, if we can keep the fae quiet, it will limit the amount of wounds it inflicts on the tree itself. It seems to know the difference in ways to maim as opposed to dealing a lethal blow," Gert said. "But the poison itself is lethal if left untreated, should the beast move on to another fae that takes the bait, the previous fae would succumb to their wounds unless the antidote is given swiftly."

"How long would someone survive until then?" Sian asked.

"We don't know, exactly, as there has been a range in the amount of deaths we've seen. Not a single fae had the same level of injuries, or the same amount of toxins in their system when they were found." Grin paused before adding, "The ones that were able to hide until the sun rose were the only bodies we were able to find at all." They all shuddered at the thought, and Willow held her hands to her belly again.

"What about the other thing we talked about - has that been successful?" Sian said after a few quiet moments.

"Yes, it has proven to be successful. Stóngrast will be safe because of this," Grin told them.

"What will keep the port safe?" Juna leaned forward toward Sian, her hands white as she clasped them together nervously.

"I think I mentioned it to Willow long ago, but the beast seems to be unable to cross stone and other hard earth elements, like gems and amulets," Gert began. His brother continued for him, their voices nearly identical.

"Stóngrast was built many, many generations ago. In the in-terim, there have been families of witches, mages, and fae that have made their homes here, and one of the things the matri-archs of Sian's bloodline were able to begin were sigils and runes to protect the members of the town by encasing every foot of this land in stone." Gert explained.

"Because the town was built on stone, I was able to work with Sian in creating the perfect protection rune on a large scale, completely underground in the form of a tunnel system," Grin took a sip of water, and Willow realized again how hungry she was and began to pick at her food despite the queasiness in her belly. "The Teg bloodline is the eldest of trolls and we have been blessed with the gift of manipulating the earth in such a way that we've completed the tunnels quite easily, and completed that which hadn't been done before."

"So even if the beast is strong enough to penetrate stone, it would still be unable to enter the port," Gert added.

"And because of Sian's ability to create the perfect rune for any situation, Sian was able to protect and prevent the demise of hundreds of fae in the Kagdah by having me recreate the runes on a larger scale while Sian stayed here with Grin to help protect our home here. Around the base of the trees I manipu-lated the stones underground to mirror the sigils, so as to keep the protection spells hidden. This has been the final piece we've been able to find to protect our families, and have given as many of the fae as we can in our travels from there to here with these preventative measures." He concluded.

"But the runes will only work if they're wide enough to en-compass the furthest branches of the trees, so anything outside of the circle would be accessible to the beast," Sian looked at Willow as they spoke. "I am hoping the fae that were given a drawing of the rune were able to successfully recreate it with their own stones on their own," Sian added.

"I can't believe this," Juna murmured to herself as she looked at her hands. Willow immediately felt awful for having brought her to lunch today. She hadn't known the direction the conversation would go, and indeed a lot of information was uncovered.

"I'm sorry, Juna," she said, and tried to reach a hand to her. The table was too wide, but Grin and Sian each took one of her hands and gently held it within their own. She smiled gratefully and squeezed their fingers.

"No, don't be sorry, I'm glad you're here and not in the forest. I've had a bad feeling about the woods for what feels like years at this point, but couldn't explain it," she told Will, "and after Arden's broken heart over the Cahlin tragedy, I wasn't willing to entertain thoughts of the forest beyond the emotion of fear. So many victims over the last year, but no explanations and no hope. The port was dying, I could feel it, and had nothing to hold on for - but life goes on, and so do we all, and I tried to help my mother and brother as best as I could," Juna said solemnly. "I knew he found you after the first time he came home, and I was *so* grateful to see the light back in his eyes. He holds himself to a way too high standard, and I couldn't get through to him. But you did," she said with a watery smile. Willow laughed and tried not to tear up at her words.

"Trust me, your brother is more stubborn than anyone I've ever met. He did not easily allow me to get through to him at all," she snickered. "And for a moment, I didn't think he'd want to try," she said thoughtfully as she thought back to the day he told her he was ready to get marriage over with. "He came around eventually, but I was worried about how dense he could be," she grinned. Juna burst out laughing, Willow knew it was a combination of nerves and relief at the same time. Sian chuckled too, and they finally finished their now cold plates before they looked at the Teg brothers expectantly.

"There is actually another thing we have to discuss," Gert told them while looking at Willow, "Willow do you have the dagger I gave you?" Her heart skipped a beat as she thought about the dagger, of how it felt almost alive.

"Yes," she said hesitantly, before reaching into her bag and finding the deepest pocket, and slid it from where she had hidden it for the last few months. She had been carrying it around silently, afraid of being without it. Gert took the wrapped blade and handed it to Grin. He reached for something in his pocket and drained it over the cloth. The dagger seemed to glow for a moment before fading, and they handed it back to Wilmayra who sat in astonishment.

"This dagger is the only thing left that is capable of ending Riuvilish permanently," they said simultaneously, their demeanor icy and solemn. It felt like the room had dropped ten degrees in that single moment.

"It seems that the last time this creature was seen, it was not properly dealt a finishing blow. It can only be killed by piercing it in the heart. It can be injured by any kind of weapon, but it will heal itself quickly depending on how large of a wound it was. We may be able to make a potion that can incapacitate it but it has grown stronger and I am not sure we could make anything strong enough to match it," Grin said.

"But, I do have ideas on where we can find that information," Gert nodded. "Check with the apothecary and their oldest books of recipes. I think we'd be able to find it in the Faelwyn directory." Juna perked up at the mention of the name, and glanced at Sian. Willow knew she wanted to mention it, could see the words on her lips, but paused. Willow could tell that she would wait until she thought the moment was right.

"The last thing we have to tell you is this: only a treeborn fae is able to wield the dagger," Grin looked at Willow sadly as he took in her flowers, and the hand resting over her tummy protectively. "I know what this means, and I wouldn't wish this on you. But our lives have all led us here and we all seem to have a purpose in the near future to protect the lives of those we love most. I only hope we are able to work together to ensure both of your safety, and the safety of others for many generations to come."

"Give us a few days to complete the Sarsen, and work on the antidote on as large of a scale as you can on such short notice. After your wedding, and we have what we need, we will all go to your tree." Gert concluded.

"We have an idea on what we can do to capture the beast, but everything needs to be aligned," Grin agreed.

"Wait, I have two questions," Willow said as she reached a hand out to Gert. "What did you pour on the dagger?" Willow asked quietly as she held it in her hand, wondering at the weight of it. The gentle hum that came from the strange hilt was both unsettling and comforting.

"A wake-up tonic, so to speak," Grin smiled, "it is very old magic, that blade, and after centuries have passed it needed a little something."

"A little something to give it the strength it needs to help you fulfill this impossible task," Gert finished.

"My other question is, only Treeborns can wield it, right?" She asked. They nodded slowly so she continued, "the both of you are also Treeborn. Why do I have to be the one to deal the final blow?" They glanced at each other and frowned before Teggrin reached for the blade and unwrapped it. He placed the bare dagger on his palm as he held the hilt in the opposite hand.

The blade that was just seemingly alive in her hand, thrumming and gently glowing, was now silent and dark.

"We are of Troll blood," Grin said, "and have too much stone in our blood to be truly Treeborn in the way it's important. The blade won't respond to our magic simply because Trolls aren't fae. The magic we have is different, it stems from something different. Your father is a witch, yes, but he is fae no matter what." He paused for a moment as she blinked at him, a bitter understanding of what he was saying finally making sense to her. "A Treeborn and a fae made you, a Treeborn fae, and so your blood is connected to what lies within this hilt. So long as the tree nymph bloodline is there, it doesn't matter if myself, my brother, and you, are only half tree nymph. You are still entirely fae born and have the magic that the blade needs to work."

"Why aren't trolls considered fae?" Juna asked as she looked at Will. Will looked to the ceiling to avoid seeing anyone's reaction to her expression as her face crumpled, knowing what he was going to say.

"Trolls and Trees are opposites, rocks are simply too hard, heavy, and unyielding compared to the adaptability of a tree. Our magic lies deep within the earth and Will's comes from within her core - a place we all *feel* more than see. We reach deep underground in similar ways but we come from different worlds. We are just not compatible with this specific type of magic. And so, it falls to you, my dear," Grin finished as they sat there and looked at eachother. Sian cleared their throat, hands sliding across the table.

"I know this isn't the best time to ask, but may I *please* hold the dagger?" Sian said, eyes wide. Teggrin smiled obligingly and handed it over. Sian gasped as they looked over the hilt, running a hand over the gemstones. They leaned closer, eyebrows raised in curiosity as Sian stared into the blade.

"This stone," they said reverently, "this is fire opal. If you look closely, there's a sigil inside of the opal. It almost looks like it grew that way," Sian's eyes twinkled. "It really looks like..." they trailed off for a moment with wonder on their face.

"What?" breathed Juna, inching closer.

"This fire opal has *my* family sigil on it," they whispered.

"Oh yes, the first witches, nymphs, and humans all collaborated on this dagger. The magic infused was stemmed right from both of your ancestors," Gert told them, his voice rumbling.

"I can't believe this," Sian stroked a finger over the opal, before continuing their observation of the knife. "This stone is smokey quartz, and this one is honey calcite. They both have different sigils inside of them, too, maybe from the other witch's families," the gems twinkled as Sian stared at them, taking in their beauty and details. The blade was quiet but the magic in the stones sang to Sian, you could see it in the way they held the hilt, fingers trailing over each stone.

"What's the last stone?" Juna asked, head nearly bumping Sian's as they both tried to get a closer look.

"This isn't a stone, it's amber. Fossilized tree sap," Sian explained, "if this dagger was made with a tree limb, which it certainly looks that way, the sap was maybe made during the forging."

"I've never seen a sword with that pattern on it," Juna murmured, reaching a hand out to run along the metal.

"This is Damascus steel, an old forging technique now nearly lost to time," Sian said. "It's very old and in our current environment in Kronevalta, there's a heavy need for easy and consistently produced weaponry. It naturally tapered off, though it is still very popular in various Ports, and especially in the Royal Guard."

As Sian spoke, Willow rubbed her eyes for a moment and tried collecting her thoughts. She leaned her elbows on the table and rested her face in her hands, sighing deeply. Every bone in her body suddenly felt as heavy as stone, just as solid as the tile beneath her feet. She wanted to find Arden and tell him everything, right that second, and run screaming into the forest to save her tree and start their family the *right* way, without fearing the creatures lurking in the dark.

"I'd offer you a drink, but, considering your current state, here's some tea," Sian said quietly. Willow looked up blearily and accepted the tea Sian gently placed on the table. She noticed Juna sitting next to her, the Teg brothers gone. They must have left while she was lost in her emotions, letting her take in everything they had explained without pushing her. She was grateful Juna sat there stoically, looking as though she were on guard and ready to protect Willow from whatever may come their way. She slid her hand across the table and held Juna's fingers, the same size as her own, and wiped the tears she didn't notice until then that were drying on her cheeks.

"Whatever we have to do, we can do it together," Juna said softly. "Arden will do whatever he has to, and so will we," she told Willow. Sian sat back down with more tea, a heavier brew for themselves and Juna, offering her the mug. Juna took it and sipped it gratefully, before she looked to Sian and quirked an eyebrow at Willow. Willow snorted, but nodded that now was a good time despite the raging storm inside her.

"How do you know that, Juna?" Willow played along.

"I'm just always right about everything," she laughed, and looked at Sian expectantly. Sian spit the mouthful of tea out of their mouth in surprise, and looked at Willow with wide eyes as they wiped their face.

"Okay, we're going to have to talk *a lot* more after we deal with the whole wedding and this beast situation," Sian said finally. "And maybe take a trip to Lexman at some point," they added before delicately sipping their tea again, trying not to spray the table a second time.

"I told you," Willow snickered, as Juna laughed.

"Well now I want to know about Lexman, what's that?" Juna asked.

"It's a school for people like us," Sian said. "Not specifically a school but there is an actual school that's there."

"I'm also wondering about Alvenia and Arden - they must have Gifts, too," Willow said thoughtfully.

"Oh of course, my mother definitely has something too. And Arden, I'm not sure. He rarely lets on what he's thinking or planning so it's hard to see if he has anything *magical* about him," Juna thought out loud.

"Oh, I'm sure there's *something* magical about him, eh, Twig?" Sian said with a sneaky glance at Will, their expression teasing. Juna howled laughing before pretending to gag, making Willow giggle.

"Well, maybe he does," she said, pretending to toss her hair over her shoulder. They all laughed before quieting down.

"I have to tell him," Willow said, one hand still resting on her tummy. The urge to run after him during patrol was all consuming though she knew it was a bad idea.

"He won't be home until the sun's down - but he promised he wouldn't be in the woods after sunset. He said he would be training in the barracks," Juna told them. "I think he and my mother are also having lunch today together, to talk about our father coming in for the wedding." Will looked at her in surprise and wondered about why she was having a meeting to tell Arden about that, and had waited until they hadn't been home to do so.

"I'm imagining she didn't tell you, and you 'just knew' that was happening," Sian said with a laugh. Juna only grinned and nodded.

"Arden doesn't have a good relationship with your father, does he?" Willow asked, not wanting to pry but curious all the same.

"He has an idea of what he thinks my parents' relationship is, but he's wrong," Juna nodded. "He thinks he abandoned her and left for the King's Guard because he didn't want to marry her. But the truth is, neither of them wanted to marry *anybody* and so married each other as friends in order to keep the lifestyles they preferred," Juna explained. They looked at her with intrigue, unconsciously leaning forward as they listened to the gossip. "I shouldn't know, but I do, and that's why I have no problem telling you two now - you understand that I'm not 'making up stories,' or something," she paused while they nodded at her. It was clear to both Sian and Willow that she had a Gift of Knowing, intuition and a grasp on what was true and real, a Gift that was indeed very strong. Juna continued, "they still talk as much as they've been able to and even have their own messenger birds they've used for years to talk. Arden thinks they have a love-less marriage due to the distance, but they do love each other. It's just not the same as the way you two love each other, and that's why he's upset. For our mother's sake, he wants her to be treated the way he thinks a wife should be treated. But mother is very happy the way things are and so is father," she finished.

"Do you know why they like it the way it is?" Willow asked, wanting to understand better but not quite grasping it.

"Oh, wait, Alvenia doesn't like the company of men, does she?" Sian asked.

"No, she doesn't like the company of *anybody*," Juna clarified, to which Sian and Will both exclaimed.

"Oh, that makes sense," they said together before laughing.

"And your father?" Will asked

"Well, I haven't been outright told, but the last time he was here I saw him wink at his Guardsman, so I'm imagining he's also quite happy where he is, too," Juna laughed before sipping her tea innocently. Sian and Will threw their heads back and laughed, the stark contrast of the earlier conversation almost gave Will whiplash but she held tight to the laughter as it was desperately needed in order to keep herself from crying again. Her thoughts circled back to the small life she was growing, and she once again fought the urge to run after Arden and find him and tell him everything.

"Don't worry, if we see him tonight when he gets home we will tell him," Juna said as she saw Willow's face, "and if we fall asleep before then, I can tell him in the morning for you if you want me to."

"That's kind of you," Sian murmured as they looked at Will.

"No, the wedding is only at ten o'clock so I wouldn't have to wait that long. I just feel like I'm lying to him if I don't tell him right this second," she confessed, the guilt sitting heavy on her chest.

"We only found out hours before the wedding, and have no way of contacting him safely, I promise you this is not you keeping secrets," Juna told her sternly. Sian nodded in agreement and stood, offering their hand.

"Let's maybe take a walk and see about those recipes," they suggested. Willow smiled and stood, taking their hand and Juna's in her own before walking out of the tavern.

"Do you have to tell anyone you're leaving?" Will asked.

"Oh, you know no one is going to say a word about me not being here. They're too scared to even say my name, let alone reprimand me for not pouring the ale," they laughed.

"You've got a good point, there," giggled Juna as they stepped into the sun, "but are you sure you won't melt under the bright sky?" She laughed, making Sian roll their eyes. Sian let out a laugh though, and nodded in appreciation at the jab.

"Good one," they snickered as the trio walked toward Fasomalo's store. Will noticed the sky was still cloudy and after being in the dimly lit tavern, it was drastically brighter outside and Willow's eyes burned at the sudden change. She laughed quietly to herself at Juna's teasing, also wondering how Sian was able to stand the light at all. Sian looked over the recipes as they walked.

"We can definitely make a lot of this today, it doesn't look complicated," they said, mirroring Will's thoughts. "I can also do this during the wedding and during the party, just for peace of mind, if you'd like," they offered. For a moment, Willow felt bad for wanting to accept their help, but she knew Sian wouldn't suggest it unless they meant it.

"It would actually make me feel better if you made as much as you could," she accepted the offer gratefully. "If you want to come, though, you know I'd love you to be there. But, we already are married and it's more symbolic than anything so I don't want you to feel as though you're missing out," she said softly, as they paused at the door. "And our outfits are ready to go, you just have to pick it up. I think you'll like them," Willow smiled. It wouldn't be the first time that Sian stayed up all night and also went to a celebration the following day. Willow had seen Sian stay awake for three days, once, and she had been so scared for Sian's safety, she finally tricked them into drinking a sleeping tonic.

"Thank you for saying that, it does actually make me feel better. I do want to go, though, so I'll be having an energy tonic tonight," Sian laughed.

"I think you need to make as much as you can, as fast as you can," Juna said abruptly, in a serious tone. Her face seemed to change for a moment before she realized what she said. She put a hand over her mouth, a confused expression on her face. "I'm sorry, I don't know why I said that," she murmured as her cheeks turned pink. Will and Sian looked at each other seriously, knowing immediately that it was the Gift speaking directly through Juna.

"I'll be staying up all night to make sure we have it in excess," Sian nodded to Juna before continuing, "but I will still go to the wedding even if I don't sleep," Sian laughed. Willow felt relieved, but felt bad Sian would take so much time to do this for her. Her veins felt icy, drained, as she thought about Sian not making enough, and also of Sian not being at the wedding with her. She was scared, absolutely terrified, of what this would mean should there not be enough antidote because Sian stayed for the ceremony, but knew she needed her friend in both places at once, no matter how impossible it felt. She knew it would only be a matter of time before the beast came back to her tree. How many days, weeks, or even *hours* more would it take for it to be here?

"Thank you Sian, I know it's asking a lot of you to stay up all night *and* go to the wedding, but I don't think I could do it without you there for me," Willow admitted softly as she glanced at Sian.

"I'll be at the wedding even if I drink every last energy tonic in the Port," Sian said solemnly. Willow couldn't help but laugh at that before rolling her eyes.

"No, you will not," she told Sian with a laugh, before gripping their hand tight. "Even without the beast lurking around my tree, I'm still dealing with the terror of the mere *idea* of being wed in front of so many people watching. It seems impossible, especially when I'm holding in so many secrets. I really need you there," she told Sian. Sian smiled and gave Will a much needed hug, the two clinging together as Juna rubbed Will's back. After a minute, they separated and finally stepped into the apothecary. They found it empty, with a note on the counter from Fasomalo stating he'd be back this evening. They collected the ingredients that had already been stored in the pantry thanks to the doctor, and began making the antidote.

"Why don't you make the sleep tonic and Juna can help me with the antidote? You look like you need some time to yourself, but I don't want you to feel alone," Sian offered gently. Will smiled gratefully, knowing she really didn't have the energy to talk anymore for right now. She sighed and set off to make the tonic, squeezing Sian's shoulder as she walked past them.

After she had what she needed, she began mixing the Moon Milk in the mortar, grinding the cherries and other herbs and spices to make the strongest sleep medicine she'd ever seen before. It was slightly different from the gentle one she would give someone for insomnia, in the way that it was purely a knock-out shot of a viscous liquid. Blood red from the cherries and sharp scented from the ginger, she knew it would be a terrible taste should she ever have to use it. She shuddered at the thought, continuing to grind the pestle until everything was fully combined and pureed.

They continued this way for what felt like hours, though was closer to only forty-five minutes. Fasomalo made it back into the building before long, and Sian told him what they needed to do.

"Can you show me the Faelwyn Directory?" Juna asked him, before he led her to the book shelves he kept in his office. Willow remembered a lot about that room, though she didn't use it much, but the thing she loved most about it were the book-shelves. Stacked all the way to the ceiling, there were hundreds of books from long ago. Staring at those books, she was over-come with disbelief that she'd stayed in her cottage alone all these years. Suddenly, Willow's belly clenched at the thought of having moved to the Hanlan Outpost that Gert had suggested so long ago. She remembered the feeling of terror at the thought of Arden making it all the way to the cottage and finding it completely empty as he was left to fend for himself in Tonsilta on his own. She tried to shake the thought from her head, as it was useless to think about a what-if scenario that would never have occurred as she had been in love with Arden from the first moment he placed his hands over her bark.

The ache in her stomach changed from dread to nausea so quickly, she almost didn't realize in time that she needed to vomit. She jumped out of her seat quickly with a hand over her mouth as she ran for the small bathroom. She didn't even have time to shut the door before she started heaving into the toilet. Tears came to her eyes as she purged the meal Sian had given her, the sting in her throat unbearable. After her stomach settled, she leaned back from kneeling on the toilet and blew her nose as tears fell quickly down her cheeks. She knew she was making noises, but she couldn't control them. She only held her tummy and wept as she sat on the cold floor, and noticed someone come in from behind her.

"Here's some water and an antacid," Juna murmured as she sat down on her knees next to Willow. "Are you feeling okay now?"

"I think I'm okay," she said shakily, "I really want to tell your brother about the baby, and I'm also very scared," she told Juna honestly.

"I know, it's good that you're scared," she leaned her head on Will's shoulder. "It means you'll be prepared for whatever will come next. Arden will know as soon as the time is right, whether tonight or tomorrow - he will know. And we will keep our family and our home safe," Juna's voice was soft and re-assuring. She sounded older beyond her years, though she was just shy of twenty years old, her birthday only a few months away. Wilmayra was only a few years older, her twenty-third birthday quickly approaching though she rarely noticed when it came and went after living alone for so long. The need for a calendar was almost non-existent, and any trading at Hanlan always coincided with the moon phase as opposed to a date and time. She only ever kept track of the years by noting when the seasons changed, and by then she knew the date of her birth had come and gone. She was a summer baby, and though she never really knew what day it was, she celebrated for herself when autumn came, as seasons were the only sign she had for the passing of time.

They sat on the floor for a few minutes together as Willow cried softly, not even sure how or why she was crying at all anymore, but supposed it was all catching up to her and her emotions hit a breaking point and needed to be released. Juna's soft strokes on her back were soothing, and she leaned her cheeks on her knees until she was able to calm herself down. She sighed and blew her nose on some of the tissue paper, and wiped her eyes. She sniffed the air and looked around, realizing she smelled ginger tea.

"Sian said she'd make a pot for your upset stomach," Juna murmured as she saw her sniff. "We know it might not do any-thing if it's just morning sickness, but we didn't know what else to do," she continued rubbing Will's back.

"Thank you," Willow told her honestly, also not knowing what to do but grateful for their support in the only way they knew how. Finally, Willow found the strength to stand and they made their way to Sian and Fasomalo as they sat around the small fireplace with a teapot and cups and offered them some when they emerged. They smiled softly at her as they all shared the quiet moment. After their cups were empty, they wordlessly were shooed off by the doctor.

"I wrote down copies of the recipes you're compiling, I'll work on them for you tonight and make as much as I can," he told them, "I'll bring them to Sian when they're complete."

"I'll take the recipe too, and do the same," Sian told Willow, pocketing what they were able to make in the short time they had been there. Sian pulled Will into a tight hug, kissing her cheek gently.

"I won't tell you not to worry, because I think it's safe to say none of us will be able to keep from worrying. But know that we will do whatever we need to do to keep you and your baby safe," Sian told her. Will sniffled into Sian's shoulder and nodded, grateful to hear those words.

"Thank you," she whispered. She felt tears pricking at her eyes and knew if she spoke any louder, she'd cry again. It seemed she had cried more today than she had in months, and was not in the mood to cry for a third time.

"I'll do whatever you need me to, as well, Miss Willow," Fasomalo said in his chirpy voice, always a smile on his lips. She let go of Sian to smile at him, and noticed his eyes held just a bit of sadness in them. She hugged him, too, giving him a squeeze before reaching her arm out to Juna. They linked their elbows and made their way back home, the sun still high in the sky. Wilmayra knew it was getting close to suppertime, the midday heat finally tapering off as the air cooled. A wave of nausea hit her again, but she ignored it and prayed to make it to their house before she needed to be sick. She just wanted a glass of water and to lay in the dark for a while, completely wrapped up in blankets and hide away from the world.

When they made it inside, they made a beeline for the kitchen where Will drank glass after glass of water. Juna giggled after the third glass was emptied, almost making Willow spit the water out as she laughed, too.

"Gods, I cannot believe this day is happening," Willow said as she burped after drinking a fourth glass of water.

"And I can't believe you're going to wet the bed," Juna snickered. "Who drinks that much water at once?" She burst out laughing as she sat on a nearby stool. Will giggled, suddenly hungry as well.

"I need snacks, or dinner," she told Juna, making her laugh harder.

"It's going to be a long pregnancy, I suppose," Juna replied. "Go upstairs and I'll find someone to make us dinner. The last time I tried, Arden yelled at me for using too much salt," she grinned. "It was *awful,* but the way he coughed and hollered was worth it."

"You're such a little sister," Will laughed before heading upstairs. After a while, Juna came up with a large plate of food, and a basket of bread. They ate everything at the table by the window in Arden's room. It had become Will's safe place and she didn't want to be far from Arden's scent that lingered throughout the room.

"Do you want me to find Arden, or send a message for him?" Juna asked as they looked out the window and watched the sun set behind the houses.

"No," Willow sighed, "it's okay. He would worry too much and probably not let me out of his sight. I think it would mess up the traditions, he would want to see me in the morning, too," she said sadly.

"Will, those traditions are not actually important. I can find him right now if you want me to, a superstition is not a good reason to keep you from your actual husband the day before a ceremonial wedding. You're already married," Juna urged, and Willow looked at her in surprise for a moment. She sighed again, knowing she would love to have Arden hold her tonight, the fear of the beast almost too strong for her to even consider closing her eyes in the dark all alone. But she knew that even if they already were married, this was important to Arden. While he didn't love the idea of being separated until tomorrow, she knew he had been excited to have a wedding of his own with his culture's traditions. And she wanted to give him that, the only thing he'd asked for this whole time had been for an early hour wedding, and to wear his formal uniform.

"No, Arden was excited about all of it, I can't break the tradition just because I'm scared. I do have a question for you, though, and I'll understand if you say no. I won't feel bad at all, so don't feel like you have to," she told Juna.

"What do you need?" Juna asked.

"I'm scared of the dark, and was hoping you'd sleep in here with me tonight," she said sheepishly, feeling like a child for asking at all. Juna laughed, and raised her eyebrows.

"If the sheets have been replaced *today* I'll sleep in here with you," she said and pretended to gag. Will could only laugh, before glancing at the bed to see a whole different set of blankets than the ones that were there when she had left in the morning. They were all a soft yellow, and this morning they had been blue.

"They're different sheets," she snickered. She went to the bathroom before changing into her pajamas, a long nightgown, and slid into the bed. Juna went to her room for her own pajamas, and came back with a tray of snacks and books, and a set of candles.

"I thought we might need these," she said as she bit into a cookie Felisia and her son made. Will dug into the snacks and laughed as she nodded.

"We definitely needed them," she said through a mouthful of chocolate chip cookies, the best thing she'd ever tasted in her life. They ate the snacks before leaning back on the pillows with the books that Juna had brought them. Will laid it on her chest as she looked out the window on her side of the room and stared at the stars.

"I don't actually know the last time that I saw the night sky," Willow admitted.

"I'm sorry," Juna murmured as she scooted closer to peer out the window, too.

"I've been so afraid of the dark that I can't even believe I ever went outside during the night before, willingly. I think it's actually warping my thinking, the fear just never goes away. And right now, I keep wondering, is it tonight that the beast will find me again?" She whispered, reaching to her candle to blow it out and sat in the dark. "My home has been boarded up, no sun or light in any room at all. I hadn't been able to use my fireplace, for the fear of it becoming a beacon to the creature and telling it exactly where I'm hiding," she vented, and Juna took her hand. "And I can remember it's horrible face," she said in a harsh voice, a shudder going up her spine at the memory.

"You saw it before?" Juna gasped, peering at Will in the near dark as her candle sat on the side table.

"Yeah, one time. I told Arden about it after some of my friends said it was just a bear. But because of Arden, I realized it was way more than that. It had these awful, awful eyes. Pupils that went up and down instead of like our own. And it looked like a bear, but it was *huge*. And it was just, looking into my cottage without blinking and I was scared to even move so I sat in my doorway without even a muscle twitch, just waiting for it to go away. Before sunrise, it ambled off but it was the longest night of my life and I haven't had the shutters open at night, since," Willow finally finished. Juna shuddered next to her, the chill up Will's spine must have traveled to her, too, the fear palpable in the air.

"I couldn't even hear its name spoken today without wanting to cry," Juna told her honestly.

"It was disturbing, I felt like it was watching me as soon as its name was mentioned." She trembled at the memory as goose-bumps trailed up her arms.

"Do you want to stay awake and wait for Arden to get home?" Juna asked. "I'm sure he'll be here soon, it's still pretty early."

"I'll try to stay awake, I don't remember being this tired before," Willow yawned as she opened the book, an old apothecary recipe list for things she already knew but there were a handful that were new. She flipped through the pages, wondering what the ingredients would be and started laughing as she realized it was a mix of herbs that couldn't possibly be used for what the recipe entailed.

"What is it?" Juna asked curiously.

"These are really silly ingredients, for what they say the use is for. This one is supposed to be a remedy for a headache, but it has only ingredients for an upset stomach. And this one is supposed to be for sleep, but it is a caffeinated tea with cham-omile which is not exactly a good idea to drink at night if you want to feel sleepy, even if it does have *one* sleepy ingredient," she said as she flipped through more pages. "There's also not a single recipe in here for menstruation cramping and pain man-agement, which is unheard of in a text like this where I went to school. It's just very interesting to see the difference in the healing methods from here and there."

"I guess I never really noticed," Juna murmured as she peered at the book in a new light. Willow yawned again and rubbed her eyes before she closed the book and laid it on the end table. She rolled over, facing the window. She never liked to have her back to them while she slept, so typically curled herself toward them to keep them in front of her. Juna yawned too but kept turning through pages as Willow dozed, the day catching up to her.

"Goodnight," she whispered.

"Goodnight, in the morning Annie and Alise will wake us up to get ready for the wedding," Juna warned her about their early schedule.

"Thank you," she replied. Within minutes, Willow fell asleep to the sound of Juna's breathing and the book's pages rhythmically being leafed through.

~ Seventeen ~

CEREMONY

Arden spent the day going over patrol scheduling and training the new recruits, having been given a shift of busywork to hold him over until the wedding ceremony. His fellow officers had wanted to make sure he was safe until the wedding, knowing that the forest had been a hotspot of violence and tragedy in the last year. Arden would have been able to handle himself, of course, but they all had told him that they loved Willow for what she did for everyone and made sure to give Arden an 'easy' day. He would have argued, but they had all been telling Arden what the mothers had explained in the market the first day, their fears absolved and their children safe. They also told him that since she had brought those resources, the physician had been readily stocked with all of the supplies consistently.

Fasomalo and Willow had decided that the only monetary trading they would accept for the medicine would be what the ingredients cost on their own, plus the time it took to be prepared. It wasn't much that they were asking for even with the cost of labor, and Arden was concerned. Arden knew this was unfailingly kind on Willow's part, but part of him thought it would open the doors to financial issues. He had mentioned it to Willow once, but was surprised by her response to his suggestion.

"Why would it be a bad idea to make everything affordable?" She asked.

"Well, if your product is high quality, it should be charged at a higher price, right?" He had asked her back. She pursed her lips, before effectively silencing him as he pondered her thoughtful words.

"By making medical care expensive, you're telling the poor and the sick that their needs don't matter. The only ones who would suffer are the working class in this port - their children would die off quickly without a doctor, and their families would fall into debt because a child had a simple fever. Fevers are easy to cure, but they can take the lives of those young and weak. Would you go to the poor, hard working citizens of your home and tell them personally their sick, dying baby is not going to live simply because they were a few dollars short of the fare? Would you tell your soldiers their health means little to you should they also fall ill?" She raised her brows at him, and he kept his mouth sealed.

He never spoke out on it again, and now knew that Willow didn't see her skills as a way to make a profit. She only sought out to help those in need, no matter their living situation. He also felt guilty for having thought of it in a way that was so oppositional to Willow's views, his perception so black and white on the topic. He wondered at his own mindset, that he'd been prepared to insist she have some sort of capital gain from the business, completely overlooking the implication that there would be a family in the port that *couldn't* afford the care they needed to be healthy. That would have set a dangerous precedent in the community, a stark contrast between the upper and lower classes and the already crumbling society would not have survived it. There had already been too much loss, both in funds and in populous, due to the attacks. Arden was grateful for everything Willow had done for them all, but most especially himself, as he felt like a new human being with her by his side.

He checked the clock on the wall as he finished more paperwork and scheduling shifts, and waited for his mother to drop in for lunch. As the Commander, he had a small office in the barracks commissary building, and was able to take meetings there. Willow had all but refused to come this far into the port, but he only laughed. He didn't particularly care for this place, and it wasn't a loss to him that she didn't want to be there.

Arden found himself staring out the window, holding the handkerchief Willow had given him so long ago now. He always found it in his hand when his thoughts would race, finding comfort in the small thing. He realized he heard footsteps in the hallway approaching his door and tucked the handkerchief away before standing to greet his mother as she opened the door, but was taken aback when she saw who entered behind him.

"Father," he said.

"It's me," the man agreed solemnly, almost waiting for Arden to yell. Arden sighed and ran a hand through his hair before gesturing to the chairs in the office. He of course knew his mother had a reason for calling him to Stóngrast and would wait to hear it before raising his voice if necessary. He figured he also needed to hear the man out, as he had always been on edge when they interacted and did not have the energy to feel that way anymore.

"I invited Felton to the wedding, I thought Willow would like to meet him," Alvenia said gently. Arden made a face because he knew she was right and that Willow *would* love to meet him. He couldn't help laughing at that, and leaned back in his chair.

"She would of course like to meet you," Arden agreed, glancing at his mother and father.

"There's actually something we wanted to talk to you about, especially now that you're officially married, as Willow told me," Alvenia said with a smile. Arden was happy to see how his family had taken her in almost immediately upon meeting her, and smiled warmly at Alvenia as she spoke of his wife.

"We felt it was a long time coming, and you deserve to know the truth," Felton said, voice just as calm and level as it always had been. Arden looked back and forth between them, confusion growing.

"Tell me what?" He asked impatiently.

"The truth about our marriage," Alvenia said softly. He looked at her in surprise, not making a sound.

"You seem to be under the impression that your father didn't want to be a part of your life, and I tried my best to be ambiguous and understanding without outright saying anything," she explained.

"I also knew that should I speak on the topic, it may push you away more," Felton continued.

"The truth is, Felton and I don't actually enjoy *marriage* in the way I know you and your wife do," Alvenia grinned in a way that reminded him of Juna and he immediately regretted asking what they wanted to tell him, knowing this was not going to go the way he had thought.

"Your mother and I were very close friends when we were young. We had grown up together and were inseparable. Everyone insisted that we'd be wed in time, that we were soulmates," Felton elaborated before Alvenia spoke.

"What no one understood is that we have very different..." she paused as she thought for a moment, "tastes in people, to put it plainly. But we both wanted to marry for the sake of avoiding the pressure of what exactly having 'different tastes' for people meant in our youth."

"When we were younger than you, it was evident the only way we could live was if we were married. We decided that we could marry each other, as best friends, so as to save ourselves from the societal expectations," Felton nodded at Alvenia.

"And so, we wed and were very happy with that choice, as I did not want to be forced into wifely duties when I had absolutely *no* desire to do so," Alvenia said. "Until one day, I was struck by the gods with the need to be a mother. So Felton and I were blessed with you and your sister, with only a few, shall we say, bumps along the way," Alvenia explained. "To put it plainly in a way I hope you can understand without being crass, I prefer to bed no one and Felton would've preferred someone like your Lieutenant," Alvenia giggled as she nudged Felton's shoulder with her own in a childlike way, Felton's laughter matching her own. He was dumbfounded as he sat there, not a word coming to his tongue.

"I was not expecting this," he said at last, as his brain seemed to come to terms with what they were telling him. Felton grinned with a smile that was so similar to his own, and Arden smiled sheepishly back.

"I know, and it should have been explained years ago. But we felt that with the wedding tomorrow, we wanted you to know that our marriage was *never* one with any lost love or abandonment, or really any type of typical marital issues. We have always loved each other, though admittedly in a different way than you're used to," Felton told him as he held Alvenia's hand.

"We write letters almost everyday with all of the gossip in our lives that we uncover," Alvenia laughed.

"That's what you're always writing about?" He snickered, not even a little surprised, making his dad laugh.

"Oh, and there has been *quite* the drama as of late in the King's Guard," Felton agreed before Alvenia grabbed his arm.

"Speaking of, I'm still waiting for the finale of that conversation we had before the invitation," she said. Felton's eyes lit up at that, and he turned to her happily in a boy-like way that mirrored the same way Alvenia had acted only a few minutes before.

"Let's have lunch at home, without any wandering ears. I have *so* much to tell you," Felton gushed. Arden stared at them and wondered how exactly he had ever thought they were in a loveless marriage, but gave himself grace in that he simply didn't understand what he didn't see, and his needs in a relationship were very different from his parents. They stood, and Arden stepped around his desk to hug them both, a little harder than he had before.

"Thank you for telling me," he told them softly as they returned his hug. They both kissed his cheeks, congratulating him on the coming wedding.

"I'm so happy for you both," Felton told him, hand clasped around his shoulder.

"I'll see you tonight when I get home," Arden told them before they walked out of his office doors as they giggled while whispering to each other. Arden only laughed and shook his head, before his Lieutenant came in and commented on his parents behavior.

"Married that long and still all over each other, eh? We could all hope to be that in love after thirty years of marriage," he said.

"You've no idea," Arden laughed.

...

The day went quickly from there, and as the sun began to set he made his final rounds before heading home. He briefly wondered if Willow was still awake, but couldn't see the light on in their room. Felisia was there with Annie and Alise, gathering the gowns for his mother and sister, and he noticed they also had matching dresses for themselves, too.

"Arden! You're home! Look at what Willow picked out for us," Alise showed him the deep pink dresses that they were hanging up on the doorway so they stayed clean. He smiled at the dresses, simple yet beautiful. He would've known they were picked out by Willow without them even needing to tell him.

"They're lovely," he told her as she hopped in delight at the idea of being in the wedding party.

"She had surprised us with this, your mother had brought them home with her after she met with you. She said Willow wanted us to be there with her, she told us we're part of her family now, too," Annie smiled softly as she ran a hand over the soft fabric.

"We were surprised, but so excited," Felisia said graciously. "She told us last week that these would be ready soon. Your mother cried when she told her why she wanted us there, too, even little Amos."

"Willow has always been one to find family with those around her," Arden agreed, giving them each a peck on the cheek as he said goodnight. He tiptoed up the stairs in case Juna was asleep in her room and he could sneak into bed with Will.

He opened the door quietly and saw Willow and Juna laying together, books sprawled out on the bed along with plates and crumbs. He almost laughed at the sight but didn't want to wake them, and quietly walked into the room to get his pajamas. Juna had a candle still lit next to her, and knew she must have been trying to keep an eye out for him when he returned. He was glad someone had kept Will company, he knew she was still afraid of the dark because of the beast and so had a hard time sleeping when she was alone. *Growing up isolated would do that to you,* he thought briefly before finding the clothes he needed and dressing in the bathroom. He wandered into the guest room and laid down in the bed, wishing Will was awake for a kiss, or even just a smile. He stood back up and padded over to his wife's side, hair tossed around the pillow with a relaxed look on her face. He leaned down and kissed her gently, on her lips and then her forehead, before he wandered back to the other room. In only a few hours, they'd be wed and their lives would truly begin. He smiled to himself before he rolled over, and tried to fall asleep. The sounds of frogs and crickets filled his ears for a long while as he tossed and turned endlessly, until he finally, gratefully, fell asleep.

...

Arden was awoken to the smell of coffee and people bustling around him. He immediately snapped awake, sitting up and looking around the room wildly trying to figure out what was going on. He saw his mother standing at the foot of his bed, with Annie, and wondered what they were doing when he remembered what was happening today.

"Oh my gods, I'm getting married," he said, immediately feeling flustered. Annie quickly handed him a steaming cup of black coffee and he smiled gratefully, taking a sip as he still sat in the bed. He peered into the bathroom to see if he could catch a glimpse of Willow, but the second door was closed. He was relieved to remember they had planned for an early wedding, as they had both agreed they would not be able to wait for an entire day to see each other, and wanted it done as early as they could.

He stood and placed his coffee down after taking another sip, mustering up the strength to get through the morning. He went to the bathroom and then bathed quickly, before his mother drew him into the room to help him with his formal uniform. The suit was always tedious to put on, as it was so pressed and rigid. He always felt like he was stifling while wearing it, but today he knew he'd feel stressed irregardless of what he was wearing so didn't mind very much. His only request had been to wear his uniform and as he struggled to put it on, he wasn't sure why he had wanted to wear it at all.

The suit was dark, royal blue, with a garnet trim along the collars, sleeves, pockets, and along the center placket. The whole suit was sewed with gold thread, a subtle detail on its own, but with the gold badges of his rank it seemed to almost glow in the sunlight. He stood in front of the mirror after he was dressed and looked at himself with a shaky smile. His mother looked over his shoulder with tears in her eyes, and gave him a hug from behind as she sniffed. She tried to tell him something, but couldn't hold her tears back when she spoke, so Arden waited for her to continue.

"I just wanted to tell you that I love you," she told him simply with a watery smile. Arden turned around to hug her back, sniffing tears away from his own eyes.

"I love you, too," he told her. Alise popped into the room through the bathroom then, looking around the room until she saw Alvenia.

"We're ready in here," she told them before winking at Arden as she turned back into Willow's room. He almost chased after her but his mom held tight to his elbow, and he couldn't move very far. She looked like she would cry should he let go of her and so he let it be for now. With one more once over in the mirror, they all deemed him acceptable for the wedding and led him to the door. He stopped suddenly before turning around and took the handkerchief from the nightstand, placing it delicately in his pocket. He linked his arm through Alvenia's feeling much better with that small addition to his attire, and they made their way downstairs.

"I'd offer you something to eat, but you look like you'll toss it up mid ceremony," Arrick snickered as he saw Arden enter the dining room. He laid out a large breakfast for everyone to enjoy as they got ready, and Arden laughed at what Arrick said. He knew he was right, if he took a bite of anything this morning besides coffee, he knew he would make a fool of himself in front of everyone.

"Good call," he told Arrick as they sat down together. Felisia stepped into the room with a coffee carafe and placed it on the table in front of them.

"For you," she told Arden.

"Thank you," he told her before pouring himself another cup. He hoped he didn't start trembling as they said their vows. He was feeling more and more jittery as the minutes passed. Arrick went back into the kitchen to make lunch for the reception and left Arden to his thoughts. He kept watching the clock, waiting for it to finally be time to go. After what seemed like an eternity, his mother came to find him along with the D'Misio family. He sent a small prayer that this would be a quick and flawless wedding.

"Arden, it's time to get outside and take our places," Alvenia grinned as Felton joined her wearing a simple black suit, and took her arm.

"Ready, son?" Felton smiled as Alvenia led him closer to Arden for a small group hug. Arden laughed and hugged them back with everything he had, he knew he needed the support and was grateful that they were both here.

"I'm ready," Arden said as he took a deep breath and let them lead the way to the back yard. They had had a lot of people that wanted to come to both the wedding and the reception, and so in the end needed to use the Fairwood Estate's large backyard as a way to host everyone that would come. Arden was blown away by the decorations and the amount of hard work that Mitri had put into making the ceremony beautiful. There were rows and rows of chairs, lined with a deep garnet red and pink ribbon in the shape of flowers along the inner and outer aisles. Each ribbon bouquet was tied together with a strip of gold fabric, the exact color of the thread in his uniform. There was a trellis arching over two flower beds, strategically placed, bridging over the small raised platform that was covered in a dark blue rug, flowers and ribbon lining the whole thing. The arch was breathtaking, dark red roses and blue hydrangea threaded through it, with pink peonies and delicate ribbons looping through in the same colors as the aisles.

Beyond the arch, the reception tables were set up. Blue table covers with gold runners, and red napkins. On each table were small vases with only a few flowers in each, the containers very small. He walked under the arch and onto the platform, looking at the table settings closer. He could see that the plants were inside of actual pots, and would be able to be planted after the ceremony instead of watching them wilt. He knew Willow must have collaborated with everyone in a perfect way to make the entire plot of land feel elegant and also practical. He could see her touch in everything around him.

Despite all the beauty and hardwork of the quick engagement, he wanted to get the wedding over with so he could finally breathe again. The anticipation alone was torture, as he had never much been one to sit around and wait for anything in the first place. Waiting for ten o'clock to roll around was going to surely kill him. He looked around as the guests filtered in, some of them even carrying their own chairs to make room for more and more people. He wondered if the entire wedding would be joined by every member of Stóngrast. He wouldn't be surprised if they were. After a while the entire yard was full of people waiting, including himself. Felton stood behind Arden as he joined him on the patio, his suit blue under the sun. It had been so dark of a color, he couldn't tell it was blue until they were outside. It looked perfect with the decorations and Arden smiled at him, though still nervous.

"Are you ready?" Felton asked with a toothy smile as the musician started to play on the violin. The wedding party emerged as the music began, the bridesmaids and groomsmen lining the aisle leading up to the platform. The maids wore a dress in a blush shade of pink, delicate and beautiful, with lace flowers along the hem of the dress in a darker pink, red, and cream colored lace. His mother and sister were wearing the same gowns along with the D'misio girls, all of them grinning as they made their way to the front with their groomsmen who wore red, matching the small strips in his uniform perfectly. Alvenia and Fasomalo, Felisia and Mitri, Annie and Arrick, all walked towards him arm in arm. Amos and Alise followed behind, walking slower for Amos' small legs. When they reached Arden, they smiled at him and Amos clapped his hands before running to the side and held his father's hand, standing with the groom's party.

Behind them, Sian wore a floor-length over shirt that had a waist high slit in the front, and faded from a soft pink at the collar to a midnight blue at the bottom. The pants underneath were iridescent blue, as dark as the night sky. They wore knee high black boots with a gold bracelet and arm bands on both arms. With their hair pulled back into an elegant braid with gold strands weaved through, they glowed as if they had stepped right out of a sunrise. Sian held Juna's arm graciously, smiling as they made their way down the aisle before they both winked at Arden and fell to the sides with the rest of the party. Finally, the musician played the song that Willow would make an entrance to. Arden couldn't help but hold his breath as he waited for her to emerge from the back door of his home. After a moment, she appeared.

A goddess in a wedding gown.

His mouth went dry as he took in the sight of her in her gown, a dark ivory, almost nude in color. The bodice of her gown hugged her curves, modest yet enticing, the neckline swooping around her breasts, the sleeves tight along her upper arms. Her entire gown was covered in the same lace flowers as the bridesmaids, only hers were gold. They glittered in the sun as the gold thread that lined her gown caught the light in such a way that she seemed to *glow* from within. There was a sparse sprinkle of red and pink flowers within the lace, a striking and ethereal sight to behold. Wilmayra also had a long, long veil that swept along the ground behind her, almost floating in the light breeze. The veil was completely saturated with the lace flowers, the colors radiant. He felt his mouth hanging open and closed it quickly, but was unable to stop staring at the beauty of his wife as she approached him with garnet stained lips. She reached him at the base of the platform and he offered her his hand to help her step up, never breaking eye contact. She smiled shyly at him as he looked at her in awe.

He noticed her flowers had changed color again, different from yesterday's light purple in the center of the flower. They still had the light lavender shade on the innermost part of the petals, but the outer petals were all a fair and gentle pink like an azalea freshly bloomed, darker than the tinted pink of the last few weeks. He smiled at her, reaching a hand out to her cheek as they began their vows. Arden hardly recognized the words Felton was saying, to them and to the people watching from the seats. He saw Willow seemed nervous too, her hands fidgeting with her veil and so didn't feel bad for being nervous, too.

"It is my honor to be the one to officially wed my son and his beautiful bride, an honor I could have only ever dreamed of. Arden has always been a kind and hardworking young man, and for him to have found such a perfect match is truly a blessing," Felton began in a deep, commanding voice. His words carried to even the furthest in the back, after years of practice from directing his forces. "The lovely Willow has proved to us all how equally kind and hardworking she is, and the pair have the most beautiful future ahead of them that I know we are all grateful to be a part of, too. I hope this day is the beginning of a truly happy marriage, as I can already see the good you have brought into each other's lives, on top of the good you have both done for those around you." Arden reached for Wilmayra's hands and clasped them together, stepping closer toward one another. Will giggled quietly as he squeezed her fingers while she looked up at him with her moss green eyes.

"The world has grown more beautiful for having known you both, and Willow herself has even gifted me a large store of medicines and recipe books to share with the Royal family as well as the King's Guard and their families. A gift beyond measure that could not be thanked for properly without moving heaven and earth around us in gratitude. I am humbled by the love my son and his bride share, and will now offer the bride and groom to drink from this chalice to symbolize their intentional joining of families, and the desire of creating a new one all their own." Felton offered them a large goblet full of cider, each of them taking a sip before Juna took the glass and placed it to the side with a grin. "By sharing a drink from the chalice, Arden and Willow begin their lives as a team, their first mark of unity as husband and wife. We will begin the vows with Willow," she glanced at Felton with a smile, a dimple on her cheek as her eyes crinkled with happiness, the nervousness almost gone from her body as they held tight to each other's hands.

"Willow, you may declare your vows," he told her as he returned her smile, his voice dropping lower. Willow looked at Arden, stepping closer, before raising her chin and announcing in a clear, direct voice, the traditional vows of his home, with not even a trace of wavering in her voice.

"In this life and by this design,
My home and my love do you I assign,
I shall bind thee to me,
Beginning anew and carefree,
And so our lives do entwine
With you in my heart and in my mind,
I will be all you need me to be,
My vow and my decree,
Together as one,
Forever has only just begun."

Arden felt tears prickling at his eyes, and vaguely heard his mother sniffling from the side as she stood with the brides-maids. He refused to look away from Willow, knowing he'd cry should he see his mother weeping. Felton then turned to Arden as Wilmayra finished her vow.

"Arden, do you accept Willow's oath?" He asked in a large voice again.

"I do," he smiled at Will, eyes watering. She laughed as a tear spilled over her eye, but she blinked it away and waited for him to continue.

"Arden, you may declare your vows," Felton told him in a softer voice.

"In this life and by this design,
My home and my love do you I assign,
I shall bind thee to me,
Beginning anew and carefree,
And so our lives do entwine
With you in my heart and in my mind,
I will be all you need me to be,
My vow and my decree,
Together as one,
Forever has only just begun."

"Willow, do you accept Arden's oath?" Felton asked her. Will never looked away from Arden's eyes as he spoke, another tear trailing down her cheek. He reached his hand out and used his thumb to wipe it unconsciously, as she answered.

"I do," she told Arden, leaning into his hand.

"The vows have been accepted, their oaths have been fulfilled. Their lives begin as they take their first moments as a married partnership, a team, a new family in which they may grow together in ways they didn't know two souls could grow. The future greets them with open arms as they face their new lives together in matrimony. Arden and Willow, you may kiss your partner," Felton smiled as he took a step back.

Arden wasted no time in sweeping Willow into a gentle kiss as everyone cheered, the sounds of clapping and crying surrounding them. Her lips were soft and warm, and he pulled her into a deep hug before pulling away and kissing her cheek before glancing down at her.

"You are so beautiful," he told her as she ran her hand over the collar of his uniform.

"You are so handsome," she grinned before they were pulled into hug after hug as seemingly everyone from the port congratulated them. Arden was grateful the tables were already outside and set for brunch, as he wanted to have a moment with Willow for the first time in a day and a half and thought everyone would make their way in that direction quickly. He was wrong, and after a few hours passed Arden was exhausted. As person after person sought them out, thanking them both for everything they did in the port, and to thank them for the beautiful wedding they all were able to witness, Willow and himself were slowly pulled away from one another. During a conversation with one of the soldiers and his wife, Willow was completely whisked away by Sian and Juna, leaving him behind. He felt sad for a moment, but he was having fun with his friends and family and actually found he didn't mind much as he and Will danced around each other in the crowd. They shared glances with each other, small smiles and gestures, waiting for the moment they'd be reunited again.

For the rest of the afternoon, he watched as Will made her way through the crowd and gracefully greeted everyone in her gown, her veil folded and placed on a table after Juna had removed it for her while Sian fixed her hair, the flowers looking pinker every moment. She always seemed to know when he was staring, and would turn to meet his eye with a cheeky smile, mischievous and adorable each time. He also seemed to feel her gaze on him and would turn to see her looking in his direction, waiting for his eyes to meet hers.

Eventually, after grazing on small appetizers and meeting with each of the guests, it was time for a formal lunch to be served. Sian and Juna urged them to the table that had been placed on the platform they had said their vows on, and everyone else slowly made their way to their own chairs. As they sat beside each other, they pulled the chairs as close together as possible and leaned into one another.

"I have to tell you something," Will told him seriously as she looked him in the eye, her face serious with a faint nervous smile on her lips, "but I don't want to tell you until we have a minute alone." He was about to respond when his mother and father stood at the base of the platform, holding glasses in their hands.

"We wanted to say a few words before we had our luncheon, and send off our newlyweds for a relaxing evening at home," Alvenia spoke, her voice drawing everyone's attention.

"Here's to young love and new beginnings!" Felton raised his glass high, clinking it against his wife's. The guests yelled in excitement as the sounds of glass met their ears, everyone toasting to Arden and Willow.

"We'll be able to leave soon, and you can tell me then," he told her as plates were brought to them with lunch by Juna, along with a table set with large portions for the guests to make their own plate. They ate quietly, starving after a long morning, and just leaned into each other instead of talking. He hadn't realized how drained he was, but knew the reception hadn't even really started yet at all. The musicians were setting up in the corner, and they'd be pulled into dancing when they finished eating. All too quickly, Alvenia held her hands out for them and led them to a spot in the yard that they had laid wood and a carpet for them to stand on.

"Let us join Arden and Willow in their first dance," Alvenia cheered as the violinist and the harpist began to play. Arden smiled widely at her, wrapping his arms around her waist before slipping one of his hands into hers, her other hand gently draping over his shoulder. They swayed to the music for a moment as Arden felt comfort in her closeness.

"What did you want to tell me?" He asked as they danced, but Willow's cheeks grew pink as she glanced around the crowd.

"I don't think it's the right time yet, there's too many people watching," she whispered, "I'm sorry, I really want to tell you but I just want us to be able to share the moment together, with only each other."

"Of course, my love," he told her as he leaned down to kiss her, as cheers and whistles filled the air.

"Go, Will!" Cried Sian from the side as Juna jumped and clapped next to them. Willow laughed before wrapping both of her hands around Arden's neck and pulled him in for a deeper kiss. She snickered when the whistles grew louder, but Arden only held his hands on her hips and smiled against her lips before pulling away, dancing to the gentle music. Before long, everyone began to join them in dancing and the music picked up a more suitable pace for everyone to move to. Laughter and delight showed on everyone's faces and they all took turns dancing together. Willow joined Felton and Alvenia joined Arden as the music filled the air in the late afternoon sky. After a few songs, Willow excused herself into their home needing to use the bathroom.

"I'll be back," she told Arden with a grin, and headed inside with Sian and Juna. Arden kept dancing, feeling more carefree than he'd ever felt in his life and couldn't believe the sun was lowering in the sky so quickly. While Willow had gone inside, Arrick and Mitri brought out more food for dinner. Arden raised his brows at his mother who he had started the next dance with and she laughed.

"Everyone insisted on being a part of the ceremony in some way. All the food was provided by the families here, with help from the D'Misios of course, and from the Cahlins, too," she told him. Arden was surprised, in a good way, that his home had been so eager to host such a beautiful ceremony and that they were all willing to provide them with warm company, too.

"They love Willow," he said to his mother, gratefully.

"They all love her, and they love you, too," she said easily as they swayed together. "I'm proud of you," she told him, but he couldn't look at her directly as he felt his eyes pricking with tears. He lost track of how many times he'd been left speechless today alone, not believing his luck in this life to have found so many people who loved him. He especially couldn't believe that he had found Will at all, and how their fates had been entwined since the day they had met.

Will found him sitting at their table, sipping water and taking a rest. The sun hung low over the trees, and he was close to being ready to call the day over. He wasn't sure what the usual protocol was for newlyweds making an early escape, but he also didn't want the night to end at all. She sat next to him with a sigh as they watched everyone around them having fun, laughing and singing along to the music. Willow leaned against him, half on his lap and sighed.

"I'm really tired," she yawned as Arden drew her to him, sitting her on his lap. She laughed at the sudden movement and wrapped an arm around his neck, the other placed gently on his chest. She yawned again before Arden snickered.

"You can go inside and I'll follow behind you," he told her.

"Hmm, but everyone is still here," she laughed.

"It's your wedding, you're allowed to do whatever you want today," he said.

"Oh please, you can't tell me you weren't going to say good night to everyone for me because you feel bad for making a run for it." She threw her head back and laughed at his sheepish expression. "I really do think I'm too tired to stay up much longer," she said honestly after a moment.

"Go ahead inside, I'll be in soon, too," he kissed her gently before they both stood. No one noticed as Will headed back into the house, and Arden found his mother and father to tell them good night before trying to make his escape, too. He was caught up by several people, and by the time he made his way inside, he found Willow sleeping in their bed.

Her hair spread over the pillow in a halo, making her look like a goddess in her light slip. The blanket had fallen low while she was asleep, so he covered her back up before heading back downstairs for another treat. He was suddenly hungry for the sweets he knew were in the house, as he felt less anxious now that the day had come to an end. He sat in the dining room with a plate of cookies and tarts, enjoying the quiet. As he sat, someone joined him with a plate of their own and he looked up to see Sian sitting across from him. Sian sighed heavily, leaning back in the chair before popping a small chocolate into their mouth.

"The longest day ever," Sian sighed between bites. Arden nodded in agreement as they both ate together. "I fell asleep after I helped Will with her veil, your housekeeper found me on the settee," they said with a yawn, rubbing their eyes. Arden laughed imagining Sian curled up on the settee, the chair was quite too small for a comfortable rest.

"Did Will talk to you about anything specific today?" Arden asked. "She told me she had to tell me something, but she fell asleep before I could ask," he explained. Sian raised an eyebrow before nodding.

"She told me a few things, but I think they'd best come from her than me," Sian said, "but I would tell you if she'd given me the go ahead first. Maybe you can just wake her up?"

"She was snoring when I went up there, I think she'd just smack me away," he said, making a face as Sian laughed.

"Yeah, she would have absolutely smacked you away and had no recollection of what exactly she was going to tell you," Sian grinned. "It was a beautiful wedding though, most of the decorative ideas were suggestions from Will. She really knows how to make something out of nothing."

"I wasn't sure what exactly it would look like because she said no floral arrangements, because of the ingredient scarcity but the fabric scraps actually turned out great," he agreed with a small smile. They continued to sit in the dining room, picking treats, before he noticed Teg enter the room. Sian grinned when a man identical to Teg followed behind.

"I was wondering when you'd show up," Sian laughed before gesturing to the dessert table.

"You have a brother?" Arden gasped, taken by complete surprise at the sight before laughing in understanding. "Oh, Will *did* mention the Teg family to me before, I just assumed it was more than twin brothers. She made you seem so otherworldly," he smiled at them.

Sian and Arden paused as they took in their faces, a dark, grim expression on their brow as they caught their breath. It looked as though they ran here holding heavy bags that looked more in fashion with Sian's usual dress wear. Sian stood up and shoved their chair back so fast as they noticed the bags too. Arden felt uneasy for a moment before he heard the sound of wind - realising quickly it wasn't windy and in fact, the sound was actually the trees. As soon as the thought crossed his mind, a shriek cut through the night. Blood curdling, painful cries from upstairs echoed through the walls and in seconds, he was running.

"*Arden!*" Willow cried out, "*ARDEN!*" Her shrieks made every strand of hair on his body prickle with goosebumps, and he felt as though he was moving through water, slowly, unable to speed up to get to her in time. He heard a concerned murmur from downstairs as he finally reached their door, Sian and the Tegs right behind him. He tossed open the door and the small lanterns that lit the room danced light along his wife as she writhed in the sheets. She saw him come into the room, eyes wide, grasping at the blanket before she let out another scream.

"Arden, *please!* You have to protect our baby, *please!*" She gasped as tears fell down her cheeks. He was on his knees next to her within a breath and pulled the now tangled blanket down to free her. His stomach lurched when he saw blood lining the sheets, *so* much blood, and felt his breath freeze in his chest as her words caught up to him. *That's what she wanted to tell me,* he thought with an ache.

"I'll keep you safe, my love, I'll keep you both safe," he pleaded to her as she laid back and wailed, a long painful gash blooming over her shoulder blades and down her arm. He held her tight to him and she clutched him desperately, her eyes wide with terror like he'd never seen before. "I'm so sorry Willow," he told her as he cried with her, another gash opening up on her back where he noticed more and more appearing.

As Willow screamed into his chest, the sound traveling to his bones, Sian and the brothers were dumping the bag out and jumped onto the bed behind Will. Sian reached over and pushed Will's head back against Arden until her mouth was open and clear, and forced a draught into her throat.

"I'm so sorry, honey, drink it and it'll all be okay, we promise," Sian said with tears in their eyes. Willow only coughed and cried as she tried to swallow it before another scream overtook her, thrashing against Arden's hands as he held her tight against him. After a moment, her voice trailed off into a whimper before she collapsed against them.

"Take the gown off, we need to clean the wounds immediately," Teg told him, he wasn't sure which brother it was but he obeyed, tearing the already destroyed nightgown off of her. Modesty at this point was the last thing on their minds as they cleaned off her skin, and packed the wounds with a poultice he was certain Willow must have helped make. He didn't realize he was shaking until he slumped to the floor, unable to stand as he trembled. He still gripped Will's hand in his, and even in her unconscious state, her hand clutched him back.

Juna ran to him then, he wasn't sure how long she must have been there as she held his face in her hands with tears in her eyes.

"It's here, isn't it?" She asked them, the sound of sniffling filling the room as they all quietly cried as their friend lay wounded and unconscious.

"The Riuvilish is in the forest, and was drawn to Willow's tree as the blooms changed in color. It could smell she was still nearby." A brother answered, breaking Arden from the daze he had found himself in as he sat on the floor. He stood up shakily and sat on the bed next to Will as she laid there looking pale and lifeless.

"What are your names," Arden said without any inflection in his voice. He felt aged beyond his years as Willow's pleading filled his memories.

"Teggert and Teggrin," Juna pointed at them. He wasn't surprised she could tell them apart, she had always had a keen sense of intuition.

"Will she die?" He whispered, looking down at her as he brushed her hair away from her face.

"As long as we move quickly, she'll be okay," Sian told him as they wiped a tear away.

"And the baby?" He asked as his voice broke. His sister hugged him from the side as Sian reached their hand across the bed and laid it across where Arden held Willow's.

"Your wife is the most stubborn being I know. They both will be fine, she will do everything she can to keep that baby safe, and so will we," Sian said firmly with a squeeze around his fingers.

"Right now, we need to go over a plan to make sure the beast is taken care of quickly. There will be no way to end it unless Willow is the one to do it," Teggrin told him.

"Well then," Arden said as he stood, angry and scared for the life of not only his wife, but of his unborn child, "let's make a plan."

He would do whatever he had to do to save them both, no matter the cost.

~ Eighteen ~

THE NIGHT WILL FALL

Willow felt like she was dreaming, a dark and inescapable dream where she couldn't run fast enough, and no matter how hard she tried she never moved. She was weeping, running for her life, as a dark shadow loomed behind her. She called out for help but no sound left her lips, the dark presence gaining on her slowly. She cried, desperate to save herself, to save her loved ones, but they were just out of reach. Her hand grasped at air as it tried to find her friends and family, before everything was swallowed up in darkness.

...

She slowly came to wakefulness, grateful to be released from the hellish nightmare she had found herself in and listened to the sounds of quiet voices around her. She groaned, trying to find her body and pull herself up to look around, but when she moved her body felt like it was burning. She gasped sharply as her eyes opened wide, and looked around for anyone to help her. She heard footsteps headed her way, a heavy step but fast. The bed dipped as they sat next to her and she turned to look at Arden with a murderous look on his face. She wondered what she could have done to upset him and realized he must be upset that she hadn't told him about the baby sooner.

"I'm sorry, Arden," she told him as tears fell from her eyes, "I wanted to tell you sooner but I'd only found out the day before, and I fell asleep before you came home and the wedding was the next morning and that took all day, and I tried to tell you what the flowers meant but there were so many people and I wanted to tell you when we were alone -" Arden placed a finger over her lips with a gentle shush.

"Honey, you don't need to explain anything, you told me as soon as you could," he assured her gently before kissing her forehead. She felt a sob in her chest but the pain in her back and arm was too much to move, so she cried openly without moving as best she could.

"It hurts, Arden," she told him with blurred vision, the tears filling her eyes too quickly to see him. "My baby," she cried out as she clutched his shirt with the arm that wasn't bandaged. She remembered the burning heat as she felt her skin tearing, ripping into open wounds as the beast sliced the tree. She remembered what the Tegs had told her about it drawing fae out and hoping to find their prey in a weakened state, and knew it wouldn't have killed her this time. She dreaded the thought of the sun going down - the idea of the beast finishing her off was *terrifying*. Arden laid next to her on the side with less bandages, and gently curled himself around her as she cried.

"Our baby will be okay, no matter what happens," he whispered into her hair, a sniff to his voice. She knew he was crying into her hair and did her best to pull him into a hug. The pain was still intense, despite the secure bandages wrapped over her undressed frame. She shivered under the loose covers, and

Arden reached over to grab a robe draped over the chair, and gently slid it over her.

"Teggert, Teggrin, and Sian went to your tree at sunrise this morning. They'd given you enough of the sleep elixir to keep you out for the entire night. Right now, the sun has been up only for an hour and we're supposed to follow after them when you're able," he explained in a quiet voice.

"What are they doing?" She asked tearfully.

"We have a plan, but we'll need to be in your house for it to be effective," he warned her with a sigh. She could tell he hated the idea of her having to be the one to deal the blow, especially now that she held his child inside of her. His hand moved to her belly as she had the thought, and she placed her uninjured arm over his.

"What's the plan?" She asked, knowing it would be scary one way or another. Arden rubbed his eyes, looking tired, but elaborated on the details when she asked.

"The goal is to lure it to your tree - we know it'll already be there, anyway - and trap it within a stone confinement. The Tegs said they'll use stones to make a path of some sort that the beast won't recognize as a trap. It will find a way through thinking nothing more of it, just that there are rocks on the ground," he said, "but as the beast enters the trap, the brothers will pull the stones closer together to make a circle around your tree, tightening it in place. The beast won't be able to leave, and we will be able to wear it down until you can finish it." Willow nodded, knowing that would be the hardest part for her. No matter what, though, she knew she'd do anything to make sure her family was safe. Nothing would be more important than the safety of her child and husband. It would all be worth it in the end.

A knock sounded at the door and Juna pushed it open with a tray of mugs and a coffee carafe, along with some breakfast. She saw Willow awake, and a flash of relief fell over her face.

"I brought you coffee, I thought you'd need it," she told them before she sat the tray down and placed herself carefully next to Will, a bare touch to her hand on the injured side. "How are you feeling?"

"Terrible," she huffed with a small smile. Juna couldn't help but laugh in response, and slid the tray over Willow's lap. They carefully helped her sit up with pillows propped behind her, but it hurt and she let out tearful cries unintentionally. "I'm sorry," she whispered as they finally had her upright. Arden kissed her head as his hands trembled, lifting his coffee.

"There is nothing to apologize for," he told her. A wave of nausea rolled through her at the smell of the coffee, but she tried to ignore it. She could hardly move, and the idea of retching as her back was split open made her ill, she was certain she would faint. Juna seemed to sense her queasiness, though, and quickly moved the tray and offered her water instead.

"Thank you," she said gratefully as the sensation slowly dwindled. "This is going to be awful," she said as she thought about walking to Tonsilta in this condition, nevermind fighting the beast.

"We will do what we have to," Arden told her, but his gaze was worried. She didn't want to think about the alternative, to losing to this monster, and refused to even entertain the idea. Arden was right, they would do what they needed to do in order to go home safely. At the door, Alvenia appeared as they quietly sipped their beverages. She saw Willow sitting up and sighed in relief, much like Juna had.

"Oh, thank goodness," she said as she made her way into the room. "Juna told us as much as she could last night," she admitted to Willow as she sat at the foot of the bed, "and we have been incredibly worried. Is there anything I can do to help?" She asked. Willow thought for a moment, and then wondered about a detail of the beast they hadn't considered. She furrowed her brows as she picked at the fruit she'd taken from Juna's tray, before looking at Arden with an optimistic expression.

"I don't think there's anything more to be done from inside the Port. Being safe, and waiting here are likely the best you'll be able to do," Arden murmured sadly. Alvenia sniffed, but nodded as Willow continued thinking of another way to fight the beast.

"The beast is poisonous," she told them after a minute, and they looked at her and waited for her to continue. "The beast has poison in its claws and teeth, right? If we use a similar method of attack, it may be easier to subdue it should we weaken it in the same way it weakened me," she said. Juna tilted her head, while Alvenia nodded. Arden said nothing, but sipped his coffee and waited for her to continue. "The antidote I'm imagining you gave me last night, yes?" She asked.

"Yes, I gave it to you after you were sleeping. We fed it to you as well as placing it on the wound, we thought it would be best to do both," she agreed.

"The beast will not be able to receive an antidote. It likely won't even know what they are - it is old, and it is only looking to feed. If we can administer a poison to it, as well as attack it, we can weaken it even more." She told them earnestly.

"But where and how would we even find it? We would need it immediately, and what we have is limited as it is, I won't risk your safety beyond what is necessary - and even that is too much," Arden said, his voice fierce. She smiled at him and linked their fingers together.

"I have an idea, and it wouldn't be very hard to do," she laughed at his expression. He rolled his eyes dramatically making her laugh, though it made pain lace up her body. She took another sip of her water, and continued. "We have someone in town that can make cobblestone readily, if we add a bit more water to it, and make it into a paste or essentially break it into an almost liquid stone form, we could use that as a poison of sorts. We know it can't touch stone, so maybe its magic is tied to the living. If it can walk on grass, dirt, water - it can only hold onto a specific type of earth. If we dip our blades into it, or our bodies, it may not be able to inflict a high level of injury. We could deter it, though certainly not discourage it," she explained. Arden's brows raised as she spoke, his thoughts clear on his face. He was considering this battle strategy, and nodded after a moment.

"It *could* work," he admitted.

"Actually, before they left for your home, I told them an idea I had," Juna smiled, "Teggert and Teggrin made the Textile Sarsen and left with the entirety of it. I told them to make a dress for you, a simple slip from fabric, to protect you as well as adding it to your tree." Alvenia smiled at Juna, a look of pride evident on her face that no one could deny as they sat there. Arden also sighed in relief, the idea a pleasant surprise - an obvious solution to a large problem they'd been faced with. "We can also ask the brothers to make a cobblestone mixture, since we probably won't be able to make it here in time before you leave." Will nodded gratefully as Juna spoke.

"Thank you," Willow told her. She slid her bandaged arm over and placed her hand on top of her's.

"I can arrange for a horse and cart to take you back," Alvenia said as she stood. "I'll have it ready immediately, so as soon as you are able to, you may go," she bent toward Will and kissed her forehead, a warm feeling filling Willow as she did. They thanked her, and she left the room quickly.

"I want to help, too," Juna said softly in the quiet room.

"I think you should stay here, your Gift is valuable and needed," Willow told her just as Arden spoke.

"Absolutely not," he told her sternly. She scoffed as she stood, a small smile on her lips.

"Only because *Willow* said it nicely, will I stay," she tossed her loose hair over her shoulder before taking their breakfast to the kitchen. Arden and Willow sat quietly before they tried to dress her.

"Arden, lend me your clothes," she told him as he handed her a dress. "You know as well as myself, I need pants to be able to move the way we need me to move." He nodded wordlessly before digging through his drawers for old clothing he hadn't fit in for a while, and found brown pants and a plain tunic for her. He slid the shirt gently over her head after taking off the robe. As she slipped her arms through the sleeves, she groaned in pain but ignored it and kept moving. There was nothing more she could do except bare with it, after all.

"Do you think childbirth will hurt worse than this?" She asked Arden. He looked at her for a minute, perplexed, but he broke into laughter as he processed what she said. She grinned, trying to shimmy herself into the pants without moving beyond a certain point.

"I honestly don't know, and I'm scared to find out," he said finally.

"*You're* scared," she scoffed with a laugh. After they managed to put her socks and boots on, with an overshirt, they attempted to stand her up. She gasped as the bandages pulled at her skin, the poultice still bound against her. She grit her teeth and made it to the door with Arden all but carrying her. Tears fell from her eyes without her control, and by the time they made it to the stairs, her vision was spotty.

"Arden, I can't do it," she told him as she swayed on her feet. "I'm sorry, Will, this is going to hurt one way or another. I'll carry you down the stairs," he said as he paused their steps and lifted her in his arms. She cried out, a sob in her throat, but Arden kept moving and gently apologizing into her hair.

Her vision went black and she woke on the downstairs couch as Arden looked down at her with tear filled eyes. Juna ran into the room with a tea cup, still steaming, and waited for Arden to sit Will up before she offered it to her.

"Drink this before you go," she advised, "*all* of it." Willow obediently drank the tea in quick gulps, but gagged as she swallowed the last sip.

"What *is* that?" She asked, a yawn escaping her lips. Her eyes widened in understanding, but it was too late, her eyelids were too heavy to hold open.

"Sorry, Willow, it'll be best for your safety on the road. You need your strength," Juna said sadly.

"Sleep well, my love," Arden said, but he sounded so far away. Her eyes shut and she was left in complete darkness.

...

Willow woke to the feeling of someone tugging on her dress. She tried swatting them away so she could sleep but the tugging was insistent. She opened her eyes groggily, trying to see what was going on.

"Would you g'way, m'sleepin" she said. Arden looked down at her with a fond smile, and waited for her to come to her senses. She blinked at him before she looked around.

"Oh, we're home," she said as she rubbed her eyes. She felt surprisingly well, the pain in her wounds significantly less than before.

"We gave you more antidote, and more pain relievers while you were sleeping. It seems the dosage wasn't enough for your metabolism," Grin told her. She sighed in relief, moving to sit up with Arden next to her. Sian bolted into the room and sat on her other side, holding her hand softly. Sian pulled something from their pocket and tied it around Will's wrist. She ran her finger over it, looking at the delicate rune, and smiled gratefully at her friend.

"It's a safety charm for you and Sprout," Sian told her. Wilmayra teared up, nodding as she pulled her hand and rested it on her belly. "I also made one for the rest of us, too. It will help protect us from lethal blows. I wasn't able to completely protect us from harm but I did my best to limit the harm we *could* experience."

Willow noticed then that they all were wearing their charms on their belts, and then looked around in surprise as she took in the brightness around the home.

"You opened the shutters?" She asked, fear evident in her voice. She had them closed for so long now she felt so bare and open to the world. A chill entered her spine and she tried to push the sensation away.

"We figured, it already knows we're here so we might as well give ourselves the extra visibility where we can," Gert supplied.

"I suppose," she said warily. "What's the plan now?"

"The plan is halfway complete, we had just gotten you inside when you started to stir but we administered the extra medicine before you fully came to, to spare you of any unnecessary pain. The next thing we need to do, is put you into this," he continued as he held up a strange looking fabric. She looked at it in surprise and reached her hand out to feel it.

"It's not like I expected it to be," she said when she felt the cold and smooth Sarsen through her fingers. "It's softer than I thought."

"It's quite an interesting material," Grin agreed. She stood and took the fabric before heading to her room to put it on. She wasn't sure if she should wear it over her clothes or if she should wear it under, but as she tried them on she knew it would need to be under her pants as it was tighter and not by any means a stretchy material, there was no way she could fit her current pants into them. After she pulled the tight Sarsen pants onto her, she pulled her hair into a tight braid and pinned it to her head in a crown. She did not want to create a hairstyle that the beast would try to hold onto like a handle, the fear of being grabbed and eaten by this beast was all consuming. Her hair needed to stay tight to her head, ideally the entire time the beast was attacking. She knew no matter what, this creature would be coming back to try and finish her off.

As she stood in her room, she noticed out the window that the horse that must have brought them here was grazing in the field, tied to a tree. Around the horse and tree were a large circle of stones, a protection paddock of sorts. The beast wouldn't go after the horse as it had begun eating fae and non-magic creatures were pointless to it now, but she figured the extra protection around the animal would be a place they could use as a safe zone, for either a get away or to take a moment to breath during the fighting that was imminent. She shuddered at the image in her mind of the bear coming back for her, and quickly put the rest of her clothes on over the stone slip so she could prepare more with her friends. When she left her room, she saw the front door open and headed out to find them.

She turned her head toward where she heard their voices, before feeling a strange sensation over her body. She walked toward her tree and saw Gert and Grin climbing high into the boughs as they wrapped the stone fabric around each limb, the trunk already bound tightly. When they saw her, they smiled.

"You were asleep for most of the wrapping, and this morning when you were in pain we had already finished the trunk," Grin called down to her, answering her unspoken question as she hadn't noticed the feeling earlier and wondered how they had completed as much as they did.

"The only problem is your flowers, and all of the leaves. We won't be able to cover every single one of those unless we bind as many as we can together. We've made sure your vital areas are secure and protected, and can only hope there's enough Sarsen to cover all of your branches." Gert added as she placed a hand over the tightly bound bark.

"It feels weird on my skin," she said uneasily, though she was grateful despite the feeling.

"That may be because of the difference in troll and fae magics, it must feel quite unsettling for you as treekind to be held so tightly by stone," Grin said apologetically.

"I wonder how you must feel with both in your blood," she wondered out loud, curiosity bubbling inside her even though the mood was somber. Arden was helping bind the branches hanging over her roof, Sian nowhere to be seen. Arden's face looked as though he was preparing for a funeral as he tightly wrapped as much of the branches as he could.

"It's comforting for us in both worlds," Grin told her with a smile.

"Arden, is there a way you could secure the fabric to the roof as opposed to wrapping it around the further edges of the branches?" She asked as she tried to think strategically on their placement.

"We actually tried that first, but there was a lot of space underneath that left room for entry. If the branches were bumped into, the fabric would fall off and leave it vulnerable even if we nail it to the roof," he said, wiping his brow.

"Hmm," she thought as Sian appeared behind her as they pushed a wheelbarrow full of heavy stones.

"Where did that come from?" She laughed. Sian winked at her before dumping the stones out and wheeling it away. Will trotted after her, intending to help.

"You shouldn't be lifting things in your condition," Sian said but Willow shrugged.

"I'm going to attack a fae killing beast when the sun sets, and I've already been attacked by it. What's the difference if I pick up rocks?" She asked. Sian tutted, but acquiesced all the same. They wandered to the river bed where rocks were abundant, and dutifully filled the wheelbarrow. It was quicker with two, anyway, she supposed and they'd have more time to prepare other things once they had enough.

On the way back to the tree, Gert jumped from the lowest branch before moving his hands in a peculiar manner and Will's eyes widened as she saw the stone *moving* when he moved his hands.

"*What the hell,*" she gasped as the stones rolled to the base of the tree, seemingly on their own. Grin laughed from the top of the tree, and Gert only smiled knowingly.

"That's what I said, too," Arden called down as he wrapped the last thick bough with the fabric. Willow only gaped at the stones as they formed a protective circle around the base of the trunk, and noticed then that all of her roots that had been exposed around the moss were completely covered in the Sarsen, the stones pushing deep into the earth and securing the fabric tight to the ground. She kneeled to feel the ground, the entire circle around her trunk bound tightly. She felt relieved despite the strange feeling over her own skin, the double protection made her feel heavy yet light as she sighed, knowing she would be safely protected with Sarsen holding her together.

"You'll all save enough Sarsen for yourselves, right?" Will said suddenly in a panic.

"Don't worry, Willow, we changed into ours when you were asleep," Arden told her as he climbed down from the roof. He lifted his tunic for her to see the fabric underneath and she closed her eyes as the panic faded.

"Good," she told him as she leaned into him for a hug. He wordlessly wrapped his arms around her, almost too tight but not tight enough. She felt his fear radiating from his skin but knew there was nothing she could do to reassure him everything was going to be okay, especially as she wasn't sure it was true.

"I'll do my best to protect you and everyone, and myself," she told him instead. He kissed the top of her head as he rubbed her back.

"Me too, I promise," he told her in the same tone. He knew what she was saying even if she didn't say it - there were no guarantees in life and the only thing they could do right now is try their best to overcome what they were being faced with. She knew though, that if anything happened to her, Arden, or her baby, she would be devastated. They'd only just begun their lives together and it was unfair she'd spent so much time living alone, devastatingly lonely, only for it to be taken away in the same moment. She felt a growing anger in her chest, an all consuming fire of unfathomable rage as she finally came to terms with what she needed to do. She pulled away from Arden and started back to the house, the trees around her trembling as they felt her emotions. They all whispered to her in solidarity, and warned her of what they'd seen when the beast had come the night before.

In the house she looked around before she saw the dagger laid out on the counter, sharpener next to it, as it sat ready in its sheath. She wrapped it around her waist, tightening it, and headed to the secret door hidden away under the carpet between the kitchen and living room. She pulled the blanket back, and the door, and climbed down into the cellar as she sought out the weapons she'd acquired over the years. It was more a hobby than anything - she could hardly wield any of the weaponry, anyway - but knew they would need as much help as they could. She could hear grinding around the foundation of her home and stones clunking along the outer edges, and wondered if Gert was also wrapping them around the base of the house, protecting it from the beast finding a way inside. She heard footsteps behind her as she gathered what she could and heard Arden whisper as she held a bow and a sword.

"I didn't know this existed," he told her in awe. He had followed her into one of the storage rooms, it was full of mostly jarred and dried foods but the upper shelves were filled with random weapons of protection. The other storage room, no bigger than this one, was the medicinal store room. It was certainly barer than it had been, but still held quite a bit of supplies should they need them later on.

"It was made when I was young, a bunker of sorts. But I only ever used it to keep the medicine, and food. It wasn't until I was a teenager that I felt the need for these," she gestured to the shelf with the assortment of weaponry. Arden helped her carry them back into the living room, and they laid them onto the table.

"I told them about your idea to poison the beast," he told her, "they'll be crushing rocks and water together soon to make the sludge of sorts, just like the man that makes the cobblestone in the Port." She was glad the idea had been a good suggestion, and hoped it worked the way she wanted it to.

"I wonder if we soaked a wild animal in my blood, and filled it with the stones, would we trick it into ingesting the poison?" She asked Arden. He stared at her with wide eyes, and she raised her brows. "Arden, we have to think through this logically. You're a Commander, this is a battle. Nevermind that we're expecting a baby and that our lives are on the line - we *need* to make as many tactical decisions that we can. Now, is it a plausible idea or shall I practice my aim with this bow?" He sighed heavily before running his hands in his hair, and rubbed his eyes before nodding.

"It would work, it would be a disgusting and unpleasant task, but yes it would work," he agreed. "I do *not* want your blood to spill, though, so I would beg you to try something else. We will think of another option," he said as he sat down with his elbows on his knees.

"You know as well as I do, there are no other options that would guarantee the beast would willingly consume a poison *without* my blood's scent on it. My wounds are still open, my blood is already spilled. I'd rather be in some discomfort now than eaten alive later," she told him honestly. He put his face in his hands and sniffed, his shoulder trembling. She felt awful for being so cold and detached as she spoke of her body being harmed in such ways, but she knew it was important. She walked over to him and sat beside him on the couch, wrapping him in a tight hug.

"I'm sorry," he told her as his tears stained her shirt.

"No, *I'm* sorry," she murmured, "this is hard for you and I'm not being very gentle about it."

"I just don't want you to be hurt, and it seems that my biggest fear is approaching very quickly - the ones I love being taken away, and I am unable to help," he wiped his face with the back of his hands, but hugged her back. After a minute, he pulled away and grabbed his own bow that had been resting on her side table. "Tell the Tegs what you thought of, and I'll go and find as many small animals I can find," he told her as he kissed her softly. They both walked outside together, sharing one last kiss before he headed behind the cottage, past the river. She found the brothers breaking down rocks as Sian carved into a large stone, and quickly launched into her idea. They all shared a look of alarm, but they agreed quicker than Arden had. Sian looked slightly pale, though, and she didn't blame them for feeling disturbed by it.

"How much cloth and medicine did you bring?" She asked them.

"We used a lot on your tree, the antidote at least, but we had been making a lot of it for this moment. So we still have a lot leftover," Sian said in a strained voice. "You actually have all of the ingredients here, should we need more. I don't think you'd be able to succumb fast enough to the poison even if we ran out of antidotes after an hour, so we would be able to make more in the morning if you need it. We also have a lot of the sleep elixir, and the pain draught. We hardly touched those stores yet," Sian explained. Willow nodded before making a face before she spoke.

"Which one of you will help collect the blood from my wounds?" She asked as she pursed her lips, knowing they'd all want to avoid it. Grin sighed as he looked at Gert and Sian and turned to Will.

"I'll do that for you, Willow. Gert and Sian, get started on the sludge mixture. And find small enough stones to fill the animals with," he added with a shudder. Sian looked entirely green as they shook their heads in disgust, but followed Gert toward the riverbed.

"I have bins and buckets somewhere," she told them. Sian waved their hand and went looking for them. Will knew they probably remembered where they were kept from the times they had slept over when they were children, and turned to Grin as he looked at her stoically.

"We should do it quickly, or Arden will have a heart attack," she warned him before turning back into the house. The sun was hardly at its apex in the sky, so she felt better knowing they would be ready for whatever the night brought them. With the changing of seasons and summer nearly at its peak, sunset was later than it used to be but darkness would fall quickly once the sun lowered over the trees. She was also uncertain how strong the beast was now that it had been able to consume the lives of other fae, and was worried it would appear before it was completely pitch black.

"I'll be right back, I have empty jars we could use, and fabric scraps that we can use to absorb as much blood as possible, and tie it around the animal carcasses," she said easily. Grin made a face at her nonchalance, but she had no choice but to separate herself from her emotions. Her body was trembling, and had *been* trembling since she'd been attacked last night and knew she would certainly die if she didn't look at this with *no* emotions clouding her actions.

"There will be time tomorrow, after we've ended this for real, to scream and carry on," she whispered to herself as she fought against the dread in her stomach as it sat there like a loaded weight. Even the nausea that she'd felt for the last few days was suspiciously absent, and she refused to allow herself to worry about the baby.

"Everything will be okay," she ran a hand over her tummy before she found the jars in the back of the guest room closet, along with the bag of fabric strips she had saved from past sewing projects. She brought them out to Grin and laid the jars on the table. She sat on the kitchen stool, straddling it and holding onto the seat back and counter to brace herself for the coming pain.

"Will you lift the hem and hand it to me?" She asked as she leaned her elbows on the counter, hands held open over her shoulders in a slightly awkward position. He pulled the tunic and Sarsen up to her hands and she pulled until the fabric was entirely rolled up, and then laid her head against the table. Grin began to peel away the bandage slowly so as not to hurt her.

"Sorry if it hurts," he apologized.

"Grin, pull it off hard and fast in small intervals. Disrupt the scabbing and healing and you'll be able to collect it more efficiently. I'm sorry, but right now isn't the time to worry about my pain and comfort, no matter how much I appreciate your concern," she told him calmly. She clenched her jaw so she wouldn't bite her tongue, before Grin pulled the bottom most bandage off first. She flinched in response and groaned, but it worked and the near-dried poultice, bandage, and light scabbing released a flow of blood. She panted as Grin collected as much as he could from the weeping wound before he closed the bandage back over her and began with the next one. She felt tears spilling from her as the pain intensified over and over, but she tried not to make a sound so as to keep Grin from feeling bad as he caused her pain. She knew this was the best bet to weaken the beast, and would sit here for another hour if she had to.

After a few minutes she heard footsteps in the kitchen and a hand ran along her head as she rested it flush against the cool countertop, now wet with tears. She peered up to see Arden looking at her from above with his own tear-filled eyes, and he wordlessly stroked her hair as Grin finished his gruesome task. Finally, Grin closed the last bandage and held the half full jar in his trembling hand.

"Thank you, Grin," Will croaked as she wiped her eyes and dropped her top back down over herself. Arden pulled her into a hug as Grin rifled through the bag he'd left on the floor, and found the bottle of pain relief medicine for Willow. As Grin closed the jar, Sian and Gert walked into the house. Sian's eyes caught the macabre scene, the dark liquid glinting in the sunlight beaming in through the open windows.

"Oh, gods," Sian gasped before covering their mouth and running to the bathroom.

"Maybe I'll make everyone some tea," Will suggested with a trembling voice. She wasn't actually sure if she could get up and walk anywhere at the moment, her entire body shaking from adrenaline, or pain, she wasn't sure. Gert placed his hand over hers and shook his head.

"I'll do that," he said softly, before he looked through her kitchen and found two kettles, and readied them in the sink. She told him where to find the tea, and before long the kettles were placed in her long abandoned fireplace.

"I don't know when it was last lit," she murmured mostly to herself. Arden nodded sadly as he heard her small voice and led her to the couch where she stretched out. She put her head on Arden's lap as he joined her, and he quietly rubbed a hand over her head, the only place she knew he felt was safe to touch. His hand trembled where it stroked her, but she tried to pretend nothing was wrong for the moment and enjoyed his comfort, even if it was a thinly veiled illusion she wasn't fooled by. His presence was real, his heartbeat real, too. And for that moment, right then, their baby too was real. She tried to drown out everything her mind was screaming to her, every thought in her mind telling her all the ways in which she'd fail, or how her loved ones would also succumb to a gruesome fate, and shut it all out. It wasn't the time, and she couldn't allow herself to feel even a miniscule amount of despair, or she would lose before they'd even tried.

When the tea was ready, she sat up slowly. Still in pain, but it was fading as the bandages pressed the medicine back into her wounds and thankfully helped numb them. It was that, or she'd lost the ability to feel them at all from the pain.

"I'll handle the blood soaked linen wraps," she said, knowing there'd never be a good time for that statement and said it quickly to get it over with. Sian came back into the room by then, and sat on the floor by Will's feet and gagged at her words. Will couldn't help but giggle at Sian's reaction, making Sian elbow her leg as they rolled their eyes.

"Laugh at me all you'd like, you're just a sick individual with a penchant for the gruesome," Sian said airily as they both sipped ginger tea. Arden had a heavier brew, though she made him add honey, but he nodded in agreement with Sian.

"I can't believe half of the suggestions she's made in battle strategy. After this, they'll want to recruit her in the King's Guard," he said with a strained smile. Sian and Arden snickered as she spit out a mouthful of tea, choking as a nearly hysterical laugh burst through her lips.

"How much time do we have until sunset?" She asked after she'd finished half of her glass.

"It's only a little past noon, and the sunset is around eight o'clock," Grin told her.

"We have time for lunch, should we harvest some vegetables?" She wasn't sure what else she had available other than the sparse wildlife and foraging options.

"I can hunt for more animals," Arden suggested. "We may get lucky and find a turkey."

"I can help with that," Gert said as he stood and placed his empty cup in the sink. Arden thanked him before they walked to the door.

"Will, I put the animals you asked for around back," Arden called over his shoulder before disappearing from view.

"I suppose that means we have to make the sludge and add your blood next," Grin said, making Sian gag again. They all walked around the back of the cottage in search of the animals and easily found rabbits, squirrels, and birds.

"Sian, why don't you make more runes so we can have more protection, and you won't have to witness this," Will offered.

"No, I should help you with this so that Grin can make the rock and water mixture. I won't be able to do what he can, and I think it would make more sense this way," Sian said.

"You can hardly look at what's in my hand in the first place," she said as she gestured to the jar she carried. "It's okay, we can't do this part until after the sludge is done and added, anyway," she said gently as she placed her hand on Sian's shoulder. They looked seconds away from tears, and Wilmayra knew how much they hated to cry in general so she didn't push further than that. After a moment, Sian gained composure and nodded before walking to the river to find more stones to engrave. Will put the jar down and followed them, figuring she should be useful in some way, too. Grin had walked ahead of them and pulled the wheelbarrow along with him to the water.

"We're going to need lots of jars and bottles," he warned Will, "maybe you should gather every empty vessel you own."

"Good idea," she said, "what will we do with them once we've filled them all?"

"You'll need to go shopping for new items, I'd suppose," he winked, though his lighthearted demeanor was hardly convincing. "We will throw them directly at the Riuvilish and hope for the best," he added. Will laughed, though she was sad she'd most likely use all of her glassware in an attempt to keep the beast at bay. Glasses and jars were a small price to pay for her life, though. She headed inside and collected everything she could find that could store liquids. It took a long time as she filled glasses and cups and everything she could think of into a bag before bringing them outside and dumping them on the ground for Grin.

Arden came back with a large bird, though it wasn't a turkey, and began to prepare it for cooking. She noticed next to him on a cloth were knives from her kitchen, as well. While she watched him, she wondered about how they'd add stones to the animals' bodies as she watched him for a minute, before she thought of something. She walked up to Arden as he defeathered the hen, and told him what she needed him to help her with.

"I wasn't sure how to fit rocks inside of those, but I think what we should do is make a cut in their abdomen and fill them that way, and then use the blood soaked linen to tie it closed. It's disgusting, I know, but I want to make sure it *works,*" she told him earnestly. He looked into her eyes for a moment before nodding.

"That would be the most efficient way to do it, we'd need to talk to the Tegs to see how good their sense of smell is so we know how heavily we need to saturate them," he responded. "If we don't disguise the smell of death and stone, the beast may well know what we have planned." Wilmayra nodded and continued to watch as he then cut into the bird with the knives and smiled at how efficient and smooth his movements were.

"You look like you've been a butcher your whole life," she said with a soft voice. He looked up at her with a proud grin before looking back down at the bird.

"I actually always wanted to be a butcher, I helped the Cahlins when I was a child. It was my first job. But with my father, I thought it was more suitable to be a soldier instead, so I pursued that," he told her.

"I don't think they would have minded what career you chose," she said. "They told me how proud of you they were before the wedding. I think they just want you to be happy with the choices you make."

"If the sun shines on us tomorrow, I'll take that into consideration," he smiled back at her, and despite the sombreness of his words, she knew he wasn't kidding.

"You can't take it back," she warned with a smile, though she wasn't sure if it went to her eyes. He smiled back, his lips wavering for a moment before he looked back at the bird.

"I can cook it, if you want," Sian said as they made their way over with wide round stones. Arden nodded gratefully and carved the last of the bird before heading inside to wash his hands.

"Set up an area for us after you ask the Tegs, then I'll help fill the stones," he grimaced before walking away. She quickly found the brothers as they broke down rocks into a fine powder, though it was quieter than she expected.

"Teggrin and Teggert," she called to them.

"Yes?" Grin responded as they turned her way with dust encompassing him in a small cloud. Gert looked to have the job of mixing the powder with water and was significantly less messy. She let out a laugh in surprise at the sight of them.

"Oh my," she giggled before focusing on her question. "I actually had an idea on how to poison the beast," she said as she explained what she had told Arden. "Do you think it would work?" They glanced at each other with raised eyebrows, slightly impressed.

"Actually, yes, I think that would work very well," Gert told her. "From what we learned from the other fae it seems to only have a vague awareness of fae lifeblood. After it attacks the tree, they listen for their screams before going in for a final attack," he explained. "It doesn't seem to have a particularly keen sense of smell outside of that basic awareness."

"So it would easily be fooled by my blood, thinking it was successful on the first try?" She wondered out loud.

"Essentially, yes. It is very simple in its intelligence, even with its strength increasing. It only wants to feed, that's its only prerogative. If we lead it toward your house with, as it would look, 'pieces' of you - it would eat them thinking it was what it hunted," Grin agreed. "Though, we should probably keep as much of it together as possible. We don't have anyone to tell us how well its sense of taste works, we only know that it can't smell very efficiently from behind closed doors."

Willow grinned, a flood of relief filling her body. If they could manage this, their fate would be drastically less dire. If they were able to poison the beast before it attacked again, her family would be safe. She put a hand to her tummy, sending a small prayer to Ivokorresh. *Goddess, please keep my family safe,* she repeated in her head over and over as she made her way back to the jar and animals. *Please.*

She thought about the best way to soak the fabric efficiently, and opened the jar to add the fabric directly. She thought if she added it to the jar, sealed it back up and shook it for a moment, each strand would surely be equally covered. As she opened the lid, the smell of her own blood was so strong she gagged, closing it quickly before running to the river and heaving into it. She kneeled on the bed, knees deep in the mud and moss, and threw up the tea she'd just drank. She dipped her hands in the water and wiped her face, cooling herself down. She trembled for a moment before shakily standing back up and headed back to the jar, feet heavy.

"You okay?" Arden murmured as he walked toward her, arms open. She walked into him, arms wrapping around his waist as he held her and rubbed circles into her back.

"I'm okay, I just smelled something awful," she told him. "I think I need to wear a scarf to cover my nose," she sniffed. Arden laughed, and Wilmayra couldn't help but smile as her words painted a silly picture of herself for him.

"I can get you something," he offered.

"I think I'll pull my shirt over my nose and see if that helps," she said softly before pulling away from him to continue her task. Arden wordlessly began preparing the animals with stones so that Will could finish them with the fabric, though both of them made faces as they completed the task. When Arden's part was done, she covered her nose with her shirt and held her breath before adding the fabric. She shook it for a minute before each one looked completely saturated, and frowned as she considered how to remove it from the jar.

"I deal with blood every month, and I have healed hundreds of injuries in my life, on hundreds of people, helped birth babies and animals. How is *this* such a difficult task?" She couldn't help but grumble as she thought out loud.

"Because its fucking *disgusting*," Sian said as they walked over, hands outstretched as they offered her a pair of gloves. Arden let out a surprised laugh and nodded in agreement.

"It's way more disgusting than a bodily function or a scraped knee," he made a face and stuck out his tongue while Sian shuddered.

"Thank you for the gloves, both of you get out of here. If you could pick me some fruit for after this, I'd be grateful," she told them, offering an escape from the dreaded task ahead of her.

She shook her body for a moment to build herself up to remove the fabrics from the jar she'd begun to refer to as the abomination, as it felt truly heinous to be holding her own blood on the outside of her body. She said a final prayer before diving into the task, grateful for the gloves. As she twisted the lid open, the Tegs called out to her.

"Before you do that, Willow, we should wait until it's closer to dark to keep it fresh," Grin advised as Gert nodded.

"We don't want it to dry out too much," Gert said, "and if it's fresh, it will be more likely to eat it and not question what exactly it is."

"Maybe a few handprints on the trunk, though, to make it seem as if you're closer than before," Grin added after a moment. Will nodded, grateful to put the task off for later, but dreaded it even more as she had to wait. Her belly churned at the thought of waiting until the last minute to complete something this important, but she tried to shrug it off and made her way inside the house where Sian had used the fireplace to cook. She hadn't noticed the smell of chicken until then, distracted by the nauseating scent of blood and death, but gratefully sat on a stool as she watched Arden from the window, gathering berries from a nearby bush before he came back inside. He sat next to her and offered her the procured fruit, and she smiled before standing to wash them.

While she washed the fruit, Arden made her a plate of chicken and vegetables that looked quite like the food in the tavern, the recipe certainly made by Sian. She remembered how Sian liked to cook when they were kids, and how they always liked to try new flavors, so wasn't surprised that her friend would find a tavern to work. She was grateful that Arden had wanted to bring her to the market all those weeks ago, because their lives would have been drastically different had they not gone.

She shuddered at the thought as Arden sat back at the table, his voice breaking her out of her thoughts as she stared into the woods, thinking of what-ifs.

They ate their meal quietly, the five of them eating as much as they could to ensure their long night wouldn't be affected by hunger. Will had to force herself to eat anything despite the growling in her stomach, because it was too hard to push the nausea down. No matter what she did, she had felt a constant sense of queasiness that made it hard to focus on anything besides that. She wished nausea would have been enough to destroy the beast in the woods, because she surely had enough of the sensation to be able to share.

After they all had finished the light meal, they looked out-side to check on the sun's progression in the sky. Low, but still mid afternoon. They still had a ways to go before the sun was completely set. She wondered briefly on how many more hours that meant and tried not to think about it too deeply and instead hoped that they had enough time to make sure the sludge was finished, the runes, and the animal poison traps. Logically, she knew they had it all completely together with nary a hair out of place. Emotionally, though, she felt she was running on absolute fumes and would not be able to keep her thoughts calm as she went over the plans again and again in her head. As she was thinking, Arden placed his hand on hers.

"Are you okay?" He asked softly as she looked at him in almost surprise. She frowned, not sure how to answer because she knew they were depending on her ability to finish the beast off herself, and end what should have ended centuries ago. She couldn't lie, though, and found herself shaking her head.

"No, I'm worried I won't be strong enough," she told him. He looked at her sadly, before nodding in understanding.

"We can go over where you should aim the dagger, if you want," he said gently. She smiled and nodded, it would be a lot more feasible if she felt like she knew what she was doing. She still wasn't sure she'd have the physical strength to properly use the dagger in a lethal way, but no matter what she had to try. She followed Arden outside and ignored the flip of anxiety in her stomach, the way her hands trembled as she moved. It wouldn't help her to focus on the doubt and insecurity floating within her like a swarm of bees, and so took a deep breath as Arden laid out a dagger of similar size on a nearby stone.

"I'm going to find another animal for you to practice on," he warned her before turning away with his bow, having placed it against a tree before having lunch. She waited patiently and looked around as the trees whispered to her. They warned her of the fierce creature they had seen tear apart her tree, and how they knew she'd be able to free them of the terror it had plagued on them for eons - though to her, it had only been a year or so. It wasn't the first time they'd seen it lurking, but she prayed it would be the last it would ever see the world again. She whispered back to them to give her warnings on the coming sunset and the beast, knowing their input would be immeasurably useful. They agreed, and sent the message to the furthest reaches of the woods, the leaves rustling in waves until one tree notified her of where the beast had last been seen before sunrise. As Arden came back into view holding a large rabbit, she told him what they said.

"It was last seen at the riverbend between here and Hanlan, a few miles away from here in that direction," she told him as she pointed. He nodded as he listened to the wind, before his brows rose in understanding.

"The trees warned you," he said. "Good, we'll know at least where to expect it. Here," he placed the rabbit on the stone and took the dagger before handing it to Will. "You need to plunge this in hard, fast, and deep. You need to reach the rock on the other end. That is how you know you'll be strong enough to do what needs to be done."

She took a deep breath before nodding as Sian and the Tegs stood to the side to watch. She held the knife, the same length and weight of the enchanted dagger, and placed the hilt in her palm. She took a step forward before jabbing the knife into the rabbit, grunting at the force. She knew it didn't hit the stone on the other end and pulled it back to try again.

She tried again and again as sweat poured down her brow until finally she screamed and used her whole strength to strike the blade into the rabbit, a jolt running up her arms and into her shoulders as the tip of the blade cracked the rock. She straightened her back and looked at it in surprise as Arden kicked the animal off the stone to look at the mark left behind. There on the blood stained rock, in the center where the knife had met it, was a large fissure. Pieces of the stone had broken away and left a divot, a perfect match to the knife still resting inside the rabbit. She gaped at Arden, but he only looked at her proudly.

"Now do it again, when the time is right," he said sagely, his eyes bright with hope. She hoped he kept that look throughout the next few hours. If they were able to work together, she too would keep her heart hopeful. The trees began fluttering around her in warning, their leaves shushing them all as they looked around and noticed the growing darkness as the sun dipped lower beyond the tree line. They all looked to one another and began dashing around the woods to finish the final steps in preparation.

Will quickly ran to the animals they filled with rocks and dipped her hands into the jar without hesitating. She didn't care about the blood, or the smell of death, or the fact that she had just torn apart a rabbit for the sake of a lesson on strength and force of will. She tied each bloody ribbon of cloth around the squirrels and birds, as Arden took the rabbit and filled it with more stones to place in the pile they hoped would fool the beast. She placed the pile on the backside of her home, hoping it looked as though it was *her* body lying there for the beast to feast on, thinking its attack had worked. She dumped the remainder of the jar onto the pile before smashing the glass against the foundation of the cottage, spraying the remnants around the ground. It certainly looked as though a corpse was lying there, and smelled like it, too. It was altogether foul, but the task was complete. She walked over to the wisteria and wiped her hands on the trunk before looking at Arden as he reached his hand out to her. She placed her hand in his, and he pulled her into a tight hug.

"No matter what happens, I love you and I'm proud of you," he told her earnestly before pulling her into a deep kiss.

"I love you too," she told him as he pulled away. She wished the moment had lasted longer, but knew there was nothing to be done for it now. Whatever happened next, they could only pray and do their best. Whatever it took to make sure they'd be able to raise their child together, and live out the life they'd always dreamed of having. The Tegs and Sian had managed to line the perimeter of the home with the stone and water mixture, the glasses and bowls along the ridge of the roof for them to throw during the fight. Arden donned his bow and quiver, filled with pointed rocks instead of arrows. She wondered at the perfect curvature of the stones, sharp and pointed, and knew the brothers had a hand in making them. It was full to the brim, and Will was relieved that at least Arden stood a fighting chance against the fae eating beast.

Sian manifested a dark web of energy around the base of Will's tree. Though it was hard to see with a naked eye, the witch's blood in her gave her a small glimpse of the power Sian had long held within. As they walked past it, she saw Arden glance over in surprise as he also caught sight of it. She told herself she would make sure he learned about his bloodline when they were safe in Stóngrast once again, her chest feeling tight as the fear of the impending fight with the beast edged closer and closer, as the sky continued to darken.

As they had agreed earlier, Willow would stand with her tree as they all took their places around the home. Sian stood inside Will's home, in the window directly next to the trunk of the tree, and held the line of magic for Will's protection. Arden and the brothers laid on the roof under cover of the Sarsen, camouflaged by both the wrapped branches and the strange fabric. They had all unanimously thought that the beast would need to smell Wilmayra for it to successfully take the bait, and by leaving her seemingly out in the open to single handedly protect her tree, they would entice the beast into following along the trail they had set for it. The Tegs faced the direction towards Hanlan, where they'd left the opening of the stone circle. As the beast crossed into the stone path, they'd pull the stones tight and flush, flattening them so the beast could not escape.

They waited, and waited, for the moon to rise high enough to wake the beast. Her mouth felt dry as the trees whispered to her that the sun was at its lowest point before sunset, and breathed into the emotions in her heart. The tree seemed barren as it was bound nearly in its entirety in Sarsen. Almost every branch had been covered in the fabric, leaving the sky above her clear. A few of the branches at the top of the tree were the only ones left untouched, the petals blowing in the breeze.

As she stood there, the early summer heat dissipating into a chill around her, she allowed herself to feel her emotions fully, a deep, burning rage billowing inside her like a forest fire. A deep, all-consuming anger as she faced the inevitable in order to protect her family. Icy, determined, and steadfast fury, pure and fierce, for a fighting chance at a life full of love. Her child's heartbeat growing inside of her, a child with their father's smile, the life so new and only just beginning, being threatened by this evil creature. Her hands tightened into fists as she thought of her child, whether it was a boy or a girl, it didn't matter. All that mattered was that baby *living* because she and Arden had overcome what threatened them.

She breathed into that rage, she bit down on her teeth and ground them together, jaw clenching and creaking under the force. She would not end like this, for she would do what must be done. She sent a *promise* to Ivokorresh that their lives would be safe and she'd rid the world of the beast with every ounce of her will, that she'd protect the lives of all by protecting her child, and as the sun finally set, she waited for the beast's imminent approach. The night grew darker and darker as the sun fell beyond the horizon, the deep blues of the sky giving way to black, stars shining bright. Clouds moved in suddenly, darkening the night even more. Her eyes adjusted slowly, until the glow of Sian's magic was all she could see. The moon peered out behind a cloud, a single ray of light along the forest floor.

As if the world were listening to her inner thoughts, a soft patter of rain began to fall around the forest. Though it was dark, and she was dry under her tree despite the Sarsen covered branches interspersed with the unprotected leaves, the rain posed both a threat and a beacon of hope for their efforts. The scent of blood filled the air as petrichor sent a concentrated wave through their noses, and as the smell caught in the wind, a deep, horrifying snarl filled the air.

It could only be the beast shrieking as though it held a thousand voices within its body, though she supposed it truly did. The hair on her body raised as she felt Arden flinch against a branch on the roof, the sound unnerving even the battle hardened soldier. She exhaled a slow breath, concentrating on her emotions and controlling them as the sound came closer and closer. They could hear and feel the unsettling gait of the beast, and the moment it crossed over the border they had set up, a heavy pit of dread filled her belly.

The trees had continued to whisper as it moved closer and closer, repeating to one another so as not to alert the beast of whom was hidden nearby, but the trees trembled in fear as they looked upon it. She knew without seeing it that it was horrific, otherworldly and disgusting. She heard a large sniff in the air as it smelled out the pile of blood soaked fabric and animals behind the house, and heard its awful bellow before it began swallowing piece after piece after piece. It let out a satisfied scream after it consumed the last bite, a horrifyingly gleeful sound.

Another sniff filled the air and Willow told herself to breathe, desperately holding onto the control of her breath and emotions, to hold onto the anger inside of her and make sure this creature paid for what it had done. As it finally sniffed out the scent of her, she listened as its footsteps made their heavy way to her. Its gait was odd, the sound of its body meeting the ground was almost light as it walked in a hobbling gait, slow but forceful. As it made its way around the tree, sniffing the air for the dried blood on her hands and trunk, it turned its monstrous face toward her.

The blood drained from Wilmayra's face as she looked the demon head on. The Riuvilish looked different than it had when she'd first seen it. Before, it had looked like an unsightly bear with unusual eyes. Staring at her as blood dripped from its mouth stood a demon with an abnormally large bear body with the face of a moose and extremely large antlers. Its fur was that of a bear, and its strange pupils were still shaped in an up and down rectangular fashion, bright yellow, with an empty, hollow gaze. As Wilmayra took in the beast as it stared at her in that blank gaze devoid of any emotions, she took in the last of the horrific and gruesome details on the demon's body.

Where the paws or hoofs of an animal should have been were human hands and feet. It walked on them as a bear would have, but the sound of its gait was *wrong* because of the repulsive appendages attached to its body. She could see that the wounds on her trunk had come from teeth and antler, and not from the beast scratching at the wood like an animal would have. Her body wanted to tremble, to escape, to be sick. But she knew as she looked at its horrid face, her fate had been sealed. It was now, or never. She waited another moment as it took its first step toward her, avoiding the Sarsen as it lined the ground over her roots. Its eyes locked on her form, before she took a step backward with a hand against the hilt of the blade hidden in her waistband. She had hidden it there during lunch and was glad it still was concealed, in case the demon could smell its magic. The creature lazily continued its odd gait, and Will continued to walk along the stones covered in runes of protection as she took each backwards step toward the river bed. As she came out from under the branches of her protected tree, the demon emerged with its nose sniffing the air for her. She wondered if it had poor vision, especially in the now heavy rain, and planned on using that to their advantage.

As she crossed the threshold of stones that the Riuvilish avoided, Arden loosed a pointed stone into the back of its neck. The demon was startled at the movement and looked up, shrieking in its revolting way again. As the Riuvilish had opened its mouth, the Tegs threw sludge straight into its throat. The demon gagged and coughed before screaming again, howling loudly in anger before Arden stabbed it with another shot, this time to its ear. The demon rubbed its face to the ground to loosen the stones, still sputtering from the sludge. It shrieked before charging at Wilmayra, but she dodged it as it leaped through the air where she had been standing.

She managed to stand up before it turned around again, allowing the rage in her soul to overtake her. She screamed as it came to her again and waited for it to scream back. As it did, the Tegs threw another sludge filled bowl into its mouth, followed by another as it coughed again. Will refused to allow the trembling in her legs keep her from winning this battle, but she wasn't sure how much longer she could wait for the demon to be overcome with poison to finish it off. She sent another promise to Ivokorresh to rid the world of the demon, before pulling out the dagger she'd used with Arden earlier as a distraction from what she really intended to use. She bared her teeth at the Riuvilish and waited for another round of howling so as to fill it with more poison. Arden aimed another stone arrow, aiming for its stomach and hind legs. In quick succession, he hit the beast in the legs repeatedly until its hind quarters were raw and opened, weeping a sickening and putrid scented blood. Willow hardly had the presence of mind to be nauseated by the smell, and continued making gestures with the plain dagger as the beast was led to a specific place they'd be able to all overtake it. By the gait the demon used to walk, it was clear to see it had already decided the outcome of the interaction, that it had every part of the fight decided and was only playing with its food.

Wilmayra was not about to let the hellish demon fae harm her family any more than it had already, and though the pain medication had begun to wear off and she knew she would be aching soon, it would not stop her from fulfilling her role in this battle. She sidled up the walkway, keeping her gaze locked on the demon as she walked backwards through the dark and rain with the tree's guidance in each step. The demon limped after her with its lip curled, head tilted to the side as it looked at her. A wave of uneasiness filled her as she realized the beast intended to leap at her, and finish her as it landed. She could see only *one* emotion on its face. Like a cat with a mouse, a coyote with a chicken, it had locked its sight on her and she knew it. She made a move to jump toward the river, the bed of stones a safe place for her to land as the demon leaped at her. She heard Arden scream before she saw the beast hit the ground, a sword within its flank.

"Arden, *no!*" She cried - but it was too late. The demon righted itself and swatted Arden away, his body rolling on the ground lifelessly as she could only watch in horror. As Arden's body came to a rest, she saw the stones on the ground pull inward, keeping Arden outside of the ring and safe from the demon until she could help him. From where she stood, and the rain filling her eyes, she couldn't tell if he was breathing. She wanted to run after him, but the Riuvilish turned to look at her, mouth open. It made no attempt to follow after Arden and she was relieved, but only for a moment. Of course the demon would only go after fae with treeborn bloodlines, and had no use for Arden. It would go for the meal with the most reward.

The golden and glowing eyes blinked at her before it made an attempt at jumping toward her, but with the damage from the stone arrowheads and the sword in its flank, it could only move in a slow and broken gait. It reached its hand to grasp the blade and pulled it out quickly, hardly making a sound as it did. The smell of the putrid blood filled the air again making her feel like she was going to be sick, the scent debilitating. It only salivated as it limped toward her, and she wasn't sure how she should attempt stabbing it in the heart without causing great threat to herself - she was not a battlefield warrior, nor did she know what exactly to do in a position such as this, with a large opponent and a lot to lose.

She felt the hair on her body stand up as a flash of lightning pierced the night, followed by a long and billowing thunder. The demon looked up at it, and Sian used the distraction to their advantage and used the sigils on the nearby stones they had planted, and kept the demon frozen in place for a moment as Will contemplated her next move. If she could get the beast to lay backwards, she could aim for its heart, in between the ribs, right in the center of the abdomen. She braced herself for what she was about to do before nodding, and ran full speed toward the demon. She leapt onto its back, sliding the dagger along its injured side and prayed it wouldn't be able to reach her for the duration of her sitting there. It screeched as it tried to shake her off, but she used the knife to lock herself onto its back. She reached up, ducking her head to avoid its massive antlers, as she cut the base of its neck.

"Here!" She called toward the Tegs, hoping they understood what she was intending. Thankfully, they did, and a wave of the rock and water mixture landed on the beast's wound. It screamed again before she was flung from its back, and landed on the wet moss. She rolled onto her side, spitting the blood from her mouth from where she'd bitten her lip on landing, and called to the Tegs again.

"Sarsen on the antlers!" She cried out to no one in particular, hoping for a rope of sorts to be tossed around the antlers and held in place. It was Sian that brought the excess fabric, a braided piece of Sarsen, and Will reached out to catch it as it flew from Sian's hands to her own. She almost dropped it and let it roll away accidentally, but she caught it in the end. As the demon swung its head down, Wilmayra looped a braid through its antlers before jumping back onto the ground. The synch tightened without her needing to do it herself as the demon pulled it taut. The demon screamed, its piercing sound numbing her ears as its volume increased. From the side, she heard a quiver and bow being filled, before another stone arrow pierced the demon in its right eye. Another howl filled the air, indignant and violent, but Wilmayra only felt relieved as the arrow could only mean that Arden was very much alive. In the dark and rain, she couldn't make him out from where she stood, and so held onto the hope in her heart. She turned toward the demon and waited for the Sarsen to snag along the earth, for a stone to lock it against the ground and hold it there.

The Tegs had instructed her on where to stab the demon when the time came, but the position had to be perfect. If not, they risked only sending it into a temporary hibernation much like the one it had been in previously. After a moment of the demon shrieking, the rain began to lessen and she could finally make out everything around her clearly. The demon's eye on the right side was no longer an eye, but a single stone in the socket. The rest of the wounds had begun to bubble and ooze as the sludge and poison bombs filled its bloodstream. The left eye, the only functional eye, stared back at her as it snarled. Where once the demon held no expression, there was now a horrifying amount of loathing in its gaze as it looked upon her. She placed her feet firmly on the ground as she heard the Tegs behind her as the Riuvilish stepped toward her slowly in its injured state.

It was no less terrifying in this form than it had been at first glance, and as her friends stood behind her, she knew it was still a very close fight. She wasn't certain what she'd do, but the Tegs held their arms up and out as they pulled the Sarsen with everything they had in their bodies. The demon was flung back, landing on its side as it struggled against the Sarsen as the fabric was pulled deep underground with the other stones buried there. For a moment, they all held their breath as they waited for the beast to be flattened to the ground, and Wilmayra pulled the magicked dagger from her waist. She took a tentative step toward the struggling beast, when the Sarsen snapped under the strain.

~ Nineteen ~

THE SUN WILL RISE

Arden watched as Gert and Grin collapsed. The magic they used to guide the rocks slipped violently from their grip. They were left weak in the mud as they gasped for breath. As he stood just outside the protective ring, he aimed at the demon but missed. It bounced off of one of its flailing antlers and it turned its eyes back to Wilmayra. He saw as she gripped the dagger with her whole strength, and held his breath as it snarled. It made its way toward her. His stomach twisted as he watched, with only his arrows to help from where he stood. As he stared, he noticed its movements, disjointed and unsteady.

Its sight was limited with the stone protruding from one eye socket and the heavy rain. It couldn't see much, and tripped over a gap in the ground, a groove in the moss. It sniffed the air to follow after her, its only reliable sense left. He watched as it hobbled in her direction, the broken movements sending fear through his veins. She put the dagger back into her waistband hilt, before turning and running in the opposite way. She glanced in his direction before nodding at him and led it toward the front of the cottage. He followed after her, remaining outside the circle. If she needed him, he would get her out safely. No matter the cost.

His attention was brought to a glow around the trunk of the tree. He saw Sian with a pulsing magenta light exuding from their hand. The flash lit the night, the orb striking its mark. Sian ran toward the demon, another glowing ball of light in their hand held up toward it. They threw it, and the ball of energy hit the demon with sapphire embers filling the air like ash. The strike sent it into a frenzy. The demon roared as it was forced against the stone border. It kicked at the ground, screaming as it fell on the rocks. Arden held his breath as he waited for the beast to stand. He saw Will creep toward it before he yelled after her. It wasn't time yet, it wasn't weak enough to be finished this way. If she struck now, she would be lost along with all hope.

"It's not down!" He bellowed. She could not take the risk yet. He had to make sure she was safe. His voice cut through the air, surprising even himself. He was raspy and harsh in his tone. There was no control or thought involved in his voice. He needed to *express* and *direct* his wife as she was faced with an impossible task.

He leaped forward and pushed Will out of the way as the demon swiped blindly through the air with its sickening hands. It knocked Arden against the cottage, sending him to the ground in a daze. He tried to command his limbs to move. He tried to blink his vision back. He couldn't see. He could hardly hear as his mind was filled with a piercing sound. He was sure it was only his head, as he could still vaguely hear Will calling his name. He slumped over and focused on his breathing. He tried to stand, but his body wouldn't follow his directions. His eyes felt as though they had darkened, the forest hard to see. He wiped his face and noticed blood on his hands. He wiped again, trying to clear it away. He rubbed his head, rubbed where it ached. He had hit the shutters with a lot of force, and he knew from experience this was a concussion. He had to ignore it, power through. He had to do whatever it took to get to Will and keep her safe. He made a promise and he intended to keep it. He pulled himself up and stood on his feet, wobbling, but alive.

He followed the sound of his wife. He strained his ears to find her, the sound of his blood whooshing in his head blocking out all other sound. He tried to walk toward them, following the light of Sian's magic, but dropped to his knees as a wave of dizziness rolled through his body. He spit the blood from his mouth. He held his hands over his head and groaned, the pain intensifying in a heartbeat rhythm. He would not be taken down by a demon fae. He would not let his wife and their family be taken by the demon. He would stand. He *would* stand. He reached into his pocket and pulled out the handkerchief Willow had given him, wiping his brow with it. His hand was shaky and unsteady, but he held it to his head as he fought the wave of dizziness that threatened to pull him to the ground.

"I will prevail," he said through gritted teeth. A soft blue light emanated from his wound, only to disappear. His head stopped swimming just as suddenly as he'd been thrown into the wall. He gazed at his hands, still coated in his own blood. He looked at the once white fabric, now stained dark and hard to see in the night. The wound was real and yet healed all the same. He wondered in amazement at what happened. What it could mean, for their future and their children. His thoughts raced with questions. He shook his head clear and stood on his feet again. It was not the time for this. He continued forward, placing the handkerchief in his pocket once again, searching the night for Will. He would worry about whatever that meant later, and sent a small prayer of thanks to whatever god or goddess had given him the strength he needed to continue. The small piece of fabric would forever be his charm of luck, a tie to Willow, an undeniable source of comfort. He ran faster as he heard Will and Sian as they screamed.

"Your power is nothing to mine!" Sian spat as another orb hit the beast. Will had the dagger in her hand. Its soft light made her look ethereal. A warrior goddess. The closer she came to the demon, the brighter it shone. A heartbeat of light. She was encompassed by the glow entirely. Arden set his feet firmly on the ground. He would protect her. He pulled his bow back with another stone, and aimed for its damaged leg. If he were able to ground the beast, it would have nowhere to run. They would be able to take it down that much quicker. He let the stone loose and it hit its mark. The demon wailed and flung its body to the ground, every limb flailing. Dirt and moss tossed through the air. He felt a brief moment of victory before it righted itself. It turned its eyes to Arden, its empty gaze taking him in.

A brief swell of panic filled his chest but he stood his ground. He saw its eyes flick toward his bow. It locked eyes on the weapon. He held the bow that had caused the majority of damage to the demon, and it knew it. It limped toward him. It didn't blink. Step after step, it hobbled after Arden. He stood his ground. When it came to the stone ring, it snarled and let out a horrific screech. It started to dig at the earth. Scratching and reaching for Arden but unable to pass over the stones. Each frantic movement of its hands sent dirt through the air, raining down on them in a wet and muddy mess.

"Get the Tegs!" He heard Will shout to Sian. Will's tree was just behind the demon as it tried to get to Arden. He knew she saw a chance, but the timing wasn't right. He watched Will sneak up on it but shook his head at her. *Not yet.* She paused but nodded, accepting his guidance. She stepped back toward her tree, an ear pointed toward the Tegs and Sian. They'd wait for the brothers and Sian before continuing. It seemed the beast was distracted enough as it tried to reach him. Will sighed as she stood, panting in frantic breaths. He couldn't see beyond the tree, or hear beyond the beast as it flung itself through the dirt.

Suddenly, the demon roared and reared onto its hind legs, spraying another wave of dirt everywhere. The force of its movement sent Will backwards into the ground, landing against the trunk of her tree. With the branches held tight by the Sarsen, he could see her land without the hindrance of the leaves and flowers. She didn't move. She laid there, crumpled in the dark. The beast flung its body again, spraying more debris before standing and swiping at the loose branches they weren't able to protect. Arden felt something catch in his throat as flowers filled the air.

"*No,*" he cried in dismay as the demon swiped at another branch before falling back to the ground, the broken branches hitting the ground with a heart breaking *thwump.* Will hadn't moved yet. He felt himself panicking before he saw the demon looking at him straight on. He turned his focus away from Will despite the ache in his chest. The worry seeped into every limb, but he met the beast's gaze. As suddenly as the rain began, it all but cleared up around them leaving Arden bare and open to the beast.

Fear filled him, but he could only stare the beast down. He'd keep its gaze locked on him. He notched another stone and let the demon watch. He held it, aiming for its face without moving. He kept the position. The second it noticed her lying there, it would be the end. No matter her current state, if it found her now everything would be lost. He let the stone go after an extended moment, keeping its eyes locked on him intentionally. It flew through the air before hitting the Riuvilish in the under-belly. It recoiled, landing on its side. The smell of its blood filled the air. Sickening, putrid. A smell that would haunt his night-mares for years to come.

As the demon stood, he saw Will lifted up by Grin. Gert and Sian held their hands toward the demon. He didn't see Grin and Will make it to safety, but as the demon stood between himself, Sian, and Gert, he knew she had to be a safe distance away. They needed to get her away from this area, far enough from the trees to keep her and the cottage safe from its destructive and disgustingly human hands. Sian sent another orb toward the Riuvilish, a ball of fuschia light and energy disorienting the demon in its only functional eye. It swayed where it lay, before righting itself and standing slowly. It turned to them, groaning. It was confused, not sure where to attack first. It was outnum-bered. It had relied on sneak attacks its whole existence and was unequipped for battle. It's only thought had been to consume, since its creation.

As Gert hit it with another stone, it screeched. It scanned the area looking for Will, sniffing the air and peering around them. But it was only met with more energy and stones. Arden locked eyes with Sian as they sent another orb at the beast. Sian cocked their head to the side. After they sent another orb toward the demon, Sian gestured for Arden to head the other way around the cottage. He took off running. His breath heaved as he turned the corner around the cottage, to the small clearing he remem-bered seeing on a map long ago. He wasn't sure how, but he knew a new plan needed to be implemented. By just Sian's nod, he knew what they were telling him wordlessly. The demon was too strong. With Sian's magic, they were sure to start a fire. They needed to move. They needed to try something different. They needed to protect Will's tree. It could not knock another branch off of the wisteria, his stomach rolled at the thought. He ran harder, straight into the woods. He felt Teggert follow behind, a rumble in the ground wherever he went. He was pulling the circle *with* the beast. Pulling it away from the tree, away from the cottage as it charged after Arden. It thought its prey would be easy to catch, but Arden was fast. It was injured, moving slower but still gaining on Arden. His lungs ached as they made it to the meadow.

The demon bellowed as it neared the clearing. The trees were sparse, and the ones still there were long perished as they laid about the ground. As if the earth fissured out beneath the clearing and had set a large slice of land apart from the rest. Arden slowed to a stop as he realized the further into the clearing he went, the closer he was to the fissured cliff face. It had been in a far reach of Will's home and they'd never come this way. He now knew why. He turned to face the demon head on, entirely cornered with nowhere to go before looking to the side of the cliff face one last time.

He wasn't much of a climber, but the grooves of the stones looked promising. Without thinking, he leaped and began scaling the rocks. If he could make it to the small outcrop overlooking the field, he'd have the upper hand. The beast breathed heavily as it caught up to him, screeching indignantly as he rose high above it. The demon threw itself toward Arden, but the cliff face was made of stone. It recoiled from the rocks as if burned before standing on its hind legs, screaming to the furthest reaches of the forest. He was certain it could be heard from Stóngrast. He couldn't cover his ears to protect them from the volume of the beast. He kept climbing until he was finally over the cliff, grasping onto the outcropping stones and pulling himself over. He let himself gasp, catching his breath before he rolled over to shoot the demon with the last of his stone arrows. As he aimed the first one, Sian launched a fierce red orb directly at the Riuvilish. The ball of magic energy erupted into flames, encompassing it in fumes and ash. It screeched and flailed, grabbing at its face as its fur burned. The stink of singed hair filled the air, blending with the putrid stench of its blood.

Teggert rumbled into the clearing, rolling through on a wave of stone. As if the earth had become water. His movements were both fluid and rigid. With the cliff face, he was able to easily block the demon within a new circle. The tree would be safe. With a heaving movement, Gert pulled loose stones from the cliff face. He grunted under the weight. Though it was dark, Arden was able to see Gert's strained expression. He pulled, heaved. Arden was jolted onto his hands and knees as it quaked beneath his feet. Gert had a firm grasp on the stones that weren't integral to the structure of the cliff face. He pulled them again, finally loosening them. Arden peered down, laying on his stomach to keep from tumbling over. He watched as Teggert pulled, sending the loose rocks tumbling down. A crash reverberated through the ground, and dust filled the air. Arden coughed, waiting for it to clear. The beast bellowed in agony, screaming the loudest they had heard it through the night.

The stones landed heavily on the beast. It was crushed to the ground, the sound of rocks hitting its flesh echoed through the night. In a sickening *crack,* the demon finally buckled under the pressure of the stones. As they fell onto the demon, its bones snapped and splintered through its fur. Its bones broke as it was pinned beneath the stones. Its voice gurgled in its throat, bubbling up fluids. As it spit rancid blood and bile, Gert pulled down harder on the stones. It let out a wail, struggling against its prison of rock and earth. Its hind legs were completely shattered, the human feet bent at odd angles. Its front hand was exposed to the night, broken and bleeding. Arden almost breathed in relief, but knew better than to think anything would be this easy to finish off. There were too many close calls. There was too much to lose.

Grin ran into the clearing, holding Will. She looked weak, but Arden saw her head lift up and search the clearing. Looking around, she finally saw him on the cliff. Grin stood her on the ground. She wobbled, but stood on her own. Gert grunted as the demon pushed against the stones. Sian threw another incendiary ball at it, singeing what was left of the fur on its face. As it flailed under the stone, its antler cracked. The broken antler hit the ground, the demon screaming as it scrambled to free itself. It was held fast by Gert.

"Stand up, Arden, I'll bring you down," Grin called up. Arden stood hastily, looping his bow over his shoulder. Grin pulled the stone off the cliff face and pulled Arden down. He was pulled over and away from the demon before he was close enough to the ground. He jumped down and ran for Will.

"Are you okay?" He asked her as he scanned her face, holding her cheeks in his hands. Her hair had fallen from the braid she'd wrapped around her head. It fell loose around her shoulders, and realized then that the branches the beast had knocked over had cost Will her hair. He brushed a loose strand from her face. It reached just under her ears, short and cropped. He was grateful it was only her hair the demon had been able to take away, and nothing worse.

"Jus' hit m'head that's all," she murmured in a daze. Arden was scared, despite the relief of seeing her standing there before him. Her words were slurred, terrifying him. Though only her hair appeared to have been damaged, her head was certainly hurt like his had been earlier. Concussion. He thought for a moment, but he wasn't sure what they'd do. She was unbalanced, teetering where she stood. One wrong step and she'd be splayed out on the ground. She would never be able to wield a weapon in that state. But when he felt his thoughts spiraling, he remembered what he had done not long ago to his own head for a similar injury. He wondered if it would work again. He knew he needed to try. There were no other options - Will *had* to finish the beast that lay screeching and gurgling beneath the stones. He pulled the handkerchief out again, still stained with his own blood, and placed it over her forehead before whispering like he had done before.

"We will prevail," he breathed into her. It had worked before, and he'd try again. After a moment, a soft blue light pooled from his hand and onto Will's face. She blinked in wonder as she gazed up at him. Her eyes were wide and a small smile creeped onto her lips.

"Thank you," she said before stepping away from him. She pulled the dagger from her waist. It was time. The trees around them fluttered, and Will looked around in dismay before her face quickly hardened. She held the dagger tight before nodding to no one in particular. He put his handkerchief in his pocket, patting it down as he looked at the sky as the trees whispered.

"The sun will rise soon," he said. Without understanding what the trees said, he could see the movement of Will's eyes as she looked at the horizon. Though it was still dark, he could see the blackened sky giving way to a deep blue. Will stepped forward, ready for the inevitable. Arden sent a prayer to any of the gods that may be listening, begging for her safety.

Grin and Gert pulled at the stones, sending the demon into another fit as it was contorted against its will. It screamed and pulled against its confinement. It fought against them with everything it had left in its body. Despite being broken beyond recognition, it pushed hard against the weight of the rocks. The Tegs pulled the rocks apart, piercing the demon's flesh as they stretched it out. Pulled tight against the ground with stones littered through its body, it let out a furious groan.

Will walked forward with her eyes narrowed, holding the dagger. Her arm was outstretched as she brandished it, the soft glowing light of the blade enveloping her. The Tegs shifted the demon one last time, covering its body in stone as its belly was exposed to Will. She looked it up and down, noting its movements, its frantic breaths. Arden watched her scan it, searching for the heart as it beat in its chest. Arden saw her gaze lock onto the center of its ribcage, distorted now from the bones inside its body that were broken. He knew she had her mark locked. He held his breath as she tightened her grip on the hilt of the blade. She stepped forward with her head held high, not an ounce of hesitation in her demeanor.

"I will you to return to the dark from whence you came," she growled, her grip tightening around the hilt of the blade. "I will you to *never* return," she stalked closer to the demon.

"I will it by the stars and the stone," she lifted the dagger high. She held it with her two hands before arching it through the air. Using her entire weight, she swung it down. It landed inside the Riuvilish with a sickening squelch.

"I will it by the hearth flames of my home," Willow cried out as she pushed harder, sending the tip of the blade deep into its chest cavity. The demon gurgled, its face lifting through the stones it was buried by. It looked at Will, golden eyes burning into her with a look of pure hatred. She met its gaze unblinkingly before heaving one last time, pressing the hilt as far as it would go, until a shriek filled the air.

"I will you to *die*," Willow screamed as she pressed harder still, sending the hilt through its broken skin and bones.

"*This is the Will of the Wisteria*," Willow howled with one final twist, collapsing onto her knees.

A wail filled the air before it echoed through the trees as the demon gurgled its final breath and collapsed beneath the weight of the stones, the fight leaving its body in one heaving breath. As the blade met the demon's heart ending it for good, a shock wave of power exuded from its body. They all fell to their knees as it reverberated through the ground, knocking them all down. They looked around uneasily, but the only thing left before them was its broken body with putrid blood as it oozed from its corpse.

Will stood up suddenly and ran into the clearing behind them. She held a hand over her mouth and ran into the thick grass before bending over and heaving over the ground. She vomited, a painful sound and Arden ran up behind her to stroke her back. She sniffed after a moment, and Arden handed her a handkerchief. She wiped her face and blew her nose before tossing it to the ground and leaping into his arms. She held tight to him, her face buried into his neck. He held her just as tight, her feet raised off the ground as he hugged her. Sian and the brothers walked over and placed their hands on Arden and Will, letting her cry for a moment.

"What *was* that?" Willow asked after wiping her face, dismayed by the force that had sent them to the ground as her nerves finally settled.

"It may have been from the power of the blade," Gert suggested. They all looked at one another uneasily before Sian broke the silence.

"Lets burn the son of a bitch," Sian said. Will peered down at them, and nodded. She let go of Arden and stood on the ground as the Tegs helped move the stones from the demon, exposing its broken body to them. Will gagged again but pulled her shirt over her nose to avoid the smell. Sian threw more energy at it until it was engulfed in flame. It was centuries old, and it had already begun to rapidly decay before their eyes.

The fire made quick work of the demon. The sun began to rise over the horizon, the sky turning a light blue. The sun's rays were still hidden beyond the cliff and trees, but the lightening color of the sky was a breath of fresh air. Will sighed against Arden, holding his arm as she rested her head on him. As the ashes of the beast filled the clearing, the dagger was left laying in the center of the ground. Gert stepped forward over the embers and lifted the dagger, its glow ceasing in his grip. He handed it to Sian who placed it in their belt. The Tegs pulled apart the ground and sent the ashes deep underground. The ground rumbled and shook them on their feet before they flattened the cliffside onto the ground, creating a large meadow.

They stood there and watched the sun rise, hands held between them as they breathed in the new day.

~ Twenty ~

NEW BEGINNINGS

As the sun loomed high in the sky, they found themselves in Wilmayra's kitchen. They had walked back to Wilmayra's cottage, stumbling and exhausted, and began making themselves breakfast. They had taken turns in the shower with the Tegs opting to leap into the river and wash themselves along with their clothes under the morning sun, basking in the light. As they cleansed themselves of the battle and washed away dirt and blood, they all were silent. Even Sian hardly said a word, and Wilmayra wasn't certain she'd ever seen Sian *not* have words before. They were bone weary, too tired to talk, hardly able to move. They laid about for a while after they were cleaned up, with wounds patched up and bandaged. By midmorning, they went in search of food. Will and Sian gathered up spices and filled up a pot with water to boil in the fire, readying noodles and spices as Arden went to hunt for them. He brought back a quail, small but enough for them to share.

It felt odd to be making a meal in her kitchen with all of the windows open, with people milling about her home. She couldn't remember the last time she'd had anyone here, aside from Arden, without the shutters locked tight. Sian helped season the bird with Will, and cooked it next to the pot of noodles. The Tegs brought in a basket of vegetables and washed them off before dicing them. Will added them into the pan with the meat and sauteed them before pulling it out and resting it on an oven mit, letting it cool. Sian lifted the large pot of noodles from the flames and brought it to the sink, pouring out the excess water. Will grabbed bowls from her cabinet and laid them on the counter, and they all filled their bowls to their preferences. Will added more vegetables than meat, preferring the produce, but Arden added extra meat to his own. They ate at the counter, inhaling their food before drinking some water and tea, and continued to lay around the house.

Will walked into her bedroom and laid down, stretching out on the large mattress. She sighed contentedly before she heard boots on the floor, tossed to the side. The bed dipped under the weight as she turned to see Arden. He lifted the blanket and crawled in next to her, yawning and stretching beside her. She was tired, too tired to talk but she raised her lips in a gentle smile as Arden kissed her cheek and closed his eyes. She followed suit, and they napped peacefully until the sound of snoring woke her up.

...

Will sat up and rubbed her eyes, running her hands through her now short hair. For a moment she was sad, mourning the locks she'd grown through the years but her hand rested over her belly. Though the night was full of stress, she'd managed to keep her belly safe from harm and had only sustained a head wound in the end. Though she knew it was too early to know if the baby was growing properly, she trusted in her intuition that the small sprout was safe and sound inside of her. She slid from the bed, trying not to rouse Arden as he snored with his mouth wide open next to her. She giggled quietly before walking to the kitchen to make more tea. Sian greeted her with sleepy eyes, rubbing them as they smiled.

They brewed a pot of tea together before sitting on the couch and lazily waited for the water to boil. Sian laid their head on Will's lap, feet hanging over the couch arm. Will played with Sian's hair, braiding it like she had when they were children. When the kettle whistled, Will stood and filled their mugs, and brought them back to the coffee table before sitting shoulder to shoulder with her closest friend. They sipped the tea quietly, enjoying the peaceful silence.

Teggert walked in the front door, smiling brightly when he saw them sitting there. He noticed their mugs and perked up, filling himself one, too. He joined them in the living room and sat in the chair across from them.

"The horse is ready to take us back to Port. Grin went to Hanlan to spread the news. I suppose you two had a good rest in the time being?" He asked them, eyes glinting. Sian laughed and nodded, laying their head on Will's shoulder.

"I've never been so tired," Will murmured with a yawn, "It's your turn in the port then?" She said with a smile. The brothers would always swap places periodically, though she supposed the human port had never been the wiser. The brothers were identical, it was near impossible to tell them apart unless you knew them very well, or had the trees listening for them in the woods like Will did. She imagined as children they must have been pure menaces with their charade.

"It's my turn to take watch," he grinned.

"It might be a silly question, but can I leave the shutters open now? I never want to close them again," she said with a pout. The mere idea of being trapped within the confining walls of her dark home was enough to terrorize her. Thankfully, Gert nodded.

"There's no more need to worry, the windows are enchanted. Nothing could be strong enough to break them, now. Leave them be, and make a bag. I'm sure you have more things you'd like to bring with you for the time being." He told her gently. Sian gasped and turned to Will, startling her.

"We have to plan your Binding Prayer Ceremony!" Sian breathed. Will rolled her eyes.

"You had me worried," she huffed, "no gasping until my paranoia wears off," she laughed. Sian stuck their tongue out at her, making Will laugh harder.

Arden stumbled down the hallway as Gert headed back to the horse and cart. He rubbed his eyes and looked around with a confused expression. Will and Sian snickered as they watched him take the seat Gert had been sitting in.

"You look just like Sian right now," Will giggled at him as he yawned, adorably sleepy. She stood before heading to her room to fill up a bag. She brought only a handful of dresses, knowing more were at Arden's still. She wondered where they'd live after everything was settled completely. She knew for herself at least, it would take a while before she felt safe again. She was just glad she had the opportunity to be safe at all, and knew there would be plenty of time for them to make their own home, wherever it may be.

She brought Arden's boots with her to the living room and gently placed them down by his feet. He pulled them on, his eyes looking less sleepy by the moment. She saw a mug sitting on the end table next to him, and smiled knowing Sian must have made him a cup. Will threw sand into the fireplace, the bag she kept in the kitchen had been unused for a long time. She hadn't lit a fire for fear of summoning the beast to her home, but now didn't have to worry anymore. She coated the ashy embers in the sand and they made their way to the door.

Will locked the cottage behind her before they followed Gert to the horse and cart that trailed behind it. Arden sat in the middle of the small cart, and Will and Sian climbed onto either side of him. Their smaller frames squeezed next to him easily, his arms going around them as they settled against his side. They talked for a bit but before long, their eyes grew heavy and they dozed off on the ride to the Port.

...

Will woke to the sound of yelling, and looked around blearily before realizing they were in the market. She recognized the voice crying out their names, and she scanned the crowd to see her.

"Arden! Will!" Juna gasped, not seeing Sian as they were tucked under Arden's arm. "Where's Sian?" Juna asked worriedly as she ran to the side of the cart. She let out a sigh as she saw Sian nestled against her brother and rolled her eyes. "Of course you're fine, I don't know why I worried," she scoffed. Will giggled as she climbed out of the cart and gave Juna a hug. She squeezed her sister in law tight, and Juna squeezed back just as hard.

"We handled it," Will told her without elaborating as everyone in the market saw them. She knew they already must have an idea about what she is, and what happened, but she wasn't ready for that many eyes to be on her. Gert looked behind him as he sat on the horse, guiding it through the mass of people.

"I'll take the cart to the Fairwood Estate and then the stables. Don't worry about anything else," he told her. She opened her mouth to ask him something but he continued, "*and* I'll handle the gossip and make sure to clear things up," he told her. Will smiled gratefully and turned to walk with Juna, arms linked, as they followed the cart along.

"What happened to your hair?" Juna asked before running her fingers through the shortened locks.

"We missed some of my tree, and apparently it came at the cost of my hair," she told her, pouting despite knowing much worse could have happened.

"You're entitled to feeling sad about losing a piece of yourself, no matter how big or small it is. It's okay to mourn your hair, and it's okay to be grateful for life," Juna told her kindly. Will felt her eyes prick with tears at her words, knowing she needed to hear that. She was grateful, beyond grateful, for the gift that she'd been given. The gift of a life she'd only ever dreamed of, certain it was only a dream that never would come true. She nodded to Juna in acceptance of her kindness before she frowned.

"I think Gert is going to tell everyone we're fae," she said in a deadpan voice. Juna looked at her with furrowed brows before she cocked her head to the side.

"Oh, he definitely is," she watched as the cart pulled up to Arden's home, way ahead of them. Gert peered over the horse and looked at one of the D'Misios before gesturing to Willow, and all they could see was a shocked expression on Alise's face, followed by the rest of them.

"Oh goddess," she muttered as Juna laughed next to her.

"Well, considering you brought and supplied us with a continuous flow of medicine, you're entitled to having a quirk about you," she snickered.

"A *quirk*," Will groaned as they laughed and met the rest of their family at the doors.

"I was so worried," Alvenia cried as she pulled her and Arden into a warm hug, sniffling against their ears.

"We're okay," Arden told her warmly, though his voice was still thick with sleep as he yawned. Sian looked like they'd fall over but Juna guided them inside, laying Sian out on the chaise in the lounge. Sian fell asleep again quickly, buried under a blanket that Juna draped over them. She snickered as Sian snored, but let them be.

"We have dinner ready," Alvenia pulled them into the dining room and pushed them into chairs, handing them both large glasses of water and plates stacked high with food. They all dug into the meal, but grew tired before long. They were sent to bed quickly, and gratefully rested their weary bodies until the sun was high the next day.

...

Will woke up feeling ravenous, and quickly dressed before she all but ran to the kitchen. She was met at the doorway by an equally hungry Sian and Juna, who both had their plates stacked high with all the food you could imagine served at a brunch. Will looked at them, very impressed, as they dug into their plates before hurriedly grabbing her own. She sat down with them at the table in the kitchen, too hungry to leave the room. It was louder, but it was closer to the food and they didn't mind.

By the time Will had finished her second plate, Arden waltzed through the doors with the same look of hunger they'd all had, making Will laugh through her bite of pancakes. She hastily covered her mouth to maintain her manners, but Juna and Sian held no qualms as they teased Arden for his bedhead. When he sat down, he smiled at them before eating, unbothered by their remarks. If Will hadn't known any better, she'd have thought Arden had *always* had two siblings by the way they interacted.

"So when are you two having your Binding Prayer ceremony, Will of the Wist?" Sian asked after gulping down orange juice. Arden looked at Will in confusion, making Sian laugh.

"Will of *what?*" He asked with a sleepy voice, running a hand through his curls in an attempt to tame them.

"Wilmayra of the Wisteria," Sian snickered. *"Obviously."* Arden sighed, hiding a smile as he pretended to roll his eyes in mock irritation. Will laughed as Sian repeated their question.

"So, Wilmayra of the Wisteria, when are you two having your Binding Prayer ceremony?" Sian said, biting into another piece of the pancakes.

"Oh, we don't really have to do that," Will waved her hand in the air, brushing the idea away.

"No, you *have* to," Juna said through a bite of bacon.

"We've already been technically married *twice,"* Arden shrugged.

"Well I'm sorry, but I don't make the rules. You have to finish the job," Sian said with their nose in the air, sending Juna into a fit of laughter.

"I'm *pregnant,* I'd say the job was finished a while ago," Will said with faux haughtiness.

"Ew," Juna groaned, but Sian only cackled as Arden spit out a mouthful of his coffee.

"Oh, gods, *fine,* we can do another ceremony," he coughed as he wiped his mouth. Will wiped the mess off the table, and also on her face. Arden smiled sheepishly at her but she only laughed.

"Hurray for planning another wedding!" Juna clapped, before diving into question after question in regards to the traditions and customs of a fae Binding Prayer. Arden made his escape after letting out a large belch, shooed away by the trio. When Alvenia came home from her meeting, they'd tell her what they were going to do. Willow also thought her and Arden should tell her about the baby, officially this time. She knew during the first attack her mother in law had to have heard her desperate cries, but she deserved to hear the news in a much happier light. They all did.

After breakfast, Will went in search of Arden and told him she wanted to tell Alvenia properly about the baby. He agreed easily, but began anxiously pacing as they waited for Alvenia to get home.

"Arden, she already knows," she said, but he waved her off. Will just giggled, but allowed him to worry, knowing there wasn't much she could say to relieve him of the irrational fear of telling his mother that his wife was with child. By lunchtime, Alvenia was home and they followed her to her bedroom.

"Mother, we have something we want to tell you," he said hesitantly, knuckles turning white as he squeezed Will's hand. She had to squeeze him back for him to loosen his hold, a nervous smile on his lips. She raised her brow to him, waiting for him to announce it. Of course, she wouldn't have minded being the one to say it, but she was having too much fun watching him squirm under his nerves, with the false idea of pressure on the announcement all his own doing.

"Arden?" Alvenia asked as he said nothing. Will let out a snort before covering her mouth. She looked at Alvenia and shared a mischievous smile with her, it was clear what he was trying to tell her to everyone but Arden, but they let him sweat for another minute longer before he finally let the words out.

"We're going to be parents," he said through clenched teeth, sending Will into a fit of laughter.

"I'm having a baby," she grinned, as Alvenia wrapped an arm around each of them, kissing their cheeks.

"I'm so happy for you both," she said through watery eyes, voice wobbling. They hugged her back tightly before she declared that she needed to tell *everyone* immediately.

"Oh gods, Mother, please don't -" Arden began, but she was already sweeping out of the room and running downstairs to find Felisia.

"Let her have her moment," Will rubbed Arden's back as he wiped his brow, sweating needlessly.

"I'm more concerned about people knowing we *made* a baby. How improper for people to know that information," Arden shuddered. Willow bent over laughing, entirely in stitches, as Arden stood there shaking his head. A small smile creeped over his lips, and he playfully rolled his eyes. He reached his hand out to her, and they wandered into their bedroom. Arden went to the bathroom and showered quickly. She knew she needed a bath, too, and when he left the shower, she hopped in after him. The warm water was soothing to her aching muscles, though it stung the wounds still fresh on her body. She did her best to wash them but knew water would have to be sufficient for the ones she couldn't reach. Just as she was about to turn the water off and give up, Arden opened the shower door and peered in.

"Let me help," he told her, already undressed. She smiled gratefully and turned around, letting him gently wipe away the old poultice she wasn't able to remove. When they were done, he helped dry each wound before adding more of the rub and bandages to them.

"Thank you," she told him. He leaned into her, kissing her deeply and desperately before guiding her to one of the chairs by the window. He closed the curtains and with the door shut, it was almost completely dark. He sat down on the chair first, and pulled her onto his lap. She easily straddled him, knees on either side of his hips.

She found herself already dripping for him, and guided his cock inside of her before slowly lowering her weight onto him. They both gasped as he filled her, and she shifted slightly to align their bodies flush together before she rose up and away, only to slam back down. As she tossed her head back, he kissed along her neck and covered her mouth, preventing her from making any noise in the middle of the day as they fucked desperately. He held his hand at the small of her back and tilted her backwards slightly.

Her eyes rolled as his angle deepened, rocking against her as she met his thrusts. He uncovered her mouth as she gasped, before sliding his hand to her neck. He put a faint amount of pressure over her throat, halting her noises. She clawed at his shoulders, pressing against him as hard as she could. The angle was *divine,* she was sure she'd come from this alone as her hand trailed down between them. She used her wetness on her clit, rubbing herself gently before Arden pushed his legs out further, and slid her deeper onto his cock.

She came without warning, a frantic cry escaping her lips as Arden kissed her to soften her noises. He used his hands to lift her hips and pull her back onto his cock as his tongue plundered her mouth. Tears filled her eyes as the sensations became too much, but she moved her hips against his to make him finish as hard as she had. Arden stood, holding her still as he carried her to the bed, his cock still deep inside her. He laid her at the edge of the bed, a perfect height for him to stand as he pounded into her. Her knees were tight around his waist, holding him to her. She bit her hand to keep from screaming as he stroked her core, deep within her, and laced their fingers together with her free hand.

"I love you," he breathed into her, a kiss between each word pressed softly to her breasts.

"I love you," she gasped, tears escaping. It was too much, and not enough all the same. She wanted to come again, greedy and desperate for it and pressed her feet into the edge of the bed to meet his thrusts. Arden huffed out a laugh, kissing her deeply before looking at her with his brows raised.

"Please," she said, trying hard not to make any noise beyond a whisper. He pushed her knees higher, pinning them almost to her shoulders and thrusted hard before coming, his delicious groan filling her ears. She whimpered and squirmed against him, so close, trying to find her end. He pulled out of her and sat on his knees, before delving his tongue into her folds. Her thighs tightened around his face as her hips involuntarily rolled up into his mouth. He leaned forward, putting more pressure on her clit as he reached to cover her mouth. Her frantic mews had escaped, but his fingers laid against her tongue and as she sucked on them she quieted herself. His fingers filled her pussy, stretching her and finding the spot that sent her eyes rolling. He sucked her clit as he curled his finger and she came violently against his mouth, nearly biting his fingers as she fought against making a sound. Her body trembled as his fingers continued to curl inside her, causing wave after wave of aftershock to roll through her body. She didn't think it was possible to come again, but if he kept moving the way he was, she would certainly find out.

He took mercy on her, though, as he lifted his head and saw the tear tracks rolling down her cheeks. He kissed her, the taste of him and her on his tongue. She ran her fingers through his hair and kissed him breathlessly, before laughing as she trembled. He pulled the blankets down and helped her onto her pillow before pulling her next to him, sweaty and sated. He wiped her tears and kissed her nose, brushing away a strand of her short hair as it laid on her forehead.

"So beautiful," he told her, making her blush.

"Love you," she yawned as she rolled over, Arden tucking himself behind her with a hand over her belly.

"Love you too, and you," he said as he rubbed the soft skin of her stomach. She fell asleep warm and happy, with a smile on her face.

...

The next few weeks were spent much like the previous: with dresses, swatches, planning, and for Willow, fucking. The baby was somehow making her libido insatiable, and she wasn't sure how she could possibly feel that way *all* the time, but Arden wasn't complaining. She was sure it wasn't anything to be worried about, and knew before long they'd be too tired to do anything like that anymore, anyway. She would enjoy herself while she could, but would be relieved to have the cottage to themselves with no one to hear them through the walls after the Binding was complete. It had been hard to focus during fittings and flower arrangements when all she could think about was her husband, and had to tell people who saw her getting flush that she was just feeling very warm. The only one that hadn't believed her was Juna, of course, but Will only laughed because it made her so uncomfortable to *know* Will and her brother were intimate at all.

The day of the ceremony came, though, finally. While it seemed as though the ideas they had were easy, implementing them seemed to be harder when it came to arranging the wisteria and the cottage for guests. The tree wasn't very large as far as trees went, and since it had grown almost over the cottage there left only a small amount of space for people to view the binding. The solution they came to was to pull back a lot of the branches, in a braid-like pattern, giving a perfect view of Arden's handprints on the now healed bark. During the attack, the handprints had thankfully been spared, with the back of the tree having been the area that was primarily wounded. With the

Tegs help, the scarring on the bark was minimal, and the skin on her back was nearly healed, too.

Will held Arden's hand as they took in the sight of the wisteria willow, flowers and branches parted with a row of blankets set out along the moss. There were no chairs, and everyone was wearing simple clothes in whites and creams. Arden wore a tunic that lightly matched his eyes, a fair blue, with white pants. Willow wore a pale green dress, with embroidered flowers made by her mother and siblings. Traditionally, the dress is made by the family of the fae being Bound, but with her blood relatives so far away, they had to make the dress first and add the lace and flowers made by her family later.

Unfortunately, her parents weren't able to make the trip, nor were her two youngest siblings. But the older two of her younger sisters, the ones born just after her when her parents had returned to their orchard, were escorted by Teggert and Teggrin to join her for the Binding Prayer. She was grateful the Tegs had brought them to her, and as they gifted her the beautiful, handmade flowers made with different stitches, she had cried real tears as they sewed it to the simple gown she'd wear for the ceremony. The tiny stitches made by her baby siblings, each tiny blemish on the flowers, had filled her heart with so much peace that she couldn't look at the dress for *days* without weeping.

Her sisters were playing on the moss, making flower crowns out of the wildflowers nearby, picking some from the bouquets and floral arrangements to add to them. In their cream dresses, with flowers wrapped around their heads, she began to weep again. Arden only rubbed her back, used to her frequent emotional outbursts. He told her it was important to let those feelings go when she felt them, because it was too short of a life for them to hold it in especially when she had a family who loved and supported her. They knew it was primarily the pregnancy hormones, but it was still an important ideal they held, to be entirely open with their emotions and to tell one another the whole truth.

Sian and Juna began guiding people onto the blankets, handing everyone a small flower as they sat down. Alvenia and Felton sat to the side, where they were joined by Will's sisters, Kyvéreth and Jeravelle.

As everyone sat along the moss, only the ones they deemed *family*, present, Arden and Willow took their places at the tree. Beneath the canopy of now pink flowers with purple in the center, they seemed to glow in a blush color as the sun rose directly overhead. It cast the flower's color across their forms, making them look young and innocent as they held hands before everyone. When they saw that Juna and Sian sat on the blankets next to the D'Misios, filling each place with their smiling faces, they looked to each other with raised brows. They nodded as they giggled nervously and stepped to the trunk of Wilmayra's tree.

Willow stood with Arden right behind her, his hands on her shoulders. They walked to the tree and kneeled before the handprints left behind by Arden, so long ago. They both took in a deep breath before laying their hands out against the bark, Wilmayra's in between Arden's hands, fitting in the space perfectly between them. As they sat, they began to recite the Binding Prayer, their voices soft but proud. As their voices recited the prayer together, their gentle words brought tears to their family's eyes as they watched. Will felt her own eyes pricking with tears, and tried not to let her voice waver as they spoke.

"I open my hands to you,
I invite you in my heart,
I pray that through all that we do,
Never shall we be apart,

From this day and onward,
Our souls will be entwined,
Forever we will move forward,
Together and always through this Bind,
My heart is yours,
  Until the end of time."

As they finished the Binding Prayer, Willow sank to her bottom as Arden rose higher onto his knees, and they pressed their foreheads against the rough bark of the tree. They held their position for a long moment, breathing each other in as they sat so close together, before falling back to their original positions and standing, hands laced together. Willow couldn't hold the tears back any longer and weeped into Arden's shirt collar, holding him tight around the neck. He ran a hand through her hair, only just starting to grow, and twirled a lock in his fingers. She smiled against him as it tickled her neck, and sighed as the smell of wisteria blooms filled her nose.

Their family rushed up to hug them, and they stood under the tree under the warm summer sun, together, finally. Arden's eyes crinkled as he smiled at her, his fingers trailing down her cheek. She lifted her head to look at him for what felt like the first time. Using the handkerchief that she had given him the first time she met him, so long ago now, he wiped away another tear that fell from her eye. She smiled up at him, leaning into his hand.

Her heart was full with gratitude and love, a peace within her she could have never dreamed of. As her sisters laid a messy flower crown over her head with petals raining down her face, she laughed and leaned up for a kiss. Arden met her lips soft and sweet as their hands rested over Will's round belly. The little one squirmed under their touch, bringing a delighted smile to their faces.

"My heart is yours," he told her, kissing her forehead.

"Until the end of time," she breathed as he met her lips once more.

~ Twenty-One ~

EPILOGUE

It was raining, but the windows were open. The humid breeze ruffled the curtains as Wilmayra sipped her tea. The little one was sleeping, he had tired himself out as he had played with his aunts all week before they left for Lexman. They'd spend the next year at school to learn just as she had as a child. One of her sisters had been able to uncover a way to safely transport pieces of their trees with them by propagating a nymph's roots, so that they could visit anywhere for as long as they liked with no fear for their health. She'd been able to take a part of the tree and plant it inside a pot, and took it to travel to Will for the first time in years since her Binding Prayer ceremony. Her sister had wanted nothing more than to be able to spend more time with her and to travel for her education so she had stopped at nothing until that dream was realized. It had given not only all of her siblings freedom, but *all* of the nymphs more freedom and opportunities to roam the world and explore in ways they hadn't before.

She was proud of her family for overcoming the large divide between them, and waited for their visits with excitement instead of with fear and worry. She never knew who would blow through the front door, but she was always ready for any guests that came by as they added more buildings around the cottage, filling the forest with cabins and stables around them. They had easily become a hub of activity, creating new lines of trade through Hanlan and Stóngrast that hadn't existed for decades by being present directly in between the areas. It was a gratifying process that they had all worked hard for over the years, with friends old and new always circulating through.

The baby in her belly squirmed and stretched and she ran a comforting hand over them, shushing the baby gently before sitting down next to the window with her tea. The baby had a month or so left before she'd join them, and her big brother was growing impatient to meet her. A petal fell from her hair as the wind blew through the window, making her smile. She put her mug on the table as she held it up to the light and admired the purple flower, with a streak of pink in the center. The opposite of her flowers with little Georgie, and they knew it would mean a little girl this time around. Arden had been a nervous wreck when he saw the colors fill in, ready to both dote on and worry for the little one as she grew. The baby stretched again, pressing against Willow's hand as she gently soothed over the elbow jabbing her ribs.

"Soon, my love," she murmured, making the baby wiggle some more at the sound of her voice. "You're running out of room," she laughed. She glanced at the clock and knew Arden would be home soon. She also knew he'd storm into the house frantically before he saw that she was still pregnant, and did not in fact go into labor while he was at the butcher shop. She had laughed at him for his needless worries, but kissed his brow each time he told her he had been on edge all day, imagining her giving birth without him and needing his help while he wasn't home.

"We'll wait for you, papa," she told him lovingly. She wasn't sure how she knew, but she did. Baby would be here soon, but she'd wait for her papa before making an entrance.

The rain continued to fall and she sat there peacefully, picking up a knitting project while she hummed to herself until she heard sleepy footsteps from the hallway. George stood in his shirt with his round belly out, rubbing his eyes with a mass of curly hair pointing in every direction. He looked like Willow, with Arden's eyes and hair, and he smiled a sweet and chubby smile when he saw her.

"Hello, sleepy head," she laughed as she stood up to get him. His belly was still warm with sleep, and he yawned while resting his head on her shoulder. She patted his curls down, kissing his cheek. He giggled as she ran a hand over his back, the sound making the baby poke against her brother. "Your sister says hello, too, do you feel her?" She asked him as he reached a hand down to the top of her belly. The baby poked against his hand, making him laugh.

"Hi, baby," he giggled as Will brought him to the kitchen for a snack. As they ate some fruit, they sang some songs and waited for Arden to come home. She heard his horse before she saw him and placed Georgie on the floor so he could run to greet him.

"Papa!" He cried as Arden opened the door, hair dripping wet. George leapt into his outstretched arms and Arden squeezed him tight, pressing kisses into his hair and tickling him.

"My son, I missed you," he smiled before leaning down to kiss Willow, "and my wife," he told her. She kissed him back with a laugh before moving back to the kitchen to make dinner.

"How was the shop?" She asked.

"It's been good, actually. We finished the storage room today and Devon officially closed the Cahlin butchery. Since our new building is finally finished, he's handed the business over to me now. The Tegs will be taking everything to and from Stóngrast starting tomorrow, delivering meats and taking orders for me while I run the shop," his eyes were bright as he spoke, his long-lived passion for the career gave him a glow that she couldn't help but admire.

"I'm so proud of you," she told him with a kiss, putting down the vegetables for a moment. He grinned as he stole a pepper from her and shared it with George, happily eating the crunchy snack together. She wasn't sure her words really conveyed how truly happy she was for him, for taking a chance and leaping into a career he'd only ever dreamed of. It was a long time coming, with hard work and determination consistently waking him up in the morning.

He had the new building built halfway between the cottage in Tonsilta and Stóngrast, with the help of their friends and family. The D'Misio's had been their most supportive friends during the construction phase, with the boys eagerly excited to work in the shop with Arden. The Cahlin family had been excited, too, when Arden had proposed the idea. Devon, who'd inherited from his father, had been the most grateful of everyone and had hugged Arden when he shared the plan. Originally he had thought the Cahlin's would want to split the business, but they surprisingly were thrilled with the proposal. They had wanted to go into their own careers of choice, and many of them had followed Fasomalo and Willow in the medicinal practice. Devon joined as a soldier under Arden's lead, before they swapped roles entirely with one another. Her husband deserved everything that he achieved, and she was beyond happy that she was able to share it with him, now that his dream was fulfilled. It suited both men more in these new livelihoods than before, and she was so proud of them all.

The baby rolled in her tummy as Arden laughed with their son as he pretended to eat his chubby fingers instead of the bell peppers. The sound of baby giggles made her heart swell as tears pricked at her eyes. She didn't think she could ever be any happier than she was right then, but knew that with Arden and their children it would only ever be magical from here and forever more. A dream of a life.

Through the window she watched as the sun's rays cast a light in the sky, the rain still falling as she washed more vegetables in the sink. Sitting there by the river's edge was a small little willow bathing in a warm patch of the sun. A sprout of a tree, but growing everyday. As her husband and child's laughter filled the room, she smiled and added water to a pot, content and completely at peace.

Thank you so much to everyone that read my story! I hope you love it!

I am so glad to finally share my love for writing with the world and hope you stick around for more!

Check out my social media accounts where I share more about my stories and characters. Art, updates, and so much more to come!

Instagram: @brittanyleannecarr.author
Tiktok: @brittanylcarr.author
Facebook: Brittany Leanne Carr; Author

With love,
Brittany Leanne Carr